GW00566591

Cambridgeshire Libraries, Archives and Information Service

This book is due for return on or before the latest date shown above, but may be renewed up to three times unless it has been requested by another customer.

Books can be renewed –
in person at your local library

 Cambridgeshire
County Council

Online www.cambridgeshire.gov.uk/library

Please note that charges are made on overdue books.

10010010487745

About the Author

The author was born and educated in London. He joined the Metropolitan Police Forensic Science Laboratory in 1966 and Studied Geology at Birkbeck College (nights) between 1968 and 1972. He joined a Cambridge-based private firm of Forensic Scientists & Engineers in 1984 and retired in 2003.

Dedication

I dedicate this book to my children, Robert and Carys
and to my grandchildren, Joseph and Seren.

Peter Pugh

Cambridge Blues

AUSTIN MACAULEY
PUBLISHERS LTD.

A CIP catalogue record for this title is available from the British Library.

ISBN 9781786128355 (Paperback)
ISBN 9781786128362 (Hardback)
ISBN 9781786128379 (E-Book)

www.austinmacauley.com

First Published (2017)
Austin Macauley Publishers Ltd.
25 Canada Square
Canary Wharf
London
E14 5LQ

Acknowledgements

I would like to thank all those friends who gave
generously of their time and encouraged me to write.

Chapter 1: First Contact

It was an average Tuesday evening in late March, in an average village pub – the Blue Boar in Grantchester. It was busy, as usual. Some customers were playing cards, others darts. All were playing fast and loose with their livers. Michael Evans and Jonathan Grey sat in a secluded corner, supping their beer quietly, lost in their separate thoughts. Michael (Mike) was listening absent-mindedly to the piped music that provided the background to the chatter of the other patrons. His gaze flitted from one table to another as he recognised faces that he knew and those that he didn't particularly want to see. He got up without a word and went over to the bar to order another round; both of necessity and as an excuse to chat with the landlord. Jonathan (Jon) hadn't been in the pub since his divorce a year earlier and while he watched Mike in quiet conversation, he reflected on how he had come to meet him and how he had come to be in the pub that evening. Michael was, in Jon's eyes, an odd, yet indispensable friend. He was a mercurial sort of guy who, despite the odd random outburst, could be genially self-contained when circumstances demanded. He had been orphaned at the age of twelve and had been brought up by his Aunt Emily, his mother's only and younger sibling, until university age. All things considered, Emily had done an excellent job and had very good reason to be proud of herself. Mike had honed his charismatic skills to perfection long before going to university and this, together with a natural ability as an academic and all-round sportsman, provided a natural springboard to start his working life. That, and his innate sense of the absurd. Although Mike had lived with his aunt in London until he was eighteen, in his late teens he had spent most holidays at the family home in Grantchester village, just a few miles up-river from Cambridge. It was there that he had forged most of his links with the local sporting fraternity – in between being invited politely to leave many of the village hostelries, the Blue Boar included. However, such was his good sense of what was proper, he never once mentioned that, but for the timely intervention of his aunt, the brewery and all but two of the other village pubs would have long since fallen into the hands of some evil faceless mega-keggery in the Midlands, whose sole intention was to sell disgusting over-priced slop to the drinking masses.

Mike was about six foot three inches high with untidy blonde hair and grey eyes. The only thing that stood between this and full admission to the Adonis Club of Great Britain was his somewhat crumpled and much lived-in face. This characteristic had been a source of great concern to his guardian-aunt who thought that it might perhaps portray indolence. It was principally this fear that led her to concentrate on what was arguably Mike's best asset: namely, his sense of humour. A well-rounded education in life plus a few object lessons in telling bald lies without causing pain gave Mike an essentially optimistic, if cynical, outlook set behind an almost permanent grin. In fact, the grin was arguably Mike's best feature and with the possible exception of such trying times as, say, going to the dentist, it became a permanent feature. He attracted optimistic people and earned a reputation for telling long and relentlessly outrageous stories with absolute and unshakeable conviction. Jonathan had known Mike for about two years and had enjoyed practically every minute of it.

By contrast, Jon was a mostly average man in his early thirties – average height, average brown hair and brown eyes and averagely disenchanted with life. It was not always this way of course. Once, in his former persona, he had been the life and soul of every party and brimming with mostly foolish optimism, but over a period of about six months almost every spark of humanity had been squeezed out of him by his wife (now ex-wife) Sara. At his most pessimistic, Jon reckoned that she had left only his brain and two shirts and he had filled the void in his life by putting it to its best use, researching and teaching with Mike. He paused from his thoughts to see Mike look over to him from the bar, answering an enquiry from the landlord, Fred Botley.

"Who's your friend, Michael?"

"Oh, a guy from work. We fancied a decent pint for a change."

Understatement was another of Mike's traits – that and discretion.

"Okay – there you are – two pints of nectar and a fiver for cash, anything else?"

"Just a bit of information, Fred. Sadly, I'm not just here for pleasure. I wondered whether you'd seen anything of Frank Graves lately?"

Fred's face darkened briefly at the mention of the name.

"Aye, I've seen 'im. He's been making a real nuisance of himself in the village these last few weeks – drunker than usual. Is there a problem at the Hall?"

"Not that I know of," Mike replied, paying and picking up the pints. "Emily just asked me to keep an eye out for him."

"Oh shit." Fred exhaled.

There was a muffled disturbance at the side door of the pub as a burly male in his mid-twenties entered, obviously drunk. It would be difficult to describe him fully in the tar-stained light of the bar. Suffice to say that he had the demeanour and smell of someone who rarely changed his clothes and probably ate raw meat with his hands. Mike elected to feign a lack of further interest, re-joined Jon at their table and passed him a pint, keeping an eye on Frank Graves as he pushed towards the bar.

"So why, out of interest, are we here rather than drinking in town? Is that the guy you mentioned on the way here?" Jonathan thumbed, in the direction of the gathering argument at the bar.

Mike's attention was drawn from Frank Graves and hovered briefly and wistfully in the vicinity of the barmaid before he replied.

"'Fraid so, Jon. You remember my aunt Emily?" Jonathan nodded, as he sipped. "Well, we are indulging a whim of hers. She called me over the weekend and asked me to keep an eye on one of her staff – the groundsman, Frank Graves. Apparently he's been spending more than his usual amount of time in the village pubs of late. He's not much liked and seemingly he has been buying beer like the world's coming to an end. Emily doesn't pay badly, but he does seem to have money to burn at the moment. I'd hoped that it would be a fool's errand, but in fact you're right, that's him at the bar – making a complete arse of himself."

Frank was now attempting to bypass the queue for the bar and simultaneously make a pass at a female customer. She was not deserving of his attention in particular, but had the figure and presence that was probably used to attention from anything human with a pulse: male or female. She was tall, blonde, and looked alarmingly fit – at least to Mike, who wasn't. He wondered why he'd not seen her sooner. From toe to top she was wearing Prada boots almost hidden by boot-fit Gap jeans, a Thomas Pink shirt and an Afghan coat that had been in, out and back in fashion at least twice. Above that level, things were much less precise. The lower half of the face was tanned surrounding a pleasant mouth, but from there to the hairline was a mystery, hidden beneath an enormous pair of sunglasses. Anywhere else she might have been mistaken for a visiting film star, incognito, but here she just appeared to be a stranger who was content to remain so. Understandably, she certainly didn't seem to want to get to know Frank Graves. The disturbance at the bar grew increasingly monosyllabic and Fred reached for the telephone to call the police. Frank, side-tracked for a moment from his quarry, turned to laugh.

"That's a bloody waste of time and you know it. It will take 'em at least fifteen minutes to get 'ere and that's only if they can be bothered. By the time they arrive I'll be safely tucked up in bed with my alibi."

Fred paused to reflect on the collection of sparkling glasses behind his newly decorated bar, but then thought how much of it Frank could rearrange before the police arrived. His shoulders slumped in resignation. Frank sensed a small but tactical victory and laughed again. At least there was one pub in the village where he wasn't barred. Any further celebrations were cut short by the woman he had been pestering moments before. She spoke in a quiet but chilling voice:

"You seem to be very familiar with the word 'alibi'. Is one you use often? I trust it wasn't a reference to me."

Michael and Jonathan started to rise, but events took over before they could intervene. They became momentarily transfixed as Frank Graves eased himself slowly away from the bar. He turned to face the young woman, reaching almost casually into the rear pocket of his jeans for his knife. He smiled menacingly as he depressed the button on the metal casing. The dirty blade flicked out and the bar hushed. Other than Michael and Jonathan, everyone had moved away slightly. Frank looked at the woman for signs of panic. But instead of backing off, she took just one pace back confidently, out of immediate range. Her tinted sunglasses reflected the bar lights behind his head and hid half her face, especially her eyes. She showed no fear and Frank began to think he had made a mistake. In the cold silence he felt compelled to speak, "Watch your mouth, bitch!"

Her reaction, when it came, took him completely by surprise. She just laughed at him derisively before speaking. "Sadly, in my experience, men carry arms for two reasons. Either they are pond-life thugs who get their jollies from hurting people, or they're sexually inadequate and carry knives to make up for the fact that they've no dicks."

Her uncompromising emphasis on the words, 'pond-life', 'thugs', and 'sexually inadequate' had dispelled any lingering doubts that a confrontation was inevitable and the more faint-hearted customers had already finished their drinks and moved towards the doors. The final reference to his lacking anatomy was too much for Frank. Having first checked his groin – hoping perhaps for a miracle – the knuckles on his right hand whitened as he gripped the knife more tightly. He attacked just as Michael and Jonathan ran for the bar, but it was all over in seconds. Frank lunged from right to left, but she anticipated his move and did the opposite, avoiding the arc of the blade by just a few centimetres. Grabbing his right wrist as it passed, she pulled him off-balance, landing a booted heel hard on the outside of his right knee. Nothing broke, but the blow was accurate and painful enough to make him drop the knife.

Frank watched her smile as she readjusted her balance. Then he saw her left foot move rapidly to the place he usually reserved for his scrotum. The agony was unbelievable. He wanted his mother and he wanted to be sick. But first he needed to curl into a ball, to stop her doing it again. Involuntarily he began to double up and, for a millisecond, he thought she was helping him. She was pressing on his shoulders, hard. He opened his eyes just in time to see a denim-clad knee rising to meet his face. He felt the cartilaginous tissues in his nose move sideways (in both directions) and assume a new and very un-nose-like position on his cheeks. The lights went red, then temporarily out. The bar was bedlam and Fred telephoned the police and an ambulance. Having reassured himself that Frank wasn't bleeding anywhere that might leave a stain, he smiled a very satisfied smile.

"Drinks are on the house," he declared, not wishing to lose punters.

In the chaos the blonde stranger detached herself from the throng at the bar. As she edged past the table to which Michael and Jonathan had returned, Michael spoke quietly, as if into his glass.

"Are you okay?"

"Now is not the time, Dr. Evans. The police will be here shortly and I don't plan to be here to greet them. Nor should you, now that we've spoken. I'm leaving now. Don't try to follow me!"

Michael sat open mouthed as the stranger disappeared. Answering Jonathan's unasked question he finished his pint, then shrugged.

"Sadly, I don't have a clue who she is or how she knew my name, so don't expect an introduction. Come on, I don't fancy seeing the police, either. I wonder what Emily will make of it. Nice floor show, though. Have to give her that. Quite balletic!"

Some short time after midnight and only a mile further north, a nondescript ancient hatchback moved slowly up the drive of Grantchester Hall. Running only on sidelights, it passed the building site on the west side of the residential block of the original red brick pile and came to a halt close to the side entrance. The driver got out. Within seconds he was joined by another, shorter man. They spoke quietly, then, as if by prior agreement, moved off to a side entrance, carrying heavy sacks. Minutes passed. The two re-emerged, this time weighed down with other sacks which they loaded silently into the car. Money changed hands and the second man returned to the house silently. Using only the moon to guide him, the driver carefully navigated his way back down the drive. Back on the metalled road he turned towards the city, turning on his lights only when he saw those of another vehicle approaching in the distance. His departure from the hall was witnessed, in turn, by a fox, vole, a hungry barn owl and a surveillance camera. The fox took no notice. The vole soon became supper for the owl, which was too hungry to care about other nocturnal happenings; especially as they had become routine of late.

Although it appeared outwardly similar, the surveillance camera, was not the same model as others fixed around the building site, differing from them in several important respects. Partly hidden by foliage, it was activated by a movement sensor detuned to ignore heat signatures of voles, owls and foxes. More importantly, it registered images in infra-red as well as daylight. Advanced to the nth degree, its digital transmitter relayed captured images via a commercial geo-stationery satellite, somewhere over southern France. The quality of the digital video signal not good enough to identify faces in infra-red. Nevertheless, in an office in London, the camera's owner viewed them in real time as well as committing a copy to disc for his client. Fast-forwarding to the best image of the car, he zoomed in on the registration number, then, using an entirely illegal connection to the Police National Computer, he determined both the name and address of the registered owner. He also learned that the car had been reported stolen in London two days earlier. Then, refilling his glass for the third time that evening, he e-mailed the Hall's owner in Italy.

Emily

Given the hour I'll keep it brief, but you've had visitors at the Hall again – which makes it the sixth time in three weeks. If we are still agreed not to involve the police yet, I propose – reluctantly – that we involve the 'boys', as discussed. Please call to confirm.

Best regards, P

PS. Cathy has 'bumped into' Frank Graves. It was in one of your pubs and he did not enjoy the experience. Will explain more when you call.

The sender, Peter Stagg, didn't expect an immediate response, given the time difference in mainland Europe. Emily, however had just returned from a party and her reply bounced back almost immediately. *Hello Peter. Michael phoned me about Frank at the Blue Boar and the call transferred to my mobile. I admire your use of the phrase 'bumped into' and am glad that Cathy was unhurt. I'd not guessed that it was her. Nice girl. Whilst I understand your reluctance to involve the police until we have hard evidence, I need your assurance that Michael and Jonathan will not be placed at risk. As you know well, I'm no happier about this than you, but if you need better cover to operate covertly, I don't see any other way. I'll fly in before the weekend. Will let you know my E.T.A. beforehand. I trust I can rely on you in this as all other matters.*

Regards, E.

P.S. We seem to have a complication, although I am not yet sure if it is related to the problems at the hall. I have just received a massive capital gains tax demand via my accountants.

Please, if at all possible, look into this before the weekend via my solicitors and accountants – I won't go into details now, but suffice to say that I've not realised any assets in the last five years or more!"

Peter was not at all pleased at having to assume responsibility for Michael and Jonathan, but there was little choice. Ms Emily Pollard was proving to be a difficult client. Being a sleuth for an unforthcoming client was difficult enough, but now he also had to deal with her accountants and there was no way that he or they would be able to arrange an interview with the Revenue in a matter of days. His normal philosophy for investigation was simple, elegant and had never failed him. The credo was to establish the facts, determine possibilities and likely eventualities, cast the net and draw it in. With Emily, he was not convinced that he was told all the facts and now the net had to be redesigned to involve accountants!

Chapter 2: A Pint Too Far

Jonathan had passed a mostly uneventful thirty-six hours since the unexpected entertainment in the Blue Boar until, after at least three pints too many, he fell out of the 'Don't Feel Bitter - Drink It' public house and into the arms of an unsuspecting woman who he later came to know as Lisa Adams. Ordinarily, being a quiet, recently divorced, and frequently disappointed sort of person, Jon would not have trusted himself to go drinking alone at lunch-time, let alone have three too many. But, following another telephonic row with his ex-wife Sara the previous evening, he had been persuaded by Mike to let someone else cover his Friday afternoon lecture and, with the weekend looming, Mike and Jon could thus retire in freedom to perform a liquid review of the many injustices of life, the price of beer, the wholly inadequate salaries offered to university lecturers and anything else that came randomly to mind.

Like so many of Mike's well-intentioned plans, this one was fundamentally flawed. Not only had he forgotten to check his own diary, but against his own better judgement he had eaten a thoroughly outdated freezer meal for supper the night before and spent the rest of the night at the hospital being pumped out, re-hydrated and a few other unmentionable procedures besides. Not surprisingly, the whole experience left him both thinner and exhausted and he slept through his two appointments; the first in the pub with Jon; the second being to collect his delightfully rich aunt from the train station on her way back from Italy.

Jonathan, of course, knew nothing of any of this when, on a completely empty stomach, he bought the first two pints. In fact, such was his unshakeable if, misplaced, belief in Mike's organisational skills, Jonathan drank them both and then bought two more in the certain knowledge that Mike would not be much longer in arriving. After the third pint, a few serious doubts started to loom unsteadily on the horizon. After the fourth, thoughts of his ex-wife preoccupied him, as they often had of late. With the help of a fifth pint, Jonathan indulged himself with a few dark thoughts about Sara, her latest be-muscled toy boy, her crone of a mother and, most of all, her bloody cats. With these half-formed images in his mind, three more pints in his now swollen stomach and failing to choose the right door for the toilet, Jonathan collapsed, less than elegantly, into the unsuspecting arms of Ms Adams.

Beauty, they say, is in the eye of the beholder – a rare example of a true truism. Since it was clear to Jonathan that he had no prospect of focusing both eyes, he used just one to take in the contours and promise of what appeared to be a very friendly face. So far, so good, but now came the tricky bit. The downside associated with being frequently disappointed is that it lowers expectations. This is not so much a truism as a fact and, depending on how completely disappointing the last complete disappointment had been, Jonathan, when confronted with, for example, a new friendly face would:

a) Not try very hard.

b) Not try at all.

c) Panic.

Predictably this type of negative thinking usually led to disappointment, but of course the simple logic of it all had passed Jonathan by, leaving him with a profound sense of non-fulfilment bordering on paranoia, combined with a total lack of self-esteem. It was a bit like an inward sigh that tails off in the general direction of somewhere that you really shouldn't explore without a tame psychiatrist to hold one or both hands. That aside and while still gazing intently with one eye, Jonathan started to realise that he had several pressing problems, namely:

1. He was not handling this at all well.

2. He badly needed a pee.

3. His one-eyed gaze might soon be mistaken for something worse.

4. He couldn't think of anything to say.

5. His brain and mouth did not appear to be joined in any vaguely functional sense.

6. He should perhaps also have had some lunch.

7. He badly needed the first pee and a second.

Jonathan swayed gently in Lisa's arms, failing manifestly to resolve any of his problems. Thankfully, however, Lisa spoke and by doing so dealt, in no particular order, with problems 1, 4 and 5.

"I'll be back in just a minute," she said. "Don't go away."

While she was gone, Jonathan dealt with problems 2 and 7, forgot the remainder, ordered a large black coffee and sat by the window to await his destiny. He had nowhere to go anyway. Destiny took a little while to arrive and Jonathan was well into his third cup of coffee when the friendly face reappeared inside the bar. By this time he had managed to train both eyes to focus in the same general direction, while at the same time convincing the rest of the bar not to spin. Telekinesis was not one of his strong points and the mental effort made him almost forget his manners. Lisa was almost upon him when he leapt to his feet and slumped back into the chair followed, dutifully, by his stomach.

The friendly face was surrounded by masses of red hair and had as its focal point two large green eyes and an unremarkable, but perfect nose. Beneath that, a pair of tensed lips were saying, "I suspect, on balance, you shouldn't have tried that. Why don't I get us both a coffee?"

"I'm okay," he white-lied. "Too much beer without any breakfast or lunch."

He felt strangely good about correcting the lie with a bit of uncluttered truth. It had a sort of novelty value that felt somehow pure. He'd almost forgotten the experience.

"No, I should be apologising for keeping you waiting. I wasn't sure if I'd locked my car and then I took a huge detour to avoid someone I didn't really want to see."

Jonathan was transfixed by the moving lips and nodded his head obediently in pretended comprehension, but he was still incapable of coherent speech owing to the beer being too strong. In addition to which, she was beautiful and he, addled or not, was a man. Lisa's lips stopped moving and Jonathan, still agog, lifted his eyes to meet hers. He beamed encouragingly. Thankfully she continued:

"My name is Lisa Adams. How would you feel about being plucked from obscurity?"

Sensing the confusion behind his eyes, she helped. "Sorry – I'll start again."

He nodded a quick 'yes'. She rearranged the words in her mind, engaged his eyes and started. "Right – I'm Lisa Adams. I work for Cambridge Promotional Videos."

There was still no obvious response – not above the neck anyway. He looked about thirty-something and that didn't seem to qualify as a secret, but she realised with more than a slight blush that the seconds she had spent supporting him had caused her imagination to go into overdrive. Arguably his most alluring feature was the eyes. There seemed to be a lot of recent pain on the surface, but equally there appeared to be a lot of potential in waiting, buried somewhere, deep, beneath. She looked at them quickly to see whether she might have added to the pain or they had seen her blush, but all was well. She'd made a mental note of the lack of wedding ring and observed that, despite the chewed fingernails, he had pleasant-looking hands – those of an artist perhaps. Anyway, no harm done – he was still amiably drunk. She wondered whether her internal confusion had resulted from seeing her ex-husband and the attendant detour to get back to the pub, but it felt as though she had been supporting this stranger with nice eyes and hands for ages, when he fell into her arms. Yet curiously, it didn't seem to bother her. She had concluded, on the basis of absolutely no evidence at all, that he was probably quite a pleasant drunk. She had been down that road herself all too often and was in no position to criticise others. She ploughed on, describing her work in selling the city to American tourists and others. Jonathan was not only amiably drunk, but after so much coffee, was also embarking on a monumental hangover. He had, of course, been told many times that the very last thing one should do when drunk was to take in caffeine, since it increased the heart rate and pumped proportionately even more alcohol to the already befuddled brain. But medical gems like that tend to be forgotten after eight pints and, often, several less. Jonathan was having enough trouble keeping up with the conversation without trying to be clever as well. He was wondering how he would come to terms with a permanently deformed bladder when the words 'plucked' and 'obscurity' crept slowly into his brain. He remembered vaguely what she had said, up to and including 'Americans', but he was still well behind on responding. He badly needed a diversion and even more badly, another pee. Why was it that, film heroes never needed a pee? It took considerable concentration to muster the words. "Jonathan – Jonathan Grey. I'm very sorry; I'm forgetting my manners. Sorry about collapsing on you earlier – as you've probably gathered I've been having a bit of a bad day. Well, a bit of a bad year, if truth were told."

It struck him that, for the second time, the he felt comfortable about telling this complete stranger, the truth. It was probably the drink. Funny how uninhibited you can be with strangers (and drink).

"Why do I have to give up obscurity just when I was getting used to it? Joking. It sounds like fun and God knows I could do with a bit of that right now. Where do I sign?"

"Well, nowhere, actually," she replied. "What we do is keep a list of what we call 'cast volunteers' – on account of the fact that we don't pay them – and ring them as and when something suitable crops up. Would you mind giving me your phone number?"

Jonathan couldn't think of anyone else in the world he would rather give his phone number to. After a brief rummage in his pockets he produced a battered card, which he handed to her without looking at it. His eyes, he realised, were still locked on hers. Even through his burgeoning hangover, she didn't appear to mind too much. A little voice that usually appeared at such times coughed politely somewhere near the back of Jonathan's brain and reminded him of the statistical probability that he was likely, once again, to make a complete arse of himself. Since his divorce he had adopted the habit of examining his thoughts in detail before voicing them. Having considered his thoughts about the current situation, its short and long term implications, he ignored them and murmured, "What the hell, life's not a rehearsal."

This uncharacteristically optimistic piece of wisdom was intended only for the little voice at the back of his brain but it also registered with Lisa, who looked up from her bag where she had carefully placed Jonathan's card. She smiled inwardly, hid her own thoughts and said, "I couldn't agree more, but you look as though you need some sleep. I'll ring you when something comes up. 'Bye."

Lisa's complexion did little to hide her blushes at the best of times and the onset of a particularly furious one sparked her rapid retreat from the pub. Disappearing behind a shock of red hair she ran outside in a state of confusion. Jonathan, shaken briefly from a darkening headache, got up quickly and ran to the door, but she was gone. Lisa ran to her car, did something unspeakable to the clutch and drove off. Jonathan sighed, retrieved his belongings from the bar, unlocked his bike and pushed it over to the common. Reasoning it was still light and there was no-one much about to run over, he wobbled off, whistling tunelessly into the late March afternoon. Home, since the previous summer, had been in Mayflower House.

Jonathan had never been able to reconcile or articulate fully his residual feelings for Sara, either to himself or anyone else, even Mike – it was just too personal and painful a subject. The relationship had started off in the normal way – the ritual progression from chance meeting to visual interest and fascination, then a voyage of discovery encompassing physical desire and a basic gene-controlled need for companionship at every level and for all time, preferably with a little judicious procreation thrown in. The order varies, but the elements remain the same and attain different degrees of supremacy in the mind, depending on the individual, and all of it is called love. The 'L' word. In Jonathan's case the elements equated to unswerving devotion. This scenario works invariably for swans, but sadly not for humans, who lack swan genes. Sara had laid her trap and baited her hook with care and precision. Jonathan had seen the sunlight glint on the lure, had felt a primeval desire to chase it, did so and was caught. There is no way for us to know whether fish agonise when the inevitability of this occurs, but humans are at liberty to agonise and do so. Jonathan had idolised Sara – an emotion that appeared to be reciprocated initially, but after the honeymoon it was as if there was a massive sea change in Sara's attitude. Gone was the charming young woman who sent him amusing texts and emails, who took him on surprise weekends to lovely places and who never failed to scatter rose petals on their bed each Sunday. Quite clinically and ruthlessly, she set about destroying him in every way and at every level. She lied to his family, shunned his friends, simultaneously tried to encourage him to promote himself while cynically attempting to undermine his career and, when that failed, started to have affairs – sometimes sleeping with several people each week. Bit by insidious bit, she destroyed him. The rose petals that once adorned his pillow were replaced with poisoned thorns and eye of newt, as the magic of the early romance turned to witchcraft.

Initially, Jonathan could not/would not believe it, but then when he had to face the truth, he just slid into denial –

a typically emotional failure to acknowledge the obvious. Even now, a year after the divorce, he could not decide whether he had somehow brought it on himself. This, of course, was an accolade to Sara's success. She had reduced Jon's self-esteem and confidence to a level barely supportable without medical intervention. His self-worth was clinically dead in the water. So low was his net value, he blamed himself completely and thus her failure as a wife/life partner/lover/reason for being – was redefined, conveniently as *his* error of choice. This is what he could neither admit to himself or Mike. Mike of course, having more than half a brain, knew most of this without being told and simply sent Jon to see a friend who worked for Relate. She was a thirty-plus-year-old divorcee who had been twice around life's block and then parallel parked without assistance. She listened patiently to Jon's story without interruption for twenty minutes and summed it up by saying, "So, Dr Grey, what you're telling me is, she's a bitch. You'll probably hate me or yourself for saying this, but there is universal truth that you must face. There are some unscrupulous women who, being unable to gain or hold down well-paid jobs, have only one means of getting on the property ladder. They marry someone who can afford to buy a house, make his life a complete misery, divorce the poor bugger and keep the house."

"Ouch."

"There's more. Would you permit me have a wild guess?"

"By all means."

"Okay – did your ex like cats?"

"Yes, but how could you know that?"

"It doesn't matter now, but did she ever say anything about her own animal sign?"

"Animal sign?"

"Yes – it's a bit like astrological signs, but even less credible."

"Yes, I think she mentioned something like that once when she called me a pig type. I thought it was a joke at the time."

"And she referred to herself as a cat type?"

"Well – yes, but how did you know that?"

"Just a wild guess, but probably relevant. You know the expression that people choose dogs that look like them or grow to look like their dogs? Well, there is also a theory that people - usually women - who really like cats start to behave like them."

"Now, that is scary."

"Yes. Imagine the average domestic cat. It does pretty much fuck-all all day, seeks and takes affection from anything with two legs, bites your hand afterwards and probably shits on your bed."

"Yep. That sounds a lot like my ex, but I hope that doesn't apply to all women!"

"Of course not; but then, not all men are dogs. I hope that you are not shocked."

"More surprised than shocked. I never imagined that I'd meet someone who dislike cats more than me."

"I don't dislike them. I hate the little fucks!"

"Ah, right."

"Did you know there is a school of thought which holds that people who like cats are incapable of maintaining normal human relationships?"

"And whose school of thought is that?"

"Mine."

Jonathan, it was true, had fared badly in the divorce. He had escaped with his credit cards, a depleted CD collection, his books and the car. Because of the difference in their earnings, Sara had kept the former matrimonial home to share with the cats and whichever of her paramours happened to be flavour of the week, plus a third of his salary. This is quite normal in a mostly abnormal world. However, despite the injustice of it all, it was slowly dawning on Jonathan that things could actually be worse. There was a very fine view from the window of his bed-sit and it was, so he had discovered, warm all winter. Best of all, there were no cats. He left his bike downstairs and took the lift to the fifth floor. His headache had receded to sleepable proportions and that was exactly what he had in mind. However, the answerphone clearly had other ideas. It was winking at him in a red, seductive sort of way intoning: 'I have messages for you'. He was sufficiently curious to listen to them. He hoped there might be something distracting for a thirty two year old, recently-divorced male to do on a Saturday once he'd slept Friday off. But, being still less well than he cared to believe, he hit the wrong button and was obliged to listen to his own honeyed tones before the answerphone kicked in. Although he did not realise it, this was the second time within the space of the same hour that Jonathan had indulged himself in an uncharacteristically optimistic thought. The little voice in the back of his head barely had time to clear its throat when the white noise on the recording gave way to Jonathan's very subdued monologue:

"Hello, this is Jonathan Grey's answer phone. If you're selling: a) life insurance, b) double glazing, c) time shares or d) religion, please hang up now. Anyone else can leave a message after the tone."

BLEEP!

"Hello Jonathan, this is Emily Pollard — I got your number from some hysterical woman whom I take it is no longer your wife. I remember thinking that she was perfectly awful when we last met in London — she was the same wife, I suppose? It's so easy to lose track of these things. My errant nephew Michael should have met me from the train station this morning and didn't. I'm at the City Hotel. I'd be very pleased if you could both join me for breakfast tomorrow, say, at nine. I think I may need your help."

Jon had always had a soft spot for Mike's aunt. Although richer than Croesus, she never flaunted it and always spoke her mind. Jonathan rang Mike, but there was no answer. He considered his headache and whether it might benefit from some more coffee. It would. He was pouring it when the phone rang in real-time. 'Bugger', thought Jonathan as he had forgotten to reset the machine.

"Hi, it's Mike – do you fancy a pint?"

Jonathan thought briefly and picked up the phone. He reasoned that if he worked on it for a little while, his present indisposition could be laid squarely at Mike's feet.

"Not especially, if I have to drink all yours again. Where did you get to at lunchtime? I've only just got home."

"Sorry about that; I've been in hospital since last night. Can you come?"

Jonathan felt suitably embarrassed, agreed, hung up, phoned a taxi and then phoned Emily Pollard to confirm arrangements for the next morning. Ten minutes later the taxi arrived: his stomach was still slurping violently as he pulled himself into the back seat. By the third speed ramp, his complexion was starting to clash with the car's upholstery. After checking his fare's condition in the rear view mirror the driver said, almost engagingly, "Accident and Emergency? Of course, we get a lot of fares at the hospital since they introduced the new parking restrictions – especially after the staff started sabotaging the ticket machines."

Jonathan groaned inwardly.

"Really?" he said, in polite yet disinterested way, but it was too late.

Sensing that he had a willing listener for the next three miles, the sort of kindred spirit to whom one could pour out one's heart, spleen and possibly one's entire viscera, the driver launched into his undeniably tedious life history. Jonathan groaned inwardly and made a mental note to use a different taxi company in future. He considered briefly the idea of adding the man to his very select but growing list of people who would qualify, for a cell on Death Row when someone finally got around to privatising capital punishment. He pictured the taxi driver on the gallows with about ten other people, blindfolded and gagged. With the hospital in sight, Jonathan's spirits rose above the tide of beer and coffee. When the taxi hit the first of the speed ramps at the entrance to the hospital, his spirits sank as the beer and coffee rose once more. Hanging was too good for the man – he would be sent instead on a three-month body-building course followed by an introduction to Sara Grey. They arrived at the right entrance. Jonathan paid the driver, took great pleasure in telling him not to bother to wait and set off in search of Mike. His stomach followed two paces behind.

Chapter 3:

Teddy Bears and Ducks

Lisa's near encounter with her ex a few hours earlier had left her typically confused. She knew that one day fairly soon she was going to have to discuss things with him – or at least sort out not only her feelings about him, but also her life in general. It was now well over two years since they had split. Lisa's parents were supportive, but she had enough trouble admitting to herself that Greg had left her for a man, without sharing that fact with them. Although fairly liberal and worldly-wise in many respects, they seemed to be on a different planet from hers and the rest of us mortals. On the few occasions that Lisa had taken her problems home, they had taken an almost patronising delight in opening every emotional wound in sight and applying salt at random. Lisa loved her parents to distraction, but at the same time had acquired a keen sense of self-preservation where they were concerned. Thus, so far as they knew, the beast Greg had run off with someone from the theatre (that was quite close enough) and their poor little Lisa was making the best of a very bad deal.

Perhaps naturally, she had become something of a recluse. The days were full of challenges, self-imposed deadlines and petulant clients, but at night she hid in books, assuming the identity of first one and then another fictional character in an effort to avoid her skewed perception of reality. This critical self-appraisal and her ongoing recovery was thanks largely to her boss, friend and constant mentor, Jenny Overton. Jenny had been wonderful from the very start. As soon as the news broke, she left flowers in Lisa's office with a note saying: 'In my office as soon as you can.' When Lisa, arrived Jenny sat her down and said, "I won't presume to know how you feel or even what you need right now, but take it from me that we're all with you. If and when you want to talk, just ring – it doesn't matter what time of day or night. Meanwhile, since I'm still nominally in charge around here, you are on holiday as of right now."

Lisa started to protest, but Jenny continued: "You have a hair appointment in ten minutes and that will leave you about an hour to pack before you have to leave for the airport. Bill has offered to drive you, as he has to pick up some equipment nearby. Here is your ticket confirmation and the key to the flat. See you in about a week, then."

The last words had such a ring of finality to them that Lisa didn't even bother to protest. She gave Jenny a hug that spoke volumes and left quickly. Four hours later she was bound for Paris. The experience was extremely therapeutic. She spent the days in museums and galleries and the evenings simply walking around, not taking too many liberties with her credit cards. When she returned to Cambridge she took Jenny to lunch to thank her and then threw herself into work with renewed enthusiasm. Two weeks, too much wine and countless pizzas later, she finally took up Jenny's offer and phoned for help. Her boss arrived twenty minutes later, armed with a toothbrush, the next day's clothes, a carton of cigarettes and three bottles of wine.

"Well, it sounded serious," she said, pretending to look shame-faced. "Besides, I didn't know if you'd have any wine left."

"Have I been looking that bad?" said Lisa, grateful that she had remembered to take out last week's empties the previous day.

"No, of course not." Jenny replied. "To be honest, I've had a crummy day. Two of these are for me! The cigarettes are in case you decide that you haven't given up after all. I take it I wasn't expected to bring tissues as well?"

They talked, or rather Jenny listened, for hours, as Lisa went over all the old resentments, anger, grief, self-doubt and the full depth of Greg's deceit. Jenny probed gently when Lisa seemed to be lacking direction and eventually encouraged her back to the present. That, on reflection, had been the easy part. Unfortunately, it offered no obvious clues for the immediate future. Jenny emptied her mind and the second bottle, lit a cigarette and closed her eyes for a long time before speaking.

"Well, I suppose you could move away and start again, but speaking personally, I don't want to lose you as a colleague or a friend and somehow or other you've got to get yourself a life. Just don't rush it! Have you any more tissues?"

Afterwards, Lisa certainly felt clearer as to what her immediate movements should be. She decided to set about buying out Greg's half of the flat. She also took up Jenny's offer of some of the follow-up work in overseas marketing. This gave her detached time to think when she wanted to and none when she didn't. She endured a few experimental dates just to see how she felt about things, but nothing seemed to happen. She found herself longing for a good book at bedtime in preference to anything warmer. It wasn't that she didn't long for a good old-fashioned hug, but at least waking up with a book removed problems such as what his name was or who was going to make the coffee. She was beginning to believe that everything interesting below the waist had atrophied, until her encounter that afternoon with Jonathan. Suddenly, spring appeared to beckon little-used parts of her body from a very long, dry hibernation. She retrieved Jonathan's card from her handbag and then dropped it suddenly as the phone rang:

"Hello, it's Jenny."

"Hello, you."

"It seems we do have a problem with yesterday's footage after all. Jason wasn't too wild about the lighting at the end of the day's shoot. We're going to have to do the last bit again. We still have the Americans and they are willing enough, but our guide seems to have disappeared."

"I don't think that should be too much of a problem," Lisa said, as she picked up Jonathan's card from the floor.

"When Jason started to whimper after the last shoot I decided to take out some insurance."

"You've got someone then?"

"I certainly have someone suitable in mind and I'll get back to you," Lisa replied, hoping that Jonathan had made it home safely.

Lisa felt herself flushing, ignored it and telephoned the number on Jonathan's card. After nine or ten rings a young male voice, utterly unlike Jonathan's, answered:

"Hello?"

"Hello."

"Hello – yes?"

This was not going well.

"Good evening, could I speak to Jonathan Grey, please?"

"Wait a minute" Long pause and muffled voices …

"This is Sara Grey, what do you want?"

The voice sounded as though it could strip paint at a hundred metres. With diminishing confidence, Lisa pressed on. "This is Lisa Adams. I'm sorry to disturb you, but it's quite urgent. I work with Jonathan and we have a small crisis with the server." she guessed, wildly. "Could I have a quick word with him, please?"

"No, you bloody can't. I've divorced the little shit and I'm tired of being his answering service! What do you do, anyway? I've never heard your name before. Another technician, I suppose."

A clue at last! The paint stripper sounded very drunk – what was it about these Greys? The line went dead and Sara hung up. Lisa telephoned directory enquiries, asked for new subscribers and tried again. This time she reached Jonathan's answerphone. His voice sounded very sad and after hearing him out, she left a message.

Outside Jonathan's bed-sit, five floors down in the gardens, a singularly evil-looking cat was stalking a duck that had taken advantage of the temporary pond which had formed over the winter. After a few minutes of furtive stalking, the cat decided that the duck probably wasn't worth getting cold and wet for and went off in search of more convenient prey. A nice little juicy mouse would do – no feathers and much easier to get through the cat-flap to disembowel on his mistress's bed.

Two fire engines thundered round the empty ring road, past the hospital and then on beyond the halls of residence. As they joined the otherwise empty dual carriageway and gathered pace, they played a duet of sirens and then another of sirens and horns, just in case anyone was trying to get in some early revision for their finals. Eventually, as houses gave way to trees and then farms and nobody was left to disturb, the duet ceased and the night closed in. Lisa lay awake wondering whether or not to ring Jenny. Even though she had no news as such, she felt a need to talk or be listened to, even though she couldn't think why, exactly. It was a 'girl thing'. She rang, but Jenny wasn't answering and there was no answering machine, or at least none that was switched on. To her surprise, Lisa felt alone, disappointed and temporarily at a loss. Another hour passed and no inspiration came. A wind picked up outside the bedroom window and Lisa swore at herself as she got out of bed in search of the emergency cigarettes and/or chocolate. "Why on earth am I doing this?" she grumbled, as she emptied bag after bag, followed by half of the kitchen drawers. "Jenny has every right not to answer the phone if she doesn't want to." The cigarettes didn't help and after several self-imposed diversions, Lisa finally plucked up the courage to telephone Jonathan again. Her nerve failed her and she took herself off to bed with a box of chocolates. As she lay there surrounded by the detritus of wrappers, silver paper and flaked chocolate, she looked up at Eric, her battered old one-eared teddy and shouted, "Well! What are you looking at?" Eric the bear had seen her in this kind of mood before and stayed shtumm, as well he might. Lisa started shaking, then wept in the way she had been meaning to do since Greg had gone. Had Eric possessed anything more sentient than stuffing between his ears, he would probably have taken charge at this point via a big hug. Suddenly, as quickly as it had started, the weeping stopped and Lisa started to laugh. She swore Eric to secrecy and fell into a fitful sleep. The street lights blazed with an unfriendly sodium glow outside her window, illuminating a noisy group of insomniac sparrows stripping the last vestiges of nest lining from last year's pampas grass. Gusts of wind shook the grass wildly, but the birds clung on with the tenacity of dedicated and professional nest builders. Much as we all cling on to one thing or another when our instincts tell us over and over again that it's really not worth bothering. In fact, had the sparrows some teeth, they probably would have gritted them. Lisa woke briefly and watched pampas shadows painting her bedroom wall. Eric sat there in a calm, reassuring, moth-eaten sort of way, his glass eyes fixed on some distant point, oblivious to the frailties of humankind and their strange habit of devising unworkable realities. Eric was at least a hundred years old and with the possible exception of his left ear, he had survived two world wars and the less than gentle attentions of four generations of the family Adams. A nocturnal painting with pampas brushes was, by comparison, a doddle. He certainly wasn't about to risk losing his other ear by saying something out of turn.

The pair of fire engines reached their destination only for their crews to find they had been called to yet another hoax. As the driver radioed in to control, a farm owner on the other side of the city looked out of his bedroom window at a small red and yellow glow beside one of his barns. As he continued to squint myopically into the darkness, there was a muffled 'pop' as a nondescript stolen hatchback burst more comprehensively into flames. He swore loudly, and went to look out his insurance policies. He smiled, thinking about his inadequate crop and, after leaving it for as long as he dared, he phoned 999.

Chapter 4: Spring Beckons

It was clear that most of the people who encountered Mike were quick to form the same view that Jon had. Three nurses were listening avidly in the reception area as Mike regaled them with one of his dubious shaggy-dog stories. Jonathan coughed politely and Mike acknowledged his presence by widening the grin then ploughing on undeterred. Jonathan followed his stomach's advice and sat down to join the uniformed audience. Despite the ravages of the previous evening, Mike was in fine fettle, leaping from one highly improbable sub-plot to the next, when Jonathan realised that he had heard this one before. Mike was approaching a particularly rude bit and Jon coughed in an unsuccessful effort to intervene. He coughed a little louder and was repaid with three stern looks and a thermometer in his mouth. The most senior of the nurses, a pleasant looking young woman with tired eyes and an undersized bra, emphasised the point by saying, "Curiously, you look worse than your friend and if there are any more interruptions I might put another thermometer somewhere more intimate."

Jonathan sank himself in his seat and let the entertainment run its course. Eventually, and only after a ritual exchange of addresses and telephone numbers and the return of a thermometer, was Jonathan allowed to take Mike away.

"How are you?"

"Well – or getting better. Food poisoning."

"Have you been in touch with Emily? She was on my answer phone looking for you."

"Oh Christ – I'd forgotten she was coming."

"Don't worry, I've already told her that you were indisposed. She sounded genuinely upset when she realised that you were really ill and not indisposed as a newt. What did you eat that could possibly offend the Evans gut so thoroughly? I didn't think there was a bug that could survive that much alcohol!"

"Actually, I've been cutting down in readiness for the cricket season. I expect it was the lack of beer that was my downfall – well, that and the ancient chicken I suppose. Quick way of losing weight, mind you! Is your car outside or do we jog?" Mike said, grinning.

"We'll take a cab. I'm still suffering from your beer I drank at lunchtime, I didn't want to risk driving. Come to think of it, I haven't eaten all day – fancy a bite to eat?"

They phoned for a cab and on the short journey to the city centre Mike recalled in graphic detail the events, such as he could remember them, of the previous evening. Jonathan seemed unusually quiet and as they approached their destination Mike observed a faint greenish tinge to his friend's complexion – rather like an avocado dip that had been left out of the fridge too long – in the sun.

"Are you sure you're up for something to eat, Jon? You look like you're wearing a face pack."

"I feel like I've eaten one. I'll be all right once I'm out of this cab – it's the bumps and the beer that don't mix."

The pasta bar wasn't busy and they were able to find a table equidistant from the toilets and the street door, to keep both options open. They surveyed the menus in search of something inoffensive. After a brief conversation with the waiter, who spoke broken Italian with a Glaswegian accent, they decided to play safe by ordering vermicelli with a cream sauce. It was neither too heavy to eat, nor too colourful if it bounced. While they waited for their food, under strict instructions from Mike, Jonathan drank a Coke quickly then ran outside to do a step-aerobic routine at the kerb. He got to about the mid-thirties before the burp came and he felt miraculously better. They ate in relative silence, listening alternately to the conversations of clandestine lovers dotted about the bar and muted rantings from the kitchen. No one could say that Cambridge was boring if you bothered to take the time to look and listen. Mike and Jonathan had eaten out a lot since Sara had declared her independence. This was not just because Mike was a terrible cook, but going out gave him a chance to get Jon out of his bed-sit, feed him and help him through a very rough patch. Mike simply accosted Jon one afternoon after lectures, presenting him with a list of restaurants.

"Shut your eyes and give me a number between one and twenty – that's where we're going tonight. I admit the approach lacks subtlety, but that was never one of my strong points."

Mike had been very patient, never pressing Jonathan to discuss or even obliquely refer to his problems. They just ate, drank, walked and talked. Although Jonathan had no reason to reproach himself, he had begun to wonder if Sara had been jealous of his friendship with Mike. She was the only person who had a bad word to say about him – several actually. At about meal seventeen Jonathan tried the idea on Mike and he accepted it quite readily. It was much kinder to let his friend believe that his ex-wife couldn't stand him than explain to him that Sara's sexual exploits had been the talk of the university. Sara's main reason for disliking Dr M. Evans was that he had resisted her charms, to wit: the offer of, 'a quick shag before Jonathan got home', only a month after she and Jonathan had got married. The lovers twittered on clandestinely and the ranting from the kitchen ceased briefly as the Italian Jock flourished their bill with his beautifully manicured hands.

"Il conto," he murmured.

"Grazie," they replied, not to be outdone.

"Prego," he oozed, counting their change.

Outside the weather was unusually pleasant for a late March evening and they elected to walk. Jonathan, because it would take care of the rest of his hangover. Mike, because he wasn't tired and it would be a good test of his resistance to temptation to pass by so many inviting pubs.

"We've been there before, haven't we?" Jonathan said, pausing from a tuneless whistle.

"Yes, I think so," said Mike, counting in his head. "Rehabilitation meal number seventeen."

"I thought I remembered it. Wasn't it the place where you spared me the awful truth about Sara?"

"Yes."

"Did I ever thank you for that?"

"No."

"Well, thank you."

"You're welcome."

"Have you ever wondered what the group noun for clandestine lovers might be?"

"No."

"Nor have I. Do you fancy a pint?"

"You really do have the willpower of a gnat, don't you?"

"On a good day – yes."

They found a quiet corner in a bar and Mike bought the round. It was a little cosy old pub, which had survived the ravages of modernisation, thanks mostly to the stolid intransigence of the landlord. He was dour, from Yorkshire and proud of it, and he wasn't having any bloody southerner from some bloody southern brewery telling him how to run his bloody pub – even if it was vaguely in the bloody south. He still had a public bar, a lounge bar and, of course, a 'snug' and that's the way it was going to stay. Gaming machines were banned and a jukebox was quite out of the question, unless of course people wanted to listen to (proper) brass band music. He served good honest bitter in good honest pints and a good Sunday roast seven days a week. You could play dominoes any day of the week, cribbage on Tuesdays and Thursdays and Wednesday night was darts night. This was Friday night, the dominoes team was evidently playing away and as a result the bar was less full than normal. Looking up, Jonathan admired the accumulation of many years of nicotine stains on the ceiling, the faded velvet curtains and the quiet simplicity of the décor. He sipped his pint tentatively then decided to go for it.

"I met someone I liked today while I was drinking your beer. Sweet girl, shock of red hair on both heads so far as I can recall, but then I did have a lot of your beer. Lisa Adams – do you know her? Late twenties possibly, works in video ads?"

"What makes you think I would know her?"

"Well, having devoted the last few years of your life getting to 'know' all the women in Cambridge, I thought it was feasible."

"Just because you spent two years in a shitty marriage and a third having an even worse divorce doesn't mean that the rest of us have had to act like monks. Anyway, the name doesn't ring any bells and, sod it; this is really about you. Are you going to see her again? It's about time you stopped being scared of women and I can assure you that they're not all harridans."

"I'm happy to concede that you know more about that than me, but my experience with Sara has left me terrified of trying again."

"True, but seeing this Lisa again cannot hurt, surely?"

"Last orders, please!"

It was eleven o'clock and a sudden chill wind greeted them as they left the pub. Mike paused for breath as two fire engines drove slowly but noisily past, toward the fire station. When the noise subsided they crossed the road outside the Don't Feel Bitter - Drink It and headed for the common. They chatted on the way back to the flats and then parted. Jonathan had avoided the subject of Lisa, not wanting to admit that he'd not got her phone number. He wandered off through the gardens under the watchful one-eyed gaze of the resident duck and decided to avoid the lift and walk to the fifth floor, vowing to be more kind to his stomach in the future. As he entered his flat he was greeted once more by the deceptively warm red wink of the answer phone daring him to press the 'play' button. He dared. Who dares – listens.

BLEEP!

"This is Sara, your ex-wife. It's no use pretending you're not there listening. Pick up the phone – loser. OK play your stupid little game, but remember this: I'm sick and bloody tired of acting as your answering service and I'm not going to do it anymore. I've got far better things to do than listen to that poisonous Pollard woman or the little tarts from your office. I shall change this number anyway, but if I get any more calls for you I'll be forced to speak to my solicitor and have him write to you."

One of the earliest solicitor's letters Jonathan had received was to complain that he'd emptied the joint bank account (before Sara had the chance to).

"I bet he'll be looking forward to that," thought Jonathan, as he checked the room for signs of peeling paint.

BLEEP!

"Hello, this is Lisa. I had a bit of trouble finding you and I think I may have offended your ex. Sorry. I hope you got home all right and that she didn't hassle you on my account. I'm ringing sooner than I thought I might because something cropped up after I left you today. If you're free tomorrow evening, can you meet me in the pub at noon? Or can you meet me there anyway, even if you're not free? If you can't do either, can you just leave a message at the pub? Thanks. 'Bye."

The evil thoughts that he'd just started to entertain about Sara melted away as he started to listen to Lisa's voice. There was nothing overtly sensual or immediately captivating about it; more that it was just pleasantly neutral, undemanding of him and thus easy to listen to. It was the sort of sound, he decided, that would soothe him to sleep if there was any justice in the world. While he waited for justice to arrive and sleep to overcome him he mused on his own circumstances and how they had evolved over the last few years. Much has been written about the meaning of life and most of it by philosophers or theologians, all of whom had their own agendas. Jonathan had never bothered to contemplate such weighty subjects as they inevitably gave him a headache. He had willingly given up independence on meeting Sara, perhaps too willingly. Having been used to thinking only for himself, friends and family, quite suddenly his thoughts had been required to consider and accommodate Sara in every situation. It was much like a painless form of schizophrenia – thinking every decision through from two perspectives. He had become quite adept at it and it was and perhaps because of that, he believed that all was well. Then, almost without notice, his whole life was upended, he was alone once more and thinking only for himself. Sadly there wasn't much justice in the world, so he got up again, took an overdue shower, pictured Lisa's green eyes and the shock of red hair and went to sleep anyway, smiling and thinking of peace.

Chapter 5: The Proposition

Jonathan woke naturally at eight o'clock and had he but known it, he was still smiling. He shook his head experimentally and was pleased to find that nothing rattled. The tongue passed the fur test, well just, and all things considered, it had the makings of a great day. This reverie was interrupted by a couple of postcards that landed on his doormat with a combined *plapp*, but his enthusiasm continued unabated especially when he realised that, unusually for a Saturday, there were none of those small unwholesome brown envelopes that most usually contained even more unwholesome bills. He looked out from his window and noticed that the temporary resident duck had found a friend of the opposite gender and that they were busily acting out a courtship ritual in what was clearly too shallow a trysting place. Seemingly, however, thousands of repetitions of genetic reinforcement were not about to be abandoned just for the sake of a few centimetres of water, and the pair of them went for it, oblivious to Jonathan and everything else, and certain in the knowledge that, if only in feathered terms, they were Mr and Mrs Right duck. Carefully planted groups of early red tulips were flattened by the sudden passage of eager plumage as Mr Right duck headed Mrs Right duck towards a singularly lush area of tulips where the chase ended and they got down to the serious business of making ducklings.

Jonathan wondered if it was quite done for him to share this moment of feathered intimacy and whether, if he continued watching, one or both of them might roll over and light up a cigarette. Anyway, neither did and he returned to the postcards. They were both from his sister in Madrid, albeit posted four days apart. She sounded happy which was good. So she was happy, the ducks were happy (although probably shagged out) and, believe it or not, he was happy. This didn't quite ring true so he finished his coffee and then, to clear up any lingering doubts, went to the bathroom to check. Sure enough, the face in the mirror was smiling, so he was happy after all and it really did look like being a great day. So what was wrong? Running down the stairs three or four at a time, Jonathan started whistling as tunelessly as ever and, hearing his approach, the caretaker's cats ran for cover. They needn't have bothered since he was in an uncommonly good mood.

Stu and Billy May Cronsev were visiting Americans in the city and had slept badly ever since they had set foot (feet) on British soil; they were not happy with their lot and didn't like – in no particular order – the food, the climate, the shops, the lack of room in British hire cars, the attitude of hotel employees and their bed. In fact, to be honest, I lied about the order of dislike, since it must be said that if there was one thing that the Cronsevs disliked more than all the other things they disliked, it was their bed. They had been vocal about all aspects of their discomfiture, but no more so than concerning sleeping arrangements. Three times, in the space of three days, they had been moved to larger rooms and it was probably on account of this, as well as their overly critical demeanour, that they had grown increasingly disenchanted with the hotel's staff.

The reverse was also true.

Sadly however, room size to them did not change the basic fact that they missed their water-bed back on their ranch in Texas. In fact, they had three and couldn't imagine why the City Hotel was unable to provide even one. The duty under-manager resisted the temptation to explain that they simply lacked imagination and positively oozed sympathy bordering on grief as he tried, in vain, to relocate them at another hotel (any one would do), but apparently the word had got out; no-one else in the city would have them for any money and it seemed to the Cronsevs that their holiday was blighted beyond any hope of salvation or recovery. Thus, with the single-minded determination that so often sets Bush-voting Texans apart from humanity, they set about dedicating the rest of their stay to showering verbal abuse on anybody who was unlucky or foolish enough to come within earshot. They wanted, in that uniquely American way, to 'share the experience'.

On reflection, one of the brighter points of their holiday was the frequency with which opportunities arose to shout at people. Friday, for example, had provided a once in a lifetime chance to thoroughly humiliate two undeserving chambermaids in the space of five minutes, followed by a stand-up row with the elderly breakfast waiter, which earned the latter a reprimand from his senior even though, naturally, he had been in the right. This was capped off two hours later with a ten-minute tirade against an unsuspecting assistant at a bespoke tailors and, to follow, an unsolicited lecture to a pastry chef on the subject of making pastry. If the Cronsevs had any friends to start with (which is itself a matter of some doubt) they were fast running out of them. They were, however not always successful in their pursuit of offering abuse and one of the few residents of Cambridge to avoid being on the receiving end of a pair of fully-vented Texan spleens was the senior guide at the College Chapel. It was a fairly close-run thing and he very nearly had his whole day ruined when luck or fate, call it what you will, intervened in the shapely shape of Lisa Adams when she plucked the Cronsevs from obscurity. If there is one thing that socially inadequate and unremittingly ill-tempered middle-class Texans enjoy more than a little gratuitous spleen-venting, it's having their inflated egos gently masturbated. Doing both, to the Cronsevs at least, obviously rated as cowboy heaven. Very suddenly and quite without warning, the vindictive amusement level of their day was launched to previously untold heights. They had wandered into the College Chapel soon after their lunch of pasta, fuelled with a thirst for some fine old-fashioned English culture and a good argument, if the chance arose. She was dressed in an ill-fitting pink number with almost matching trainers (they almost matched each other and the ill-fitting pink number). He, not wishing to be outdone on the sartorial front, was rigged out in pale blue slacks, a bright red Elvis shirt and a hideously loud sports jacket. The jacket purported to be double breasted, but the two front panels had long since given up any hope of meeting each other once off the hanger. He was, in every sense, a well-rounded man and she even more so – rounded that is. They were, in the worst of traditions, American tourists.

Like it or not, they were exactly the type of people that the residents of the fair city of Cambridge would eagerly welcome to their homes, bosoms and anything else that would separate them from their dollars. Separating tourists from their money had always been a year-round sport – almost a way of life, really – and Americans were seen by many to represent the ultimate challenge since not only did they speak a form of English, but often 'did' England in two days before 'doing' the rest of mainland Europe in four more. Consequently, unless there was a war to win or oil to be liberated, they rarely stayed more than a week. The staff at the museums and galleries dreaded the arrival of the Cronsevs and their like, but managed to remain civil, exhibiting a degree of professional detachment and creditable fortitude that bore no relation to their meagre salaries. They greatly resented the fact that the British establishment had neither the funds nor inclination to prevent English art collections being plundered to satisfy the hunger of American collectors who appeared to appreciate nothing unless it was expensive and wanted it, no matter what the cost, to hide away in their private galleries to impress their friends who probably appreciated it even less.

The Cronsevs were in no position to buy art (and had no taste), but were determined to see it, along with any building that was older than America. Their first encounter in the chapel was with the senior guide, but he had been at the receiving end of offensive Americans more times than he cared to remember and, realising his impending doom, he led them off at a brisk trot. He had an ultimate goal, which was of course to lose them. This could be achieved in various ways from which could be derived entirely different levels of satisfaction. Level one involved leading the visitor(s) attentively but quickly to an exit door of one's choice and then running like hell. Level two was a little more subtle in that it involved leading the visitor(s) attentively but quickly to an unsuspecting third party, effecting an introduction and then running like hell. On a truly tedious day (as most were) a little variation could be added to levels one and two by:

1 Letting someone else specify the exit door.

2 Agreeing to prearranged time penalties for early/late arrival at said door.

3 A combination of a) and b).

4 Any combination of the above with an unsuspecting third party.

5 Any combination of a), b) and c) with a duty third party.

It was by means such as these that the senior guide and his junior colleagues were able to engender some notion of team spirit. Sadly, however, with the Health and Safety at Work Act came tasteless yellow sticky tape, warning signs and ramps over perfectly serviceable steps and thus almost overnight, the realistic option of hospitalising unwanted American visitors was a thing of the past. It was this sort of erosion of job satisfaction that caused the guides to decline the offer of overtime generated by the presence of the video crew and made the senior guide opt for the simple expedient of leading the Cronsevs attentively, but quickly, to Lisa Adams. Lisa's elation at having an excuse to see Jonathan again had to be set against her equal dismay at having to invite the Cronsevs back for a re-shoot. It took all of her concentration to remain pleasant to them when, in truth, she would have given a year's salary to have them deported as undesirables.

On the Saturday morning at their hotel, the Cronsevs were reviewing the previous day's events under the quietly disapproving gaze of Emily Pollard, who was seated only two tables away. She had considered whether or not it would have been more prudent to have arranged the meeting with Michael and Jonathan in the privacy of her room, but decided on balance that doing so might alert Michael to the possibility that there was more at stake than she cared to reveal. Knowing him as she did, she sensed that he could react in one of two ways – he might behave with typical generosity to her request and agree without reservation, or, he might revert to type and indulge in one of his charming but testing mind games; trying to second-guess what she was really up to. She feared the latter and didn't want to provide that excuse. For the first time in her life she was not looking forward to seeing Michael and it was this that put her in an unusually irritable frame of mind. This was not helped by the repeated porcine noises coming from the Cronsevs' table. She was about to move to a more distant one when, to her great relief, they finished troughing and left. The elderly waiter advanced at her glance and replenished her glass of juice without a word being spoken. He smiled briefly, as if to acknowledge that there were still some people of proper breeding in the world and she returned his smile saying:

"Will they be staying here long, Charles?"

"We do so hope not, madam," he replied, with great sincerity.

Emily was anticipating the first of many croissants when Jonathan and Michael arrived. They had made no plans to meet up en route, but somehow knew that they would, since neither would willingly keep Emily waiting. She embraced both of them enthusiastically and invited them to be seated as Charles hovered attentively, waiting to take their orders. He observed that both young men were wearing sensible corduroy trousers, brogues, shirts, ties and befitting jackets, and therefore suitable company for Her Ladyship (as he liked to think of her).

After a lengthy exchange of pleasantries, the three set about an equally lengthy breakfast. Emily was hungry because she had somehow managed to miss out on dinner the night before and was looking forward to seeing her 'boys'. Michael was hungry because he rarely wasn't and needed some replenishment after the ravages of the previous two days, and Jonathan was hungry for the simple reason that on this morning, and for the first time in a while, he hadn't woken up wishing he was dead. It's a feeling that is greatly underrated by the congenitally well-in-the-head.

"Jonathan, I'm sorry if I appeared unnecessarily rude about your ex-wife, but I've never exactly hidden my feelings about her and – well – it's all over now and I'm sure it's all for the best. My only regret is that you had approached me sooner instead of letting me find out via Michael. You know I've always been very fond of you." Emily said, as she started pouring a fresh pot of coffee.

"There's no need for an apology, Emily, I've thought and said much worse."

Jonathan knew sufficient of Emily to appreciate that Sara was not a subject for the breakfast table and her concluding comments were nothing more that code-speak for, 'you're much better off without the bitch', so he changed the subject to pouring the coffee. There was very little point in pursuing the subject of his failed marriage and anyway, it was becoming blindingly clear to Jonathan that for some reason that he just couldn't wait to understand, he had just stepped over the ridge of an emotional watershed that, previously he had thought existed only in the mind of his therapist. Ever since he had woken up just a couple of hours earlier, he had been giving in to or giving himself up to bursts of spontaneous optimism. He hadn't a clue why, but he was enjoying the sheer novelty of it all too much to care. He certainly wasn't about to curtail the moment by talking about his ex-wife. Reason and reality would no doubt follow at their own pace and in their own good time. Life, he decided, was like that. He was still gazing into near space when Emily beckoned Charles to bring another bowl of fruit and he, Charles, suggested that they might all be more comfortable eating in the morning lounge. This, of course, was his code-speak for, 'Why don't you three bugger off so that we can lay the tables for lunch'. Once they were all seated in the lounge, Emily attempted to explain why she had convened the meeting. "Thank you both for joining me this morning – especially at such short notice. I'm only in the country for a short stay and I need your answer to a proposition."

Michael and, to a lesser degree, Jonathan were familiar with Emily's propositions and answered, "Yes, please," and "What is it?" though not both in the same order. They lacked practice.

Emily smiled, having just won a small bet with herself and ploughed on. "Well it's like this," she said, knowing that it wasn't, and covering her embarrassment by toying with an imported strawberry. "I'd really like the two of you to set up residence at the Hall or, at least, the Stables. My solicitors have given me the final go-ahead with Romulan Business Systems regarding their offer on the Hall. To bring you up to speed, Jonathan, Romulan already have a production and marketing facility just outside the city and are looking to open a corporate training centre at the Hall. They are acknowledged to be ahead of their peers in the race to produce certain types of cheap, user-friendly software, and have had the foresight to realise both the revolution and upheaval that this will cause in business, not least in the secretarial job market. Their advisers see this as an inevitable and even a long-term problem, but are trying to make the best of it by diversifying into combining product sales with a training programme. The aim is to select and train a force of super-aware secretaries to, as it were, pass on new skills to the ultimate end-user while, at the same time, making themselves entirely indispensable; and that's where we come in. They will start to occupy the Hall on a short-term rolling lease starting next month – just a few days away now – and, if possible, I'd like you both to be around to see that everything runs smoothly."

"And what's happening about the staff?"

Michael posed this question while watching Emily carefully. He had shown no obvious reaction to her sales pitch, but found it a little more imprecise than he had come to expect from his aunt.

She had been uncertain how to handle the situation and in her indecision, she had forgotten one of her nephew's best skills. He was an excellent chess player and she had too easily exposed a weakness which he could exploit. It was quite out of character for her to ask him to watch out for a member of her staff and his disquiet about doing so was compounded by her request for a meeting. In good chess fashion he had planned his game and she had made a poor opening.

"Oh, they're staying on," said Emily, "But actually, that's part of the reason why I'd like you both to be around. There is, I suspect, some hostility among the staff and I thought it might ease the tension if there was some increased evidence of family. Jonathan would be there for your company, Michael."

Emily carefully selected another grape as she failed to avoid Michael's eyes. She knew that he would guess that her earlier request to watch out for Frank was connected in some way. She was right, but more importantly, by mentioning hostility she had given Michael an excuse to ask the question that she least wanted to answer. Jonathan sensed something in the air and decided to stay quiet as Mike went for the Queen or, more likely, the throat. He had never beaten Mike at chess and this meeting was not his game.

"I don't mean to sound negative, but would it not make more sense to hire a professional manager, or expand Bill's terms of contract? You trust him, don't you?"

Despite every effort not to, Emily hesitated and appeared flustered. It was not in her nature to lie to anyone, and lying to Michael was not something that could be done lightly. Thankfully, but not entirely so, he saved her from doing so.

"So what is it exactly that you are not telling us, dear aunt?" he asked, putting his grinning face down to grape level for emphasis. "I mean, it's no real bother to me to move out of my rooms at college and go back to the Stables, but it's quite another thing to ask Jonathan to uproot from his flat so soon after he's got used to it."

Emily sighed, looked around carefully to ensure that nobody within earshot then leant toward Michael and Jonathan and whispered, "Actually, I'm not quite sure what is going on at the Hall, but I have a very bad feeling that I'm not going to like it much when I find out. Thinking about it, I really should tell you both all there is to know and then, perhaps, you will understand the real reason why I need you, both of you, at the Hall."

Emily smiled innocently at Michael and Jonathan hoping that they had missed the rapid promotion of, *like you to set up residence* to *need you, both of you.* She smiled again, but they had not, which is to say that they had not *missed it.* Emily blushed. Michael and Jonathan looked at each other, performed a synchronised shrug that didn't require any practice and looked back at Emily with a pained, joint-expectant, but politely quizzical gaze. Seconds passed as Emily looked first at the depleted fruit bowl and then the ceiling and then the windows and drapes and then, finally, the garden. Michael broke the silence by rising slowly to his feet and saying, with a barely suppressed grin, "Well, it really has been swimmingly wonderful seeing you once more. We really should have breakfast and these informative little chats more often. Ciao."

Jonathan could see that Michael and Emily were acting out some much-rehearsed little ritual of dancing round each other, both urging the other to capitulate first. He had seen Michael do it so often with other people, but he usually failed at the last hurdle, only slipping into a fit of laughter. That said, the stakes were obviously higher here, as if there was some form of long-standing stand-off. Having lost far too many games of chess to Mike, Jonathan knew that Emily's only option was to topple her King in submission. He was right, but only when Michael added, "Are you coming, Jonathan?" did Emily appear to give in.

"Oh very well," she said, laughing. "You win – I'll tell you everything. Two months ago, when I was last in the city, I told the staff what was likely to happen if and when Romulan were to come to the Hall. The games rooms would be used for lectures, formal training and seminars and the like and the rest of the Hall would be unaffected except for much increased use of the kitchens and bedrooms, for those from out of town taking residential courses. Then, of course, there is the other refurbishment to be supervised. I was a little tired and preoccupied at the time, but looking back on it, I'm now fairly sure that what I had to say did not provoke unbridled enthusiasm. I'm not really sure whether they were displeased because of the extra work – they would have been helped of course – or that the presence of outsiders might interfere with some other agenda of which I still know nothing. So the real reason I need you there is that I want you to act as decoys while someone else finds out what's going on."

The problem with telling one lie or non-truth is the inevitable necessity of having to, or feeling that one has to, embellish or support it with others even less credible. Generally, it works for a while with the likes of politicians and other professional con-artists, but not for comparatively more gentle souls like Emily Pollard – for which reason Mike asked, "Well, that's all very fascinating, but you seem to have avoided telling us whether or not you trust Bill – that's Bill Edwards, the butler, Jon. And who is it, actually, who is going to do your sleuthing while we act as decoys?" He resumed his seat at last. Emily capitulated.

"Yes, I'm sorry, both of you. A few years ago I had a tip off from the police that there was a gang going around burgling stately homes. A crime prevention officer gave me some advice on increasing security and I reported a few prowlers. The police set up surveillance but then nothing else happened. I was obviously happy about that, but the police told me, off the record, that Bill Edwards was, as they put it, 'known to them' and might have alerted the gang. Bill had no criminal record, all of his references were genuine and he had been in-post for several years, so I had no legal grounds to dismiss him. Obviously, however, I lost any reason to trust him. Nothing further happened for several years and then, two months ago when I was here, I gained the impression that something was wrong. I could not involve Bill and I didn't want to involve the police with only suspicions, so I hired a private investigator. He tells me that things are being stolen, yet I am not aware that anything is missing. The investigator wants to do more and has persuaded me to let you divert Bill's attention while he does so."

"And the sleuth?"

"Well since you are so intent on knowing everything whether or not you need to, perhaps you would care to drive me to the airport so that I can catch an earlier plane and then you can go to meet him."

"Checkmate, I think, and yes of course I will, if you think it'll help," Michael said, rising once more.

"In fact, it will help me no end, as otherwise I might miss tonight's plane and have to stay over in London – and I find that such a depressing prospect these days. I have to revise my reservation, pack and check out, so could you collect me at noon or soon after?"

"I certainly can if I go now – back soon! Ask Jonathan about his love-life." Michael left the last words hanging in mid-air as he left the lounge like a man who had just eaten too many croissants.

"I'll do nothing of the kind," she replied.

Emily watched the doors close through the space just vacated by Michael. She still wondered whether or not it was wise to involve him or, for that matter, Jonathan, in all this intrigue. Well it was too late now and her jumbled thoughts were interrupted by the elderly waiter, who coughed politely before enquiring whether there would be anything else. Emily replied that there would not, but said that she had enjoyed her stay as much as ever and would be leaving soon. He expressed his pleasure at the former and obvious sadness at the latter and backed away in the manner that only emotionally confused elderly men can. With her attention wrenched back to the present, Emily turned to Jonathan and asked, "Are you really quite sure that this is not going to be a huge inconvenience to you, Jonathan? I feel that I'm taking you a bit for granted at very short notice."

Jonathan had left all of the talking to Michael, but this had given him plenty of time to marshal his thoughts. At Emily's question, he was able to articulate them quite unlike a man who had drunk a bucket of beer only the day before.

"I really can't think of a single reason for not moving into the Stables." he said. "From what I recall, there will be more than enough room for me to collect all of my books from storage, the view is even better than that from my bed-sit and if I choose to, I can even canoe to college. It all sounds perfect, so when can I start?"

"If you're that keen, you can start today," Emily smiled.

"I am that keen, but as Michael was trying to hint in his own, very unsubtle way, I have a date, of sorts, and if I'm not very careful I shall be late for it – would you forgive me?"

"Yes, of course. You should have said sooner and it was rude of me to impose – in fact I shall have to go and pack, otherwise I shall not be ready and checked out when Michael returns. It's been lovely seeing you again, Jonathan."

"You too, Aunt Emily."

Jonathan escorted Emily to the lift, where they embraced fondly and then parted. He ran all the way to the pub and arrived just as the cracked church bells across the road clanked twelve.

"That was close," he said, almost to himself.

"Just a little," said the friendly face next to him.

Jonathan looked quickly round and saw Lisa's green eyes peering out from behind the curtain of red hair. He realised with a jolt that he'd been looking forward to this moment and its implications. He had completely fallen out with the little voice at the back of his brain about an hour earlier, probably during the second jug of coffee. When Emily had mentioned the idea of moving into the Stables he had lapsed - or was it leapt - into another burst of uncharacteristically optimistic thought and the poor little voice was lost in the onslaught. Lisa and Jonathan looked at each other as the rest of the world went on outside theirs.

She looked wonderful and he looked confused. She looked wonderful because she was; and he looked confused because he had every right to be. It's a 'men' thing. It was not simply because he was a man confronted, simultaneously, by his own hormones and a wonderfully beautiful woman. It was both of those things plus the fact that he was still wearing his cycle clips, but had mysteriously left his bike at the hotel. Lisa felt a blush rising and adjusted her curtains in an effort to hide as much of it as possible. She failed manifestly and tried toying with her clipboard instead. Moments and silences slid into each other and yet, miraculously, the world still kept spinning. Babies were born, mountains were thrust up from murky depths only to be washed back down again by acid rains and peoples around the world slaughtered each other in the name of their Gods/football teams/lacking oil reserves.

"Do you fancy a drink?" he ventured.

"Yes," she replied, laughing, as the tension eased.

"I've been looking forward to seeing you," he offered.

"Me too," she replied as more moments and silences slid together.

"I don't think we can keep this up much longer," Jonathan said, "or at least, I doubt that I can."

"Me neither," she replied, "but I think that the hardest part is over. Now about that drink . . ."

Chapter 6: Gotcha

"There's actually very little left to do." Lisa said, as she pushed a few crumbs around the rim of her plate. "It's just that the light went horribly wrong at the end of the last shoot and our director, being a bit of a perfectionist about continuity, wanted to re-shoot the last scene involving the guide. To make matters worse, he has disappeared, but it shouldn't matter too much since you have much the same build and we can fill up the sequence with a few distance shots – and that's where you come in. You don't actually have to follow a script as such, as we will voice-over most of the dialogue. All that will be asked of you is that you appear reasonably authentic. In fact, the only bit you might not be too keen on is the American couple that you're supposed to be 'helping'. They are a little overbearing, even by American standards. But once we get set up, it shouldn't take more than about ten minutes."

"That doesn't seem to be too much of a problem." said Jonathan, as he rose to buy another drink. "I work at the college and have to lecture to a few first year students who are distinctly American and once they get used to the idea that they're not being taken too seriously and that no-one will ever forgive their parents for electing Bush, twice, they either join the human race by the end of the first term or go home − which is even better. Do you do this sort of thing all the time? I mean, with Americans, or do you extend the service to other countries where English is not the first language?"

"Most of it is for the American market because that's where most of the money comes from, but we also do quite a lot in French, Spanish, Italian and of course, Japanese and Chinese. The English speaking market is much the easiest to handle because much more effort has to go into the production if you know from the outset that you will have to end up using sub-titles or voice-overs. It all looks a bit clumsy if you don't use discrete sound bites, but then, if you do too much of that it can look more like a political broadcast − and everyone knows how contrived they appear. Thanks," Lisa said, as Jonathan passed her a fresh drink.

They chatted on peacefully as the church bells clanked 'one' and then they parted reluctantly; she to shop and make final arrangements for later and he to sort out letting his flat and thoroughly enjoy the prospect of surrounding himself with books once more. Lisa gave him her address (without even a hint of a blush) and he quite eagerly agreed to call for her just before five. With only a slight diversion to collect his bike, Jonathan made it home in twenty minutes to be greeted by his voice mail. There were two messages; the first from Michael on his car phone, suggesting a pint later and the second from Sara, suggesting that he could avoid a solicitor's letter and the threat of much worse to follow by giving her his car. He smiled and made a mental note of the former and wiped both. He remembered the message that he'd found in one of the good luck cards occasioned by his divorce. It read, *Life is but a shit sandwich and I guess it's time for lunch!*

Jonathan misspent the hour that followed entirely failing to find sufficient bags, crates and boxes to accommodate his belongings and was about to play yet another CD too loudly as, some eighty miles away, Michael found himself having just fallen through a door that was opened for him and gazing down the undeniably ample cleavage of the investigator's assistant. He had already spent a relatively unusual Saturday in a battle of wills with his aunt and followed this with an unexpectedly rushed drive to Heathrow only to discover that her plane was, in any event, delayed. His subsequent inability to park anywhere near the investigator's office, even on a Saturday, had prompted an unscheduled sprint that, despite his recent efforts at getting fit, had left him breathless. Michael was thus not only gazing down the aforesaid and undeniably ample cleavage, but was also breathing heavily. Somewhere about a foot above the object of his immediate attention there was a noise. It was a very nice cleavage as cleavages go and this fact more than made up for the inconveniences that so far had blighted his day, but Michael realised that the noise was a voice, moreover a voice that belonged to the cleavage and it said,

"In my short, but relatively fulfilling life, I have always found that I can have a much more meaningful conversation with someone if they do me the courtesy of looking at me while I am speaking to them − preferably, that is, at some part of my face."

Michael snapped up his head, hiding his embarrassment and most of his reluctance. "I'm very sorry," he said, lying, "but I wasn't expecting to be here at all. It's been a rush all day, I couldn't get parked and I've just had to run half a mile so's not to be late."

He looked plaintively into her eyes which, though not as interesting as her cleavage, were nice eyes nonetheless. He saw no glimmer of imminent forgiveness, but the pupils were starting to dilate which, he told himself, was a sign of something. He'd forgotten what it was a sign of, but went for the punch-line anyway: "And besides, you've a button missing."

She looked down very briefly, returned to his gaze, relaxed her stance a little at last and said, "Well, the last part at least was honest. I think perhaps you came here to see Mr Stagg. I'll just take you through if you'd like to follow me. Would you like some coffee?"

Michael followed her through the maze of grey filing cabinets and computer screens to a small ill-lit office with a brass plate affixed to its door.

"I'd wait until he's off the phone if I were you, just in case it's confidential. I'm sure he'll be done in a moment; he knows you're here. I'll see you a bit later." She smiled and he returned it saying,

"I hope so − my name is Michael."

"I know," she replied. "Mine's Tess. Bye for now."

Michael watched Tess weave her way back through the office and wondered why she knew his name. She had that sort of predatory manner that was at once scary and irresistible. In fact, he was so preoccupied with her departing rear that he didn't hear the door behind him open.

"It's quite a view isn't it, but then your aunt said that you had a healthy interest in beautiful ladies. You must be Dr Evans. Peter Stagg. Please come in and take a seat."

Peter Stagg rarely left the same impression with any two people that met him and rarely left any lasting visual impression at all. It was, I suppose one could say, all part of his trade. He was of average build, height, middle-age etcetera and had the somewhat unnerving habit of attracting your attention to his hands when he spoke, so that it was difficult to assimilate any clear picture of his extremely average face; at least none that was likely to be remembered. Perhaps the only lasting recollection that most new acquaintances had of him was that of a calm inner confidence that required no external trappings – and certainly none that would be remembered. Today he was dressed in tattered blue jeans of unknown designer make, very expensive looking trainers, a single-breasted jacket of a nondescript light dun colour and a silk tie that screamed, 'I cost a great deal of money in Rome'. Michael liked to think that he could deal with most people in an equal way, but found himself almost at a disadvantage when trying to deal with Mr Stagg. It was almost as if he was, in some strange way, being manipulated and he found the experience quite bizarre. There was nothing sinister about the situation, or at least there didn't seem to be, but it was only with considerable effort that he forced himself to look straight at the face of the investigator and say, "Nice tie. Did you buy it in Rome?"

It broke the tension and Michael realised quickly that possibly the best weapon for a 'private eye' was the ability not to be remembered. He followed Peter into the office and was ushered into a large brown leather chair facing the window. It all fitted the pattern: with most illumination from the window, he would have to squint while the investigator would remain, partially at least, in silhouette. He was warming to this game, though not appreciating immediately that it wasn't.

None of this was lost on Peter, not least because he was and had to be a keen observer of humankind, but because Emily had, at his request, briefed him most thoroughly on her nephew. The point that she stressed more than any other was that Michael was a very fast learner. So to try to keep Michael's attention away from facial contact Peter lied effortlessly and said, "Florence, actually. Did anyone offer you coffee?"

Michael nodded as the door opened and refreshments were brought in. Peter continued, "Your aunt was good enough to provide me with a lot of background material on the case, but I now understand that you and Dr Grey will be living nearby, at the Stables. That was mostly at my suggestion and I hope it's not going to cause either of you any inconvenience. It's just that we're going to find it far easier to operate if whoever it is we're looking for is otherwise occupied worrying about you, or you two. Your aunt has also provided me with detailed personality profiles of the staff. I've had copies made and I'd like you to go through them at your leisure, just in case there's anything she's missed. I doubt that there is – she seems to have been very thorough."

"No problem," Michael said, accepting the folder, "But I've a few questions, if you don't mind."

"Question away. Your aunt said to expect it."

Michael's heart sank as it began to strike him that he'd been had.

"Thanks. Firstly, has my aunt been any more forthcoming with you about what she suspects than she has with me?"

"I don't believe so, but I do sense that there is something that she has told neither of us. That said, I often find that clients simply fail to mention some suspicions and even salient facts. I don't think it's intentional in your aunt's case, but in my business it's important that I know everything and make decisions and decide what's important."

"That doesn't surprise me. Second, roughly how long do you think this is likely to take?"

"Pass – it depends entirely on what we find out in the first week and, of course, how that affects whatever we do thereafter. Your aunt has set no particular time limits, but neither of us is anxious to have an investigation running on indefinitely. The one thing that we agree on is that the police can't be trusted to do their usual half-arsed investigation on their own. In view of recent events she wants a concrete case put to the police as soon as possible. I am instructed to report to you weekly and bill her four-weekly. What she and I have agreed is to place one of my staff – Tess – on a Romulan residential course and see what she can achieve with minimum effort."

"That sounds very sensible," Michael acknowledged. He decided not to enquire what was meant by 'recent events'. If Emily wasn't eager to tell him he didn't expect to learn anything more from Mr Stagg.

"It was your aunt's idea," Peter answered, forcing a smile.

"Yes, it does sound like her. OK – third: how exactly do we help? I mean do you want us to make complete nuisances of ourselves or just let it be known that Emily is not completely giving up the running of the Hall in her absence?"

"I've been giving a lot of thought to that and, on balance, I think our purposes will be best served if you do mostly the latter. The first thing you could do is to appoint a replacement maid. Your aunt has requested one of the existing staff to 'do' for her in Italy for the summer. No one could question you taking a hand in the interviews and you can appoint one of my assistants."

"With pleasure," Michael said, grinning stupidly. He was quite warming to Peter Stagg and could well see why Emily's solicitors had recommended him.

Peter returned the grin, saying, "A friendly warning though – quite apart from how odd it would look for you to be seen fraternising with the staff, Cathy Everet is trained in self-defence and also has a very short fuse. Here is her photograph – you met her in strange circumstances last Tuesday, I believe."

It took a little while for Michael to reconcile the face in the photograph with that of Frank's near nemesis. She was not blonde and had penetrating eyes. But it went some way to explain why she, at least, knew him. She had been briefed. Michael returned the photograph and Peter continued, "Anyway, with luck you won't have much time for that sort of thing. Look."

Peter handed Michael hard copy of an email that Emily had sent from the executive lounge at the airport. It read:

Dear Michael,

I forgot to ask you one further favour concerning the Hall. The new occupiers want to do some remodelling a few days before they open. They will use the same contractors that are doing my refurbishments. Could you liaise with them and make sure that everything goes smoothly and that none of our fixtures are damaged. My solicitors have names and details and are expecting to hear from you. They have also had a quiet word with Antonia and Owen Drake in Dorset about a reference for Miss Everet.

Love,

Emily

P.S. I know it will be difficult, but do try to keep your hands off her and don't do too much liaising!

"I take it, then, that my aunt has already met Cathy?"

"Yes."

"And she has most probably spoken to her about me also?"

"Most probably."

"And this meeting between you and me was arranged some weeks ago, my aunt never intended to be here at all and I have been, in every sense of the word, had!?"

"Er – yes."

"Well, I'll be buggered."

"Right answer, apart from the tense, I'm afraid, Michael."

Chapter 7: A B movie

His ears still ringing from an over-excess of digital decibels, Jonathan parked his bike outside Lisa's flat. To say that he'd parked it was perhaps stretching a point since, in reality, he had left it slumped casually against a bald spiky-looking pampas grass and told it to wait. Grasping a fine-looking bunch of daffodils in one hand and his courage in the other, he entered the foyer and announced himself at the intercom. The door buzzed, clicked and then opened to his touch and Lisa appeared at the door to her flat. She looked as though she had been beautifying herself for hours (which she had) and Jonathan flourished the flowers. He had intended to say that he hoped he wasn't late and that he didn't know what kind of flowers she liked so he'd got daffodils because they always reminded him of the onset of spring and the renewal that it promised. In short, he was babbling to himself. Anyway, none that mattered because somehow all the words got even more jumbled up in his head and when, finally, they came out they sounded suspiciously like, "You look beautiful."

It seemed to be received well up until the point when Lisa started to laugh, cough and then cry. She waved him inside and motioned that she would have to get herself some water. Jonathan seized the opportunity to look for signs of cats, but to his great relief, found none. She returned from the kitchen still laughing, but with rivulets of eye make-up decorating her cheeks.

"Do you make a habit of complimenting people in your cycle clips? Look what you've made me do to my face."

Jonathan thought about telling her that she'd managed it perfectly well on her own, but then, he did see her point. Lisa collapsed onto a large multi-coloured beanbag and made pretence of hiding behind her hair. He looked quickly round for a box of tissues and found one beneath a coffee table, but as the moment was not yet right he just gazed helplessly around the room and waited. Lisa continued to laugh and sob at the same time and when, after a few minutes, it all seemed to subside, Jonathan squatted in front of her, parted her hair and offered the box. She wiped away the worst of the streaks, still tying her best to be a bit cross, but the persistent bouts of giggling somehow let the whole scene down. More minutes, sniffs and giggles passed and the floor about them started to take on the appearance of a municipal waste tip. Jonathan felt his ankles start to ache and sat down. He eyed his cycle clips disapprovingly and pocketed them. He saw that this was not going quite to plan, but not knowing what the plan was and being undeterred, he looked once more at Lisa and said, "For what it's worth, you still looked beautiful."

Their faces were now no more than inches apart and closing. Someone once said that the first kiss is no respecter of age. It matters not whether one is sixteen or sixty-six, the expectation and thrill remain the same (and sometimes the disappointment). But they were not to find out just yet. Lisa started to lean forward, but then caught her breath, hurled herself backwards and then sneezed loudly. It was Jonathan's turn to laugh and the moment was gone in an instant.

"You don't have cats, do you?" she asked. "Only I'm allergic to cats."

"No cats, I promise, but I was attacked by your pampas grass on the way in. Could that be it?"

"No, I don't suffer from hay fever and it's too early in the year anyway, but the local cats pee on the pampas and I'm extraordinarily sensitive to them. I guess that's what did it."

Lisa had at last regained her composure and went out to the kitchen to put the kettle on. She asked Jonathan to make them both some coffee while she retreated to the bathroom to carry out what she later described as 'emergency repairs'. Jonathan found the wherewithal for coffee, made two mugs and carried them back to the sitting room to await Lisa's return.

"I've made yours black. Is that alright?" he asked, to mid-air.

"Fine, thanks. I'll not be long."

He browsed idly through the sparse collection of books on the shelves not yet knowing that a more comprehensive collection adorned Lisa's bedroom. He was most-way through the CD stacks when she returned fully repaired.

"I'm really sorry," he said, passing her mug. "I suppose it must have looked a little odd."

"Please don't worry. Our only real problem now is not being late. You don't wear cycle clips to drive, I suppose?"

"Not knowingly."

"I was afraid not. We'd better take my car then. Finished?"

The inside of Lisa's car and, in particular, the front passenger's foot-well looked much like the sitting room floor that they'd just left behind. Jonathan pretended hard not to notice the mess and deftly buried his feet in the small but welcoming pond of tissues, not daring to contemplate the myriad of sci-fi species that no doubt eked out some form of non, four, six or eight-legged existence there. The map compartment was replete with all manner of sweet papers and wrappings and it was quite evident that whatever feelings Lisa Adams lacked with respect to felines, she more than made up for in cravings for chocolate. Jonathan pondered briefly how many hectares of trees had been felled in some remote and distant part of South America to satisfy the cavernous interior of the glove compartment, but decided that this was not a good time to air his 'green' credentials. It would, in any event, have been a little hypocritical given what he had just done to the pampas grass with his bike. He looked instead at Lisa and wondered why it was that so many women always seemed to adjust the driver's seat so that it was bolt upright and as close to the steering wheel as possible. Apart from the fact that it looked so bloody uncomfortable, it left no room for the seat belt to operate in the event of a crash and this car was too old to have an airbag. She wouldn't stand a chance. It wasn't as if Lisa was particularly short; her knees looked too high for that, and the car wasn't one of those where the front end was curved sexily to satisfy some functionally aerodynamic whim of an Italian designer. He continued to dwell on these morose thoughts as they drove off and then just dwelt on looking at Lisa, which was a much more pleasant train of thought.

"I hope we'll find somewhere to park," Lisa said, glaring at a taxi driver who had just launched himself out of a side road in the certain knowledge that it and all other roads were his by royal decree. She had got about as far as mouthing something beginning with 'F' when she remembered that she had company.

"It shouldn't be a problem." Jonathan assured her. "Many of the shoppers will be heading out by now and if not, I've got a staff parking pass that I hardly ever use. I usually go everywhere by bike unless it's tipping down or I've too much to carry."

In the event they were able to park very close to the college chapel and spent a few minutes running through once more what would be expected of Jonathan. When finally they entered the building, the lighting crew were just about set up and were amusing themselves at the expense of the director who was, it appeared, having an unsolicited lecture on the struggle of the free world against communism and Islam throughout the ages and the role played by Hollywood and Fox News in bringing to the public the full role of Uncle Sam in this and many other good causes besides. It was thus also a lecture on how to direct films given by an unfortunately dressed male American. He was encouraged, or so it seemed, by an equally unfortunately dressed female American.

"They," Lisa said, grimacing, "for your sins, are the Cronsevs – your charming guests from the Atlantic."

"I think the world will be safe just so long as we don't let them breed." Jonathan replied.

"Let's hope that they haven't already." Lisa agreed. "I think Jenny's going over to intervene."

Jonathan studied the person to whom Lisa had referred. With a few quiet words and determined gestures, Jenny separated the Cronsevs from their prey and walked them over to greet Lisa and Jonathan. Lisa embraced Jenny and introduced Jonathan. Jenny opened her eyes slightly wider and tilted her head almost imperceptibly at Lisa. Lisa had tried to prepare herself emotionally for the inevitable unspoken question, but failed as expected. The smile barely won out over the blush, as she replied with deliberate ambiguity:

"Yes Jenny. This is whom I had in mind."

Jonathan was careful to watch this interplay, fully intending to read between the lines – spoken or not. He was aroused at the near kiss only an hour earlier and was conscious that he found Lisa very attractive. It was evident that Lisa and Jenny were very close and adept at speaking without words. What he heard or perceived he heard pleased him sufficiently for the moment. The women continued to talk and exchange meaningful glances and Jonathan excused himself to walk over to what he took to be the set. Some of the ancient pews had been rearranged slightly, presumably to create an illusion of more space, and four arc lamps had been placed discreetly to fill in some of the naturally shadowed background and thus reduce the sort of severe contrast that makes amateur promotional videos look like amateur promotional videos. An earnest young man clutching a light meter advanced quickly towards Jonathan, saying, "I don't know what your day has been like so far, but unless you want the rest of it to go tits-up you'd better come outside with me to discuss light levels."

Jonathan recognised the look of impending doom on the man's face and knew that the Americans were about to pounce if he did not comply. He moved toward the young man, not daring to look left or right and together they almost sprinted out into the last of the early evening sunlight.

"Thanks," Jonathan smiled. "I take it that was a near thing."

"Very, but from the look of the sun, we'll have to go back in anyway. Do you know what you have to do?"

"More or less." Jonathan replied. "They are going to put some sort of obscure question to me and then I have to bullshit them for about twenty or thirty seconds until you think it will be okay to fade to a sequence showing three hundred and fifty adiposally-endowed tourists squeezing themselves into a wide bodied jet in the States, all eager to buy as much culture as is humanly possible in two days."

"You've been warned, I see!"

"No, I just guessed. Come on – they're calling us in."

The director ushered Jonathan and his co-stars to their places and before any of them had the opportunity to consider second thoughts, he called for 'lights' and 'action'. Jonathan was aware of a lull in the background noise, spoilt abruptly by a fairly predictable and entirely unoriginal question from John Cronsev. The man's face filled Jonathan's vision like a familiar bad dream and given the low but distant camera angle, he understood why it really wouldn't have mattered what he (the guide) looked like. Lisa had indeed been looking for 'height' and 'build' just as she had said. Jonathan wondered briefly who the poor bugger was who had been plucked from obscurity to endure the Cronsevs for the earlier parts of this epic tale and whether or not he had since taken an overdose, but the predictable question ground inexorably to its predictable end and he found himself duty-bound to offer some sort of plausible reply. Slightly behind and to the right of the Cronsevs Jonathan saw the director making a quick winding gesture intimating that the question had over-run and that he would therefore have to bullshit even more authoritatively in order to finish in time. Jonathan therefore adopted his very best contemplative, scholarly pose, took a deep thoughtful breath, and said, "Well, that's a most interesting, unusual and, if you will permit me to say, perceptive question; I must say. Most interesting indeed. My. My. Why did the chapel take so long to build? Quite by accident you've chanced on an old pet subject of mine that hasn't been debated fully since my great-great grandfather's time. Now let me think … well you know, for Lord knows how many years, it was thought that most of

90

the delays were caused by the sudden and greatly lamented deaths of ruling monarchs – I don't suppose you get much of that – while others, of course, claimed that it was more to do with the fact that there was a complete lack of power tools and cranes, and that all the materials had to be transported here and erected by sheer dint of human effort. Anyway, we now know that those ideas were just a load of outmoded, jingoistic, sentimental cack. Modern-day computer based research carried out right here at the University Department of Occupational Psychology has shown to a probability of slightly less than eighty two percent, that the delays were in fact the result of entirely, not to say readily foreseeable, degenerative interpersonal relationships between the diverse groups of ethnic Patagonian, Cuban, Celtic and, to a lesser degree, Persian migrant workers, generations of whom were pressed into service to complete the task. I mean, you might think you've had problems with those Mexican chappies in Texas, but compared with the difficulties we had here …well, need I say more?"

Jonathan continued to gaze in an entirely scholarly way at the Americans as the light of truth finally started to dawn in their eyes. Finally Stu Cronsev gathered what was left of his limited wits and said, "Thank you young man. Thank you very much indeed!"

He grasped his wife's plump hand in his own, guided her out of the chapel and walked her quickly and wordlessly back to the hotel, where they packed, checked out and took a taxi to Heathrow for the first available flight back to America. With the mention of the words 'Cuban' and 'Persian', Jonathan had succeeded in confirming their worst fears. Clearly, England, for all its famed, envied and much vaunted culture had, throughout history, been riven with communists and terrorists. Worse than that; it probably still was. It was no place for them. No place at all!

Chapter 8: Reunion

Jonathan watched the retreating backs of the Cronsevs as they squeezed hurriedly out of one of the chapel doors. The little voice in the back of his head had warned him urgently about the potential consequences of saying anything along the lines of, "Come back, I haven't finished," so he didn't. The arc lamps went out with a resoundingly unanimous 'phuttt' and he realised that all eyes were upon him. He looked around incredulously and asked, "Was it something I said?"

The laughter and discreet applause that followed his question raised a few eyebrows among the chapel staff and it ceased at a gesture from Jenny. Instead, the crew circled Jonathan, offering their congratulations and thanks. Lisa stood, admiringly, at one side.

"That was quite brilliant." Jenny said, beaming at Jonathan.

"The acting?" he said, hopefully.

"Well, that as well, I suppose. Was that OK, Jason?" Jenny asked, looking at the crew in general. They nodded approvingly.

"Great," she continued. "I'm buying!"

The crew, helped by Lisa, Jenny and Jonathan, dismantled the equipment, re-packed it in appropriate trunks and boxes and took it out to the waiting van. Jenny thanked the senior guide and promised not to return again until after exam time. This news was received well. The video crew and cast offered a welcome diversion from time to time, but their continued presence was beginning to be a nuisance. The bulk of the crew pleaded prior commitments and disappeared leaving Jenny, Lisa and Jonathan to seek liquid refreshments. Jonathan still had less than fond memories of his hangover of the day before and suggested food. There were no objections and the three set off in search of a newly opened tapas bar. They found it, only with some difficulty nestling in a side street in a refurbished milliner's. Although it was still only early evening, the bar was already heaving and they were shown to the last available table. They chose a selection of seafood and lightly spiced pepper dishes and pecked at them while they chatted.

"Thanks again for stepping in at the last moment, Dr. Grey – you got us out of a real hole."

"You're most welcome – and please, it's Jonathan."

"Right, thanks, and what is it exactly you teach? I had no time to talk to you before you dismantled our friends from across the water."

"Polymer chemistry for the most part – it's a bit tedious over supper though. I mean, it has no documented reputation for sharpening appetites and I've never heard of it used as a main theme in an after dinner speech. I expect I'll chuck it all in and do something different one day, maybe some VSO, once I get my life sorted out."

Jonathan knew that Lisa had first-hand experience of Sara, albeit by phone, but he hoped that he had said enough and that Lisa understood. The look in her eyes said that she had – probably only too well. Jenny, of course, knew of Lisa's distress and changed the subject.

"Well, I won't expect you to chuck it all in just yet, but if you can avoid the subject next weekend you're more than welcome to come to dinner. In fact, after what you did with the rest of the cast, I won't mind being lectured all weekend. Lisa's going to come and some of the crew too."

"I'd love to," Jonathan replied, almost squeaking as Lisa's knees touched his. "I'll get the bill for this and then, if I recall it right, you are buying."

Jenny and Lisa went to the 'Girls room' while Jonathan waited for the bill. He tried contemplating his napkin and then the wallpaper, but there was no avoiding it; he was going to have to contemplate his life. He was only too aware that he found Lisa very desirable, but he was worried that everything was happening far too quickly. Quite apart from the fact that at almost a moment's notice he was about to move again and play at being a detective's decoy, he found that, more and more, he was becoming preoccupied with someone whom only two days previously, he hadn't even met. He was over thirty and thinking like a teenager. By any standards, it was quite ridiculous. He toyed briefly with the idea of running away, but that was even less adult and anyway, the option was unavailable. Ultimately, he was saved by the bill – it arrived, hotly followed by Lisa and Jenny.

"You choose this time, Jonathan." Jenny said, as the waiter helped her into her coat.

"Fine," said Jonathan. "If it's alright with you two we'll go to the Don't Feel Bitter - Drink It – I arranged to meet a friend there."

First they drove to Lisa's flat to dump her car and then walked briskly back to the pub. Michael was seated in a corner of the bar, deeply engrossed in a book on second year thermodynamics. A good beer chaser, if ever there was one. He looked up briefly to locate his drink and caught sight of the three of them as they picked their way slowly toward him through the crush of customers. He gestured the universal sign for drinks as he rose to his feet to welcome them, but Jonathan, by return, gestured that the ladies were buying. Jonathan, at Lisa's suggestion, joined Michael while she went to the bar to help Jenny.

"Hi, Mike," Jonathan said, sitting down. "How did it go with the detective this afternoon?"

"Fine, I think, but I no longer see it as one of Emily's whims, so I think we should keep it under wraps for as long as we can. She has given the man what amounts to a blank cheque, so I'm sure we should take it very seriously."

Michael's face lapsed into its more familiar grin as the women slowly peeled themselves away from the press at the bar.

"You don't seem to have been wasting time since we parted company this morning, but I didn't know you'd be bringing Jenny Overton as well."

"You know her then?"

"Ah yes!"

Mike and Jonathan rose as the women finally reached the table, clutching pints.

"I believe you two already know my friend, Michael Evans."

"Well, I certainly do," Jenny said, kissing him lightly on the cheek. "Good to see you again, Mike, it's been a long time."

"It's been too long," Michael agreed, "and it's also been a long time since your cousin's wedding – it's Lisa, isn't it?" he added, turning to look at her.

Lisa looked blankly for a few moments as she searched her memory. Recent experience had shown there was a whole chunk of her life that appeared to be just a nasty grey blur. It was that chunk which coincided with the last year or so of her involvement with Greg, when things started to go seriously wrong. She could vaguely remember a wedding, but nothing in detail: certainly not this man. Michael sensed her obvious embarrassment and helped out.

"I wasn't there very long actually and, as I recall, the photo session was curtailed by an awful thunderstorm."

"Ah, that wedding," Lisa said, at last recalling where she had seen Michael before. "Didn't you abscond with one of the older bridesmaids?"

97

"Ah – yes – on reflection, think I preferred it when you couldn't remember me."

Jenny sat down very close to Michael and rubbed her right middle finger up and down his glass, teasingly. He had appeared a little discomforted at seeing Jenny and now that she was almost sitting on his lap, he looked as though he wanted to be several miles away. Lisa and Jonathan saw the entertainment value in this unexpected encounter, glanced at each other for agreement and smiled. Jonathan opened the inquisition thus:

"Well Michael, in the two or so years I've known you I've not seen you quite so ill at ease in the presence of someone whom you've obviously, how can I put this?, 'known'. I think I pitched that just about right, don't you Lisa?"

"Just about word perfect, I'd say," Lisa replied, warming to the task. "Though in the four years or so that I've known Jenny here, I would not have described her as the bridesmaid type, nor the sort who would have such a disorientating effect on an old acquaintance, unless of course he, the acquaintance, had something to be disorientated about. I think I pitched that just about right, don't you, Jonathan?"

"Just about word perfect, I'd say. Shall I go on, Michael?"

"I think you've both gone on enough already. Just take it from me that Jenny and I knew each other a long time before either of us knew either of you. We were both very young at the time, me especially." Michael blushed, grinning. "You can carry on talking about me while I get another round of drinks, if you really can't think of a better subject for a Saturday night. Same again?"

Once Michael had returned with the drinks they moved onto less controversial subjects and caught up on the exploits of other previously unknown shared acquaintances. As the evening wore on and remaining barriers went down, two sets of conversations dominated as Jenny gravitated towards Michael and Lisa towards Jonathan – they discussed ex-spouses. As it transpired, this was all part of a plan that was hatched by Jenny and Michael quite early in the conversation, having realised that they had been acting out similar supporting roles for their respective friends.

"I've never seen you blush before, Mike," Jenny said, quietly.

"I don't do it often," he replied, "but seeing you again took me a bit by surprise and I had always meant to apologise for running off like I did."

"You could try now if you like." Jenny said, fluttering her eyelashes at him mockingly.

"Not if you're not going to take me seriously, I won't." Michael countered, trying to look hurt.

"OK," she said. "Answer just one question and we'll call it quits. Was there someone else or were you just running away?"

"Which answer would you prefer?" Michael asked, trying to guess which would hurt less.

Jenny looked at Michael and smiled with an echo of something hidden just below the surface of her emotions. Even after all this time he was trying to protect her; trying not to hurt her. She took his hands in hers, moved even closer and whispered:

"I'll make it easy. You weren't running to anyone else – even though you let it be known that you were. Also you weren't running away from me. I probably drove you away by trying to rush you into a marriage you thought might not last."

"You and your father, in fact, but do you always answer your own questions?"

"These days – yes. Are you doing anything next weekend, only Lisa and Jonathan are coming to dinner?"

"I can't make it next weekend, I'm afraid. As of this morning I'm moving back to the old Hall – well, the Stables really – remember them? And I'll be humping furniture across town on my own from now until Easter if I can't prise Jonathan away from Lisa to help. They do seem to be getting along alarmingly well, don't they?"

"Happily, they certainly do, but I'd better have a word with Lisa before she makes too many plans for next week. I need her to go to the States for a few days. Don't go away; I'll be back."

Lisa wasn't overjoyed at the prospect of going abroad again, but she took it passably well. There was an almost unanimous decision not to have another round of drinks and they left on the clank of ten o'clock. Michael had brought his bike and set off still clutching his book. Jonathan joined

Jenny and Lisa and after they had dropped Jenny off at her flat, they went back to Lisa's to untangle his bike from her pampas grass.

"Thanks," Lisa said. "You were great and I enjoyed meeting your friend Michael again. It's a bit of a surprise about him and Jen though – she'd kept that one very quiet."

"Him too." Jonathan replied. "Look, since I won't be able to see you beforehand, what time should I call by on Saturday? If the weather holds, we could walk."

"It'll be a very long walk if we do. Dinner will be in Paris! Didn't Jenny explain? The company has an office there with a huge apartment above it. Much of the time it's used by visiting clients, but they rarely stay at weekends so it's free for us staff to use. You'll need overnight stuff and there will be an early start. Why don't you come round for breakfast about seven?"

"I'd love to, and Paris will be great," Jonathan replied, "but for now I'd better be getting home to do some more packing. Michael and I are going to move to the Hall – his ancestral seat – and I'll probably be there by the time you get back from America. I hope you manage to avoid the Cronsevs."

"So do I."

During this exchange Jonathan had retrieved his bike and was making ready to leave. He had purposely avoided thinking about kissing Lisa goodnight. He wanted to, of course; it was just that he didn't want to plot, plan and anticipate in case the end result was disappointing. Lisa had taken the opposite view and had used the loo break in the tapas bar to encourage Jenny to keep Jonathan's friend, whoever he was, preoccupied. In the event, things went to plan, albeit for entirely different and unexpected reasons. Jonathan's expressed desire to go straight home was a little disappointing, but all it did was bring the moment closer – and now it was upon her. She took Jonathan's bike from him, parked it back on the bruised remains of the pampas grass and wrapped her arms around his neck. Jonathan was surprised – very pleasantly. They were still glued together some minutes later as two fire engines sped past, sirens screaming.

"That's the third time this week," Lisa said, coming up for air and pulling herself reluctantly away from Jonathan. "They seem to be earning their keep just lately."

Jonathan was still dazed at the unexpected passion and was relieved by the interruption. He picked up his bike, again, squeezed Lisa's hands and left. There was a fine spring mist in the air that thickened as he crossed the river and then thinned again as he pedalled up the hill past Michael's rooms. The light was on in the sitting room, but he was tired and didn't want to disturb Michael this late at night. He cycled on over the common and at last, into the car park of his block of flats. For all the grief and generally bad times that living there had meant, Jonathan was almost sad to be leaving the place. It was warm and, to coin estate agents' terminology, it was certainly very compact. He would miss those strange and uninformative conversations with other inmates in the communal laundry room. Also he would miss the view of the gardens with the transient pond and its even more transient inhabitants. He would miss the ducks. He got off his bike and stole quietly towards the pond to see how the pair was getting on. He wasn't quiet enough and disturbed them causing a flurry of feathers and irate quacking. He backed off and blundered into the pond itself. Yes, he thought as he walked through the car park leaving a trail of muddy footprints, he would miss all of this, but most of all he would miss his car. It was nowhere to be seen. Jonathan carefully removed his shoes and socks before entering his flat, and laughed at his own misfortune. After taking a hot shower and making himself a coffee he telephoned the police to report the theft of his car.

"And it was locked, sir?"

"Yes."

"But there was no alarm or immobiliser?"

"No – it is quite old, really."

"And what sort of value would you put on it sir?"

"Oh, about a thousand, maybe twelve hundred at the very most."

"Well I'm afraid it's a very common make of car, sir. Are there any special extras or distinguishing features that we should look for?"

"None that come to mind. I think my ex-wife took everything that wasn't welded on. What happens now, anyway? This is the first time that anything like this has happened to me."

"Well you should inform your insurers as soon as possible, but after that, there's little more that you can do other than wait for it to be found. We'll be in touch with you as soon as there is any news. That other number is a work number, I take it?"

"Yes."

"And can we contact you there?"

"Yes, or leave a message."

"Fine, Mr. Grey. We'll be in touch."

Jonathan hung up and laughed again. 'There's no way that Sara is ever going to believe this,' he thought. He set his alarm and went to sleep thinking about what might be his last ever Monday at the flat and the prospect of a weekend with Lisa.

Chapter 9: Moving In

With only one more week before the Easter vacation, college was very quiet and Jonathan had only three lectures to give – one each on Monday, Tuesday and Thursday. None of the work was new, as such, so no heavy preparatory reading was needed. At lunch with Michael on Monday they agreed to hire a van and then spend as long as it took to move all their belongings to the Stables. Jonathan's greatest pleasure came from retrieving his books from storage. He had missed them in the same way that you miss old friends who go to live or work abroad. It wasn't as though he used to read every day, it was just that they had always given him a sort of warm, cosy feeling and a familiarity that was just difficult to do without. And for no more rational reason than that, Jonathan's first van-load to be moved comprised just books.

The Stables had been very tastefully converted years previously and the gardens had matured well, hiding any trace of residual evidence that there had ever been a well-trodden paddock. The buildings were of local white brick set in a square about a mostly grassed garden, with a reasonable-sized swimming pool set at its centre. The north, west and east wings had been fully converted, the north wing being raised to two floors. The breach at the mid-point of the south wing had been widened to allow vehicle access, some of the stalls at either side having been converted into open garages. The east and west wings were all given over to use as bedrooms with en-suite facilities and the larger north wing contained two sitting rooms, a spacious dining room, a well-appointed kitchen and a study. It was the latter that Jonathan had earmarked for most of his books.

Michael looked rather ruefully at Jonathan as the room quickly filled with a seemingly topless mountain of books during the course of Monday evening. After lugging in the sixteenth heavy case-load and with no obvious end in sight, he sat down with an exaggerated grunt saying:

"I don't suppose this -" he waved his hands around the room generally, "- any of this, is up for discussion, is it?"

"Absolutely not, Michael. This -" he looked round fondly at the burgeoning heap of prose about them, "- this is a small part of the price you have to pay for the pleasure of my company."

Michael stopped grinning. "You mean there's more?"

"No, I didn't mean more books. I meant that you would be able to share some of the less attractive moments of my life like the weekly, manic, vitriolic and thoroughly pointless telephone calls from my ex-wife. I've had the flat number diverted here – as of ten minutes ago. So if it rings, I'm in the bath."

"Any other surprises I should know about, or can we leave this lot and go for a drink?"

"We can go for a drink when I've unpacked this lot and you've cooked. I promise you that's the last surprise today."

As it turned out, there was one further surprise for both of them, as on returning from an unusually brief drink they let themselves into the Stables to find the lights on, the alarm off and Cathy standing in the kitchen busily cutting up the remains of her jeans and feeding them to the Aga. She looked for the entire world as though she had just returned from an average day at the office and not the least as though she'd taken up freelance plastic surgery as a hobby. Michael gave her a quick glance of reverence tinged with fear.

"Hi!" She said, looking up briefly. "You must be Michael's friend Jonathan. We met briefly last Tuesday. There, that's got rid of the last of the evidence. They were nearly new, too!"

She shut the hearth of the stove and looked up at the stupefied expressions on the two men's faces. She was standing in Michael's kitchen wearing, seemingly, only an oversized rugby shirt.

Michael's grin reappeared by default. "I seem to be making a bit of a habit of meeting Peter's colleagues partly dressed," he said, as seriously as he could. "How long have you been here?"

"Since late Tuesday night."

"What? Peter said that I should see you soon, but mentioned nothing of you being here."

"Well, I imagine that he just overlooked it. I had booked in at the Fox, but after that unfortunate encounter with Mr Graves, I had to change my plans quickly. So I decided to hide out here – Ms Pollard had given me the keys in case I needed a bolt-hole, which I did."

It might have been that he was tired after carrying so many of Jonathan's books; it might also have been because Jonathan had restricted him to two pints, but the main thing that was really pissing Michael off was an increasing belief that he was not being told everything – i.e. being kept out of the loop. He might have expected it from his aunt, but he would have expected better from Mr Stagg. He had kept his cool at Stagg's office, but now he was visibly annoyed and without much attempt to conceal it he announced, "Well, I can't cope with this now. I'm for a shower and bed."

Cathy saw that she had lost the initiative and also left the kitchen, clutching her shirt as low as possible around her thighs. She returned minutes later wrapped in a dressing gown. Jonathan thought he preferred it when he could see her legs, but having seen her in action, he wasn't about to say so – he wasn't feeling that brave. She was gorgeous, but he wasn't about to tell her. Instead he changed the subject and said, "I'm afraid we haven't unpacked as far as real coffee yet so it will have to be instant if that's OK with you."

"Anything as long as it's black without sugar, please."

Jonathan moved the remains of the boxes and a few books that he had overlooked so they could be seated in comfort. He had reached the conclusion that this Cathy person, whoever she was, was very easy on the eyes, but he wasn't too happy about the circumstances in which they had met. He looked nervously at the window but was reassured when Cathy explained that the room was not overlooked other than from the enclosed garden and that if anything larger than a fox was out there, it would be detected by some clever sensors and software. She explained that in the few days she had been there, she had upgraded the intruder alarm equipment and that more was planned over the next week or so. Jonathan appeared mollified and said, "Well, that was a bit of a spectacular entrance to village life, Cathy. Do you put a lot of men in hospital on your first night in town?"

"Not if I can possibly avoid it." Cathy replied. "Until Tuesday evening I had intended to spend a few days quietly in the area just getting the feel of the place when that moron decided to follow me from one pub to another trying to buy me a drink – or worse. He was thrown out of two that I know of and I thought I'd lost him."

"So you weren't following him then?" Jonathan asked.

"Not at all, although I think I recall the previous versions of his face from some of the client's photographs. As I said, I was just familiarising myself with the area and I wasn't intending to meet him – or you two for that matter. So I really had no choice but to come here. Do you think that Mr Evans is really upset? Are you, too?"

"Me? – no I'm more confused and bemused than upset, though I can see why Mike is miffed and I can confess to being a little apprehensive myself. As you get to know Mike better, you will understand that beneath the apparent easy-going exterior there is someone who takes his responsibilities very seriously. His problem at present is that he's been given too little information, would dearly like to take it out on you, but knows that it's probably not your fault. He'll get over it, but if we are all to get on and work together it would help if you or Mr Stagg could have a word with him."

Jonathan had come across with a little more authority than he'd intended and Cathy surprised herself when she head herself say, "Yes – I see your point. I'll apologise to him in the morning."

"That'll be good, but what will you do for clothes?"

"I took some of them into the inn, but none that I'll miss. I still have quite a few in the car."

Clearly it wasn't Jonathan's place to raise any further objections to Cathy staying, but he was still not particularly happy with the developing situation and, still trying to work things out, he asked, "And there's nothing at all at the inn from which you can be identified?"

"Nothing at all." Cathy replied. "The clothes and the bags are unmarked, all from chain stores – and paid for in cash. I told the people at the inn that I arrived by taxi, so no one will have even thought to look for a car. I pre-paid for three nights with cash and no one in the village, other than you two, has ever seen me out of the wig and glasses. The only person to have looked at me for more than a few seconds was Frank whatshisname: he was very drunk and isn't going to remember, or probably see anything much for a few days yet. So you will see that despite this evening's colourful diversion, I can act like quite a professional."

"I wasn't questioning that." Jonathan replied, without a hint of apology. "It's just that a great deal seems to have happened this week and, speaking for myself, I wasn't expecting to have a quiet drink and end up with someone having their face remodelled by a woman who looks alarmingly like my ex-wife. The last bit's not your fault, but I'm not at all used to this spy stuff and, speaking again for myself, I do find it all a bit discomfiting."

Cathy carefully put her coffee mug down on a small space on the floor between the boxes of books, counted inwardly to ten and looked straight at Jonathan. "I wouldn't want you to take this the wrong way, Jonathan, but it's precisely because you are confused – both of you – that you will be such good decoys. Believe me, there should be no danger to either of you and, as of now, I promise that you will be kept informed of anything, everything you need to know. Please don't worry and just pretend nothing is going on. It's the best way, so just try sleeping on it. Speaking of which, judging from the number of books outside it, I seem to have taken the liberty of choosing the room next to yours. Will that be a problem?"

"Not for me – shall we?"

Jonathan led Cathy round the east wing of the Stables and willingly accepted her offer to help make his bed. He toyed briefly with the idea of offering to wash her back and other bits in a nice warm bath, but he had a recurring vision of Frank's new two-dimensional nose and thought better of it. Thus he returned to the main room, where Michael found him thumbing through his books and trying his best to avoid this new version of reality. He appeared not so much absent-minded as detached from it in the way that he had been so often in the bad days with Sara. During that time Michael had tried to offer counsel as well as friendship, but found, as like in so many other aspects of his life, that with all the best intents and determination in the world, he lacked the vision, training and the right words to deal with the problem. He had also been aware that, desperate though he was to do something, there was too great a risk that he might only make matters worse and maybe push his friend over the brink. So he adopted the policy of simply 'being there' as often as possible and making damned sure that when he wasn't able to, someone else would 'be there' instead. It wasn't too hard an exercise in logistics and he would have cut off a metaphorical arm to see Jonathan happy, really happy, once again. It was an absolute bloody crime, what Sara had done to Jon and a tribute to him that he'd not gone and flipped out completely. Lisa (another one), the professional counsellor at Relate, had helped greatly and Michael thought it possibly the best idea he'd ever had to get her involved. He had met her years previously at one of those end of term parties that usually ended up with a hangover in a strange bed, but strangely hadn't. Funny that – they were rare. They had just chatted and drank sensibly and although she was lovely, he'd not entertained any biblical intentions toward her. That was rare too, very rare. He'd taken her number of course, like you do, but had happily consigned her to the category of *person worth keeping in touch with*. Initially, she thought Michael was really talking about himself, but when that was put right and the introduction was made, Jonathan's rehabilitation really started.

Chapter 10: Undriveable

"Good morning. Department of Chemistry."

"Hello, Susan, its Jonathan, is Dave Ellis about?"

"Hi – yes I believe he's in, hang on a moment while I try his room; I think he was looking for you yesterday."

"Yes, so I heard – thanks."

"No problem, if this doesn't work I'll put your call straight through to the labs – hold on."

"Hello, Dave Ellis speaking."

"Hi Dave, it's Jon. I'm not due in until this afternoon, but I heard I should talk to you."

"That's right, I took a message for you yesterday from someone at the police station – something about a car. Hang on; I have it written down somewhere. Now where did I put it? Ah yes here it is, it's from someone called Jones, WPC 243 Jones, she says they have got your car. It can't be driven but it's on a trailer, so if you turn up with a tow bar and identification you can take it away."

"OK, thanks, Dave, I'll be in after lunch, 'bye."

"Bye."

Jonathan wandered through the Stables feeling fairly impressed with the Police at having found his car so quickly. Initially, he had visions of the thieves being so disenchanted with its performance that they had brought it back in disgust after attempting the first hill, but the report that it couldn't be driven didn't bode well. He followed the smell of fresh coffee to the kitchen where he found Cathy still wearing a bathrobe which was Michael's, but thankfully, looking a little less like Sara. She looked quite innocent with multi-coloured toast crumbs around her lips and certainly not the man-slayer of the fateful night in the village pub.

"Morning, Cathy; I see you managed to find the real coffee."

"Mmmmm. Want some?"

"Please – black. Have you seen Michael yet?"

"Yes, about ten minutes ago and I managed to get an apology in, so we seem to be on terms again, at least for a while. He came in looking for his bathrobe, I told him he'd have to fight me for it and he went off muttering about not hitting women."

"That figures; he hates people who do. Do you know where he's gone now?"

"He didn't say but from those awful 'singing' noises, I'd guess he's in the shower. Does he really get that upset about people hitting women, Jonathan? I hope I didn't touch another raw nerve."

"You probably wouldn't believe it from the way he behaves, but Michael gets upset at quite a few things – and that one the most, I think it all stems from something that happened when he was very much younger. I almost got him to talk about it once, but beneath that pampered and very flippant exterior, he can be very deep. Don't worry about upsetting him though, if things start to get him down, he just starts 'singing'. It's usually so bad that either people start throwing things at him or he realises things could be a lot worse. Listen!"

They listened to the strangled version of an old Beatles lyric wafting from some distant part of the Stables. Cathy looked at Jonathan and winced.

"And he really believes that anything could be a lot worse than that?"

"Absolutely. He's completely tone deaf."

"No kidding, but isn't there anything we can do?"

"Well we could join in or go outside, or if I could work out where the stopcock for the hot water tank is, we could give him a cold shower to remember."

The noise grew worse as Michael lapsed into what was just about recognisable as a melody of the Rolling Stones' greatest hits. Cathy took off the bathrobe and handed it to Jonathan, while revealing what seemed to be just like he imagined army underwear would appear. He looked in appreciation as she blushed and asked, "You want me to give him back his bathrobe, don't you?"

"Yes."

"And you want me to tell him I'm sorry – again?"

"No" 'da da da da dum – Brown Sugar! "YES!"

"And you want me to do it now?"

"No. OK, YES! And Cathy, just one more thing. Did you learn to fight in the army or do you just like wearing brown?"

"Jonathan, are you taking advantage of the situation to come on to me, or am I right in thinking that there is probably someone somewhere who would be quite pleased to know that you are not?"

"Well, it's very early days yet, but probably the latter. You could say that I'm undecided, gullible and of course, male."

"Well that really doesn't clarify anything. Anyway, I just had an accident with Mike's washing machine, okay? So stop gawping at me and take Michael his sodding robe! Or have you forgotten what I did to Frank's nether regions?"

Jonathan could see that Cathy wasn't entirely serious, but as a precautionary measure he just grabbed the robe in both hands and ran. By the time he reached Michael and completed the delivery the 'singing', such as it was, had stopped and he took a short cut across the garden back to his own room where he picked up his own bathrobe for Cathy. He knocked on the door of her room, but this time she really was genuinely undressed and only her face appeared at the door. Jonathan merely held out his robe while pointedly looking away.

"I thought you might like a peace offering in case you stay a little longer. And besides, my hormones can't cope with all this early morning excitement."

"Thanks, Jonathan, you're very thoughtful," she said, accepting the robe, smelling his body on it and closing the door softly. "It's just a shame that you're not available as well as undecided, gullible and of course, male." she added, once he was well out of earshot.

Jonathan realised that all the morning's diversions had so far prevented him from having breakfast and he wandered back to the kitchen to find food and, so he hoped, Mike. He, for all his lacking vocal prowess, had a car with a tow bar. The kitchen overlooked a small 'U' shaped rockery and an even smaller pond in one corner of the garden. It was a warm sheltered corner and even though it was not quite April, the pond was seething with tiny legless tadpoles clinging, or so it seemed, to any available leaf edge. It was just as if the whole pond had been brought to the boil like a saucepan of black-eyed beans and then turned down to simmer. Then the image disappeared in a surge of ripples as a large frog belly-flopped from its hiding place among the rocks into one end of the pond.

"You're looking very pensive this morning, Jonathan. Is there a problem or was the singing too much for you?"

"I didn't hear anything that I would remotely call singing. No, there's no problem other than persuading you to take your bike to work so that I can borrow your car."

"Well that's no great problem," Michael replied. "I was thinking of doing that sort of thing quite regularly as part of getting fit for the new season. Remember; we have our first game in six weeks."

Jonathan wondered whether he should react to Michael's use of the 'we' word, but decided against it. Instead he established that the keys were in the car and bade his friend farewell before the conversation could take a turn for the worse. With the morning rush hour done, it was a pleasant drive into the city and Jonathan experienced no problem until he tried to drive into the cramped car park at the rear of the police station. He was at once confronted by a surly man in uniform who looked far too young to be a constable.

He was about six feet two with a spotty complexion and a leer that suggested that he would be more at home hurling abuse from a football terrace than doing point duty. Jonathan laughed at himself, as it was the first time that he'd admitted that a policeman looked young and hence he was getting old, but the moment of humour disappeared when the surly-faced officer spoke.

"You job, mate?"

The single syllables and peremptory style of delivery appeared to be in keeping with the man's demeanour, but unfortunately for Jonathan he had not the least idea what the words meant. It was only the fact that the last word was pitched slightly higher than the two preceding it that gave Jonathan a clue that the whole three were meant to be some sort of question. As Jonathan wound down his window he toyed briefly with the idea of replying in similar vein, with something like: 'Yes – you work bench?' but on looking at the vacant stare on the officer's eyes, Jonathan guessed rightly that among the many bits of software not installed behind them was a sense of humour. Instead he put on his best, polite yet not non-condescending smile and said, "Good morning, officer. I've come to collect my car."

Initially it seemed that he might just have given the right answer. There was nothing in it with more than three syllables and the leer seemed to waver momentarily.

"You job, mate?"

"Pardon me?" Jonathan replied, wondering if perhaps the first word might have been a mistake. Either way it didn't matter, as the officer was firmly attached to his limited car park attendant repertoire and pressed on, "Are you 'Job'? Are. You. Sir. A. Mem. Ber. Of. The. Police?"

Jonathan listened carefully to the question while at the same time reassuring the little voice at the back of his brain that he wasn't about to do anything rash. Straining to maintain the smile he answered slowly, "Well actually no – I'm not a member of the police; I'm a member of the public. I've simply come, as requested, to collect my car."

"Well you can't park 'ere mate. See that sign there?" He pointed with a flourish. "It says, 'Police Authorised Vehicles Only', and yours ain't, so you can't park it 'ere mate."

Jonathan was in far too happy a mood to start an argument, but instead made a mental note of the officer's number from his epaulette, just in case there was a vacancy on death row. His smile now gone, Jonathan gave him one more chance to reason. He rustled in his pocket to find the note that he'd made of his conversation with Dave Ellis and said, "No, sorry, perhaps I didn't make myself very clear. One of your colleagues, WPC 243 Jones, suggested that I should come here to collect my car. It was stolen a few days ago and now, apparently, you've found it."

This was clearly quite a lot for the officer to take in at one go and he shifted uneasily from one flat foot to the other as he struggled to come to terms with the longer words. He looked briefly at the no parking sign as if seeking inspiration, but none came. He shut his eyes, hoping that when he opened them again this difficult member of the public would have gone way, but he hadn't. Eventually he reached into his tunic to look at a crumpled copy of the duty roster that he'd carefully stuck together with chewing gum, pulled himself to a semblance of authoritative attention and said, "WPC 243 isn't on my relief, is therefore not on duty today and you can't park 'ere, mate."

Jonathan felt his heart sink, knowing that there was nothing to be gained by continuing to use reason. He thanked the young officer for his 'help' and reversed out of the car park without even a sight of his car. After a brief tour of the surrounding streets he found a parking space and jogged back to the front office of the police station. There the service was far better.

"Good morning, sir. How may I help you?"

"Good morning, officer. I've come about my car, which I believe you have, here. I reported it stolen a couple of days ago and yesterday I had a message from WPC 243 Jones to say that I should come and collect it."

"Fine, sir. Can I have a look at your papers and some form of identification?"

Jonathan produced his passport, driving license and photocopies of the insurance, M.o.T. and registration documents, explaining that the originals for the last three were in the car when it was stolen.

"Well, that all seems to be in order, sir, if you'd just care to sign the release form here and here," the officer said, pointing. "Fine. Now the remains of your car are your responsibility once more. You may collect them from the rear yard."

Jonathan knew deep down that he was going to have to brave the rear yard again sooner or later, but the word 'remains' threw him completely.

"I'm sorry to have to trouble you further, officer, but as I understood it the car was just undriveable. So why do you refer to it as having 'remains'?"

"I take it that you've not seen it then, sir?"

"No, I've not."

"Right, well, according to our records it was reported stolen by yourself last Saturday evening and was next seen on Sunday evening, when it was found dumped and alight in a field about six miles out of the city. By the time the fire brigade got to it, it was all but burned out together with the three farm buildings surrounding it. There's been a spate of this just lately and yours was just one of three this week. You'd better have a copy of this report for your insurers, sir – they'll only ask for one anyway."

Jonathan was too shocked to say anything more than, 'Thank you'. He picked up the papers and left quickly. Having collected Michael's car and driven twice round the block, he entered the rear yard of the police station and was confronted once more by surly officer who seemed to delight in being a spotty and self-appointed car-parking attendant. True to form, the young man asked the inevitable question and, flying in the face of the advice being shouted from the back of his brain, Jonathan replied, "Yus, mate. Come to collect vehicle number Charlie – three.ah – four.ah – seven.ah – bravo – foxtrot – victor."

"Right, mate. Jus' back in over there," he said, pointing to something barely recognisable beneath a tarpaulin, "and I'll hitch it on for you."

"Right, thanks, mate."

Having towed the remains of his car back to the Stables and left them in one of the vacant garages, Jonathan separated the charred heap that was once his car from the police trailer by the simple expedient of attaching the former to a stout hook in the wall with a chain and towing the trailer out from beneath it. The noise was pretty awful, but it worked. He was now running a little late and wondered whether he could have saved himself from rushing by simply dumping the car outside Sara's place. However the memory of Cathy all but castrating Frank was still fresh in his mind and common sense prevailed. He eventually returned the trailer to the police station following the afternoon lecture and was pleased not to encounter the surly young officer once more. No doubt he was having a nice cup of tea and a fresh bag of hay. After that and being on the south side of the city Jonathan decided to go to his flat to collect any fresh mail and load anything that was small enough to fit into Michael's car.

That done, he drove to Michael's rooms and together they loaded the van with furniture. Something important was bugging Jonathan, but for all he tried he couldn't get it to approach the surface of his mind. Instead he ribbed Michael about taking the van rather than his bike, as discussed earlier.

"I think," Jonathan said, quite seriously, "we'll have to put you on beer rations if there's to be any chance of getting you fit in six weeks."

Michael grunted as he squeezed one last small box into the van and straightened up with an expression of resignation tinged with thirst.

"Yes, I suppose you're right, Jon. I'll try making a start, say next week or better still, next month. I've been getting quite enough exercise humping your books and this stuff around without going to cruel and ridiculous extremes like that. Besides which we; that is, you and I will be starting training tonight."

It was Jonathan's turn to use the resigned expression, although it looked a much better fit on Michael.

"I have this nasty memory of you using the 'we' word this morning, but I kind of hoped that it was just a mistake, as I don't recall having remotely agreed or volunteered to do anything."

"Well your recollection is correct, Jonathan, and you neither agreed nor volunteered for anything. What's more, if it makes you feel any better, neither did I. It's Cathy's brainchild really. After you left this morning we started talking about lots of things and among them was fitness, or more to the point, our lack of it – fitness that is."

"Michael, why do I know that I'm not going to like what comes next very much?"

"Because you probably know that it will do you good. Did you know that Cathy was in the army?"

"I sort of guessed she might have been. Is there some kind of connection between the two or have you lost the plot?"

"Oh, right. Anyway she was, and finished up as a qualified P.T. instructor. I sort of happened to mention that we were trying to get fit for cricket and -"

"There's that 'we' word again," interrupted Jonathan.

"- and she said that she'd help out with a few ideas, here and there."

Michael was clearly on the defensive and Jonathan, still hiding his amusement, pressed home the advantage: "Michael, have I ever told you that I never feel exactly safe when you're being this evasive? In fact, on a scale of one to ten, the effects of you being evasive are about seven worse than your casual use of the word 'we'. Now I know why your aunt tries to keep at least two countries between you and her for most of the time – you just seem to attract one disaster after another. What on earth have you volunteered us for?"

"Well, when you put it like that, I didn't actually volunteer either of us for anything, really. It's just that I wasn't brave enough to say 'no' when Cathy suggested it."

"Suggested what?"

"The swimming."

"What swimming?"

"The swimming we have to do every night before she cooks our supper and every morning before we have breakfast."

"So you won't be cooking supper then?" Jonathan asked, all too hopefully.

"Not while Cathy's here." Michael replied.

"Or breakfast?"

"Or breakfast."

"Great!" Jonathan smiled. "When do we start?"

Chapter 11: Air Guitar

Perhaps predictably, Jonathan's enthusiasm for swimming, or to be more honest, someone other than Michael cooking, was badly misplaced. When Michael had left Cathy earlier in the day, she was busily overhauling the solar heating for the pool. Unknown to her however, someone who for the sake of argument we shall call 'Michael', had completely forgotten to tell her that during the previous long hot summer, the re-circulating water supply to half of the panels had been electronically wired out to prevent the pool overheating. Thus although Cathy had finished her check-list by ten o'clock and the sun had obliged by shining relentlessly all day, the pool temperature didn't manage to climb above seventeen degrees centigrade by the time that Michael and Jonathan dived in to complete their twenty length entitlement for supper. For some reason that was never made entirely clear, Cathy told them that it was at least twenty and since the air was cool and neither of them was brave enough to question her on the subject, the best thing they could (and did) do was to just dive straight in and swim. If nothing else, the extreme coldness of the water concentrated their attention on completing the specified number of lengths as rapidly as was possible.

Michael was the more powerfully built of the two, but Jonathan was the more natural swimmer – thus by agreement, they stayed together throughout the ordeal. As they commenced their last length Cathy wandered up to the side of the pool dressed rather pointedly in jeans and a thick warm jumper and handed both of them bath robes as they climbed out, shivering noisily. They both looked a bit blue at the edges and she ushered them indoors quickly. Michael was the first to be able to control his chattering teeth long enough to speak, and enquired tetchily, "Why did you tell us the water was warm when you knew quite well that it wasn't? One of us might have had a heart attack!"

Cathy opened the kitchen door to let them in and then gave them each a mug of hot milk before she answered.

"I figured that if I told you the real temperature you would never have gone in, so I took the liberty of lying a bit. Before you complain I should point out that it's probably Michael's fault for not telling me about the modifications that he or someone else made to the heating system. I only discovered the problem about an hour ago, otherwise the temperature could well have been nineteen or so by now. I would also point out in my own defence that lying is an underestimated and much maligned form of communication. Anyway it hasn't done either of you any harm so instead of standing here dripping and shrinking in unmentionable places, why don't you both take your drinks with you and have a hot shower? Supper will be ready in twenty minutes."

Although still numb with cold, Jonathan and Michael realised that they had come about as close as they were ever going to get to an apology – which was to say, nowhere near, and went and did as they were told. Their discomfort was made complete when having each finished a fairly generous portion of fish salad about thirty minutes later; they were told that they had also finished supper! As it transpired, Cathy was unable to secure a hotel room in the city and so she stayed on at the Stables, mugging up on maids' duties in general and the finer points of silver service in particular. The continued presence of Cathy ensured that the fitness regime was adhered to strictly. With all the solar panels now working, the pool temperature quickly became more tolerable, but no sooner did it do so than Cathy increased the number of lengths to be swum. Food portions improved a little, but there was a voluntary ban on beer – volunteered by Cathy. Thus it was a very much leaner but fitter Jonathan who packed his shoulder bag and cycled into the city to breakfast with Lisa on Saturday morning. Lisa was very jet-lagged and had only just awoken when Jonathan arrived. Despite being obviously pleased to see him again, she remained quite subdued during breakfast and once in the minibus, she promptly draped herself over Jonathan's shoulder and fell fast asleep. There were eight souls in total and all but Jonathan were in various states of fatigue. They reached the Kent coast at much the same time as Peter Stagg arrived for his first appointment of the day. The office was spacious, square and compellingly drab. Its two side walls were lined with old indistinguishable filing cabinets of grey painted metal that merged effortlessly into a slightly darker carpeted floor. The single window in the rear wall gave a forgettable view of a supermarket car park, while the opposite wall, which was shared with the typing pool, had a door at its centre flanked by out-sized prints of uncompromisingly kitsch art. The leather-topped table which dominated the room's centre was tidy, supporting only a laptop and two or three closed files each in grey covers, no doubt arranged in alphabetical order. In front of the desk was a comfortable chair, behind it a more formal seat and behind this stood the room's occupant, Theo Plummer – Chartered Accountant. Either by choice or so as not to clash, he wore a drab grey suit. He was an odd looking man – not quite ugly, but distinctly off-world in appearance, almost like the runt of a litter from some fiendish genetic experiment conducted in a secret laboratory in Slough. He had a pronounced forehead supporting a thatch of unkempt mousy hair. Beneath this were a pair of sharp darting blue eyes and small reading glasses perched on the end of a slightly uplifted nose. Despite or perhaps because of his odd looks, Theo had legendary success with women, and perhaps because of this he was unmarried. Having a busy mind and sharp sense of humour, he just seemed to attract intelligent women – the sort that preferred grey cells to six-packs. In truth he had no time for a full-time relationship as two loves occupied most of his waking hours. The first was accountancy and the second, air guitar. This might seem an odd pairing, but as Theo rationalised it, he badly needed the latter to offset the unremitting boredom of the former. So there he was: bored by his first love and unfaithful to it with his second. Playing air guitar was not greatly favoured and even less well understood by his colleagues, but he and they were fully aware that he often did his best work after a three-minute rendition of some nameless rock great. Besides which, he was the boss. His client, Emily Pollard, knew nothing of either his sexual prowess or his second love: nor should she, as they were not her concern. She employed him because of his loyalty and fastidious attention to detail – two traits that appealed to her in roughly equal measure. Theo had just finished a particularly stirring rendition of a track by ACDC when the intercom buzzed to announce the arrival of Peter Stagg. Miss Pollard had alerted Theo to an approach by Mr Stagg, but had been unusually reticent regarding the precise nature of the enquiries that he was undertaking on her behalf. Theo muted his mp3 player, rearranged his tie and advanced to the door just as Peter knocked.

"Mr Stagg. Do come in, Miss Pollard emailed to say that you might want to see me."

"That was kind of her, and even more so of you to see me at such short notice."

"That's not a problem, she is a valued client and, I like to think, a friend also. I am more than happy to help if I may. Have you been offered coffee?"

Peter affirmed and cast his eyes around the office, which seemed to focus attention at the desk. Peripherally, he noticed a couple of neglected pot plants on the filing cabinets near the windows and small dried stains where attempts at watering had missed the mark. Concealed behind the plants were a pair of high-tech loudspeakers which seemed oddly to conflict with the surrounding ambiance of complete unremitting banality.

"Yes, thank you. I understand from Miss Pollard that you have some interesting news for me."

"Interesting yes, but I'm not sure whether it is good or bad. Please have a seat. You should perhaps have a look at this."

Theo passed Peter a Revenue demand for some two million pounds and noticed a brief look of incredulity pass over the investigator's face. Emily had indeed used the word 'interesting' in her email to Peter of the previous day and he paused to question what she might regard as most interesting.

"You see," Theo continued, "apart from its size, this demand poses something of a conundrum. Miss Pollard has always been careful with her financial affairs and invariably has sought my advice on matters much smaller than this. Moreover, she assures me that she has not disposed of any assets without my knowledge. On the other hand, assuming that they have not made a basic blunder on a grand scale, the Revenue would not issue such a demand unless they had hard evidence. I can and will look into that in my own way and that is something perhaps we should discuss. I imagine that this is why she has suggested this meeting. I wouldn't want to duplicate your own enquiries, but to be quite frank, I don't know exactly what they are or what part I should play."

Peter gathered from this that his host probably knew nothing of his own investigations and if Emily had not told him, then he would and should probably also be discreet. He didn't want to alienate Emily's accountant, but he had too much on his own plate to sideline a potential confederate, even if Emily had chosen that course. Peter had the unnerving sense that a hole was forming rapidly in his investigative net and it would be helpful if it could be plugged before it gaped and swallowed too many resources. He therefore decided to be tactically indiscreet on this occasion. He reflected on the demand once more before replying.

"I think perhaps that our mutual client spoke little of my work because it is still at an early stage and she didn't want to mislead you. If it will help I can share a hunch with you, which is that this demand and my enquiries are linked and with your help I will discover how and why. If I am right, the outcome of your work will inform mine. Would you be able to obtain some unofficial information from the Revenue? I don't want us to rattle any cages, but I imagine that it would not be unusual to seek particulars."

"Yes, that's in order. I know a few people at the Revenue and I could perhaps arrange a lunch if you were able to come. We should be able to able to have sight of any evidence, even though we would not receive it formally for some time."

Peter considered the offer, but with his current workload he concluded that it would be better if he left the accountant to do the leg work. If Emily trusted the man, there was probably little to be gained by committing his own time.

"Lunch would be a good idea, but it would probably be better that I was not present. I am not that happy about pretending to be an accountant and even less so, to appear undisguised and raise potential suspicions. If my hunch is correct, it would be preferable for you to go alone and then I can act quietly on whatever you discover. Whatever else comes to light I doubt that my work will be of direct interest to the Revenue. Miss Pollard has told us both that she has made no disposals and, for now, I shall assume that the evidence the Revenue has is false and was provided by a third party, possibly even an anonymous one."

The last few words were sufficient to claim Theo's continued attention. He gratefully accepted the carrot that Peter dangled under his nose and unknowingly was co-opted to the team. Business cards and the usual pleasantries were exchanged as Theo guided Peter back through the typing pool to reception. He then returned to his office, put away the files and picked up his phone.

"Geoff. Good morning. How're Sally and the kids? Great! Are you still dealing with my client Miss Pollard? Good. I wondered if you were free for lunch today or tomorrow? Today? Excellent, then I'll see you at one in the Crown."

Theo had found the encounter with Mr Stagg all very fascinating and felt the sort of buzz that he'd first experienced on qualifying. He slackened his tie, selected a particularly rousing track by Lynyrd Skynyrd and picked up his air guitar. He needed to do some serious thinking. Curiously, he'd already forgotten Mr Stagg's face. He reflected later on what he'd meant by act quietly. Peter took a cab back to his office thinking that it had been too easy.

Chapter 12: A Wet Dream

The company apartment was not located in a particularly fashionable area of Paris, but had the advantage not only of off-street parking in a private courtyard, but also a large, square roof garden with a reasonable view toward the city centre. The food was taken to the kitchen by Lisa, Jason and Jenny, while the others looked around and sorted out rooms. Lisa, to no one's surprise, then took a shower and caught up with even more sleep. The rest went off to be tourists, leaving Jenny and Jonathan to cook.

"Jonathan, do you think we should have a sorbet between the soused herring and the liver?"

"I would certainly choose to, given the total difference in flavour between the two. Do we have time to make some or would you like me to nip out and buy some? I think I saw a shop nearby somewhere."

"No need. I think I just about have time if I make it now. Can you pour us some drinks? We might as well make full use of chef's perks since we are welded to the kitchen for the next two hours or so."

"Sure! Is red okay with you?"

"Yes, fine thanks. Jonathan?"

"Yes, Jenny?"

"Would you mind discussing Mike in his absence?"

"That depends, rather."

"On what I want to discuss, I suppose?"

"Mostly, yes."

"Are generalities, allowed?"

"In general, yes," Jonathan grinned.

"Would you say that he's happy – generally?"

"Yes – generally." Jonathan replied, hesitantly and only after some moments of thought. It wasn't that he was unsure of the answer or whether it was appropriate for him to give it, it was more that he was a little reluctant to discuss anyone in their absence. He didn't feel that he knew Jenny well enough or long enough for such a conversation and most of all, being a man, he didn't quite understand just where it was all leading. He was about to ask why she wanted to know when she beat him to it by getting another question, the real question, in quickly:

"What I mean is, is there anyone – I mean anyone special – in his life at the moment?"

"That hardly qualifies as 'general', does it?"

"No, I suppose not." She flushed, and busied herself making the sorbet. "I'll try putting it another way. Is there anyone else as well as you two staying at the Stables at the moment?"

Jonathan thought very carefully before he said: "No" – so much so that Jenny began to think that he was playing games with her. Jonathan didn't help by adding: "Well, not on a permanent basis, anyway."

Jenny gave Jonathan one of her legendary withering looks but either he didn't recognise it for what it was, or he was immune to such things as a result of his failed marriage. She wondered briefly if his inclination to answer more helpfully would be improved by the addition of half-made sorbet to his drink, but decided on the balance of probabilities, that it wouldn't. She couldn't blame Jonathan for displaying loyalty to his friend, but equally or even more so, she couldn't understand why Michael hadn't been in touch since their reunion the previous Saturday.

She mulled it all over in her mind a little while longer before giving in to one last question:

"Jonathan?"

"Yes, Jenny?"

"One last question?"

"General?"

"General."

"Go on then."

"Well, why has Michael moved out to the Hall when his rooms are so handy for college?"

The question threw Jonathan a little, since although he had no reason to mistrust Jenny, he had no particular reason to trust her either. Of more importance, he and Michael were supposed to maintain a united front of pretence, however implausible, about Mike's presence at the Stables, and this was the story that he gave Jenny. After all, it was in many respects true, and he was in no mood to lie or even bend the truth slightly. Not a hint could be given about Cathy, the very temporary house guest, as there was no way that Jonathan could see of explaining her presence without either spilling the beans, or outright lying. He shouldn't really have made reference to her earlier to Lisa. No, there was nothing for it, he was going to have to bullshit his way out of this – bullshitting didn't qualify as bending the truth and certainly not lying – well not quite.

"It was all quite sudden for both of us really. Last Saturday morning Michael and I met his aunt – you may know her – and she asked Mike and me if we would mind moving into the Stables for a while to make use of them and in Mike's case, to look after the Hall during the refurbishment and oversee the tenants as they move in. Normally his aunt would have taken care of everything herself, but seemingly she has some unavoidable business abroad. Mike was happy to help out, and I must confess I was more than happy. I have been cooped up in a bedsit since my ex-wife and I parted company and apart from the fact that Mike and I have always got on well, I've really missed the space and freedom of having several rooms to spread around in, and an out-of-town life-style probably more than anything else. I expect that Mike didn't have time to contact you because we spent the whole week packing and moving our possessions across from the city and, what spare time we had, was spent avoiding pints of beer and doing fitness training in readiness for the new season – I'm sure you can remember how Mike is about his cricket."

Jenny had finished her glass of wine and Jonathan poured her another one and replenished his own glass while everything he had said had time to sink in. He stopped short of suggesting that Jenny and Lisa should come round for supper sometime soon as it was an idea that he would really like to be able to bounce off Michael first, just in case he really didn't want to see Jenny again. Anyway, it was probably going to be difficult maintaining any kind of a social life at the Stables with all the subterfuge going on. He thought that the reference to cricket was an inspired move, since, in his previous experience, it was almost guaranteed to be a conversation stopper in the presence of women. In the event, it backfired badly. Working as she did in the media, Jenny could recognise incoming bullshit at a hundred metres. She was wondering how long she should let Jonathan drone on before interrupting, but the final reference to cricket was a real gift, and far too good an opportunity to pass up.

"Funnily enough," Jenny said, as funnily as she could, given that it wasn't, "It was Mike who introduced me to cricket several years ago in London. I think he had me lined up for making sandwiches or some such nonsense, but I soon put him right on that score. Anyway, after the first few matches I was hooked and formed a ladies' eleven. I've lost contact with most of the original team, but I still watch regularly and the company often sponsors county matches. I'll make sure that you're both invited to the next one. Where do you get a net when you're at college?"

"Oh, errr … Wherever we can, really."

Jenny could see that he was struggling and changed the subject to food and Lisa. Jonathan found both easier. After a while, the rest of the party started to return and Lisa awoke without any prompting. The sorbet delayed the meal by more than an hour but most of the time was spent in playing board games and drinking unnamed aperitifs with interesting cumulative effects. Formal eating commenced at nine o'clock and wound up about two hours later. Jonathan was beginning to feel the effects of too many chef's perks and, for that matter, wine at lunch. Half way through the main course he started alternating wine with water and by the end of the cheese course, he regained control of his wits. In stark contrast, Lisa appeared to be bent on emptying the EC Wine Lake single-handedly. There was nothing ill-mannered or ugly about the way she did it, but Jonathan was nonetheless surprised and perhaps a little disappointed by it. He realised that to think like that was somewhat hypocritical, given the way they had first met, and tried to put the thought out of his mind. Another thought that he was busy trying to suppress was the one about what was going to happen – or not happen later. Although he had tried not to think too much about it, there appeared to be a certain inevitability about the way the evening was going. During the rare moments that Lisa had been awake during the day, she had made no effort whatsoever to disguise her friendly body language. It wasn't that he was embarrassed by it, or didn't enjoy it and the unspoken promises it held – far from it. But somewhere inside of him, in fact not very far from the back of his brain, the familiar little voice coughed politely and waited patiently for his full attention.

"Having a good time, are we?" it said, rhetorically. "I suppose you two are about to bid polite goodnights to everyone else and scamper off to bed like sixteen-year-olds. Come on, Jonathan, you only met her a week ago. You fancy the arse off Cathy, you hardly know if you like Lisa yet and yet here you are about to jump in the sack together! Don't screw up now that you've just about got your act back together. Have you forgotten the pain that goes with commitment or are you going to convince yourself that it'll be just giving in to the lust of the moment?"

"It's not like that and you know it!" Jonathan protested.

"What isn't like what?" Jenny said, looking up from her plate of poached pears.

"Oh, err. Sorry," Jonathan said, trying to shake off his constant built-in critic. "I was just thinking out loud. It's been a long day and I think I'll hit the sack." The idea seemed to strike a chord with most of the company with the exception of Peter and Gillian, who volunteered, rashly, to clear up the devastation in the dining room. The babble of voices diminished and Jonathan kissed Lisa warmly as they reached her room. For a brief moment, he thought that he would be able to avoid the moment that he had been dreading all day. Then just as he was about to retreat to the safety of his room she whispered:

"Just give me a few minutes to shower – I'll leave the door unlocked for you."

The little voice in the back of his brain shrieked 'NO WAY' and Jonathan whispered, "yes," as Lisa slipped inside her room and slowly closed the door behind her. He turned and walked quickly in the direction of his own room. His face appeared quite calm, but just behind it turmoil was gradually turning to rage. He returned to the kitchen for yet another glass of water and continued walking and muttering the litany of the 'own goal scorer'. It went something like:

"Shit! Shit! Bugger! Bugger! Bugger! SHIT!"

As usual it didn't work and a few minutes later Jonathan was standing in his own shower, preparing himself mentally for what was about to happen. It had been a long sweaty day, first cooped up in the minibus and then on chef's duty in the kitchen, so he was glad of a shower anyway. Almost ritually, Jonathan shaved, washed his hair and dried it before cleaning his teeth and putting on the dressing gown that he had borrowed from Michael. Then with much trepidation and failing confidence, he turned off his light and left his room. The cold marble-clad floor chilled his feet as he made the short journey back to Lisa's room, and his spirits sank. The chill rose up his legs. He really was not in the right frame of mind for any of this and the closer he got to her door, the more he resolved to be sensible and listen to the little voice that accompanied him everywhere. He couldn't avoid going into Lisa's room having said that he would, but he would have to be entirely candid to avoid upsetting her. After all, it was all very well being able to justify your thoughts and intentions to yourself, but that was a far cry from being equally successful with another – especially when the 'other' in question appeared to be hell-bent on bouncing. This was going to be tricky. He was at her door now and he knocked gently before entering. A small and very dim bedside light illuminated a cascade of red hair on one of the pillows. Jonathan closed the door silently behind him, summoned all of his evaporating courage and said, "I'm sorry I took so long, but I needed to do some thinking – about us mostly. Don't get me wrong, Lisa, but I don't think I'm quite ready for this yet."

There was no answer and he ploughed on: "It's not that I don't want you – I do, badly – it's just that since we met it's been as though I've just recovered from an illness. And like I had a pain all the time – but didn't know it was there until it wasn't. I'm sorry but I'm not explaining this very well at all am I? It's just that I think it would be best for me – us – not to rush into anything, just in case the pain comes back. Does that make sense? I don't want that kind of pain again if I can avoid it."

There was no reply and Jonathan moved a little closer to the bed. Lisa was sleeping deeply and snuffling quietly as if in the embrace of a favourite dream. Jonathan and the little voice inside the back of his brain laughed at his narrow escape. He switched off the light, considered his situation, pulled up the covers slightly, returned silently to his own room, took off his robe and fell into his own bed. For what seemed like ages, he lay back with his eyes open, listening to the dim distant noise of central Parisian traffic and the barking of local dogs. As both diminished with time, he tried as best he could to go to sleep while considering the absurdity of life in general, and his present position in particular. If he had been right in thinking that the explanation he had just given could have been taken as ill-advised, the next morning was going to be far more interesting. Perhaps inevitably, Jonathan's thoughts started to stray back to the break-up of his relationship with Sara and the difficult period that had followed. He wondered if Michael had received any vitriolic telephone calls from her during the course of the day. She seemed, from past experience, to have an unerring knack of waiting until the weekend before being her most obnoxious, as if she was making an extra special effort to spoil his weekend as compared with the rest of the week. It was with such thoughts as these, and with a mental note to add Sara's solicitor to the select list of those who would be at the front of the queue for the gallows, that Jonathan lapsed finally into an uneasy sleep. The first dream was innocent enough, and was mostly to do with long balmy summer days by the Stable's pool. The second was more strange and involved Jenny, dressed in cricket whites, bowling poached pears at him. The third and final one was one of the type that you really wish you could remember in detail after, but never can. It was one of the sort that has the disconcerting habit of disobeying, or simply ignoring those fundamental laws of physics that relate to time and space. This, in a sense, was what was happening to Jonathan. For some reason he was on a guided tour of the college chapel but as he and the rest of the visitors moved deeper and deeper into the building, the masonry walls gave way to natural rock and he was in fact in a defunct mine in Derbyshire and the tour proceedings had just got to the part where the guide turned off all the lights to give the guided their first impression of absolute darkness. By a strange quirk of fate that seems to pervade the best dreams and a plethora of the worst disaster movies, the moment of 'turning-off' coincided with the long-predicted reawakening of an old, deep-seated geological fault, which succeeded in bringing part of the roof down. The air was filled with dust and he seemed to be choking on something. He tried to take a breath, but whatever it was in his mouth simply went into his throat and he started to panic involuntarily. Jonathan felt the pressure of something moist bearing down on his pelvis and remembered that the mine joined a cave used by potholers. His heart pumped as it struggled to circulate enough blood to his muscles to move the weight on him. He had to escape, but didn't know how. He woke to find that it was light outside and with not a cave in sight. Lisa was astride him and he had a mouthful of her hair.

"Time to get up!" she announced, triumphantly.

"Yes I know," he said, to the other voice. "I should have locked the door!"

Chapter 13:

An Unwelcome Visitor

Back at the Stables, Michael, by comparison, woke naturally at about eight-ten and was well into his seventeenth length of the pool before he remembered that Cathy wasn't yet up to check on him. The lack of Jonathan stomping around in search of coffee two mornings running should have provided a clue, as should Cathy's absence the previous dawn, but even in one of his more optimistic moods, Michael had never claimed to function on all cylinders before lunch – or to be exact, before his first pint. Pints had become lamentably few and far between of late, and Michael was more than content to blame his persistent lack of attention in the mornings on that particular liquid deficiency in his diet. He knew of course that such thinking was nonsensical, but he needed a bit of self-induced martyrdom to bolster his resolve to keep training, and thus make it as effective as possible. There was no surprise that in just under a week he was already very much fitter, especially since, unbeknown to either Jonathan or Cathy, he had also started a daily programme of weight training at the college gymnasium. The thing about which there was even less doubt was that this annual ritual of flab-ridding was becoming progressively more difficult and painful year by year. Two years previously, he had sought some medical advice from a doctor friend and promptly wished he hadn't.

"What you need, old son, is a bit more stress in your life. It's the best cure I know for a slow metabolic rate. Have you ever thought of getting married to a harridan, breeding some awful children, becoming over-mortgaged and taking on an expensive mistress for the sole purpose of meaningless but exciting sex? It seems to work for most of my male patients. Trouble is they all seem to be losing their hair, being stricken down with heart attacks or playing unwilling host to voracious peptic ulcers. No, Michael, there is nothing much wrong with you that wouldn't be put right by trying to live a less self-indulgent, hedonistic and outrageous life style."

Advice like that he just didn't need, but if the previous day was anything to go by, he might as well have been about to put the theory to the test. Saturday had started well enough apart from twenty unobserved lengths of the pool and the first telephone call. It interrupted breakfast and, predictably, it was Sara.

"Hello, Jonathan."

"Hello, who's that?"

"Who's asking?"

The voice was becoming less friendly and Michael recognised it.

"I asked first," he said. It wasn't very adult, but he was only fifteen in his head. Also, he didn't like Sara.

Few knew the details of the passing of Michael's parents – Emily, of course, and maybe a few others not including Sara. Michael's father had been a brute, a characteristic that emerged only after Michael was born. It could have been jealousy of course, or his lack of success in the business world -- especially compared with his wife and her younger sister Emily, but brute he was and all too often he took out his frustration on Mike's mum. She never reported it to the police, but people got to know. You couldn't keep explaining all the bruises away all the time. Eventually she snapped, and chose to do it while he and she were on a motorway. The coroner drew a convenient veil over the fact that neither of the deceased was wearing a seat belt. Michael witnessed some of the beatings as well as most of the rows and the effect was indelible. Consequently, one of his favourite pet hates was people who hit women. It was probably only that which had always kept him from having a serious chat with Sara. Another of his pet hates was soggy muesli, and thanks to Sara's untimely phone call, he was rapidly acquiring his very own bowl of it.

"Where's Jonathan and what are you doing in his flat?"

"That's two questions and you still haven't answered mine."

There was a brief silence while Sara breathed heavily. Michael used the respite to salvage and eat a lonely island of muesli that was not quite inundated. He chewed it lovingly and imagined his friend's ex-wife spitting feathers, or better still, bursting an important blood vessel.

"Is that you, Michael?"

"Yes, Sara."

There was no point prolonging the initial skirmish any further; the rest of the muesli had sunk beyond culinary redemption and Michael was now contemplating toast and something fattening.

"Did you know it was me all the time?"

"Yes, Sara."

"Then why didn't you say so?" she said, angrily.

"Because I love it when you get angry," he lied.

Saying that was a big mistake and Michael knew it immediately. Sara enjoyed, loved and just about revelled in having her vanity rubbed. Her voice and demeanour changed in an instant.

"I seem to recall that you turned me down last time, Michael, but I won't hold it against you. We could always look on it as a postponement. What do you say?"

Michael thought over her renewed offer, almost absent-mindedly, as he sorted through various jars of preserves in the cupboard next to the phone. He thought of the sheer devastation that had almost destroyed the spirit of his friend, shuddered and sighed. Then he found the strawberry jam and said, "Ah!"

His thoughts returned to Jonathan and how just after the split, he had lost over a stone in four weeks. If nothing else, it suggested his doctor friend might have been right. Then, reluctantly, he brought his attention back to the present point, his much delayed breakfast and mostly, the root cause of Jonathan's distress who, at that very moment, was very likely pouting at the other end of the telephone line.

"Michael, are you still there?" she pouted.

Michael was still there, but he was still thinking. He thought about all of the people he knew whom Sara had pouted at, bedded and discarded before, during and after her soulless marriage to Jonathan. There was nothing empirically wrong with being over-sexed – whatever the hell that meant. There was of course a huge imposed differential morality between the accepted sexual habits of men and women. If a man "'put it around' he was regarded by his peers as a bit of a lad, free with his seed, a rake or just a bit randy – all of which being vaguely okay. On the other hand, if a woman behaved in the same way, she would generally be regarded as a slut. This is what happens when the men write the rules. And after all, who sets the standards? How does one know that they are necessarily set right and how, as a 'wrong', does being over-sexed rank with, for example, one nation beating the shit out of another nation over some stupid obscure difference of opinion about, say, politics or religion, or chopping down millions of acres of rain forest to grow crops to rear cattle? He couldn't exactly claim to have been a natural role model for anyone thinking of taking up celibacy, but even with his modern views on sexual liberation, he found it difficult to understand what could motivate any human being to be so unforgivably cruel to another. In short, he had a deep and positively unhealthy loathing of Sara – not for what she was, but for what she had done to his friend Jonathan. Thus it was personal.

"Yes Sara, I'm still here," he said, wearily.

"Well?" she demanded.

"I'd rather sleep in a ditch," he replied, hanging up.

At the same moment, two lightly browned slices of scrummy toast leapt athletically out of the toaster and then came to rest half way into the slots. He liberated them, covered them generously with butter and strawberry jam and added them to his earlier breakfast in case he missed out on lunch. Fearing another unwelcome phone call, he switched on the answering machine. Then, fearing that the first two slices of toast might be inadequate, he set about preparing some nice company for them. If the beginning was anything to go by, it had the makings of a stressful day. His shower was the next excuse for an interruption and this time it was the police, in the person of a uniformed inspector – not on the phone, but at the door. Fortunately, Cathy was still in her room and stayed there.

"Doctor Evans?"

"Yes, that's right."

"Doctor Michael Evans?"

"Yes, how can I help you?"

"I wondered if I might have a few words with you, sir?"

"Well yes, of course, do come in," Michael said, stepping backwards into the hallway. "Just come through to the kitchen and help yourself to some coffee while I finish getting dressed."

"Thank you very much, sir. I'm sure it won't take very long – just a few questions about an incident in the village."

"Right – I'll just be a couple of minutes." Michael shouted, as he went off to his bedroom. He was a little surprised that he hadn't had this sort of visit before. The fight in the pub, brief as it was, had been the talk of the village all week and he was more or less obliged to announce his return to the Hall the next morning, before the staff found out via the village grapevine. As he rightly guessed, he and Jonathan had been noticed in the pub on the occasion of Frank's brief encounter with Cathy and there was nothing to be gained by trying to conceal the fact. Any pretence might be viewed with suspicion. He dressed quickly and returned to the kitchen where the inspector was waiting for him, mug of coffee in hand.

"Good, I see you found everything. Now, how can I help?"

"I am investigating an assault that took place last Monday evening in one of the pubs in the village and I understand that you may have been a witness."

Michael was a bit surprised at the officer's choice of the word 'assault'. It was hardly likely that Cathy would break her cover to press charges, and less likely that Frank would pursue the matter, and since he hadn't seen Frank actually hit anyone, he thought that a charge of affray would have been more appropriate. Perhaps Frank had hit someone earlier in the evening. Whatever the situation, Michael was interested to find out what the police intended to do about Frank, as he needed as much ammunition as possible before he sacked him. He had already sent him a letter by registered post summoning him to the Hall the following Monday and he wanted to be properly prepared for any eventuality. He therefore played dumb.

"I take it you are referring to Frank Graves' run-in with that young lady. Is she alright?"

"I'm sorry, Doctor Evans, I don't seem to have made myself very clear. We have no news of the young lady. It is Mr Graves who has made the complaint and we are trying to ascertain the identity of the lady so that charges can be brought."

Michael was amazed, but was careful not to show it. Frank Graves was long overdue a good smacking, and now he had the temerity to complain about it to the police of all people – what a nerve the man had! Still, it was just as well that he knew what was going on, even if it did make the task of sacking Frank less easy.

"I'm very surprised to hear that, inspector. From what little I saw of events, it seemed to me that Frank brought it on himself and probably got no less than he deserved."

"That's as may be, sir," the inspector said, with a hint of anger in his voice, "but the fact remains that Mr Graves was the victim of an attack on his person and I have reason to believe that you might be able to identify his assailant."

This was getting uncomfortable and Michael was glad that Cathy was keeping out of the way. There was something belligerent about the policeman's tone and Michael couldn't believe that the publican hadn't made a complaint to the police about Frank. It was probably the best opportunity he had ever had to do so. He made a mental note to see him about it later. Meanwhile he still had to 'help' the police without compromising his own position. He continued to play dumb.

"Well, of course I'll help in any way I can, but I didn't get a very good look at the lady. The lights in the pub are quite dim and to be quite honest with you, I wasn't concentrating on her face so much as bits lower down – if you get my drift."

Michael was quite pleased with himself for discovering a way of introducing an element of wholesome untarnished truth into what was otherwise destined to be a pack of lies. Unfortunately for him however, the inspector was not impressed and certainly not amused. He simply looked at Michael and said, "I wasn't referring to her appearance, sir, although perhaps we can deal with that later. I was and am more concerned with what passed between you – that is – what you said to each other. You did speak to each other, didn't you, sir?"

The question was put in a conventional sort of way but Michael was sure that not far beneath the surface lurked some hidden menace. He would have to treat this person very carefully.

"Well, now you mention it, we did exchange a few words, but there was nothing of importance so far as I recall."

"Are you quite sure about that, sir? Only, according to three of the other customers I've spoken to, you and the young lady appeared to know each other, and you and another man were seen leaving shortly after she did."

Michael was completely alert now – surprisingly so, considering that he still hadn't had a pint.

The inspector had now played his trump card and things weren't too bad. He would certainly get to see Jonathan before the inspector would and, by the sound of it, the inspector no more knew Jonathan's identity than he knew Cathy's. He really didn't like all this lying but there was nothing for it; he was committed.

"Well I certainly don't know her – more's the pity – and so far as I can recall, the conversation was to do with her need to get to the ladies to wash off some blood and the fact that I was blocking her path. My friend and I certainly left a few minutes later, but I don't believe there was anyone about when we did. We just grabbed a cab back to town."

"And who might that be, sir – your friend?"

"His name is Grey – Doctor Jonathan Grey – we both teach at the College."

"And is he about at the moment, sir?"

"No, I'm afraid not. He's gone away for the weekend."

Michael was relieved that the worst was over and that he could again slip a little truth into the conversation. The inspector gave no indication that he knew he'd been listening to lies and he appeared to lose interest in the proceedings.

"Right, thank you, sir and just for the record, would you try to describe the young lady for me?"

Michael heaved an inward sigh of relief and pictured Cathy in his mind. There was little point in attempting to be clever and trying to invent anything fictitious about Cathy. There would have been any number of people in the bar who could provide a description of the version of Cathy that was supposed to be remembered from that evening, and he would be a complete fool if he didn't do likewise.

"I would say that she was in her mid to late twenties, about five feet eight inches in height, shortish blonde hair and, by the looks of things, no bra!"

Michael was determined to get this miserable policeman to at least smile a little, but it was useless, his face remained motionless.

"And can you describe her face, sir?"

"No – not really. She was wearing a large pair of dark glasses if I remember rightly."

"You do, sir. How about clothes, can you remember what she was wearing? – when you and she had your...conversation?"

The last part of the question sounded ominous but Michael managed not to show his discomfort. There was little doubt that he would have to brief Jonathan very carefully before he and the inspector met.

"Well, I can't really be sure about it, but I think that it could have been jeans, some sort of thick shirt and maybe a trench-coat and boots. But as I say, I can't really be sure."

"Right, thank you Doctor Evans, you've been most helpful. Could I ask you one last thing? Could you get your friend Mr Grey to contact me at this number?" He handed Michael a card. "When he gets back. I'd like to see if he can help me, too."

Again there was an ominous emphasis on a single word, this time on the word 'help', which made Michael's flesh creep. He wondered if Cathy could be sponsored to rearrange the inspector's nose for him, but that was just idle thinking, and he mustn't lose concentration now that his unexpected interview with the long arm of the law was nearly over.

"Yes, I'll make sure that Doctor Grey gets your message. Now, if you'll excuse me, there are some things that I should attend to. Please see yourself out."

Michael had by now endured more than he could take of this humourless person hiding behind a uniform, and he watched his back go out of the door. He thought that he may have missed something important but couldn't quite put his finger on what it was. He remembered his curtailed shower and went back to his room to take another one. Outside in the garden the inspector was looking around nosily on the way back to his car and appeared to be preoccupied by the sight on Jonathan's burned-out car in one of the garages. By the time that Michael had finished his uninterrupted shower, he had completely forgotten that he may have missed something important and was instead thinking very seriously about a pint. He had at least got some justification for going to the Blue Boar. Following his encounter with the man in blue, he wanted to see Fred Botley, the landlord. Checking that the answerphone was switched back on, he left the Stables, vaulted the fence at the end of the lane and walked through the meadows to the village. He arrived at the pub just after Martha Botley opened the bar doors. The village was quiet apart from a small white van that was being driven slowly up and down as if its owner was thoroughly lost.

"Good morning, Martha," Michael said, as he pulled a stool up to the bar. "I'll have a pint of bitter, please."

"Master Evans, I thought it was you as you came up the street. Fred said you were in the other night; I'm surprised you didn't come up to see me like you usually do."

Martha and Fred had run the Blue Boar since before Michael was born and having no children of their own, they had always looked out for him when as a child, he and Emily had travelled to the Hall during school holidays. For as long as he could remember her, Martha had always struck Michael as being essentially a warm round person who was one hundred percent heart. It had become almost a habit that Michael and she would have little chats over tea and cakes whenever he was in the area. He felt a little chastened that he hadn't been to see her the previous Monday – it must have been the first time he hadn't in years.

"I'm sorry, Martha. I didn't come in 'til quite late and then, what with all the excitement…"

He let the words fade as the bar door opened and a man in a plaster-splattered boiler suit came in. Michael caught a glimpse of a white van parked just outside and smiled to himself as the man approached the bar. He had about three days of stubble on his face, greying hair and a cigarette hung vacantly from one corner of his mouth. It was Peter Stagg.

"Sorry if I broke up your conversation, folks," he said, in a flat Midlands accent. "Only I'm lost and I was wonderin' if one of you could give me some directions."

He was looking straight at Martha who dutifully smiled at him.

"Where is it you were looking for then?" she asked, warmly.

"It's a place called Grantchester Hall Stables. I've been up and down this street three times and I haven't seen any signs for a Hall or Stables."

"Well, you're OK now. This gentleman lives there and I'm sure he can help you." Martha gestured at Michael, who was beginning to have fears about being able to finish his pint. He put it down on the bar and assumed what he thought might pass for a look of surprised recognition.

"You must be Jo Phillips!" he said, hoping that he was right.

"That's right – and you must be Dr Evans." Peter replied, holding out an authentically plaster-caked hand.

"Well this is most impressive, Mr Phillips – I didn't expect you to turn up this quickly. We only spoke - what? an hour ago. Look, I have to see a couple of people here in the village, so would you mind letting yourself in and making a start? I'll be back in a couple of hours at the most."

"Fine, but I'll still need directions."

"Yes of course. Just go up the hill to the church, go about fifty yards beyond the next building, then immediately left and third left after that. Here, take this key; it'll work for the gate to the yard and the house itself. The walls that need fixing are in the garage just south of the fig tree. I'll see you at about one o'clock."

Peter agreed, took the key, thanked Michael and left quickly.

"Problems with shrinkage cracks," Michael explained. "Is Fred about? I'd like a word if possible."

"Yes dear, he's out the back in the store, bottling up. Do you want me to top that up before you go through?"

Michael found Fred struggling with some crates and helped him finish before they went into the back room for a quiet chat and, in Michael's case, another pint.

"Is everything back to normal after last Tuesday, Fred? I seemed to choose the wrong evening to come back to the village, I'm afraid. Emily told me that Frank had been making a nuisance of himself, but I had no idea things were that bad. Have you banned him now?"

"I have, Master Michael. In fact, he's now been banned from all the pubs in the village and not before time, I'd say. After what happened I'd be surprised if he showed his face hereabouts for some while. Mind you, after what that young lass did to him, I'm not sure that many folks would recognise his face. According to the police, he's going to have to go back into hospital once the swelling has gone down to have his nose rebuilt. I'd hate to think what his other bits look like though. She certainly gave him a good kicking, didn't she? Perhaps that's why the police are so keen on finding her."

"Have they been asking questions then?" Michael asked, innocently, from behind his rapidly diminishing pint.

"Questions? It's been more like the Spanish Inquisition around here. You'd have thought there'd been a bank robbery the amount of uniforms we've had up here the past week. Did you know she'd booked into the inn and then just vanished into thin air – left a load of clothes there too."

"Really?" Michael said. Fred was a great source of reliable information if one had the time to listen and, today, Michael needed as much as he could get. If he, or for that matter, Jonathan, was going to get into another session with the inspector, research would be vital. The hotel wasn't news of course, but Fred was bound to know more.

"They even sent an inspector up here, and we haven't seen one of them in years. It was him who interviewed me and the other bar staff. Strange sort of cove he was too. The whole village reckons Frank had it coming, but according to this inspector bloke, it was Frank who was the victim and that girl, whoever she is, has to be found and punished.

161

He was quite put out when he discovered that it was me that made a complaint about Frank. He had me withdraw it, of course."

"Really, why was that Fred?"

"Well he reckoned that there wasn't much chance of a court convicting him of anything, being as how he came off worst. Also, he said I'd have to make several appearances in court and with my heart and all … well, you know, Michael … I'm not as young as I was."

"But what about the knife – surely that would show intent?"

"Well, that's a strange thing. We were told to leave everything in the bar as it was and do you know, the knife was never found even though I saw it with my own eyes."

"Really?"

Michael was beginning to get a bad feeling about what was going on, but he didn't want to alert Fred – not with his natural talent for spreading news. What he really wanted was to have an urgent conversation with his newly acquired plasterer.

"Look, Fred, I'd better be getting back to the Stables to sort a few things out. I'll pop back and see you one evening in the week if that's alright?"

"Of course young Michael, you know you're always welcome here, whenever. Just don't leave it so long next time."

Michael almost ran back to the Stables, a morass of thoughts, fears and awful ideas bouncing around in his head. He found Peter looking quizzically at the burnt out car in one of the garages with Cathy at his side.

"Good afternoon, Mr Evans. I got bored looking for your drinks cabinet and came out here for some fresh air. Is this – was this – yours?" he said, pointing at the charred heap.

"No thank goodness – it's Jonathan's, although technically by now it probably belongs to his insurance company."

"Did it happen recently?"

"Yes, very."

"Can you make sure that nothing happens to it for a while? I'd like to have a colleague take a look at it, if you don't mind."

"Surely – but I don't suppose you're going to tell me why?"

"No – or at least not yet. It may just be a false suspicion. I would like, however, to keep all options open at present."

"Fine, but we really do need to talk."

Michael led Peter and Cathy indoors and they sat down for nearly an hour exchanging information. Most of the trade was from the former to the latter and Peter listened avidly as Michael recounted his long interview at the hands of the inspector, and even more avidly as he went on to detail the extent of enquiries carried out among the bar staff and customers at the pub. When it was done, Michael introduced Peter to the drinks cabinet while Cathy fixed the three of them some lunch.

"When we've had this – and thanks by the way, I'd appreciate it if we could go through it all over again but this time, I want to get it all on tape."

"But that's it!" Michael exclaimed.

"What's what, Michael?"

"That's what was wrong. He didn't take any notes."

"I'm sorry, Michael, you've lost me momentarily."

"The inspector. He didn't take any notes when he interviewed me. That can't be right, can it?"

"No – probably not, although he may have a very good memory."

"Maybe so, but even if he has, surely it's normal procedure to take what they call 'contemporaneous notes', isn't it? Unless, of course …" Michael jumped up, took a card out of his pocket, grabbed the phone and dialled the number. He had never asked the inspector's name and read it from the card, when he got through. He pushed the 'conference' button so that Peter and Cathy could hear the conversation.

"City Police Station. Good afternoon," said a pleasant voice.

"Good afternoon. Could I speak to Inspector Cotting, please?"

There was a brief pause as the owner of the pleasant voice looked at a duty roster.

"I'm sorry, sir, he's not on duty today, but he's on early turn tomorrow. Can I take a message?"

"No thanks, no problem, it can wait. Bye."

Michael put the phone down and smiled at Peter who said, "I suppose you're expecting congratulations, aren't you? It's just as well Cathy's already checked that your telephones weren't bugged, isn't it?"

Michael's smug look faded as he realised the implications of what Peter had just said. He was not the only person with keys to the stables. He had gone to the Hall the morning after the fight to announce his return and, although many of the staff seemed reasonably happy to see him, Edwards the butler – or, as he liked to think of himself, staff resource manager - was quite cool, verging on hostile. He blustered about having received no word on the subject from 'the mistress' and went on to say how many of the staff were inconvenienced by all the changes that were going on. Michael had never cared too much for Edwards and came close to telling him that most of the staff, including himself, were paid very well for doing very little, but he let the moment go. Instead he explained that the main reason for his presence was to liaise with the incoming tenants and the contractors so that he, Edwards, wouldn't have to deal with it. The explanation, so far as it went, appeared to find favour with Edwards until Michael added that since he was about, he would also deal with recruiting a replacement maid for Trisha, who was about to go to Italy to work for Emily. When he said this he thought that he saw a nervous twitch in Edwards's face – he certainly flushed as if trying to conceal some anger.

Michael knew that Edwards had a daughter who was out of work and thought that he might have earmarked the job for her.

"But of course, if you've already got someone in mind?" said Michael, trying to head off a confrontation.

Edwards flushed even more, knowing that he had been cornered and would have to declare an interest if he was to get his way.

"Well actually, Dr Evans," he said, with stiff formality, "I was hoping that my Betty could have the job, seeing as how she's local and knows the place."

Michael knew or at least, knew of, Betty and she was a pleasant enough sort of girl, but this wasn't going to help him smuggle Cathy in without arousing suspicion, unless he could come up with some workable compromise.

"I'd have no objection to Betty working here if she gets the job fair and square. And if I do the interviewing, no-one can accuse you of nepotism, can they?"

Edwards didn't like it, but he knew that it would be illogical, not to mention improper, to argue. He agreed, and with obvious reluctance retrieved the CVs that he had consigned to the waste bin in his office. He handed them, including one posted from Dorset, to Michael.

"Thank you, Edwards. I'll get my secretary to go through these and make the arrangements for, say this time next week, so could you make sure that the mistress's study is available from ten o'clock onwards"

Michael gave the request as an instruction rather than a question. Edwards knew he had lost the unequal battle for authority and said, almost automatically:

"Yes, sir."

"Oh, and Edwards?"

"Yes, sir?"

"Do you think that it will be adequate to hire only a replacement for Trisha? I would think that with the influx of people once the tenants arrive, we will perhaps need some additional staff, anyway, wouldn't you say, Edwards?"

"Most certainly, sir."

Edwards realised – as Michael knew he would – that the more vacancies there were, the more chance Betty would have of filling one. Thus with compromise both conceived and achieved, Michael returned to the Stables leaving Edwards at least superficially happy. The earlier hostility was, to some extent, hidden by the time the two parted. However, Michael was left with a sense of having gate-crashed his own party, and was reminded of the feeling when Peter raised the possibility of bugging devices. His otherwise perpetual grin lapsed slightly as Edwards was one of those with keys to the stables.

"Lighten up, Michael," Peter said encouragingly. "I always check that sort of thing wherever I go, just as a matter of routine. It wasn't because I necessarily expected to find anything. Besides which, fascinating though it may be, this suggestion of some form of link between Inspector Cotting and Frank Graves doesn't get us any closer to what is or isn't going on at the Hall. So if you have finished playing at detective, I'd still like to get this down on tape. Right?"

"Right."

An hour of digital tape later, they were done. Peter made ready to leave, but stopped when he saw a fax machine in the hallway.

"Is that connected?" he asked, pointing.

"Yes," Michael replied. "Do you want to use it?"

"No, not now, but Cathy said she missed it when she checked everything else."

He opened his bag, pulled out a small plastic-cased instrument, which he passed briefly over the fax machine, with no comment.

"No, it's alright, it's just that it might be useful if I send you a transcript of this tape to show to Jonathan when he gets back tomorrow. Is that the number?" he said, pointing.

"Yes it's the same as the phone but it only intercepts fax messages – or you could simply email it to me."

"Okay, thanks – and one last thing, Michael. What are your movements next week, in case we can work together or I need to contact you in person?"

"Monday and Wednesday I'm at college most of the day and you have that number already. Tuesday I'm at the Hall, probably all day, interviewing Cathy and God knows how many others. Thursday I'm back at the Hall talking to the clerk of works and a fire prevention officer about the new accommodation and Friday I plan to do as little as possible!"

"Will you have an architect at the hall on Thursday?"

"I wasn't planning to – why?"

"Because you should."

"The ubiquitous Mr Phillips, I suppose?"

"The very same. What time is your appointment?"

"Ten, but the clerk of works knows the architects – Emily's and the prospective tenant's."

"Fine, I'm from English Heritage then."

"He knows them too – and they may even be there."

"Oh, bugger it," Peter sighed. "I really am sick of pretending to be a magazine journalist!"

He finished collecting his effects together, checked that nobody was outside and departed.

Michael was left with Cathy and much to think about and he was still doing it the following day when the third interruption came. It was Sunday lunchtime, the pubs had been open for an hour, the phone rang, it was Sara again and she was drunk. Jonathan had warned him about Sara and the ritual weekend verbal abuse and although he'd not expected two calls the same weekend, Michael was glad that he had left the answering machine on.

"This is Sara, Jonathan. I expect Michael told you I rang yesterday. He was very rude to me and after he hung up, I went round to your flat only to find that neither you nor he was there. One of your neighbours, correction, ex-neighbours said that you and Michael were living together at the Stables so at least my solicitor will know where to write to you. I still intend to have my car back. I just hope that the two of you are happy together. You deserve each other! Goodbye, boys."

Cathy looked at the answering machine with some horror, but said nothing. Michael was about to give in to the inclination to phone her back with some friendly advice like, 'get a life' or better yet, 'fuck off and die', but he was saved from himself and probably his very own solicitors' letter by a slightly different ringing sound and the noise of his fax machine stuttering into life. It was from Peter and comprised a header followed by eighteen pages of single-spaced text. Yes, he had soaked up enough stress the day before to last him for a week. He could feel the pounds simply falling off.

Chapter 14: Should Have Taken The Tunnel

"I'll take the final stint if you like," Jonathan said, as he came in from the small after-deck and shivered from the cold. "The clouds look a little ominous over the English coast. It looks as though we could have some heavy rain later."

His amateur, gloomy, but otherwise accurate meteorological predictions fell on deaf ears. With the possible exception of Bill and Gillian, who were accomplished sailors but were far too drunk even to appreciate that they had left France, the rest of the party were in the toilets practising their vocal projection. The grey sea at Calais had been deceptively calm and had given no clue of the horrors to come. The captain, to his credit, had radioed to both coasts to see which might be better – whether to continue or retreat, but there was nothing to be gained either way. The weather had simply closed in and they were stuck with it. Even with the stability of twin hulls, he had to reduce engine speed such that it was just sufficient to climb up one side of each wave and then glide down, with as much grace as possible, into the base of the next one. There was no threat to life as such, but Jonathan didn't envy the person whose job it was to clean out the loos once they made land.

As they reached the relative calm of Dover harbour, faces, some green, some grey and some mottled, started to appear timidly from the toilets. Some of the less mottled faces made it almost as far as the main passenger area before going for one last throw of the diced. The 'infamous five' of his group, as Jonathan christened them, were not alone in their plight and on the vehicle deck. The crew decided to open the doors fore and aft as soon as the vessel berthed, so that the prevailing westerly gale could clear the air at something like the same alarming rate as the green, grey and mottled passengers were managing to contaminate it. Jonathan took in one whiff of the foetid odour on the vehicle deck and promptly did an about turn to round up the rest of the party. With some effort he managed to persuade Gillian to hold everyone back until all the vehicles had been off-loaded, and get them to disembark as foot passengers. Fortunately, the minibus was one of the last vehicles to be loaded, and by waiting until most of the others had driven/slithered out, he was able to run to it, start it and get to fresh air all on one large lung-full of air. Perhaps the enforced swimming was of some value after all! Jonathan collected the less-than-magnificent seven just before the customs hall and then drove off into the gathering gloom of the M20. He was of course right about the prospect of rain and he wouldn't have been far off the mark if he had predicted a cloudburst. The windscreen wipers could barely cope with the torrent, even on their fastest speed and that, coupled with almost everyone else's fragile condition, predisposed him, like never before, to drive very carefully back to Cambridge. Peter and Bill, who unwisely had foregone water with their lunch-time meal, were starting to show signs of dehydration and after much argument to the contrary, the heating was turned up to give them some comfort for the last thirty miles or so to the city. This was of course a big mistake. Jenny had thoroughly over-catered the cheese and the leftovers, which, weighing in at about 4.5 kilos, had been mouldering in the minibus for a total of about seven hours when they and she were carried into her flat. Gillian, thankfully, had sobered just a little and volunteered to stay with Jenny to make sure that she came to no harm. Since no one else was yet fit to drive, Jonathan extended his stint to include dropping everyone except Lisa outside their respective homes, and then taking her back to the Stables for some serious coffee and a hot bath. By the time he had finished acting as taxi driver and parked the minibus under cover, it was nearly nine o'clock, dark, and raining with renewed vigour. Michael had seen the approaching lights and had unlocked the courtyard door as Jonathan reached the near end of the drive. He met them with waterproof coats and ushered them quickly into the hallway. He looked back somewhat surprised at the steaming minibus, grinned at Jonathan and said, "What a very generous thought, but you shouldn't have. Belgian chocolates or a string of onions would have been enough, really."

"Please don't mention food, Michael," Lisa said, weakly. "Not for about a week or so anyway."

"Sorry, Lisa. If it's any consolation I've been worrying about you both ever since the storm started. The power has only just come back on here and it's still off in the Hall and half the village. I expect you'll want a bath, won't you?"

"Yes, please!"

"Right, I'll sort out some coffee while Jonathan shows you the way. Enjoy it – you look frozen."

Jonathan half guided and half carried Lisa to his bedroom and through to the bathroom beyond. He ran the bath and left her to undress, while he returned to the kitchen to collect coffee.

"Is she OK?" Michael asked, pouring coffee into three mugs.

"She will be if she can keep that and a few glasses of water down to follow. I can't remember seeing so many casualties since the last time we played cricket! Are these two mine?"

Jonathan almost made it to the door of the kitchen before the power went off again and the Stables were plunged once more into near darkness. Michael, in a fit of unusual foresight, had left candles placed strategically about the rooms and moved quickly to light two and pass one to Jonathan before he could come to too much grief. Jonathan accepted the small light, gratefully, and then returned slowly to his room followed by his flickering shadow lurching wildly from one wall to another. On entering his room he saw that Michael had been very thorough in his preparations and had left even more candles dotted around. He lit one, took the original and, knocking gently before he entered, let himself into the darkened bathroom. Lisa was still wallowing gently beneath about five inches of yellow-white pine-fragrant foam.

"Were you all right in the dark? I've brought you some coffee."

"Fine, thanks," she answered, smiling. "It was such a novelty being able to shut my eyes without everything spinning around that I just kept them very firmly shut, wallowed a bit more and enjoyed the experience. Is that my coffee?" she asked, leaning out of the bath toward the further of the two mugs.

The flickering candle light caught the small bubbles of foam as they flowed in lingering clumps down her arm to her wrist, on to the back of her outstretched hand and quite unceremoniously into the other mug. Jonathan smiled broadly.

"Yes. Do you want to drink it in here or shall I leave it in the bedroom for later?"

"Leave it here, but don't leave it – I mean – don't leave me in here alone. I want to thank you."

"What for?"

"Washing my back."

"I haven't."

"No, but you could if you stayed."

"Ah, right!"

Back in the kitchen, Michael was sitting engrossed, looking much like a human island surrounded by candles and reading once more through the fax that had arrived earlier in the day from Peter. He was still perplexed at the attitude of Inspector Cotting and the attendant problems of sacking Frank. He had been in Emily's employ for more than five years and would almost certainly claim unfair dismissal. Michael had no real justification for making Frank redundant and even less to waste on an inevitable appeal. If anything, there was more than enough work for two groundsmen – especially if the Hall guests were going to make use of the grounds, gardens and tennis courts. No, he would have to exert some pressure on the publicans in the village, and if worst came to worst, he would have to take legal advice. He wasn't at all sure that he liked this managerial role. He preferred simple uncomplicated decisions, like those about whether to bat first or field, when to declare, whether or not to have another pint, and if the answer was 'yes' as was usually the case – whose round it was. Jonathan wandered back into the kitchen preceded by a pair of spluttering candles and interrupted Michael's train of thought just before it led inexorably to Jenny.

"Penny for them," Jonathan said, pulling up a barstool and making a clearing for his candles.

"Oh, I was miles away and a long time back," Michael replied, putting the sheaf of papers back into numerical order. "How's Lisa feeling now?"

"Fine I think, but I don't suppose she's feeling anything much at the moment – she managed to stay awake in the bath but not for very long afterwards. She seems to have spent most of our budding relationship asleep."

"Probably the best thing," Michael quipped. "She looked a bit rough. I think perhaps you should read this lot as soon as the power comes back on. The incident with Frank Graves is still reverberating around the village and you can expect a visitation from the police in the not too distant future."

"Right, thanks. I'll do it first thing in the morning."

"Fine – better make sure you do – 'night."

Chapter 15:

Divorce Solicitors

Monday morning dawned bright, dry, calm and with a hint of warmth – almost as if the skies were trying to pretend that they weren't responsible for the previous day's excesses. No prior arrangement had been made, but just after seven, Michael and Jonathan fell out of their beds and then fell into the pool to do their duty lengths. A mystified Lisa watched in confused awe, from the kitchen window as she paused briefly from rummaging through the cupboards looking for something substantial to put in her stomach. She had a serious case of the munchies. Breakfast came and went – in Lisa's case, twice – and the three went their separate ways. Lisa retrieved the minibus from its temporary garage and Michael gave Jonathan a lift to college. Cathy had made a point of keeping out of the way the previous evening and continued to stay out of the way until the coast was clear. It was an uneventful day and Jonathan spent most of his lunch break pouring through the missive that Peter had faxed to the Stables the day before. He had intended to do so as soon as he got to his room, but a pile of mail awaited him and his urgent attention. Nonetheless he was most anxious to ensure that he was adequately prepared should Inspector Cotting call. In the event, he didn't and the only thing to sour Jonathan's day was a pointed letter from Sara's solicitor. Quite naively, Jonathan had deluded himself into believing that with the divorce behind him, and the over-generous settlement in her favour, Sara would stay out of his life. He was very wrong and in addition to the drunken weekend calls, he had also come to expect a monthly letter from Messrs Drake, Prosset and Orr, Solicitors, or whoever Sara happened to be using at the time. Jonathan often wondered how stupid, gullible or just plain old-fashioned bent one had to be to believe and trot out the nasty imaginings of Sara's sad mind. Quite apart from the fact that there wasn't a shred of truth in what she claimed and hence they alleged, what irked him most was the fact that in reality, he was funding it all from the maintenance payments. The first two or three letters had really upset him and it was only when Michael suggested that he should perhaps use them as toilet paper, frame them or use them to practise his aim at darts, that he started to see the funny side of what was going on and treat them with the contempt that they each deserved. After he had received the sixth monthly instalment of literary venom, he showed them to a solicitor friend in an attempt to determine how much it was costing Sara to promulgate her evil fantasies. The reckoning was about five hundred pounds a month, which by no small coincidence was exactly how much Jonathan was paying her monthly. He mulled it over for a few days or so and then, spurred on by an awesome hangover, he summoned up all his courage and wrote to them. His letter read as follows:

Dear Sirs,

I write to acknowledge yours of the fourth May, June, July, August and September and to reply, in particular, to that of fourth October. Hitherto it had been my understanding that persons in your profession were obliged to act, so far as was reasonably practicable, within the strict bounds of certain rules of engagement. Since what you allege in your letter of fourth October is in direct contradiction with almost everything that you have alleged previously (see yours of fourth June and August), you will by now have realised that you have made a fundamental error, either previously or more recently, or that you have been completely misinformed by your client. I am aware that potentially, this places you in conflict with yourselves and rather than reporting you immediately to the Law Society, I wondered if we could reach some form of mutually acceptable arrangement. I am advised that your regular monthly letters probably represent a fee income in the sum of five hundred pounds or so and I view, with mounting incredulity, the fact that this equates with the monthly maintenance payments that I pay to your client. What I thus propose is that the maintenance payments should be remitted directly to yourselves. This would obviate the need for your client to pay tax on them (she does declare them, I suppose?), and would also remove the need for you to write to me and vice versa – and save a few trees in the process.

Yours in eager anticipation.

Jonathan had to wait nearly two months for the reply which was both brief and to the point. It read:

Dear Sir,

We write to acknowledge and thank you for yours in reply to ours of October last, and are most obliged for your most helpful comments contained therein. Inter alia, blah blah blah. Suffice it to say that we have impressed upon your ex-wife, now also our ex-client, the advisability of seeking new legal advisers.

Yours faithfully

Grovel, Grovel Arse-lick and Slime

The latest firm of leeches, Messrs Digby, Smith and Dorren, had an equally dismal grasp of the English language and as with prior incarnations, they exercised an unnerving habit of practising the computer equivalent of joined-up writing once a month – usually on the first Friday. The first Friday of April had just passed, the letter was posted and, as the result of an arrangement with the Post Office, it duly materialised in the post box at the Stables. After the usual preamble based, very loosely, on Latin it read:

We are instructed to inform you that as a result of your repeated refusal to return our client's car, she is faced with no alternative but to return once more to the Courts to seek a revised Order to have returned to her what is rightfully hers – namely the above aforementioned vehicle referred to previously above. Please be so good as to arrange for the above aforementioned vehicle referred to previously above and all relevant documents pursuant to legal road use of the above aforementioned vehicle to be returned to our client within one week of receipt of this letter, otherwise we shall have to act as set out in the above.

It occurred once more to Jonathan that it might be quite fun to arrange to have the remains of the car gift-wrapped and placed in Sara's front drive. As before, however, common sense and an absence of bravery got the better of him and he put the thought to one side. He had received an acknowledgement from his insurers but nothing more bankable. There was also the matter of letting Peter's company have a look at the remains.

Late in the afternoon, Jonathan rang Peter to discuss what was to be done with the car and whether what he had in mind would be jeopardised by any legal wranglings. There was no problem and a tentative arrangement was made for the Wednesday morning. Peter didn't have any inspiration about Sara and her legal dogs, but he suggested that he should talk to Michael about instructing Emily's lawyers in London. She had used one of the top three litigation practices in the capital and Peter thought that a letter from them to Sara's solicitors would cause sufficient chaos and rampant diarrhoea to delay matters for a few months, and might even scare her off.

Chapter 16:

A Slip in the Dark

The initial contact from Inspector Cotting came at breakfast time the following morning. The telephone rang just as Jonathan and Michael were about to take a later than usual swim. Jonathan took the call praying loudly that it wouldn't be Sara.

"Hello – Hall Stables."

"Good morning. Could I speak to Mr Grey, please?"

"You are. How can I help you?"

"Good morning. This is Inspector Cotting of the City Police. I expect that Mr Evans said that we would be in touch."

The voice and the tone grated in unison and Jonathan wondered if this man was congenitally unlikeable or if Michael and the transcript had contrived to make him appear so. Neither Michael nor he made a habit of parading their doctorates unnecessarily, mostly because of a shared distaste they had for those of their colleagues who did. Academic snobbery was easily the worst way of taking oneself seriously. Having said all that, there were always those like Inspector Cotting who could either not bring themselves to acknowledge their intellectual betters (if better was the word) or so despised them that they would go out of their way to emphasise the alternative title – in this case that of 'Mr'. Jonathan tried hard but couldn't let it go:

"Yes, *Dr* Evans did say that you were still making enquiries. Do you wish to interview me today? I can call in at the station this afternoon if that would be convenient."

Jonathan had been waving feverishly at Michael, who had hurried back inside believing the call to be for him. He covered the mouthpiece and whispered, 'Cotting'. He then pressed the speaker button so that Michael and Cathy could share the inspector's discomfort. There was a faint noise of a washing machine in the background as he replied, "No, that won't be necessary, sir. I can just as easily come out to you."

"I bet you could," Jonathan thought to himself. Michael was trying not to snigger too loudly, gave up and turned the speaker off again. Jonathan pressed home the advantage.

"Well, that's the problem, really. I won't be around very much and it wouldn't be any trouble for me to pop in and see you. Would early afternoon suit?"

There was an uneasy pause as the inspector made a sudden lunge for the washing machine before it could launch itself into a noisy spin cycle. He almost regained his composure when his doorbell rang and he muttered a curse.

"Er. No. It seems that I'm tied up most of the week. Would you be free to come in, say on Thursday morning?"

"Ten?"

"Yes, that'll be fine. See you then."

Both men hung up, one with a grin and the other with a scowl. The one with the grin looked at Michael and the pair of them burst out laughing. Cathy simply shook her head at the juvenile behaviour. Michael was the first to stop laughing and he made the superfluous phone call to the police station to confirm the inspector's next day duty. After the swim Jonathan settled down with a good book to pass the time until his lunch date with Lisa. Michael, by comparison, had a far less pleasurable day in prospect. He had to be just adequately pleasant to eight out of ten of the short list of candidates before offering jobs to Cathy and Bill's daughter Betty. Bill had tried to cook the books by putting less than helpful comments on the CVs of anyone who seemed capable, on paper, of eclipsing his daughter. The first three were pleasant enough but didn't shine. Betty was next and she had a genuine spark. Even if he didn't need to placate her father, Michael would probably have given her a job on the spot. She obviously took after her mother. After several more no-hopers, he took advantage of the brief lunch break to survey progress with the building works while, at the same time, avoiding the growing temptation to sneak out for a quick pint or three. After that, the rest of the afternoon dragged slowly on to its inevitable conclusion, Miss Everet from Dorset being the last to be interviewed, shortly after three thirty. She arrived with an altered disguise. The hair was brown again, but this time it

185

was shorter than he remembered with just a slight hint of highlights above her left eye. The biggest difference were the eyes themselves. Cathy of a week ago had cold grey eyes that appeared almost devoid of any emotion. The updated model had piercing blue ones, an appearance that must have been created by tinted contact lenses. Michael was so busy taking in the changes that he forgot his manners and Cathy sat down before being asked.

"They are," she said.

He was still looking vacant and feeling the effects of having to spend a day pretending to choose when choices had already been made. 'No matter,' he thought. Emily had probably given up a large chunk of her life to look after his well-being and it was probably about time that he started returning the favour. After all, he hadn't got anything much else planned for today anyway – and it was probably worth the wait to see Cathy again, even with the minor modifications. She was now sitting opposite him, looking expectantly for some sort of response.

"They are what?" he responded.

"Tinted. I am wearing tinted contact lenses."

"Ah." he replied, as if he had expected a different answer.

"Michael, are you feeling all right? You look as though you have just been brainwashed."

"Yes – sorry," he replied. "I've had a long hard tedious day interviewing the competition for your new position and if nothing else, it has taught me how inept an employer I would be if I ever had to take it up seriously. It certainly makes me appreciate the simple joys of imparting knowledge to willing minds. Very few of the potential employees had the necessary experience to get the job and even fewer had the aptitude, but each of them was desperate to get the position. The CVs were really depressing reading. Not including you, only two of the women I've seen today have been in work this year. So I found myself wanting to give them all jobs and unable to do any such thing. Nice CV, by the way, are the early bits true?"

"Every one. The only whopping lie is the bit about working for your friends in Dorset. That coincides with the time that I've been with Peter. Antonia sounded nice though. I spoke to her on the phone and I'm almost sorry that I didn't work for her. Is she much like your aunt?"

"Very much so. She's my second favourite lady."

"Well?"

"Well what?"

Michael had wrenched himself back to the present moment and was warming to the idea of some friendly word play. The perennial grin was taking up residence on his face.

"Well, are you going to interview me, or are we going to spend the rest of the afternoon discussing unemployment and its role in subduing the serving classes?"

"You mean we have to go through the ritual despite the fact that I have to give you the job anyway?"

"We certainly do! I've spent most of the last two days trying to learn silver service, how to curtsey, how to be politely deferential and how to make beds like a nurse."

Michael thought about the last bit for a while, but wisely dismissed from his mind.

"I suppose I shouldn't be surprised, but was all that really necessary in the circumstances?"

He realised immediately that he had said the wrong thing. Cathy flared her nostrils and gave him a withering look that made him cross his legs involuntarily. Seeing that she had achieved the desired effect, Cathy pressed home the advantage.

"First off, I always prepare for any identity – however simple or temporary the role might be. Secondly, you obviously know little of the circumstances. Have you spoken to Peter since he was at the Stables?"

The grin went back into hiding as Michael shook his head.

"I thought not. The circumstances, such as we understand them, are becoming more unpleasant the more we find out. Has Jonathan spoken with friend Cotting, yet?"

Michael's shoulders sagged visibly as his head shook again.

"Was that a 'No' or a 'Don't Know'?"

"The latter, I'm afraid. He's made contact – this morning as you know – but Jonathan gave him the runaround and is supposed to see him on Thursday. That won't stop the man turning up at the Stables, or even going to the college if he has a mind to."

"Well let's just hope that he does neither of those things; it could be that he is dangerous. Peter has been making enquiries about the inspector and it seems that he has a dark past which is linked to that of your ex-groundsman."

"He's not my ex-groundsman yet."

"Well, I don't know what advice you've had, but I see that as being strictly your problem. Inspector Cotting used to be based in London where, before his fall from grace, he reached the dizzy rank of detective chief inspector in the Burglary Squad. His rapid departure from both the squad and London was unnaturally quiet when you consider that he was put back in uniform and busted down a rank. Peter had to call in a lot of favours to discover the truth of what happened."

Michael had started to regain his composure and wondered if now was the moment to start asking questions like, 'How would you prepare turbot for serving at table?' Thankfully, insight and wisdom got the better of him and instead he asked:

"So what happened?"

"You probably wouldn't have heard of it, but about ten years ago there was an internal enquiry in the London Police about corruption in the antiques theft investigation bureau. The word at the time was that, in certain fashionable parts of London, small and valuable items were being stolen to order, with many of the losers receiving several visits a month from the same team of burglars. The link between many of the jobs was that having been deprived of their valuables, some of the losers visited the same dealer to buy replacements. These were all untraceable goods, unless, of course, you marked them. No sooner had Mr and Mrs Sloane replaced their treasures (courtesy of their insurers), than up they popped with the dealer, the owners repurchased them and the same burglars stole them again. The same goods circulated around endlessly for several months before the boys in blue got wind of it. Then only after a lot of pressure from above, the police started marking and tagging certain goods. Suspects were targeted and the net closed. More and more resources were poured into the project and just as the operation appeared to be reaching a conclusion, the burglaries stopped."

"A leak?"

"More like a very big hole drilled from well inside. The gang obviously had a well-placed policeman in their pay and the word was that they probably had two. The one who was sacrificed was a go-nowhere detective constable with a gambling habit, an expensive wife and a delinquent son to maintain. The one who remained relatively untouched was your friend and mine, the then Detective Chief Inspector Cotting. In the event, there were enough suspicions to blight his career more or less permanently, but his partner in crime got ten years. He was about to be released, for good behaviour, after three when, quite conveniently, his fellow inmates discovered that he was put inside for being, as they say, a 'bent cop'. Stories get blown out of proportion in jail, but apparently they injected him with almost enough heroin to kill a vanload of policemen and then just for good measure they hung him up by his wedding-tackle, to die."

"Shit!" said Michael, crossing his legs again.

"That was more or less his widow's first reaction apparently, but by lunch time, she had managed to overcome her grief, pack and set off to join the rest of the gang in South America.

"Anyway, once the dust settled, Cotting got a quiet move out to the country – or so he thought – and then about five years ago, his past came back to haunt him in the person of Frank Graves."

"How does he fit into...?" The question died on Michael's lips almost as he asked it. "Oh I see. For 'delinquent son', read, 'Frank Graves'. But why the alliance? I would have thought that they would have avoided each other, wouldn't they? – I mean – new city and a new start."

"Ordinarily perhaps, but not in their case. Cotting probably thought that he could start a new life without anyone from the past coming back to haunt him, but it was not to be. Frank, it appears, has been in trouble with the law since his early teens and it did not take long for him to find out his father's nemesis or the name of his partner in crime. Frank didn't move here to improve his mind or even for the work. It was to blackmail Cotting and he's been doing it all the while."

"And that's why Cotting is trying to help him? It doesn't make sense does it – I don't think I'd go out of my way to help someone who was blackmailing me!"

"You're right in that at first sight, it doesn't make sense, but Peter doesn't think it's that simple. Apparently Frank has a suspended sentence for an assault in London and it may be that by keeping him out of trouble here and making it seem as though Frank was the victim, Cotting could make a one-off final payment and keep his past where it belongs."

"And do you believe that?" Michael asked, trying to fit all the loose pieces of information into the theory.

"Until I find something more convincing to believe, yes. Besides which, Peter has an uncanny knack of reading these things right most of the time. That's the main reason why I work for him."

"How did Peter find out about Frank's criminal record? That's illegal, isn't it? Doesn't it involve getting access to a secure computer?"

"Do you ever make omelettes, Michael?"

"Sorry!"

"Shall we go back to the interview, then?"

"I think it'll be for the best."

Michael went through the motions of interviewing Cathy, offered her the job and saw her off the premises. Much as he had expected, she had prepared herself thoroughly for the interview and had stood head and shoulders and a few other bits above the rest of the candidates. He was beginning to find her very attractive, but realised quickly that this was neither the time nor the place. He set off in search of Bill Edwards and told him of the staff changes and in particular, Betty's obvious abilities as an interviewee. He stopped short of suggesting that charm and dignity were the sort of inherited characteristics that skipped a generation. Bill wasn't exactly overjoyed at the appointment of Cathy and Michael made a mental note to ask her how she had managed to upset him in such a short space of time. There was obviously a lot about her to admire.

It was starting to rain heavily again as he headed back home to the Stables. He wasn't dressed for rain and started to run to make the cover of the trees before the threatening clouds burst above him. It was a very unequal race; he lost it and resigned himself to a thorough soaking. After a further ten minutes' mud-soaked drenching, one stone wall stood between him and the last field before a clear run to the Stables. As if things weren't bad enough, the track down to the gate was doing its best to impersonate a stream. He looked at the wall and climbed easily to the top. The lower parts had been kept in good order and had been protected by clinging foliage from the ravages of frost. From about a metre upward it was all down to faith and mechanics and neither could cope with the additional load of Michael. Loosened by a winter's frost and lubricated by the recent rain, the stones gave in to gravity. All things do that in the end. As he lost his footing, Michael fell, heavily gashing his left calf to the bone on a sharp frost-shattered stone. He cried out with the sudden pain and lost his balance completely. Still bending to grasp his leg, he fell headlong into a gathering pile of rocks. In what was otherwise a shallow, makeshift and premature grave, Michael had one solitary piece of good fortune. The ground immediately supporting the wall fell sharply away from it onto solid bedrock. This had two beneficial effects. The first was that when he hit his head, he did so with sufficient force to knock himself senseless. The second was that with his senseless head a good three feet below the gaping wound, he neither bled to death nor suffered brain damage. Michael lapsed in and out of consciousness as the rain grew more and more heavy and the light faded. In one wakeful moment before darkness fell, he saw his leg and the blood still oozing from the wound. He tried to move but the pain was truly dreadful – he must have cracked a couple of ribs, just for good measure. With considerable effort he managed to lift his left leg just high enough to push a rock beneath the calf with his right foot. When he lowered his leg again, its weight pressing on the wound was enough to stop the bleeding. It was also painful enough to make him pass out again. His first visitor was an inquisitive cow that wanted to know who was lying down in her field. The second was a large, shabbily dressed man sporting two black eyes and a pink adhesive dressing covering the remains of his nose. It was Frank Graves. He was in a fouler than usual mood, lifted only by the sudden appearance of a newly made short cut through the wall. He climbed over the remains and almost stepped on the prone figure of Michael. For a brief moment, a long-disused spark of humanity flickered in what passed for Frank's soul and he bent down almost compassionately, to see if he could help. Despite the quickly fading light and the muddy camouflage, Michael's face was quite recognisable and when he saw it, Frank laughed and kicked Michael in the side of the chest. There was no reaction and Frank laughed again – so much so that it hurt his strapped knee. He searched Michael's clothes, liberated his wallet and credit cards and then kicked Michael once more. Steering a wide course around and then back to the Stables, he vanished into the rain thinking that perhaps it hadn't been such a bad day after all.

Chapter 17: Field Dressings

As she left the Hall, Cathy made no mention of the fact that she had still made no hotel reservation for the night. There was too much risk of being overheard for her to entertain that kind of conversation without privacy and, having been shown to the door, she took a brief tour around the outside of the building just to see how the real thing matched the plans. It was an imposing structure, but the onset of rain curtailed the tour and she doubled back to her car for cover. The rain eased a little and had more or less stopped as Michael left. She considered offering him a lift, but there were too many watching eyes near the Hall and she read the local paper instead. After a few minutes the rain returned with renewed vigour and since it was also getting darker, Cathy resolved to take the risk and give Michael a lift anyway. By the time she hit the public road, she realised that he must have left it and taken the cross-country route. So be it. They would probably arrive at the same time. She drove on down the hill, turned left and then second left and on until the Stable lights came into view. Someone was at home anyway. Jonathan opened the door with Lisa at his side.

"Hello," he said warmly. "I knew Michael was interviewing you today, but we weren't expecting a personal visit. Cathy Everet – Lisa Adams; Lisa Adams – Cathy Everet."

The women smiled at each other without obvious effort.

"Yes, I did see Michael today; in fact he should be back any time soon. I missed him on the road so I guess he's coming over the fields – if he doesn't drown en route! I meant to ask him while I was at the Hall, but I forgot. Will it be OK for me to stay again tonight? I need to call Peter and speak to both of you about what we are supposed to be doing in the future."

"Well I'm sure it will be alright, but you'd better fill Lisa in; so far I've told her nothing. I'll get some drinks."

Lisa sat open-mouthed as Cathy introduced her to the conspiracy and brought her up to speed on the intricacies. Jonathan chipped in from time to time, but left it up to Cathy to fill in the fine details. She certainly knew her stuff and he was impressed. Lisa finished her drink in two gulps and poured herself another. The three talked on until the subject returned to Michael and his continued absence. Jonathan looked with squeezed eyes out over the fields but the light was very poor and the rain had diminished visibility to just a few tens of metres, even to the west.

"It's tipping it down out there," he said, almost despairingly and turning back to the women. "I'd better go out and meet him with some waterproofs. If he's got any sense, he'll be holed-up under a tree somewhere. Can you fix some hot drinks and hide the brandy? He's bound to make the most of it."

The rain fell heavily and unremittingly in cold piercing sheets as Jonathan trudged and squidged his way into the gathering gloom and up the hill towards the stone wall demarcating the northern boundary of the field. When he reached approximately midway between the Stables and the slope beneath the wall, he glanced back and made out a pale area of watery light, which must have been from the kitchen. He shuddered, put his head down, pulled his coat closer round him and trudged on. As the ground started to rise he made out a notch on the horizon and moved instinctively towards it. In the fading light he found Michael in the debris of the wall. At first he feared the worst and felt his heart start to beat rapidly. He knelt down at his friend's side as tears filled his eyes. Regaining his senses, he felt for a pulse and to his great relief, found one. It was weak and erratic, but it was there nonetheless. Michael's face felt cold and having covered the upper part of his body with the coat that he had been carrying, Jonathan took off his own and placed it over Michael's legs. The light was now so poor that Jonathan could not see that the grass all around Michael's legs was stained with washed-out blood. He knelt down once more and after whispering that he would be back, he ran, stumbled and slid back to the Stables to summon help. By the time that he fell into the kitchen, he was mud-stained, completely soaked through and gasping for breath.

"Call an ambulance quickly!" he managed. "Michael has had an accident and he's out there in the rain."

Lisa reached for the telephone and Cathy opened her mouth as if to say something, but ran outside to her car instead. She returned some moments later with a torch and a first aid kit. Lisa was repeating the address as Cathy and Jonathan ran past her into the night. Jonathan was still a little winded from his run to the Stables, but he probably wouldn't have been able to keep up with Cathy even if he wasn't. When he caught up with her she was already putting a pressure dressing on Michael's left leg, as if it was the sort of thing she did every day.

"Is there anything I can do?" he asked, kneeling down to check Michael's pulse. He glanced at the red stained grass and chalk bedrock beneath Michael's legs. "I must have missed that in the dark; has he lost a lot of blood?"

"Quite a lot, but I've seen worse. It looks as though he pushed that rock beneath the wound with his other leg before he lost consciousness, or he got dead lucky and fell that way. It's not the blood loss that caused him to black out though – have a look at his head, Jonathan. I think he may have taken a knock."

Jonathan took the torch and moved Michael's head gently, first to one side and then to the other until he found the lump. It felt the size of an egg and he shuddered as he realised that he had warm blood on his hand.

"Have you any more dressings in that box of yours, Cathy? I'm afraid you're right. He's going to have a mammoth headache when he wakes up. He will wake up, won't he, Cathy?"

The gravity of the situation hit Jonathan like a sledgehammer in the middle of his chest and he felt the panic start to rise once more. Cathy sensed his unease and squeezed his hands in as much of a caring way as she could in the circumstances.

"I think he will be OK, Jonathan, especially since you found him so quickly." She could feel him trembling and hoped that he was reassured. She needed helping more than hindering at the moment so a diversion was in order.

"Do you know Michael's blood group, Jonathan?"

"Yes it's B Rhesus positive, why?"

"Well he's lost quite a bit and it would save time if the hospital was forewarned. If I stay here with Michael, do you think you could run back to the Stables and telephone the hospital? Then you can guide the crew up here when they arrive."

Jonathan agreed without discussion and retraced his steps as quickly as possible to the temporary warmth of the Stables. Cathy watched him until he was out of sight and then returned her attention to Michael. His bandages were already sodden with rainwater but at least there was no sign of fresh blood. He was very cold, however, and as there was still no sound of an ambulance, she took off her coat and laid down next to Michael in an attempt to take off the chill. She covered them both with her coat and cuddled him gently. He stirred slightly and murmured something inaudible. Time seemed to drag, but after a final angry burst, the rain stopped. There was a brief silence and then, as her ears became accustomed to the relative quiet, she started to pick up the sounds of water trickling down from the wall above them. This and the sound of Michael breathing gave way eventually to the wail of the approaching ambulance. The rain had cleared the air and the headlights were easily visible from nearly a mile away. The ambulance's approach was tantalisingly slow because of the narrow twisting lanes but eventually it pulled up at the Stables, now well-lit in the valley below them. Minutes later she heard voices and picked out figures moving quickly up the hill towards her. She had left the torch pointing towards the Stables as soon as the ambulance stopped and, long before the figures came within full view, she quietly rose to her feet, moved into the shadow of the tallest part of the wall several metres away and crouched down beneath her coat. Although the rain had stopped, cloud cover was complete and it was totally dark. Under the cover of her camouflage, Cathy was just another large wet rock.

"You did well to leave the torch here, sir, and these dressings are very well done. Your friend owes you a lot, I think."

Jonathan stood to one side with the torches as the ambulance crew eased Michael gently onto a stretcher. Lisa had come with them and between the four of them, they lifted Michael off the ground and moved off slowly down the hill towards the waiting ambulance. Jonathan was one of the two bringing up the rear and as they moved off, he casually dropped a spare torch on the ground for Cathy to find her way back. Cathy waited for the party to move completely out of sight before she left the cover of the wall, retrieved the torch and started to pick her way down the incline. Jonathan followed the ambulance in Michael's car and so it was Lisa that let Cathy in just a few minutes later. She was mud-stained and generally soaked through and elected to leave most of her clothes in an untidy heap in the kitchen before heading off in search of a hot shower. Ten minutes later she was dry, dressed and ready to go. Lisa set the alarm and locked up while Cathy started her car and moved it closer to the door. She got out to open the yard gate and a movement sensitive light turned on, bathing her in a harsh blue-white glare. She moved her hand instinctively to protect her eyes and so missed the hunched form of Frank Graves as he darted for cover outside. Having relieved Michael of all his valuables and left him for dead out in the fields, Frank decided to turn his attention to what was left in the Stables. He had spent a few minutes or so just circling the building and was alarmed to see lights on, people within and an approaching vehicle. He was about to give up when after a few minutes he saw a man move off on foot only to return running a few minutes later and then set out again with a woman. He – the man – had obviously found Michael Evans's body. Frank thought things through and wondered what to do. There was nothing to connect him with the body and he could get rid of the credit cards in London – no problem. He might as well stick around to see what happened. It wasn't worth risking the lanes in case he was seen by oncoming traffic. Someone was bound to have summoned help. About ten minutes later the man returned alone and soon after an ambulance arrived. The two ambulance crew, dressed in green luminous waterproofs, the man and yet another woman trudged off up the hill, their torch-lights wobbling gently into the night. This was probably as good a time as any and they had even left a door open, but something held Frank back. There was something vaguely familiar about the first woman but he couldn't quite place what it was. Curiosity got the better of him and he slid back once more into his hiding place near the building in case he could get a better view of her. He was dressed in heavy waterproof clothing, but his boots and socks were soaked through and rain had been draining off his lank hair down his neck. Now that he had stopped moving he was starting to feel cold. They had told him at the hospital to avoid sneezing if at all possible and he was now starting to feel the chill. He was still avoiding the urge to sneeze when the wobbling lights came back into view half way down the hill. There were four lights and only four people – if you didn't count the one on the stretcher. The bandaged head was exposed so perhaps the bugger was alive after all. As the stretcher party moved around the building to the waiting ambulance, a pale yellow light shone out from one of the rooms, enabling Frank to recognise the second woman – so it was the first one that was missing. He moved quietly round behind them and saw the man get into a car and follow the ambulance as it accelerated gently down the drive. The second woman went back into the house on her own. Where was the other one? Frank had difficulty even dealing with simple things in life and this mystery was quite beyond his comprehension. He sat down in the bushes to think it all through. The wailing siren of the ambulance was still audible as Cathy walked past his hiding place. She was only a few feet away from him and he held his breath, frightened that she might hear him.

Cathy did not slacken her pace and was quickly out of sight around the corner of the building. He felt his heart pounding and what was left of his nose throbbing. He was still manifestly understanding nothing when minutes later, the lights went off and the two women emerged from the Stables. Frank heard the sound of them talking and then a car being started. He moved even more cautiously closer to the yard gate, all the time remaining within reach of the cover of the bushes. He was only two metres from it when Cathy walked into the detector beam that operated the floodlights. He took one step into the bushes and crouched, just before Cathy walked into view, raising one hand to her eyes. Recognition was not immediate, but when it arrived it did so with chilling clarity. If he had seen her full face he might have remembered nothing, but it was the mouth that gave it away. On the evening in question she had been wearing huge dark glasses, which covered almost everything except her mouth. He remembered the mouth and this was the bitch that had put him in hospital. His first instinct was to reach for his knife but his second instinct prevailed and that was to bide his time. Cotting had so far drawn a blank in his enquiries, especially with regard to Master Evans, so what was going on? He needed to speak to Bill Edwards before he did anything, so he stayed in a damp crouch until the two women had driven away. It was seven o'clock, he was cold, wet and hungry and he needed some advice. The clouds had started to part and he now had to decide whether to risk the fields – and more particularly the overgrown pits – or the lanes and the risk of being seen.

There weren't that many people around with a cross of sticking plaster over the middle of their faces. He mulled it over a while longer, tossed a coin in his mind and set out along the lanes – the shorter of the two routes.

Jonathan fumed inwardly at the slow progress of the ambulance as it picked its way through the lanes back towards the city. By the time they reached the ring road his spirits lifted slightly as it became clear that the ambulance crew had radioed ahead to alert the police. Several junctions were blocked off in their favour and five minutes later he was parking close to Accident and Emergency. He ran inside just as the medical crew pulled the curtains around Michael's cubicle.

"Mr Grey?" A tired but familiar face smiled at him. "We met the last time your friend was here."

"Yes, though last time was a lot less serious than this. How is he doing?"

"He will be OK. They gave him some plasma in the ambulance and we'll be giving him some of his own group before he goes for X-ray. He's still unconscious and I expect that we will keep him in for a couple of days – he took a bit of a knock on the head. We are a bit confused about some of his other injuries though."

"What other injuries? I didn't know he had any others!"

"Well, how many walls did he fall off?"

"Just the one that I know of."

"Then it looks as though someone gave him a kicking while he was down. Can you have a look at his clothes for me? You might as well look after them for now anyway."

"Sure, no problem." Jonathan followed the nurse into a small, clinical-looking room where Michael had been examined upon arrival. A large stainless steel bin held the remains of the bloodstained dressings that Cathy had applied so expertly. His first instinct was to be sick but then he thought that at least he knew the true meaning of 'field dressings'. Cathy was one different lady.

"Sorry about the mess," the nurse said, seeing his facial colour change from pink to green and back to pink. "We are a bit short-staffed at the moment and we haven't had a chance to clean up yet. Look – here are his clothes – we had to cut them off him, of course."

Jonathan looked at the sorry mess of cut textile resting in a muddy heap at the side of the room. He had never seen clothes cut off someone before and it was only because he had seen Mike in them that he knew they were his. He looked at them without a clue what he was supposed to say or do.

"Where are his personal effects?" he asked, at last.

"Nothing's been removed that I know of – that's how he came in and we just stripped him, so if there was anything on him, it should still be there unless it was lost where you found him."

"No I checked that when we put him on the stretcher – there's nothing left in the field. We should find a set of keys, some credit cards, a wallet and an old fashioned fountain pen."

"Half an old-fashioned fountain pen," the nurse corrected him, "I'm afraid the other half is still sticking in him – that's partly why we wondered if he had been kicked. How exactly did you find him – was he on his back?"

"More or less, yes," Jonathan nodded.

"Then it is as we thought," she continued. "If the blow on the head was from falling, we cannot ascribe the bruising to the side of his chest to an accident – if that is what he had. It looks as though he has been kicked at least twice while he was lying on the ground and one of the kicks broke his pen."

"Well there's one sure way to find out," Jonathan said, putting on some disposable gloves. "I'll take the trousers and you take the jacket."

They rummaged carefully, checking that no pockets had been cut when the garments were removed.

"I've got the keys," he said, shaking the empty remains of the trousers limply in one hand. "How about you?"

"Half a pen and a diary – you forgot about that – but nothing else. I'll report this to the duty administrator and then notify the police. I hope your friend can shed some light on all this, though if I'm right, he probably won't remember much about anything."

"You seem to be very certain about all this," Jonathan said. "How come you're so sure about the injuries?"

"I usually work the Saturday afternoon and evening shift, so I get to see a lot of so-called sports injuries and pub fight victims. Not that there's much difference, really, they are mostly the same people."

They emerged from the room to be met by Lisa and Cathy. Cathy was in yet another disguise – or so it seemed. She was wearing a dowdy headscarf, which aged her by about ten years, and she had also rouged her cheeks somehow to make her face appear a little more pinched than it really was: quite clever. Her cold grey eyes were wide and she was shaking her head almost imperceptibly. Quietly, but very firmly Cathy was again denying her existence.

"Penny," he said, guessing wildly. "I thought you were going to stay at the Stables and phone people."

"I was," she replied, relaxing a little, "but I thought I'd better come along with Lisa to find out how he is for myself."

"Speaking of which ..." Lisa floated, looking at the nurse.

"I'll get the doctor to see you. I really must get back to my duties now, especially in the circumstances."

She left the three of them in search of a doctor while Jonathan brought the others up to date -- particularly with respect to the word 'circumstances'.

"It looks as though," Jonathan explained, "in addition to half braining himself and nearly bleeding to death, someone has given Mike a kicking and robbed him. The nurse there is about to telephone the police, Cathy, so I guess you'd better make yourself scarce."

"Okay," she agreed quickly. "But I should see him before I leave. If it's me that has to wake his aunt in the middle of the night, I'd better have some good answers. Do you know what's been stolen?"

"His wallet and credit cards – there's an A3 photocopy of all of the cards in his briefcase, so if you get time you could start phoning around and stopping them."

Their conversation was interrupted by the approach of a young and tired-looking doctor. Her white coat was slightly spattered with blood. It looked as though it had been slept in, but she had sufficient reserves to muster a smile as she approached.

"Are you three with Dr Evans?" she asked, looking at each of them in turn.

"Yes, I'm his cousin," Cathy lied, "and these two are friends. What's happening?"

"Well it looks as though he's had a lucky break, despite his injuries. I'm told that someone provided some excellent first aid before the ambulance crew got to him. Who was that?"

Jonathan saw the familiar look in Cathy's eyes and, without any hesitation, volunteered himself.

"Well done!" the doctor continued. "You probably made his chances of a full recovery much better. So far as we can tell and working from the bottom up, Dr Evans has a badly lacerated left calf, but thankfully no damage to tendons. There is some slight damage to an artery, which is why he lost so much blood, but we have clamped that for now and will repair it properly once he's had an X-ray. There's a little bruising to both upper legs but nothing that will show after a week or two. We will know more about the pelvis once we've had him X-rayed, but there are no outward signs of damage. He looks to have been kicked twice in the ribs and I've just removed part of a pen from one of the areas. Thankfully he is quite well muscled and there was no penetration of the pleural cavity. I wouldn't be at all surprised to find that he has several broken ribs. Lastly, he has a very large lump on the back of his head and we don't know yet if there is a fracture beneath. Again, X-rays will sort that out. He is sedated at present and we plan to keep him that way, at least until we've sewn him up properly. When he does come round, he'll probably be concussed and he may even be suffering from amnesia, we'll just have to wait and see. You can see him briefly if you wish, but only for a few moments. Don't be alarmed by his appearance; he'll be alright."

She led them past a row of occupied booths to a small well-lit room, which looked at first sight like a shrine to the inventors of stainless steel and oscilloscopes. In the centre and neatly laid out on a mobile cot was the ghostly figure of Michael. His skin was white, going on blue. His left calf was covered with a large sterile dressing, his loins with a strategically placed blanket and the top of his head with a loosely placed dressing. Jonathan could see that the top and back of his head had been shaved to reveal a livid mound of flesh about the size of a goose egg.

"Ouch!" he said Jonathan, wincing visibly.

Lisa moved gingerly round the cot to see what he was looking at and then promptly slid to the floor. Cathy helped her out of the room as the doctor further explained things to Jonathan.

"Don't be put off by all the tubes," she said, waving one hand at the plumbing attached to Michael's arms. "The red one is blood – obviously – and the clear one is saline mixed with a cocktail of antibiotics. Is he up to date on tetanus jabs, by the way?"

Jonathan nodded and the doctor continued. "Right – once he's sewn up we'll start him on blood thinners to deal with any potential clots. It'll take him about four or five days to get up to speed on those and by that time, apart from some visits for physiotherapy, you should be able to take him home. Does he have any next of kin other than his cousin? I mean, is there a Mrs Evans about, or a girlfriend or both, who should be contacted?"

"Neither at present," Jonathan answered carefully, "but there is someone who will probably be a bit peeved if she doesn't find out. I'll deal with it."

An attendant entered the room and after a brief conversation with the doctor, wheeled Michael, his cot and the plumbing out in the direction of the X-ray department.

"Doctor?" Jonathan asked, as the door swung closed.

"Yes," she replied, fighting back a yawn.

"He will be all right, won't he? You mentioned blood clots."

"I mentioned possible clots, not actual ones. It's a normal precaution to prescribe blood thinners in cases of this type and there is no reason, at present, to read anything more into it than that."

Jonathan was about to ask another question, but the doctor's pager intervened and after thanking her, he went off in search of Lisa and Cathy. Lisa was in reception talking with a police officer and Cathy, not surprisingly, was nowhere to be found.

"There you are, darling," Lisa smiled at him and broke off the apparently unwelcome conversation. She was still looking a little jaded as she threw herself into his arms. "This officer would like to take a statement from you, Jonathan. I've told him everything there is to know, but he seems very insistent."

Jonathan looked over her shoulder and felt his spirits sink as he gazed upon the unmistakable early hominid and belligerent features of PC 103 'jobmate'. This was destined to be a long and tedious evening. He thought quickly.

"Is Penny still phoning people?"

"Yes!" she answered. "I think she's using the box in the car park just outside."

There was sufficient emphasis on the word 'car' for him to comprehend where Cathy was lying low, but hadn't left the area.

"Fine!" he decided. "Why don't you join her and make sure that she contacts Jenny as well as Emily and then I'll get a cab and join you both at home later. Mike's going to be alright and there's nothing that you can do to help by staying here."

The suggestion was said with sufficient authority to convey the intended impression to the waiting officer. Lisa merely nodded, kissed Jonathan gently on the lips and left. Jonathan saw that the constable had become distracted by the need to take details from the admissions register, so he took the opportunity to take a leak and raid a chocolate vending machine. His body was catching up with the fact that it had not been fed for some while. When he came out of the toilet the constable was still poring through the hospital's records and was making himself increasingly unpopular with the admissions clerk. He was tempted to stay within earshot and enjoy the sport, but his concern for Michael swayed him. The clerk was beginning to go distinctly red in the face and was starting to clash with her blouse. Worse still, it looked as though the two of them, she and he, were in for a lengthy session. Jonathan looked for a sign marked 'X-ray' and followed it. Hospitals, at night, are uniquely depressing places and, to kill time, Jonathan found himself following a succession of signs all equally marked 'X-ray', but none of which lived up to expectations. He wondered whether the much vaunted, but never really fulfilled Patient's Charter applied to this hospital and where, for that matter, he could find a complaints form. Ten minutes and five signs later, he was lost in a confusion of wards. It was about half an hour after the bell calling family and other visitors to leave. They were a sorry-looking lot, held together by ties of duty and enforced compassion and trudging out slowly, thanking nursing staff that they had never seen before and would probably never see again –

unless another ageing relative took a tumble. Most of them, the family and visitors, had driven a long way to see someone that they had ignored for years. They had spent the last hour or so sitting around on hard chairs cracking feeble jokes and eating the patients' grapes. They wandered out in file agreeing silently that he/she had had a good life and it would probably be better if ... Jonathan looked, listened, but didn't much like and made his way back to Accident and Emergency where reality was easier to accept. On turning the last corner he was pleased to find the waiting inquisitor – well, almost.

"I believe you wanted to see me." Jonathan said, reluctantly.

Chapter 18: Gravesend

As he trudged wearily along the part-flooded lanes and headed in the direction of the village, Frank mulled over the events of the evening and comprehensively failed to understand them. In fairness to his legendary lacking grey matter, he possessed only a partial framework of clues and no means of linking them. He was cold, miserable and very hungry, in need of help and most of all, he needed a stiff drink. Having just enough wit to realise that he could satisfy the last three desires by seeing Bill Edwards, he headed towards Bill's house. The parlour lights were on, and after knocking on the window Frank was admitted. Bill looked quickly up and down the road to see if his visitor had been seen but there was not a soul about. He shut and locked the door and turned to see the shabby, steaming figure of Frank who was now sitting by the open fire rolling up a cigarette.

"I thought we had agreed, long since, that you would not come to see me here. This had better be good, Frank!"

"Shove it, Bill," Frank grunted angrily, spitting spare strands of rolling tobacco into the fireplace.

"I have some information for you and I need a drink."

"It's Mr Edwards to you, son, and it had still better be good. I don't want you here because we shouldn't have people seeing us together other than at the Hall, OK?"

"I said shove it! Nobody saw me and this could be important, if you'd only listen."

Bill sighed and went to the dresser to get a bottle of whisky and two glasses. He rued the day that he had ever set eyes on Frank and had started to overlook his antisocial/criminal behaviour. Within months he found himself faced with a straight choice between being blackmailed and becoming an accomplice. He chose the latter on fiscal rather than moral grounds. Whatever else he was, Bill was a lifetime advocate of the redistribution of wealth –providing of course that it was other people's and redistributed in his direction. Well, what was done was done and he just had to live with it. He sighed again, poured out two generous glasses of whisky and sat down handing one to Frank.

"Very well, what is it that's so important then?"

Frank drained his glass in one, shuddered involuntarily and handed it back to Bill expectantly. Bill knew that he wouldn't get anything useful out of Frank without providing him with several more glasses, so he filled it willingly and handed it back without argument.

"I've found out who broke my nose!" Frank said, proudly.

Bill wondered if it wasn't too late to take the second glass back from his unwelcome guest and throw him out, but he decided that Frank would probably get nasty and start a fight, so he opted instead to humiliate him.

"Frank," he began very quietly, "do you honestly think that I give a toss who broke your nose? Although we are forced to work and steal together, you shouldn't for one moment think that I care about you, or for that matter, what happens to you. From what I heard, you thoroughly deserved it. By coming here tonight just to share your little gem of knowledge with me, you may well have got me into trouble. Who is she, anyway?"

"I don't know!" Frank snapped.

He had been so intrigued at seeing her again and seeing her, of all places, at the Stables that it hadn't dawned on him that he was no nearer to putting a name to her. His sense of guilt and deflation grew as Bill started to go red in the face and start to bluster. Feeling defeated, he added, "But I know where she is – she is staying with that rich sod Evans at those fancy Stables of his."

Bill's expression changed at the mention of Michael's name and he sat down once more, his scowling face illuminated by the flickering light of the spitting coal fire. He was sure there had been some connection between Michael and Frank's assailant after Betty had seen the two of them exchange words in the pub just before the woman vanished.

"I'll speak to Mr Evans about it in the morning," he announced, after some thought.

"You won't," Frank replied, leering. "He's in hospital and most likely half dead, with any luck. I found 'im lyin' in the rain not far from his 'ome an' he was all covered in blood."

"Did you call an ambulance?" Bill asked, pouring more drinks.

"Course I bloody didn't." Frank said, laughing. "I just helped myself to some of his things and kicked 'im a couple a times."

Bill was starting to go red again and Frank realised that he had perhaps said too much. He finished his drink and started making for the door.

"Get out, you bloody fool!" Bill shouted, "and don't ever let me find you around here again."

Frank let his shoulders droop in a show of resignation and he shuffled out once more into the damp night. There was still no one about and he reached his home only ten minutes later. He let himself in quickly but instead of getting out of his damp clothes, he searched beneath an untidy pile of papers for his phone book. He thumbed quickly to C, found Cotting's number and dialled it. The number rang several times before an ugly voice said, "Cambridge 468372. Who's speaking?"

"Hello, Mr Cotting. It's Frank."

"I thought I told you not to contact me."

"I know all that, but this is important."

"It had better be! In case you didn't know, it's nearly eleven o'clock and I'm supposed to be on duty in seven hours' time. I'm in no mood for trivia so what is it?"

"We have to meet," Frank said, almost excitedly.

"We don't have to meet. You can just tell me what you have to say and then I can go to bed, which is what I was going to do when you rang. Now say what it is you have to say and then sod off, Frank. I'm tired and very uninterested, so make it quick and then leave me alone."

Frank was tired of being ignored and he had more of a lever on the inspector than he did on Bill. He wanted to sort out who the woman was and he wanted to do it now.

"Telling you isn't any good. I need to see you tonight. Meet me in fifteen minutes on the old bridge beyond the village."

He hung up and left the inspector to fume and comply. Fifteen minutes later he was waiting on the bridge as a car parked some distance away and the shadowy figure of Inspector Cotting walked purposefully towards him.

"Well?" he demanded, still fuming. "What's so all-fired, bloody important to drag me out at this time of night?"

Frank had known David Cotting for several years now and had always enjoyed wielding this sort of power over him. He earned little enough for his needs at the Hall and the regular monthly payments from the inspector went straight into a pension fund, Frank's only concession to Thatcherism. His wages went on rent, drink, food and some of the less discriminating working girls in the city. David was also a party to his little arrangement with Bill at the Hall and although he lacked his late father's guile, Frank had come to realise the advantages of having a cop in tow.

"You never were much of a detective, were you, David?"

Understandably, Inspector Cotting was not in the best of moods and, to be addressed in first name terms by a half-wit thief when, by rights, he should have been asleep, did not help. To have his ability as a detective questioned was almost too much to bear.

"At least I've spent most of my life on the right side of the law! Now what the fuck do you want, or did you just get me all the way out here to insult me?"

Frank wasn't in the mood for listening and what passed for his brain, was locked irrevocably on transmit. He continued, "If you were a real detective, you would have found that woman by now – that bitch 'oo broke my nose."

He thumbed agitatedly at the middle of his face as if there was another nose nearby that was not broken.

"As it is," he droned on, "I had to find ''er for meself didn't I? Without no 'elp from you nor nobody."

The inspector managed to stifle a yawn as he began to see the point. He asked Frank to get to it and Frank obliged in every detail – the accident – if that was what it was, the robbery and the chance sighting of the woman at the Stables. He couldn't believe that anyone would be so stupid or low as to rob someone who was unconscious or perhaps even dead and then contemplate burgling the victim's house. Still, at least it might mean that he could end his enforced relationship with the village idiot.

"Oh I see, Frank." he said, in as friendly a way as he could manage; "you are going to tell me who she is, I am

220

going to charge her, have her put away, claim all the credit, share the compensation money with you and then we never have to speak to or see each other again. Well done, Frank. I have to hand it to you, you certainly have been a great help."

"No, that's not it at all, David," Frank said, growing in confidence, "you don't understand anything! I had to find her, you have to arrest her, I get the compensation money and we ..." he let the word hang menacingly in the air, "continue as before. I don't see any reason to reward you for failure. Good night, David."

The inspector listened with barely restrained hatred as his 'partner' twisted the knife. He had been careful to leave his house unseen and equally alert to ensure that his conversation with Frank was unwitnessed. He looked around quickly just to make sure. No problem, they were alone.

"Frank," he began quietly, "in all my years as a policeman, I must say that you are the most stupid, greedy, self-centred, low-life piece of excrement I've ever met. I've been meaning to do something like this for a long time."

The inspector was quaking with rage as he grabbed Frank firmly by the lapels of his coat and head-butted him equally firmly on what was left of his nose. The blow did not carry any great force, but it took Frank completely by surprise and the painful effect that it had on him was entirely disproportionate. He let out a yelp and sprang backwards, breaking the inspector's grip on his coat. Leaning, as he was, against the parapet of the bridge, only the upper half of him moved back, with the net effect of projecting all of him over the edge. Unwittingly, he executed a perfect double reverse somersault before plunging into the cold, muddy water below. The inspector strained his eyes to see the surface and was alarmed to see the spluttering form of Frank flailing around and very much alive just a few yards downstream. Frank was a surprisingly good swimmer and started to make for the archway en route to the jetty upstream of the bridge. Without even a moment's hesitation, the inspector closed his hands about one of the coping stones that Frank had kindly dislodged from the parapet and with a sudden effort, wrenched it off. He walked quietly to the other side of the bridge, leant out precariously and dropped it on the emerging head below. This time there was no yelp. Frank's head, or at least, the top of it, inverted from convex to concave, a surprisingly large amount of brain tissue squirted out from both ears and from the stump of his nose and he died without even knowing it. The inspector leant on the upstream parapet and sighed heavily.

"Bye bye Frank, you stupid useless bastard," he said smiling suddenly, "and bloody good riddance!" He looked around carefully, saw no one and walked to his car, whistling softly.

Chapter 19: Nil by Mouth

There are rarely any good reasons or truly momentous events that would persuade a non-believer of the complex and stunning interconnectedness of life, but now and again, there are simple examples of coincidence which believers jump on with mindless regularity and unfailing faith, as justification for one obscure theory or another. One such was that at the exact moment of Frank Graves's long overdue departure from life as he knew it, just a few miles away in a private ward in the City Hospital, Michael opened his eyes and stopped dreaming. The dream had ended at its end and had been one of those rare, stunningly brilliant yet ultimately disappointing dreams about which theses are written or, as the result of which, unsung housewives from places like Chipping Sodbury leave their doting, if occasionally unfaithful husbands, two point four children, the Volvo estate and the cat, and rush off to a croft somewhere on a Scottish island to paint a masterpiece or write about imaginary orgasms.

Michael had always enjoyed dreams for what they were – simply as unplanned voyages of the mind – and particularly those which were unbounded by mankind's frail but dependable concept of time. These were of the type that commenced at the moment of waking and were triggered, for example, by the brain's first cognisance of an alarm bell, seemed to span hours, weeks or months and ended microseconds later when one part of the brain told all others about the bell. Sometimes, just for fun, Michael would prearrange for different sounds to be his cause of waking, just to see how many different sounds could stimulate the onset, development and finale of a mind-voyage. This was not one of those dreams; this was something very different and owed much to the dosage of morphine-based painkillers inside him. It was therefore both stunning and brilliant. He was in a laboratory at the college. It was his college, but not his laboratory. The layout of furniture was wrong and it was all of an unhealthy, washed out, fleshy pink colour apart from one stool, which was greenish brown with lumps on the legs looking uncannily like broken leaf buds. The four feet of the stool stood in bedpans. He didn't think that could be right, but before he could investigate further, an old grey-haired man appeared on the stool and beckoned him to look at a slide under a microscope. The man's face looked sort of familiar, but Michael couldn't quite place him.

"Well, go on then," the man urged quietly. "You've come this far, so you might as well look."

Michael placed his eyes to the lenses and focussed them to suit his vision. A few cells swam into view.

"What is it?" he asked, without looking up.

"It's blood, Michael – your blood. You seemed to have been so careless with it, we thought perhaps you should see just what you were throwing away."

"I didn't mean to be wasteful," he pleaded, as he increased the magnification. "Anyway, what is it that I'm supposed to see?"

"You're not supposed to see anything, but there is much to be seen if you choose to," the old man intoned.

Michael increased the magnification to the maximum setting but decided it still wasn't enough and tensed in concentration.

"If you want more, just will more." the old man urged. "You may think that you understand all, but you comprehend nothing. Just do as I say and WILL MORE!"

The order shot through Michael and his eyes seemed to fuse with the glass of the lenses. Slowly at first, the magnification started to increase again, only this time it was as though he was being drawn down the microscope toward the sample. The cells grew larger until just one of them filled his vision. Ever more quickly the process increased in speed until he started to discern individual molecules scudding around first beneath and then around him. There seemed to be some order to their motion, but for the moment it was beyond his comprehension. He was thirsty for knowledge, but there was nowhere to stop and drink. He had to concentrate to avoid missing something. The sense of order started to become more tangible as the process of magnification slowed down. A lone atom came into view and gradually became larger as it occupied the entire space about his being. The sense of sound came to him and then a feeling of well-being as showers of electrons flashed around him, secure in their prearranged, preordained and entirely logical orbits. Suddenly, he understood everything known about physics and everything tantalisingly yet unknown. He saw how easy it would be to generate nuclear fusion, which would have been great, had he been also able to remember the dream later. He could understand all this and felt content here – but there was more. Before he had the chance to say 'no', the entire process was thrown into reverse, increasing, this time, with quite alarming speed. He knew instinctively that he would overshoot the eyepieces, but he had neither the will nor the means to stop or even slow down. His perception flew out of the microscope, the room and well beyond. In seconds the earth became a mere speck as part of him moved out into space. It seemed that this way was even faster than the 'getting closer' or was that just an illusion? Was it that the vacuum of space offered less resistance to the voyaging mind, or was it just that he was minded to resist it less? Anyway, he saw and understood the cosmos in its vastness. Time and distance passed until he was beyond beyond. Then the vision disappeared and all was dark for a while.

"And there you have it, Michael," the old man said. "You have been to both ends of infinity when you know full well that infinity has no bounds. Now do you comprehend?"

The man was gone and he was alone again in the laboratory. It was still not his, but at least it was the right colour and the bedpans had gone. The buds were missing from the legs of the stool but he didn't care. For once in his largely wasted life, he had learned something of earth-shattering and fundamental importance – he felt that at long last he knew something.

Ultimately, as previewed, the disappointing and predictable thing about the dream was that on waking, Michael forgot all of it and, as had been prophesied by those in real life, he had a massive headache.

He was propped up in bed with the room lights dimmed to a level barely adequate for the average cockroach to be seen. A plastic-looking artery sprouted from the back of his right hand and an anaemic-looking one from the back of his left. For a moment he thought they might be strings, and that he had died and been reincarnated as a puppet. The sight of two nurses with ragged edges reassured him that he was alive, possibly concussed and probably in hospital. For some reason, both the nurses were saying the same thing and when he focussed, one of them joined the other – but it hurt his head. He shut both eyes, opened one and only one nurse was talking. That was better. Keeping one eye fully shut he used the other one to glance about the room. He moved both feet experimentally and felt a sharp pain in his left calf. Looking back at his left hand he saw that had grown another one. Clever that! He followed the arm up to the neck and saw Jenny looking at him with tearful eyes. She lifted a finger to her lips in a gesture, but he spoke anyway, even though the back of his head suggested otherwise.

"Me, too." he said, squeezing her hand.

"You must not talk," she cautioned. "They said I could stay only if I didn't tire you – and that means not answering any questions."

"I haven't asked any." he protested, trying to look stern with only one eye.

"Yet," she finished.

"Yet," he agreed quietly, and slipped back into a drug-induced sleep.

Jenny watched him for a few moments and then leant to one side and picked up the phone on his bedside table. After a brief pause, she spoke quietly.

"Hi Lisa, it's me. He's awake"

"And?"

"And he's probably got concussion if his vision is anything to go by. There's nothing broken in his leg and best of all, his skull is intact."

"Great!"

"Yes, but he's got four cracked ribs and more bruises than you can shake a stick at. Did Emily get the message?"

"Yes, she rang back soon after."

"How did she react?"

"Just as you and Jonathan predicted. Naturally, she blames herself. She asked a stream of astute questions, threatened to castrate someone called Peter and rang back again a few minutes later with a flight number and an ETA at Heathrow. I'm collecting her while Jonathan sorts out some cover for Mike's lectures. Do you want me to save you some supper?"

"No, thanks, I think I'll stay here the night. I want to be around when he wakes up properly."

"OK, I'll catch you tomorrow. Bye."

"'Bye."

She put the phone down, moved back closer to Michael and clasped his hand again. He was peaceful and the room was quiet. Nursing staff busied themselves outside in a final burst of activity before the night shift took over. A long half-hour passed before the last three cups of coffee got the better of her, and she crept into the neat bathroom attached to Michael's private room. When she emerged, a night duty sister entered the room preceded by a drugs trolley burgeoning with all manner of sedatives, painkillers and controlled mind-benders. With obvious and much practised skill, she simultaneously lifted the clipboard from the end of Michael's bed, read and understood its contents, compared them with the handwritten instructions above his bed head, checked the name and admission number on his wristband, reached for the thermometer, inserted it in Michael's nearer armpit, checked his drips while taking his blood pressure, scribbled something illegible on the clipboard, asked Jenny if Michael had asked for any painkillers, looked at the thermometer, scribbled something else equally illegible on the clipboard, said good night and left. Jenny rearranged Michael's spare pillows on her armchair, put her feet up on the spare seat and covered herself as best she could with a blanket. It was not the most comfortable of beds but she was weary and not too fussy.

She still held Michael's hand as she fell asleep thinking of how things had been years before. She'd been in love with him then, too.

Frank, or to be strictly accurate, Frank (deceased) was, by now embarked on his final journey into the city, but despite the force of the swollen river, the trip downstream took the best part of the night. Unnoticed by water voles, postmen and milkmen alike, he floated quietly and leaf-like into the city centre, rotating first one way and then the other as eddy currents played, tentatively, with his outstretched limbs. By seven o'clock, he had progressed to the narrow weir, which in other circumstances would have been his resting-place. Not this morning, however. The torrent had already washed away the boom and, with no apparent effort, Frank (deceased) slid over the smooth lip and landed with a resonant splash in the turbulent waters beneath. Momentum and strong currents took him quickly to the riverbed where his upper half became trapped in the half-buried remains of a supermarket trolley that had been donated to the environment the previous October during someone's spectacularly drunken stag-night. His resting-place did not go unmarked however. His booted feet floated level with the surface of the river, looking like a pair of tired, leathery water lily leaves. The resonant splash did not coincide with any momentous event. It did not for example coincide with the moment that Michael woke up again. That was brought about by laughter outside his room. Jenny was fast asleep in her makeshift cot and her hand slid from his. He smiled at her presence and then lay back with his eyes shut, trying to remember what had happened. Thinking, like binocular vision, hurt his head and he lifted his right arm to put a hand to his head. Yes – it was bandaged and there was a painful lump on it. – What's more, his chest hurt; he didn't remember that. He carefully pulled the sheets down to reveal a mass of bandages. This was confusing. He tried pulling them back up again, but it gave him a stabbing pain in the side of his chest and he yelped in pain. Jenny stirred and woke up with a start.

"Is there something wrong?" she asked, letting go the remains of a dream. "I thought I heard a cry."

"You did," Michael said, trying to get himself up to a sitting position. "It was my reaction to discovering that I have been mummified. What happened?"

"That's a question, Michael."

"How many am I allowed?"

"That's your second," she replied, teasing.

"Were you always this difficult, Jenny?"

"Three."

"Oh bugger it! Did I say anything to you last night?"

"Yes."

"Ah – progress! Did I say the right thing?"

"Yes, I think so."

"Jenny?"

"Yes, Michael?"

"Do you see that mirror on the other side of the room?"

"Yes I do, why?"

"Well, what do you suppose 'HTUOM YB LIN' means?"

"You know I won't forget this when you're better, don't you?"

There was no answer; Michael just looked at her with both eyes (almost) and he didn't need to say anything. Jenny didn't need to either, but she did so all the same. It was as though all the words were rushing to get out at once. She wanted to chide him, forgive him, love him to bits and embrace him all at once and all with words. She didn't know if any of it made sense to him, but she was somehow compelled to say it anyway. There was an unavoidable conclusion coming into sight and it fell off her lips like the last brown leaves of autumn in a November squall.

"...It's just that having found you again ..."

"Me, too," Michael helped her and lay back, exhausted. "And I think this is the moment that I should propose-"

"I accept."

"And you promise not to run off like I did?"

"I promise."

They were still kissing as passionately as circumstances would allow when Jonathan came in on his way to college.

"Oh, sorry." he said grinning. "Lisa had to get up early to get to Heathrow and it didn't seem worth going back to bed, so I thought I'd pop in and see how you were getting on. Anyone for coffee and croissants, or shall I just go and leave you to eat each other in private?"

Chapter 20:

Smoke Gets in Your Eyes

Lisa was not exactly good in the mornings and this was by no means a good morning. The previous evening's game of musical cars had reached its confusing height when after reading about the latest recent increase in joy-riding in the city, Lisa decided to collect Jenny's car from the hospital to prevent thieves doing it first. Despite her weariness, she and Jonathan drove back to the city and using her own set of keys, took Jenny's BMW back to the Stables for safekeeping. After only five hours' sleep she was back at the wheel and heading for Heathrow. The first hour was driven in the half-light of dawn and she made good time. Tail lights became more frequent as she neared the M25 and after a dozen or so miles, traffic ground to a standstill as she and all the other single occupant cars jostled for position at the first set of road works. Eventually two narrow files of slow cars squeezed along in close parallel between the well-ordered avenues of unnecessary plastic cones. The white reflective strips on the cones picked up the passing headlight beams with a rhythmic monotony –

not quickly enough to be stroboscopic, but sufficiently quickly to bring on a headache. Lisa turned up the music, opened the front windows and fished around in the door bin for Jenny's polarising sunglasses. They helped a little and once the road works were passed, the headache diminished. The signs for Heathrow became more frequent and by eight-thirty Lisa had parked in the short term car park at Terminal 4 and was making her way to arrivals. Heathrow, like any other international airport of its size, was in many ways like the grand vision of a science fiction writer. Almost twenty-four hours a day, tens of thousands of people were ushered through garishly carpeted lounges and corridors into pressurised tubes and flung into the air, only to be replaced by tens of thousands who, until minutes earlier, were strapped into other pressurised tubes which had just undergone what most of their pilots referred to as 'controlled crashes', before being ushered back into the same garishly carpeted corridors and lounges and hence back to their homes, offices and little pockets of unreality. In simple time and motion study terms, it was a nightmare. Droves of cooking staff worked in shifts to accommodate the varied desires of peoples from all over the world, the majority of whom had seriously disturbed body clocks. Paradoxically, Lisa quite enjoyed being at airports simply because of the sheer wealth of life to be seen. She was, by nature, a people watcher and there was nowhere better to do it than at airports. Lisa felt at home in airports in much the same way as herons feel at home in trout farms. Large enclosed spaces like arrival or departure halls do not, by and large, have good acoustics but after some practice, Lisa found that it was possible to filter out the general babble of white noise and concentrate on individual conversations, even at a moderate distance. This was not done in any invasive sense, but since airports seemed to bring out both the best and the worst in people, it was always entertaining to observe expressions, odd mannerisms and gestures and then see if the words matched the mime. It was not always easy – for example she had witnessed at least six different gestures to accompany, 'Well, I assumed that you had packed them,' and there seemed to be countless ways of expressing the kind of exasperation that goes with: 'If I say, "Don't look now – it's Mrs XYZ -." I mean, don't look now.' Curiously enough, the very people who should have been scrutinising every scar and laughter line were those least inclined to do it. These were the Anti-Terrorist Police, or at least those of them who were unfortunate enough to have to carry arms. The majority of these blighted people dealt with their self-consciousness and receding chins by hiding behind badly designed designer beards, while the rest by simply trying to stay out of sight, perched on strategically placed galleries. Lisa could see all of them, all looking slightly ridiculous cocooned in their bulletproof jackets and trying furiously not to look like over-fed, over-armed blue-painted gnomes. She looked at their faces and saw real fear: the fear of being in the wrong place at the right time; having to flick off the safety catch and face down an armed terrorist knowing that, of the two of them, only one was concerned about gunning down innocent tourists. She had enjoyed a safe life – well, so far, anyway – and had never had to come to terms with real fear, not on such terms as these officers. They had to do it every working day, and by so doing they earned her compassion.

The moment passed and Lisa dragged her concentration back to the purpose of her visit. She glanced up at the arrivals board and smiled cynically as she read silently 'AL 643 ROME DELAYED ETA 0930'. At this point, nine out of ten people would have followed their favourite four letter word with: '... it, I could have had two more hours in bed'. Lisa, however, was unmoved, she simply telephoned Cathy to forewarn her and then went to departures for more sport. Her first stop was at the newsagent's where she bought an awful book. It took no great effort, they were all equally awful and, following a minimum of research, she had long since given up wondering how it had come to be. It just had, and that was that. It was as inevitable as rain on a bank holiday. Sport was to be found in profusion only yards away in the self-service cafeteria. There were three groups of challengers for the 'most predictable stereotype award', together with about six or seven unclassifiable. Two of the three main groups were those en route to or just returned from the Gambia. Those on the outward-bound journey were excited, pale-skinned, over-dressed and delightfully irrepressible. They were there to throw as much over-priced breakfast down their throats as possible so as to avoid the free but sanitised alternative that would be served on the plane. In stark contrast, those on the way back were dejected, painfully burnt, stung in very unfortunate places, decked out in shorts and tee-shirts bearing innovative messages like, 'PHEW IT'S HOT IN THE GAMBIA' and dying in unison for a real cup of tea. For some reason that completely escaped Lisa, neither group talked to each other despite their obvious shared interest. By the looks of those just returned, those just about to go would have done well to have learned something about how to avoid the native insects. Perhaps more understandably, neither of the first two groups talked to the third. They were in from Atlanta on the 'red eye' and were recovering from having spent the previous seven and a half hours with their knees tucked under their chins, and waking to have their body clocks tell them that it was lunchtime. Most of the men were smiling and exchanging pleasantries in the range: 'Gee ,it's great to be here!' to, 'Gee it's great to be back!' and most of the women were swapping thinly disguised lies about their Anglo-Saxon ancestry or lauding what was left of the Royal Family. They achieved this with minimum lip movement and no obvious variety or animation in facial expression. Lisa always found it difficult to read such people and had long since concluded that plastic surgery and botox had a lot to answer for. In lieu of lunch, the Americans were swarming noisily around a clutch of tables, all trying to sit on the chairs with the most leg room and complaining vigorously that their coach was late. They had, at best, only six days to see and digitally record the whole of England, which, so far as they were aware, comprised London, Cambridge, Oxford and Stratford-upon-Avon, before they had to return home. Lisa watched, listened and enjoyed, and decided that it wasn't such a bad morning after all. The out-bound Gambian flight was called and the numbers around her dwindled. She let her eyes make one last sweep of the Americans, just to make doubly sure that the Cronsevs hadn't snuck back into the country and then headed off in search of the Piano Bar. It was too soon in the morning for a drink – besides which, she would soon have to be driving again – it was just the incongruity of it all that

237

attracted her. Piano bars were few and far between as it was, found only in certain classes of hotels and the odd up-market café. Airport piano bars were very different. Although they lacked the feel of belonging that one would associate with hotels and the inevitable false relationships that developed between the pianist and certain guests, Lisa felt that nonetheless, such places had a role to play in airport life. The incongruity, if such it was, derived from the same base as all the unlikely situations that were likely to be encountered in a major airport. It was the size of a small town, though with a better infrastructure than most. The pianists, like all airport staff, were hourly but lowly paid shift workers, whose tedious lives were geared to looking after the different needs of a transient population of tens, perhaps hundreds of thousands of people. The last strains of *Smoke Gets In Your Eyes* were sucked into the ceiling acoustics and a wave of tiredness washed over Lisa. She looked up at the clock and saw that Emily's plane was due to touch down in ten minutes. She finished her coffee and went back to arrivals. Even though it was still relatively early in the morning, there was already quite a sea of black-suited chauffeurs huddled around the railings, ebbing and flowing gently in the air conditioning, each holding a clipboard bearing a hastily written name. 'Clipboard,' Lisa thought. 'Shit – I don't know her and I haven't got a clipboard.' Two minutes later, she was back at the newsagents where she found an A4 note pad and then joined a queue of people clutching awful books, heading submissively towards the checkout. Emily emerged from customs striding behind her luggage trolley like a modern day Boudicca, cutting a swathe through less purposeful fellow passengers. Her grey eyes, which portrayed a mixture of anger and relief, swept quickly through the pulsing tide of black suits until she saw her name on Lisa's improvised clipboard. Their eyes met and two smiles followed. Her course now set, Emily ploughed toward Lisa with renewed urgency, the bow wave of her trolley parting the sea of black suits in advance of her passage in a way not seen since biblical times. Lisa watched the approach in detached fascination, feeling for no logical reason at all, that she had known Emily forever. Jonathan had said it might be like this and he was right.

"You must be Lisa!"

"Yes. How was your flight?"

Emily began to answer, but her voice was lost in the developing confusion behind her. A small group of passengers had attempted to follow in her wake into the Promised Land of arrivals but promptly drowned when the chauffeurs re-grouped. Emily insisted on paying for the car park – much as Jonathan had said she would – and they set off for Cambridge and the hospital.

"Does this work?" Emily asked, pointing at the hands-free phone.

"I think so."

Emily retrieved a telephone number from her handbag and dialled it with her expensively manicured fingernails. She got through to the answer phone, but when she started to speak, Cathy came on the line.

"Sorry about that. I had to be sure it was a friendly call."

239

"That's alright Cathy, it's Emily – relax. Is there any news?"

"Yes. Jenny rang earlier and he's going to be alright."

"Jenny!?"

"Yes. Jonathan thought it would be a good idea to tell her and she stayed with him all night."

Emily glanced questioningly at Lisa, who nodded without really taking her eyes off the road.

"Fine! Is he in a private room, do you know?"

"Yes, Miss Pollard. The main number is 478363 and his room extension is 322, the same number as the room itself."

"Thanks, Cathy. We'll go straight there. 'Bye. I'm sorry, Lisa, that was a bit presumptuous of me. I don't even know what plans of yours I've wrecked."

"It's not a problem, I had nothing on that's as important as this and besides, we'll be there in under an hour. Why don't you give the hospital a ring and let Jenny know when you'll be arriving?"

Emily didn't need asking twice. Lisa navigated her way easily through the rush hour traffic and dropped Emily outside the hospital shortly before midday and, at Emily's insistence, left her to find her own way back to the Stables later. Jenny was waiting at the entrance looking, quite rightly, as though she had spent the night in a chair. She joined Lisa and together they headed for the office. This was not because of any all-pervading desire to do some work, but more because it represented the nearest source of real coffee. Lisa looked sympathetically at her friend and said, "You look as though you've spent the night in a chair."

"That's because I have," Jenny replied, adding, "But the good news is that I'm engaged!"

Emily found Michael propped up in bed, trying to drink a tumbler of water while at the same time trying to read a paperback with one eye and making a botch of both. He looked almost comical surrounded by drips and with needles sprouting from the back of both hands. On seeing Emily he gave up the struggle of trying to read, put the book down and smiled warmly.

"I'd have tried to stop you coming if I had known," he said, trying instinctively to get up. "There was really no need for you to drag yourself all the way over here. As you can see," he said, flailing both arms and making both drip supports teeter dangerously, "I'll be up and about in no time."

Emily smiled and sat down quickly in the hope that he would give up trying to be a gentleman. In the short interval since she had last seen Michael he had lost his natural colour, about ten pounds in weight – so it seemed to her – and looked some ten years older. She looked around the room quickly to see if there was anything obviously missing: there wasn't. A mixture of anger, fear and relief played with her emotions and it was only with some difficulty that she managed to speak without crying. Michael was obviously trying to put on a brave face through the fug of painkillers and still couldn't focus well enough to appreciate her distress.

"So, are they looking after you properly?" she managed.

"Well enough, I think," he replied, lying back resignedly. "To be honest, I'm not too sure that I'm aware of what's going on yet, they keep giving me all sorts of sedatives and things and I expect that I would know a lot more without them, but on the other hand I expect I would feel a lot more too, so I'll do as I'm told for now."

"Well, I expect it was worth coming all this way, if only to hear you say that."

Emily was relieved to hear him speak so coherently and she relaxed a little. All the same he looked very pale, apart from the backs of his hands both of which were badly bruised in shades of purple and orange. Michael saw her looking and said, "Don't worry, Emily, I didn't feel a thing when they did this. Apparently the one on the right was done while we were bumping along in the ambulance and the one on the left was done by a trainee doctor who had already been on duty for twenty-three hours when I was wheeled in. Colourful, aren't they!"

"I promise not to worry visibly, Michael, but I want your word that you will behave until you are fully well. Now that I've seen you I shall be able to go back contentedly in a few days – relatively so anyway, but it depends on you giving your word."

She left the last word hanging around in the hope that for once he might take her seriously, but as usual it was a forlorn hope. He just smiled at her without agreeing or disagreeing. She was forced to continue, "I know that you want to find out who did this to you, but you are not well enough and anyway, you should leave it to those who are paid to do it."

Michael wasn't about to argue with his aunt, as he had long since given up the unequal task of trying to reason with the unreasonable. Come to think of it, he didn't feel much like arguing with anyone just yet. He just played her along a bit.

"Have you eaten breakfast yet, Emily?"

"Yes, if you stretch the meaning of the word."

"Would you like some more, or perhaps some coffee?"

"Yes please, coffee would be nice."

"Good," Michael said, pulling the cord by his bed. "Look, Emily, you can rest assured that I am not about to do anything stupid in the next few days or even the next few weeks. It's true that I have no confidence in the local police, but I have too many other things to think about in the next few weeks to go chasing after some unknown assailant and besides, if I do anything to upset you, there's a good chance that I'll also end up doing the same to Jenny and I certainly can't cope with two miffed women at once. I've got to get fit again, I have got a whole bunch of first year students to prepare for their exams, and I've got this business at the Hall to see to."

There was a brief silence while Emily tried to summon up one of her stern looks. She found it difficult, because she was tired and still greatly worried about Michael, but mostly she found it difficult because, if she was to put herself in his place, she would probably have found herself bound to, or by, the same obligations, with the same sense of duty to everything and everyone. Martyrdom, it seemed, ran in the family.

"Look, Michael," she said, eventually. "You have had a narrow escape and if you want to make a full recovery you'll have to take things easy for a bit – for a while in fact – and you shouldn't imagine that the world will stop if you take a break from it for a while. As for the other matters, I shall have several big words with Mr Stagg about finding your assailant. Jonathan is at this very moment arranging cover for your lectures and he can stand in for you so far as the Hall is concerned. It will probably help him feel better if he is kept busy."

Michael lay on his bed in a resigned heap, not the least moved by what Emily had said, but not the least surprised either. In one of his rare moments of objectivity he also reasoned that she was probably right, or sufficiently close to being right to make an argument futile. Had Michael but known it, Emily wasn't entirely right about Jonathan. He had already organised cover for Michael's lectures and, thanks to another colleague's absence, was also out of his depth providing some himself. The noon bell rang none too soon and he scuttled willingly back to his room to make some phone calls. The first was to Cathy, back at the Stables. By agreement, she only answered the phone after she had recognised his voice at the end of his own taped message.

"Hi! Is there any news?"

"Not a lot, as such. Jenny rang from the hospital to say that Mike was fine. I passed that news on to Emily when she phoned from the car, and Lisa phoned from work to say that Emily had been delivered safely to the hospital and that either she or Jenny would collect Emily again when Michael had exasperated her – her words, not mine. Peter's boffin has done with your car and he is busy creating clever prose on his laptop. I'll email a copy through to you once he's done."

"Thanks. Was there anything else?"

"Oh, yes. Peter emailed through a copy of a letter that Emily's solicitors have sent to your ex. It was with some stuff he sent to me and I'm afraid I read it in error – sorry."

No problem." Jonathan said. "Was it good?"

"Well, let's say I'd rather be me than her!"

"I'll second that," he said, without thinking.

"Jonathan, did my ears deceive me or was that a compliment?"

He was caught completely off guard and didn't know if it was a serious question. Worse still, if it was, he didn't know how to respond. He was still having trouble coming to terms with the sudden onset of Lisa. He found her very attractive sexually but after the first heady euphoric days, he was less sure about the mental side of things. This was not to say that he thought he had been sure to start with – quite the reverse – it was just that much as he enjoyed Lisa's company, he didn't think that his life would fall apart if she didn't play such a large role in it. To his great relief, the 'L' word had not been mentioned – relief because he wasn't at all sure how he felt or if he was actually capable of feeling in that way. There was a lot that he didn't know about Lisa and equally, there was a lot that he hadn't told her about himself. The problem was this: He had sensed from the outset that there was something other than business lurking behind Cathy's steely grey eyes – or were they blue? – but he had just dismissed it as imagination or over-active hormones! Perhaps he simply hadn't been aware of people's feelings and he had been missing out on opportunities for want of being aware of them. Anyway, none of this was helping him at the moment so he ducked the issue.

"I'm sorry," he said, after banging his desk. "I missed that – someone just came in."

"It doesn't matter," Cathy said, smiling to herself. "Oh, there was another message from Lisa. She said to ask you if you would mind skipping the cinema, because she wants an early night."

Jonathan was disappointed at that, because it was a one night only showing of *The African Queen* at the college, and he had been looking forward to it.

"Are you still there, Jonathan?"

"Yes, sorry, I was just a bit surprised – well, miffed, really. I was looking forward to going."

"Oh well," she said, offhandedly, "We can't always get what we want. I'll catch you later. 'Bye."

Cathy's parting comment left Jonathan with the sinking feeling that he had been found out and that she knew, or had guessed, that he had ducked the issue. Oh well, what the hell, it wasn't his only problem – he had to telephone the police station to put off his meeting with the inspector.

He looked through his pocket diary and retrieved the telephone number of the police station. After a brief pause and three rings a polite female voice answered.

"Good afternoon, City Police Station, how may I help you?"

"Good afternoon. This is Jonathan Grey. I have an appointment to see your Inspector Cotting and I'm afraid that I won't be able to make it after all. Is he there or could I perhaps leave a message for him?"

"No, I'm sorry he is not on duty today, but if you could tell me what it's to do with, I'll take a message and see that it is placed on the appropriate file and left on his desk for him to see tomorrow when he comes in."

Jonathan was quite impressed at the apparent efficiency and politeness with which his enquiry was being dealt and replied, "Yes of course. It's in relation to the alleged assault on a Mr Frank Graves. Inspector Cotting wanted to see me since I was, or rather he believes I was, a witness to the alleged attack."

There was another brief pause and the sound of muffled voices before the receptionist spoke once more.

"And you say that your name is Jonathan Grey?"

"Yes, that's right."

"And may I take your number Mr Grey?"

The voice sounded just a little more animated than before but Jonathan didn't feel that he had anything to fear and had no reason to be uncomfortable, since the inspector probably already had the college number as well as that at the Stables, so he repeated both. The receptionist thanked him and hung up just as his fax machine clattered into life. It was from Cathy and it was the solicitor's letter and the forensic report on the fire in his car. After a very brief introduction the report continued with a factual account of the damage to the car and an excavation of the interior to determine 'cause'. Jonathan started to read it carefully and then, realising that the author had just been, as it were, going through the motions, he speed-read through to the conclusions which read:

➤ The driver's window had been broken before the fire

➤ There was no key present in the ignition switch

➤ The ignition may have been 'hot-wired' but insufficient evidence remained for this to be confirmed

➤ Flammable liquid, most probably diesel fuel, was used to accelerate the fire in its early stages

➤ A sample of same was retained for comparison with other incidents, as per your instruction

Jonathan was still puzzling over the final conclusion when his thoughts were interrupted by a sharp knock at the door. It was opened before he had the chance to respond and two rather ill-dressed and overweight men jostled in order to be the first in. The elder of the two puffed up his chest and said:

"Dr Jonathan Grey?"

"That's what it says on the door." Jonathan replied, with a familiar sense of impending doom.

Chapter 21:

Porridge or Salad

Just to show how perverse and unreliable it could be, the April weather had changed completely in a space of twenty-four hours and, by the late afternoon, the sun was shining brightly and with surprising vigour over the city of Cambridge. The heavy rains of the previous evening and night had both cleaned and cleared the air. This done, and with no wind to provide a chill, the sun bore down unfiltered and without hindrance on the city with considerable and unexpected power, giving a rare and tempting glimpse of the months to come. Previously damp corners of gardens became illuminated for the first time in months and their owners wondered, anxiously, when they could safely disinter their barbecues and clean away the remains of last year's snails in time for the weekend. The solar panels heating the swimming pool at the Stables creaked gently as they expanded a little in response to the welcome energy and shafts of pure, bright sunlight penetrated windows all over the city. None of this, however, did anything to raise Jonathan's spirits, as he sat in his cell at the police station. He had been watching the window-shaped patch of light move slowly across the wall for about an hour now and wondered if it had been someone like him – wrongly imprisoned many thousands of years previously – who had invented the sundial. They had taken his watch and other personal belongings, together with his belt and shoelaces and he felt a little undone. On reflection, he could perhaps have avoided all this had he only been a little more co-operative earlier. But since he had told his inquisitors the truth and yet they chose not to believe him, he didn't feel that he had been in the wrong in trying to assert his rights, especially given the words he had used. He was just too preoccupied with Michael to be civil and never, for one moment, imagined that they might be so dumb as to arrest him. Also, a lot of time might have been saved had they told him, to start with, that Frank was dead all over and not just on the nose. What they still hadn't told him was that Frank had Michael's credit cards on him when he was pulled from the river. The two officers had laughed derisively when Jonathan explained that he had seen the fight (such as it was) in the pub and that it was for that reason that he had first arranged to see the inspector and then rung again to change the arrangement. They knew not of the fight or of any such arrangement, nor did they particularly care. They simply cautioned him and placed him in a cell while they called the inspector. He felt utterly alone and wished that he could have been ploughing relentlessly up and down the pool at the Stables. In fact, right then he wished that he could be almost anywhere other than where he was. He held his head in his hands and wished, but nothing happened. Presently he heard the noise of shuffling feet followed by the operation of the lock on his cell door. A humourless uniformed sergeant beckoned to him and he was led wordlessly back to the interview room to be confronted once more with the two detectives. They sat him down on one side of a stained rectangular table whose only decorations were a microphone, some recording equipment and a particularly sordid ashtray. The elder of the two switched the tape recorder on once more, while the younger one sat down opposite Jonathan, lit up yet another cigarette and placed his hands behind his head so as better to expose the sweat-stained armpits of his ragged suit jacket. Jonathan gazed in obvious loathing and the detective flushed visibly as he lowered his arms quickly. Jonathan smiled inwardly and told himself to relax. The little voice argued loudly for bravado, but he was having none of it.

"Twelfth April, two thousand and seven, four thirty pee emm. Continuing the interview with Jonathan Edward Grey. Officers present: Detective Constable Darren Priestly and Detective Sergeant Peter Germin. Well, Mr Grey, we have some news for you, but as you might imagine, it is both good and bad. Which would you like to hear?"

"Since this is a formal interview, I would be obliged if you would address me formally." Jonathan replied, angrily. "Also, since, so far I have treated you with no less courtesy than you deserve, I would hope that you, in return would deal equally with me – and for the record, it's the thirteenth."

Jonathan was now playing for time and since, as he imagined, Messrs P&G would have difficulty dealing with anything other than a confession or an outright lie, it was the only option he had at his disposal. The mention of 'bad news' gave him cause, for the first time, to consider what he had been up to for the last few days, what of that he was prepared to share with these morons and what, as such, was his alibi. The problem with alibis, or at least his one, was that as yet, Jonathan had not been asked for one. Were they just playing with him or did they not yet know when Frank had come to his timely end? He was not the least inclined to do their job for them and sat quietly enjoying what he hoped was their confusion. At length, the elder of the two – DS Germin - cleared his throat and spoke confidently.

"Well, it's like this, Dr Grey," he emphasised the title with obvious disdain. "We've been in touch with Inspector Cotting and guess what? He has heard of Frank Graves, but surprise, surprise, he has never heard of you! So what do you say to that, *Dr* Grey?"

Jonathan was not surprised by the news, in fact he would have put money on Cotting denying all such knowledge, and thus he continued the offensive.

"There are, of course, two possible answers to your question, if any has to be given. The first is that you could be lying – I'm sure you wouldn't find that too much of an effort – or alternatively, the good inspector could be lying for reasons of his own. I leave the choice to you. The only answer I can give you is the one that I gave you earlier. It was the truth then, as it is now. I would probably be able to help you more and let us all go home sooner if you were to be more candid with me. All you have said so far is that Mr Graves was found this morning, feet-up and head-down in

252

the river. And I told you that some while ago, I saw the same Mr Graves get his just deserts in a village pub. As yet, you have not told me how or, for that matter, whether the two events are supposed to be associated. If you want me to me to implicate myself in or exonerate myself from Mr Graves's death, it would help us all if you would disclose when, exactly, he is thought to have met it. Then, at least, I would be able to give you the names of those who could vouch for my whereabouts. As it is, you are wasting both your own time and, more importantly, mine. I hope that I make myself clear!"

Jonathan was so impressed at his improvised monologue that he hadn't noticed the white knuckles and reddening faces appearing on the other side of the table. Neither had he noticed that a little prompter was at work in his head. The younger of the two detectives announced an intermission in the interview and rose from the table to turn off the tape recorder so as to give Jonathan a good kicking, when the hand of fate intervened by knocking politely on the door. The same humourless uniformed sergeant entered and announced that Dr Grey's solicitor had arrived. This caused great consternation among the detectives and equally great elation and surprise for Jonathan. The reason for both conditions was that, thus far, he had been denied a phone call to anyone, and had thus resigned himself to holding out without a solicitor for thirty-six hours, after which they would either have to charge him or let him go. Such foolish blind faith in one who really should have known better.

"Mr Phillips," The sergeant droned. "The prisoner's brief. He says he's come, specially, from London."

Jonathan managed to stifle a wry smile as Peter sat down without waiting for an invitation and engaged the two detectives in polite but formal conversation. At length he asked to be given leave to speak in private with his client and was given ten minutes.

"Right, Jonathan," he said, quickly. "I've just come from the Stables and I've spoken with Cathy and Lisa. I'm going to tell you everything that you've been doing for the last three days, as well as I can remember it, and you must correct me should my memory fail. Have they said yet what it is you are supposed to have done?"

"They've not charged me with anything as yet, but they are questioning me about Frank Graves's death."

"Frank's dead?! When did that happen?"

"I don't know – we were just getting to that when you arrived. All they have said so far is that he was found this morning, head down and feet up in the river. By the way, how did anyone know that I was here?"

"Cathy rang the college to see whether you had received her email and she was told about the row and your detention, by someone in your department. You seem to have achieved celebrity status."

"They just seemed to get up my nose somehow. Anyway, let's start."

Peter talked Jonathan through the three previous days with surprising accuracy and only a few minor corrections were needed. They were seated quietly when the two detectives returned and after the traditional formalities, the interview continued.

"I believe that when I arrived, you were about to disclose when exactly Mr Graves met his death. It would certainly be most helpful to us all of us if you would, as I am sure that my client will then be able to provide you with an account of where he was at the time."

The detectives were so surprised at the conciliatory tone and the helpful way in which the suggestion was made that they missed the fact that the newcomer had hijacked the interview with his first words. They were of course much the same words that Jonathan had said earlier, but without the anger from the back of his head. Jonathan watched the play and was very impressed. The two detectives just sat at the other side of the table, transfixed by Peter's gestures and inflexions and, as intended, they missed everything that they were supposed to miss. Emily was certainly getting value for money from this guy.

"Well, sirs," the elder detective took the lead and started to address them both. "We have reason to believe that Mr Graves met his maker yesterday evening, so perhaps you would tell us where you were and who was with you. And, as if I need to remind you, sir," he looked at Jonathan at this point, "you are still under caution, so what do you have to say?"

Peter nodded the merest of silent approvals and Jonathan recounted almost minute by minute the events of the previous evening – without of course any mention of the involvement of Cathy. He took them through his first discovery of Michael beneath the collapsed wall, his quite inspirational, if second hand, first aid and on throughout the long evening to the eventual and unwelcome encounter with PC Jobmate. At the first mention of Michael the detectives' faces showed a glimpse of animation. Apart from that, however, they showed only increasing dejection. They were fairly certain about the time of death since the pathologist's first guess of about eleven o'clock was confirmed by Frank's wristwatch. It was one of those delightfully old-fashioned types with real hands and cunningly magnified little inserts to show both day and date. It was battery powered, but not being waterproof it stopped ticking at about the same time as its owner did. Jonathan finished his tale and there followed an embarrassing silence, as the two detectives looked at each other, both bereft of inspiration. Finally Peter intervened in his now familiar conciliatory and helpful way. He even almost felt sorry for them. Almost.

"Might I suggest that while you go to check the details of my client's account with your uniformed colleagues, you also inspect the Occurrence Record Book – it'll be in the front office – for confirmation of the events to which he referred earlier."

The two detectives left the room, one to phone the hospital and the other to inspect the appropriate records in the front office. They came back together and shame-faced only ten minutes later and sat down without turning the tape recorder back on. Then the elder of the two spoke quietly and with barely concealed embarrassment. "I'm afraid there has been some awful mistake. You should have one of these." He handed Jonathan a form. "It's for making your official complaint."

The silence hung about them all as Jonathan and Peter looked at each other as if to decide whom should speak first. They weren't even that sure whether they should even speak yet. The silence didn't look as though it was finished with loitering. No decision was forthcoming and the younger detective spoke up nervously.

"Whatever you do decide to do, you could perhaps return these to your friend, Dr Evans."

He handed Jonathan two plastic bags, one containing a leather wallet and the other a small leather folder of credit cards.

"They were found on Mr Graves. I can only say I am very sorry."

Jonathan and Peter looked at each other once more and at length Peter took the complaint form and tore it into pieces with a flourish while beaming generously at the two detectives over his half-rimmed glasses.

"I'm sure there will be no need for this," he said, waving one hand at the paper debris on the table. "In fact, I am sure that my client will take the view that you were simply trying to do your job within the usual constraints of under-funding, the absence of public understanding and wholly inadequate support from the Home Office."

Jonathan watched the docile nodding heads on the other side of the table and didn't know whether to laugh or to throw up.

"Having said all that," Peter continued, more assertively, "I am equally sure that, subject to the pressure of other enquiries, you will give some passing thought as to why your colleague, Mr Cotting, chose to lie to you."

Peter let this sink in as he smiled briefly at Jonathan and they both rose from their seats in preparation to leave. They were shown back to the charging room where Jonathan collected his belongings and left, without further ceremony, in search of the nearest pub. The pub was already quite busy with the early evening crush of office workers desperate to wash away/drown the cares of the day, or simply get wasted. Peter and Jonathan spoke little as among the customers were a number of off duty uniformed police looking more than a little conspicuous. Conscious of these unwelcome ears, they drank up quickly and set off in search of a taxi rank.

"You took a bit of a risk, posing as my solicitor," Jonathan said, as they ran across the road between the slow lines of cars heading home. "Do you have a card for every occasion?"

"I usually get by with about a dozen or so most of the time," Peter replied, as they got into a cab, "but I get a buzz out of taking on a new role at short notice – it sort of makes it all worthwhile somehow."

"Even so, you got to me very quickly. When did Cathy contact you? It must be at least two hours' drive from London."

"Not 'til late afternoon actually, but by then I was already on my way here in readiness for tomorrow.

Tomorrow, for my sins, I am a member of the Press – not so stimulating as being a solicitor, that's for sure. Did I tell you I qualified as a solicitor? I never got to practise though – I didn't fancy it somehow, it didn't seem to have very much to do with the truth so I turned my mind to other things."

"Okay," Jonathan continued, "Perhaps it wasn't too difficult a role to play, but wasn't it a bit chancy drawing friend Cotting into this? – the police are hardly likely to go chasing their own kind, are they?"

Peter allowed himself a brief smile before he replied.

"Those two detectives don't know yet what they've gotten themselves into. By now, they and their very confused superior are on their way to Scotland Yard for an unexpected meeting with someone of a rank just slightly less than God. There's not much that I can do directly about Cotting, but as the saying goes, 'I certainly know a man that can!' From now on he is going to be watched like a hawk."

Jonathan said nothing for a while, finally said "Aaaaaah," and then said nothing for another while. At length they reached the Stables. The gate was open and lights were lit within, but all the curtains were drawn closed as if protecting some dark secret. The cab stopped just outside and Peter paid the driver.

"Whose is that?" Jonathan said, pointing to a very sexy-looking sports car.

"Mine," Peter said, almost proudly. "I reckon I'm entitled to at least one frippery in life and that's it. I drove

259

up from London with a colleague. She dropped me off at the police station and came back here. Her name is Tess, Michael has met her and she is booked in on the first week of training at the Hall. I know the refurbishment isn't finished yet, but enough has been finished to make a small beginning on the courses and I didn't think we should miss the chance of placing someone else on the inside."

Jonathan closed and locked the gate quietly and then followed Peter to the door. Cathy, being ever watchful, had seen the lights of the cab through the drapes of the parlour and had opened the door in readiness. Peter went in first and Jonathan followed him into the stone-flagged hallway, Cathy kissed him gently and then pulled herself away quickly. They looked at each other briefly, neither knowing which was the more surprised. He moved on into the warmth of the room beyond where everyone else was waiting. He took in the assembled faces with a quick sweeping glance. Emily was in the middle and thrust a generous glass of whisky into his hand and held it a while as if checking that nothing had happened to him during his brief stay with the police. Jenny confined herself to smiling a welcome at him and the stranger, who again reminded him facially of his ex-wife, offered a hand as she introduced herself. Lastly his eyes fell on Lisa and he was surprised. She looked as though she had been crying; perhaps that was why she had not met him at the door. She made no motion to kiss him and she looked ill at ease and perhaps a little drunk. Perhaps she was just tired; she was up very early after all.

"How is Michael?" he asked no one in particular.

There was the briefest moment of silence while the reception committee wondered what to say. They assumed wrongly that something had happened which Jonathan simply didn't want to discuss and that asking after Michael was his way of keeping the conversation away from himself. Emily was the first to speak, which was only right since she had been the last to see him and anyway, she probably knew Jonathan better than anyone else present, with the recent exception of Lisa.

"When I left him he was giving a physiotherapist a hard time about what he should be doing or to be more exact, when he was going to start doing it. She was trying to explain to him that there was no point considering doing anything like swimming or anything at all serious in the way of exercise until the stitches were out, and he was being difficult. I did think about staying to give her a hand, but by the sound of her, I don't think she would have too much trouble. Have you eaten?"

"Well, now you come to mention it," he said, pausing only to drain his glass, "I am starving. I had forgotten that I had missed lunch and, for a while, I was wondering if I was going to discover the delights of 'porridge'."

He looked around for signs of hilarity but there were none. At length it was Lisa who broke the silence. She was still close to tears as she spoke. She had been drinking, it was true, but seemingly, that was not her only problem.

"I, that is, we were very worried about you, Jonathan. It was bad enough with Michael ending up in hospital, but when the police arrested you for something you didn't do – something you couldn't have done – well, we all felt so impotent somehow. And you could have avoided it all if you hadn't been so bloody clever with them at college."

She knew that she had spoken out of turn even as she said it and as if to make matters worse, she glared defiantly at Jonathan, almost daring him to reply. Tempting though it was, he didn't. He knew of course that it had been by no means 'clever' to have dealt with the two detectives in the way that he had, but at that time he did not know why they wanted to speak with him. Neither of them seemed destined to set the world on fire, but on the other hand, a successful murder investigation would do their pathetic careers no end of good. But how could Lisa know what he had said, or whether or not he was within his rights to say it? Try as he might not to, he found her reaction surprising and her rebuke mildly offensive. Thankfully, Emily sensed the confrontation coming and headed it off at the pass. She stepped forward, slipping an arm through one of Jonathan's and led him off toward the dining room, as if their earlier conversation had never been interrupted.

"Well, we must all be thankful to Jenny and Cathy and Tess. They may not have spent such an interesting afternoon as you, but at least they have something to show for their efforts – look!"

The dining room was warmly lit with about a dozen candles, which competed for that duty with a roaring log fire. The table was set for seven and groaned under the weight of food set on it. It was all cold fare but as salads went, it had the potential to dispel any myth about their connection with the word 'healthy'. Jonathan looked at it in wonder and then at its authors. Cathy and Tess beamed with obvious pleasure and Tess said:

"We nearly emptied the salad shelf at the supermarket."

"Thank you – all of you," Jonathan said, grinning, "But how did you guess the number correctly?"

"That was mostly my doing." Peter said quietly. "There was an agreement – yes, I think that would be the best word for it – an agreement between Ms Pollard and me, that I would have you back here for supper, or forego my fee for this investigation! Faced with that ultimatum, I decided to call in a few favours in high places. Paradoxically, by denying knowledge of you, David Cotting played into our hands and quite unknowingly, has sealed his own fate. There are some people at Scotland Yard with very long memories, all of who have a score to settle with him. They see this as being their chance!"

He finished the brief explanation, smiling, as he opened a bottle of champagne. Everyone waited for Emily to sit down before they too took their seats. Jonathan sat next to Emily and opposite Lisa. Her face appeared a little friendlier in the mixed light of the candles and the log fire. Tentatively, he tried squeezing one of her feet between his own, but although there was no obvious change in her expression, he felt her flinch slightly and withdraw her foot from between his. There was a barely visible stiffening of her hands as she helped herself to a selection of cold meats. He was about to break the silence when, unknowingly, Emily came to his aid.

"Will you still be available for tomorrow, or I shall I go to the Hall, since I am here now?"

In the excitement – if that was the word – the excitement of the day, he had forgotten that he would be deputising for Michael the next morning. There had been no great problem organising cover for lectures and from Emily's description, it didn't sound as though Michael would be, could be, away from things for more than two or three weeks at most, but the events at the Hall had slipped his mind momentarily.

"I will be more than happy for us both to go if you're free," he replied, smiling at Emily. "But I have only vague memories of the Hall and not a clue about what's supposed to be discussed in the morning."

He helped himself to some salad, poured wine for Lisa, Emily and himself and then listened as Emily described the works going on at the hall and the interest of the fire prevention department of the local brigade. There was it seemed a conflict between what would satisfy the fire department and what would satisfy the architects. The latter were more interested in preserving the essential character of the building than with the niceties of self-closing door technology.

The conversation changed to lighter matters. Tess, it seemed, had spent a pleasant holiday close to the village where Emily was now more or less permanently in residence. They chatted at length and to no great purpose about local wine growers and their customs. Jenny left the table after a short while to telephone Michael and left Peter and Cathy discussing local history with Lisa. Initially it went well, but Lisa was very tired and had done herself no favours by having drunk too much wine too quickly. Eventually she gave up pretending, excused herself politely and went to bed. At Peter's suggestion, he and Emily went back to the city to a hotel, leaving the others to clear up. Once the kitchen was under control, he went off to his room, taking a large glass of fruit juice in case Lisa was as dehydrated as she deserved to be. He found her sitting by an open window, smoking a cigarette and trying to pretend that she had not been crying since she had left the dinner table. He ignored the smell of the smoke, went to her side and sat down on the floor.

"Do you want to talk yet, or is it something you have to deal with on your own?" he said, kindly.

There was a brief silence as Lisa drew on the butt and threw it out of the window. Her eyes welled with tears and she looked down at Jonathan as he sat at her feet.

"I want to, Jonathan, but I don't know that I'm sure what to say. It's about Greg – I've heard from him again."

The effort or perhaps the release of starting to talk turned the trickle of tears to a flood and she made for the privacy of the bathroom to sort herself out. Jonathan stood up and gazed out of the window at the garden. The pale bedroom light picked out the drooping heads of the last of the season's daffodils as they swayed gently in the breeze. He didn't quite understand what Lisa had just started to say, or what he might think about what was to follow, but he was starting to feel a little confused. The little voice at the back of his head had had a little to say of late but the words, 'I told you so' were starting to form. The mental exertions of the day were starting to get to him and he felt that, quite beyond his control, events were bringing themselves to an unexpected head. Lisa was still making ablutionary noises in the bathroom and he took her seat. Almost absent-mindedly, he took a cigarette from her packet and lit it. He had not smoked since his first year at university, apart, perhaps, from the odd joint at parties. He inhaled sharply and the warm smoke hit the back of his windpipe. Inhaling was a bit of a shock at first, but after the first four or five times, it no longer hurt. He was on his third cigarette and thinking how little Cathy would approve, when Lisa came out of the bathroom. If she was surprised at what she saw, she didn't let it show. She seemed, instead, to have wound herself up to say something and was not about to be deterred. Jonathan tried to look calm as he stood up and offered her a cigarette.

"I'm a good listener, if that helps," he said.

"Well, it's like this," she began. "I had a letter from Greg a few days ago and he seemed a little - well - strange. Anyway he suggested that maybe I could ring him for a chat – just to see how we were both doing – and I did. Cutting a long story short, he sounded a bit down and suggested that we could maybe see each other again and I found that I wanted to – see him that is. I wanted to tell you so that you would understand."

"And do you understand?"

"No – of course not. If I did, I wouldn't be like this. I don't understand why I should want to see him after what he did and I don't understand why I am prepared to risk hurting or even losing you when I've only just found you. In fact, I don't really think I understand anything anymore."

Jonathan ran through all his emotions and avoided giving an instinctive reaction. At length he gave in to the prompting from the back of his head and recited the words, but not verbatim. "I think I may understand or, at least, I think I could perhaps explain some of it were the situation reversed." 'God forbid', he thought to himself. "Since I've met you, I've started to enjoy feelings that I'd completely forgotten to feel. But they're not all related to you, it's just that feeling - generally much better about life, I have re-learned to see, touch, feel, care – all those every day emotions that normal people take for granted. Well, it could be that you feel something like the same way, and you've remembered that you cared for Greg. You used to love him once, didn't you?" (Lisa nodded with her mouth open.) "Well, love isn't something you can just turn off or on like a tap, is it?" (More nods.) "Well perhaps that's what is eating you… - maybe. The way I see it, you don't actually stop loving people when they hurt you, it's just that the terms of reference change. If you don't mind me saying so, your problem is working out whether you love Greg or are *in love* with him. If you love him, you can deal with it, whereas if you are in love with him, you really do have a problem and it's one that you alone can solve."

Lisa said nothing in reply but seemed to have understood something of what she had heard. "Do you mind if we turn in?" she said, yawning. "I'm beat and I've got another early start tomorrow."

"No problem," Jonathan replied, catching the yawn "I've had a long day too!"

"Yes. I'm so sorry about the timing," she said. "It's just something I have to sort out."

They went to bed somewhat further apart than usual, and soon after, Lisa was snuffling away to herself in the darkness. Jonathan lay awake a little longer, running through the events of the day until inevitably, he arrived back at the present. He glanced over at Lisa's hair, shining faintly in the starlight and wondered why he had not listened to his alter ego. Eventually, when he had its full attention, Jonathan said, "Well thanks a bunch. I wouldn't have said that if I were me!"

Chapter 22:

A Flaunt of Diplomas

When Jonathan awoke it was still dark. He searched around with his left arm but the other side of the bed was empty; Lisa was gone and it all seemed strangely final. There was no concrete evidence for such a conclusion, but his instincts told him that it was so. He thought about it a while and then shut his eyes again in a confused silent protest. This was interrupted by birds bent on twittering outside the window. It became gradually lighter and as morning became more and more inevitable, Jonathan stretched and warmed up his muscles while building up courage to open first his eyes and then the curtains in his room. He had deluded himself into thinking that there had been several inches of snow overnight, or that one of the trees in the yard had quite unaccountably become uprooted and thrown itself into the pool. But no such luck. There was no frost or snow, no wind to speak of, and nothing faintly arboreal in the pool. There was no avoiding it; he just had to swim for his breakfast. With Michael still in hospital, he could get it all over and done with a bit quicker, and twenty minutes later he was breathing heavily and standing under a hot shower trying to convince himself that it was all worthwhile. Cathy had been watching him from the kitchen and greeted him with a mug of coffee as he entered and put down his shoes.

"You seem to making progress." she said, returning to the grille. "Do you find it's getting any easier?"

"A little," he replied, nibbling at some toast, "but I can't say that I have any great enthusiasm for it first thing in the mornings. I trust you are taking advantage of the pool while you are here – you won't have much chance once you're up at the Hall, unless there's a pool there that I don't know about."

"There is, actually," Cathy said, correcting him gently, "or at least, according to the brochure there is, but I haven't seen it for myself. My interview with Michael didn't extend to a guided tour. Is Lisa on her way through, or can I finish this toast?"

The question was innocent enough and Jonathan didn't feel that he was being probed. He simply answered with the truth – or at least a version of it. He smiled inwardly as he remembered one of Sara's rare moments of wit. He had been questioning her about one or other of her many lies, when, like Cathy after the first swimming session, she calmly dismissed his protests by saying that lying was just another form of communication. Try as he might, Jonathan could not dredge up any memory of having cared for Sara. He was sure he had, of course, but everything had been blocked out in an effort to retain some semblance of sanity.

"No, she seems to have gone, already." he said, as much to himself as Cathy, but then added, "She had to leave early this morning, so we've both missed her."

"It's not my business Jonathan, but is there a problem? Lisa seemed a bit upset last night."

"You're right on both counts, but she does have some personal matters to see to, that's all. I don't think we'll see her for a while. In one sense it's probably for the best, since the fewer of us involved in Emily and Peter's business, the better."

"I'm sorry, Jonathan – I didn't mean to intrude – I just wanted to make sure that you were okay after what you've been through."

"Thanks, Cathy – that's kind. Sorry I was a bit short with you, but I'm much more concerned with Mike's health than yesterday's encounter with the police or my very brief relationship with Lisa."

"No apology needed, even I have to admit that things have not gone entirely to plan so far. Anyway, if you do want to talk about it, just remember that you do have other friends."

"Thanks, Cathy. You're very sweet and I'll certainly bear that in mind, if I need a shoulder."

Tess shambled in to preclude further conversation, looking for all the world like someone who really didn't like mornings. She grunted something barely comprehensible at Cathy who, being gifted, seemingly with language skills as well as those relating to putting people in hospital, dutifully poured her a sluggish cup of brown steaming liquid. Tess accepted it with a slightly more comprehensible grunt and sat down to light a cigarette. Cathy looked at her almost sympathetically, before explaining the situation to Jonathan.

"You wouldn't have guessed it from last night, but Tess here," she began, nodding toward her colleague, "is a self-confessed mess. As you will have gathered, she is not very good in the mornings and refuses to function before a coffee – preferably yesterday's – and at least three cigarettes. After that, she's as normal as you or me."

Jonathan liked to think that he was normal, but wasn't entirely convinced that Cathy qualified.

. He risked lifting his eyebrows as if to question her statement and she caught his look and grinned. Tess saw nothing of this as she still had both eyes screwed firmly shut while struggling to get her caffeine and nicotine levels up to proportions capable of supporting life. One hand searched purposefully for an ashtray.

"Despite her many addictions, Tess is very hard working and very quick on the up-take. Once she is back in the land of the living, she will no doubt tell you her life story – she seems to take some sort of perverse pleasure in doing that sort of thing to strangers. However, since you have to be at the Hall in about thirty minutes, I'll give you the short sanitised version so that you can avoid asking any sensitive questions. She won't mind me giving away her dark secrets as they aren't either – dark or secret – so don't bother to blush. Before joining Peter, Tess used to be in the police in London until her very promising career was brought to an untimely end by a foolish dalliance with a fellow officer. Dalliances were commonplace then and no doubt still are, but Tess had the misfortune to have conducted the best part of hers on videotape and it left her looking for a new job."

Jonathan looked at Tess for any sign of disapproval over the way the story was unfolding, but the one eye that was now open appeared unmoved, disinterested and simply in search of the coffee pot. Cathy continued.

"Tess was attached to CID, and at the time of the recording attached, in the biblical sense, to a detective sergeant. Anyway there had been a successful operation of some sort, too much drink was consumed and rather than going to his place or hers, Tess and the man made use of the snooker room. What neither of them knew was that someone had been pilfering the coin machine for the lights and as a result, video surveillance had been set up. Copies of the tape were circulated extensively and, eventually, people in high places got wind of it."

"What happened to the man?" Jonathan asked, trying not to think too hard about Tess stretched out on a snooker table or the origin of the phrase, 'kissing the pink'. "I trust he suffered the same fate."

"Not exactly," Tess said, with both eyes just open. "It was put to him that he too should do the decent thing and resign, but some of his more bullish male colleagues persuaded him to tough it out and so far as I know, he still has a job. He didn't have it all his own way though, I heard that one of his previous dalliances got hold of a copy of the tape and sent it to his wife."

"Ah. Right." Jonathan mumbled, as he put on a coat and headed for the door.

"Jonathan?"

"Yes, Cathy?"

"Aren't we forgetting something?"

"Right. Yes – er – sorry, 'bye – see you later."

"Yes, goodbye," Cathy said, patiently, "but I was actually thinking about something else."

Jonathan was now at a complete loss and stood open-mouthed waiting for light, or whatever was wrong, to dawn on him. He looked at his dim reflection in the mirror and saw that his hair was combed and that his shirt buttons appeared to match the appropriate buttonholes. So far so good. The next bit was a little more tricky, since the window didn't offer sufficient a reflection for him to tell whether his fly was zipped. He felt that it might not be quite the right thing to do to appear to play with himself and worse still, he had a nagging feeling that Cathy knew exactly what he was thinking. He looked up at her and his suspicion was confirmed. The open mouth was joined quickly by a blush and he opened his arms in an expansive and plaintive gesture for help. Cathy simply looked him down, paused briefly at hip level and then let her gaze settle on his feet – the ones with socks but no shoes on. Jonathan followed her gaze praying inwardly that there wasn't cause for it to linger anywhere below the waist. After an anxious moment, he made a dash for his shoes and then another one for the door.

"He seems nice." Tess said, shutting one eye again. "I don't suppose you've ...?" she let the question fade with a wave of the hand not holding a cigarette.

"You don't suppose right, so far." Cathy said, with a sigh that took even her by surprise.

"Anyway, this business appears to be dangerous enough without taking the risk of mixing it with pleasure – speaking of which, you have several more reports to read before you check in for your induction – it's tomorrow, isn't it?"

"Yes," Tess replied, now fully awake. "According to the bumf they sent me, we get a day's induction – introducing us to the trainers and the software and so on, and then we get the weekend to get to know each other before the serious work starts on Monday. I was beginning to look forward to it until I read the bit in the small print about not smoking. Peter didn't mention that when he asked me to volunteer – still, at least I'll have an ally in Jonathan if he's around."

"Why do you think that might be; he's not a smoker, is he?"

"I think so – or at least, I thought I could smell it on his jacket before he left in such confusion. The usual wager?"

"Why ever not?" Cathy agreed, nibbling at some cold toast.

Although the weather had not prevented Jonathan's early morning dip, it was doing its best to ruin the rest of the day by making him late. Mike's car was prone to condensation and since it had been a fairly cold night the

275

engine didn't want to fire on more than two cylinders. The battery started to fail after several attempts and it was only by pausing a few moments and threatening to give Mike's car to his ex-wife, that Jonathan persuaded it to start. Thereafter it purred its way over the short journey to the hall, almost as if it was anxious to please. As he drew into the grounds of the hall Jonathan saw Peter looking for all the world like a well-dressed but nonetheless seedy hack, in conversation with a stiff-backed gentleman, whom he took to be the Fire Prevention Officer. Jonathan flicked briefly through the file that Emily had given to him and made a mental note of the man's name and rank. He locked Mike's car and strode purposefully toward the two.

"It's ADO Duncan, isn't it?" he said, offering his hand in a way that didn't allow refusal.

"I imagine you were expecting to see Mr Evans, but as you may have heard he had an accident and I am deputising for him. I am Jonathan Grey by the way."

"Yes. I was expecting you, Dr Grey. Dr Evans's aunt was kind enough to telephone me before I left my office this morning, hence I was forewarned. Also I was lucky enough to have met Mr Phillips here who, as you know, has not only been documenting the recent history of the Hall, but also promised to provide me with some historical information about the local fire service. He also said to expect you in Dr Evans's absence."

"Yes," Jonathan answered, truthfully. "Mr Phillips and I have met on several occasions recently. Have you seen Miss Pollard, by the way?"

"Yes, she is inside, talking with her architect and Mr Caine from Building Control. We were only waiting for you and the tenant's architect to arrive before we started, but there was a message to say that he was delayed, so Mr Phillips and I decided to take some fresh air while we waited."

"Good idea," Jonathan agreed. Peter and Mr Duncan seemed to be hitting it off, but Jonathan couldn't resist the temptation to push things along a little and added, "Oh by the way Mr Philips, the police found my car, but it had been burned out."

"Really?"

"Yes," added Mr Duncan. "There's been a lot of that sort of thing of late."

"Really?"

Jonathan, seeing that he had done enough, bade them a temporary farewell and went off in search of Emily. He had not been to the Hall in quite a while and the outside was certainly looking a little crisper than he remembered. The gravel circle surrounding the fountain had grown at the west side of the Hall with an extension to the rear, presumably to allow tradesmen's vehicles to park both out of sight and nearer to where the remaining work was to be done. According to Michael, most of what little was to be done to the main frontage had been completed, early on, and the only serious outstanding structural work was in the ground and first floors of the west wing, where early stripping out had revealed signs of wood rot to an extent that some replacement was called for. Even without being told she had to, Emily insisted on using comparably aged timber and this had taken some while to acquire. Thanks to Emily's renowned powers of persuasion, the incoming tenants were quite understanding of the delay – more especially once it was explained to them that other private rooms could be made available to them in the short term. More out of curiosity than purpose, Jonathan followed the drive round to the west. He liked watching people with skills at work but also, he wanted the chance to have a good long wander about and maybe find where the pool and gym were for Cathy. In the event he achieved neither since he blundered into a heated conversation between Bill Edwards, who he recognised from years back, and the clerk of works, who he recognised from a very smart badge that he wore on his jacket, and an even more impressive label that had been lovingly taped to his hard hat. From the sound of it, this was an everyday confrontation between the two men, each trying to establish if not extend their territory/responsibility/authority, and what the conversation lacked in style, it more than made up for in volume and entertainment value. Bill was edging monosyllabically towards a small victory, to the extent that his adversary was physically retreating (backwards) towards the sanctuary and relative safety of his site hut. Here he was 'king' and none would flout his authority. The nearer he got to his beloved hut and the further out of earshot of his subordinates, his confidence returned. He was even shorter than Bill Edwards, but in gaining the first step to the door of his refuge the situation became reversed. Jonathan stood only a few metres distant as the two men, now of reversed heights, faced up to each other. Bill realised that if he was not careful, he might soon lose the initiative so he pressed on even more monosyllabically, closing the gap between the two of them. The clerk of works took a further step back and up, but this was only to gain even higher ground and as such, was just a feint. With both feet now firmly planted on the top step to his hut, he allowed himself a mildly dangerous rush of blood to the face and gripped the door handle until the knuckles on his left hand went white. This was just about as far as he was about to retreat and as if to emphasise the point to Bill, the clerk of works puffed up his little chest and waved the middle finger of his free hand as menacingly as he could at Bill's upturned face. There was a moment of silence which, apart from being welcome, gave Jonathan the opportunity to reflect upon Michael's often repeated view that, certainly in the male of the species and to a lesser extent in the female, volume i.e. loudness was inversely proportionate to height. This theory seemed to hold true more often than not as did the one, limited to the male, that height was inversely proportionate to perceived self-worth. Jonathan wondered if he should devise some means of intervening before blows were struck or before one or perhaps both men had a heart attack, but he had no need. He was not the only spectator to the entertainment. One of the contractors, who could rightly claim to be a regular viewer, was so amused at the angry finger wagging that he gave himself away by bursting into a fit of uncontrollable laughter. The clerk of works looked around angrily and Jonathan was pleased that he managed to appear unamused – well just. Bill seized on his brief moment of victory, laughed before spitting on the lower of the two steps and then stomped self-importantly back into the Hall without saying even good morning to Jonathan. His manners, it seemed, were not improved since their last meeting, years previously. Jonathan glanced at his watch and saw that ten minutes had passed since he had left Peter and Mr Duncan, so he set his curiosity aside and went off in search of Emily and the others.

As he walked past the open door of the site hut he glimpsed in and saw a small number of framed diplomas hanging on the wall, placed carefully so that a visitor entering could not fail but to see them. 'Pratt', he thought and walked on trying to think of an appropriate group-noun for diplomas. By the time that he had walked through to the font of the Hall to find the others, he had decided on the word 'flaunt', for want of any better. Emily, another woman and someone with a clipboard and wearing an official looking grey suit were deep in conversation when eventually Jonathan found them. Emily greeted him with two polite kisses, on each cheek and then introduced him to Liz Porter her architect, and to Chris Caine from Building Control who appeared, on introduction, friendlier to speak to than his demeanour had suggested.

"It looks now as if we have two people who are unable to make it," Emily said, with just a hint of annoyance. "The tenant's architect just phoned to say that he won't be able to make it at all and the representative from English Heritage left a message to say that she can't get here before this afternoon. Fortunately, I already know her views and since they are very close to my own, I speak for her. I certainly can't wait for her to arrive."

As she stopped short of saying what she really thought of people who were late for appointments. Emily's attention was distracted by the arrival of ADO Duncan and the ubiquitous Mr Philips. The two had been deep in conversation, but broke off when they heard the tone of Emily's voice.

"I think I may be able to assist a little." Mr Duncan said, as he greeted people in turn. "When I last spoke to the tenant's architect – I think I still have his card on file somewhere – yes here it is, Mr Jarvis – he said that if there was a consensus and no unreasonable extra cost or delays to his clients, he would be happy to go along with anything that fell within the requirements of the Fire Precautions Act."

With the possible exception of the little bit of entertainment that he had just witnessed, Jonathan was beginning to wish that he had stayed in bed, but he saw the tension leave Emily's face. The word 'consensus' was one of her favourites and she warmed visibly to the prospect of an early completion to the meeting. Needless to say, she wanted to run the meeting herself, but since it had been called by Building Control at the specific request of ADO Duncan, she thought it might be more polite (if less efficient) to let them run it together. She therefore raised her eyes at Mr Caine, inviting him to start, and had he but known her face better, to finish as quickly as possible. He obliged at least in the first part (the first four words) by saying, "Well, in a nutshell, so to speak, it comes down to this. While most things to do with structural changes, alterations and changes of use fall within the remit of my department in terms of the Building Regulations that is, anything vaguely to do with fire precautions, or to be more precise, 'Safe Means of Escape' is more the responsibility of the Fire Prevention Department of the local fire service, to whom all such matters are referred for advice."

Having met him several times before, Emily had suspected that it would be an error to invite the man to speak first, but she consoled herself with the certainty that he would eventually have to pause for breath or, better still, expire. She was of course far too well-mannered to do anything more than stare blankly at a point about two feet behind his head as he babbled on in a well-practised monotone. Jonathan, being less patient than Emily and certainly less well mannered, had reverted to his original opinion of Mr Caine and had added him, without second thought, to the burgeoning list for execution. He was about to lose the battle to hold back a yawn when suddenly the babbling stopped and was followed by an embarrassing silence. The ADO was far away in a world of his own and had missed what was evidently meant as a cue. Somewhat flustered, he started, gaining confidence as he went.

"Well, I'm sure that there is very little that divides us and I'm equally sure that even with our depleted numbers we can reach a compromise today. As I think you are all aware, the only sticking point that prevents me from issuing a certificate is the matter of the adequacy of fire stopping to the main stairwell at second floor level. I'll try to keep this as brief as possible, but as things stand, the options are that the fire stopping remains as it is, but this will require an additional external fire escape at the rear of the building.

This was a suggestion of the tenant's architect, requires Building Control consent, but is rejected by both the owner and English Heritage on the grounds of, for want of a better word, 'ugliness'."

Emily, Mr Caine and Jonathan nodded in unison. Peter was looking at the paintings and detached himself from the others.

"The second option," Mr Duncan continued, "which as you are aware is the one I favour, is to replace the main doors at second floor landing level with propriety self-closing, half hour fire-stopping doors surrounded each side and above with Georgian wired glass. This was proposed by both the owner's architect and the owner herself, but is rejected on aesthetic grounds by English Heritage. As of this morning, it strikes me that the tenant's architect has no vote in the matter, but we are still left with the task of finding a compromise – or for that matter, a different option. Shall we go upstairs and have a look or does anyone have an idea for discussion down here?"

There was another brief silence as everyone looked at each other for inspiration. Then, just as there was about to be an unspoken agreement to ascend the main stairwell, Jonathan shrugged off the little voice at the back of his head and muttered one of his favourite words.

"Why?" he asked, almost hesitantly.

"Because by being there and seeing the problem, we may find an answer to it." Emily chided him gently. "Is all this swimming making you too tired to walk up a few steps, Jonathan?"

"No, sorry, I didn't mean why do we have to go upstairs – even I can understand that. I meant why do we have to replace the doors at all? I've had a look at the plans. Why don't we just leave them as they are, which will satisfy one faction and then build some of these fire stopping things into a fire-wall a few metres into each corridor? – which I imagine will satisfy the other faction."

The Building Control officer, now thoroughly caught off guard, flourished a well-worn calculator in the pretence of needing to carry out some vital calculations, while the ADO Duncan and Ms Porter rushed upstairs to discuss 'feasibility'. This left Emily caught between wondering whether she should beam approvingly at her nephew's friend, or change her architects, or perhaps both. Peter had rejoined what was left of the party, and having heard most of the conversation en route, he shrugged his shoulders and said, without naming the reason why, "In my business, it's often useful to have a new pair of eyes look at an old problem. If you've been close to something for a long time, you get so used to it that you can't stand back and see it objectively."

"That is so typically profound of you, Mr Stagg – sorry, Phillips. I think I'll let you buy me lunch," Emily said, trying hard to contain her displeasure at the shortcoming(s) of her architects. "I'll just have a quick word with those who wisely escaped upstairs, to see how long it will take them to sort out the details."

"Well, there's a bit of a problem there." Peter said, with genuine regret. "I have already arranged to take Mr Duncan to lunch. He thinks we are going to have a lengthy discourse about fire-fighting through the ages but in fact, I am going to pick his brains on a subject of more interest to you – that's why I gate-crashed this meeting in the first place."

"Yes of course Mr Phillips," Emily replied. "Of course you must. I seem to have been taking too many people for granted recently. Please forgive me. Anyway, with Michael on the mend and this business sorted out, there's nothing to keep me here so I can see a few old friends, do a little essential shopping and fly back to Italy last thing this evening."

"I'm up for lunch," Jonathan chipped in. "I want to go into the city anyway to see how Michael is getting on and I should think he'll be driving them all witless by now."

"Yes, that would be nice too; I'll join you if I may."

There was no need for Jonathan to answer and so he didn't. He simply opened the passenger door for Emily and stood by it as she got in. It was all done in seconds, but it was long enough for him to let his eyes take a sweep over the front of the Hall, including the first floor window where Bill Edwards was quietly watching their departure. Jonathan wondered why the man hadn't had the decency to bid his employer farewell, and also felt the hair on the back of his neck start to prickle. Emily gave him a knowing look but said nothing, not then anyway.

"Is there anything you need to collect from the Stables?" he asked, as they picked their way through the cars parked in the village high street.

"What? Err no, sorry I was preoccupied. I was just thinking how little things had changed around here and how pleased I am that they hadn't. But did you notice Edwards as we left, Jonathan?"

"Yes. You too?"

"Yes. It's odd, but it is as if I could feel his eyes boring into my back ever since I got here. We have never got on since the day he first moved to the Hall, but he was the best candidate and I just never got around to 'replacing' him. Funny, though," she said, frowning, "I have never felt so unwelcome anywhere before. What do you think it means, Jonathan?"

"I don't know off the top of my head, but I'll think about it, and if that doesn't work I'll ask Peter if it fits into any of this theories. Come to think of it, I'll ask him anyway – I'd like to find out why he is so interested in Mr Duncan. He must be riveting company to make it worth missing lunch with you!"

"Flatterer!"

Chapter 23:

Pursuits

The foyer at the hospital was relatively quiet when, after a fruitless search of most of the wards and still replete with lunch, Jonathan and Emily pressed the bell at Enquiries and found out Michael's new room number. Being now nothing remotely like 'critical', he had been moved to a relative backwater – to a small but neat room overlooking the nurses' accommodation wing. Jonathan took one look at the view and laughed.

"How come you always manage to come out of things smelling of roses, Michael? Here you are on your back, surrounded by nurses and then at the end of the day, just when you think they'd let you get a bit of peace, quiet and sleep, you have to watch them getting undressed, taking showers and sordid stuff like that. I don't know how you cope really – it doesn't even look as though your curtains shut fully."

"They don't." Michael said, grinning and getting out of bed with the aid of a stick. He hobbled over to the doorway to greet them both and then hobbled back again with no obvious effort. "Anyone for a drink?" he added, pointing at a small fridge the other side of his bed. Emily ignored the question and tried as hard as she could to be cross with him.

"Is there any point asking if you are supposed to be hopping around like a demented barman, Michael?"

He tried to look stung by her question, but with no more success than she had in trying to look cross.

"Well actually, since you asked, I am doing exactly as I promised you and that is, doing as I was told. 'They' say that I should take as much exercise as I can without exhausting myself and to rest thoroughly in between. 'They' also say that the best chance I will have of making a complete recovery and being able to play cricket badly again, is to do as much walking as I can, given that I still have to carry this heparin pump around and then, as I said, rest up in between. I tend to do most of my resting up when the nurses go to bed, but I see that as being a reward for following orders. Was that a 'no' by the way? I'm only allowed a few drinks a day and I'd rather have you join me than drink alone."

Emily looked at her nephew long and hard, but apart from the bandage on his head, the bruised wrists and the heparin pump plugged into the left one, he seemed well on the mend. He was thinner of course, and still not perhaps his usual colour, but other than that … well, time would tell. The next bit she knew was not going to be easy, so a drink was perhaps in order.

"Michael?" she began, "I have a little favour to ask you – that is – I'd like you to consider doing something for me."

"Gin and tonic?" he replied, pressing on as if there had been no interruption in the earlier conversation.

Jonathan smiled to himself as he moved out of any direct firing line. He was surprised but quite pleased to think that Michael was so much improved that he believed he could take his aunt on in verbal sparring. He helped himself to a tonic and sat on the window ledge waiting to see if Emily could be goaded into getting to the point, or if she would simply waste time practising footwork. It was actually quite entertaining watching these two trying to edge each other into making the first mistake. Michael took the initiative by pouring drinks for himself and Emily without waiting for her to answer and then guiding her to what was clearly the more comfortable of the two seats in the room. Emily sat.

"So, what is this smallest of favours that I can do for you, dear aunt?" He sat down with obvious ease and crossed his legs with an air of open defiance. One of the nurses had found him sitting cross-legged earlier in the day, delivered herself of a semi-hysterical monologue on the subject of how to promote blood clots and threatened to sew his curtains together.

"I was going to ask you if you would care to come to Italy with me to convalesce for a few days – but I can see that you probably don't need to, so don't even think about it."

'Clever,' Jonathan thought to himself. 'She thinks she's on a loser and wrong-footed him – very clever!'

If Michael was feeling wrong-footed, he put up a good show of not appearing so. He uncrossed his legs (this time with just a hint of pain), sighed a little and then looked directly at his aunt before replying.

"Well, to be honest," he lied, "I'd rather like to come with you, but I don't think that it's fair to leave everything in Jonathan's lap at the moment." He looked at Jonathan for support, but saw from his face that it would not be forthcoming.

"There is no reason why you shouldn't go once you are a little more mobile, Mike," Jonathan said, trying to ignore the blooming scowl. "The vac is about to start so there will be no lectures to cover and with the best will in the world, you won't be up to doing anything too physical for a week or so at least. You'll probably be out by the weekend anyway, so why don't you ask Emily if there will be room for Jenny as well? And if there is, you can both go out at the weekend."

Michael opened and shut his mouth, thought briefly about saying something stupid like, "I suppose you two planned this," and then brightened as he realised that it was, after all, what he probably wanted. In any event he could see from Emily's look of admiration at Jonathan that she had not expected help from any quarter, so he let it go. The deed, done. Jonathan made Emily's day complete by taking her all the way to Heathrow. He had a loose arrangement to contact Peter later in the day but other than that, there was nothing more pressing in prospect than another thirty lengths of the pool and that could be done at any time of the day. Besides, he enjoyed Emily's company and the outward journey passed quickly and without incident. Jonathan was listening avidly to stories of Michael's earlier misdemeanours and so intent was he on both listening carefully and watching the road ahead, he completely failed to notice that shortly after he and Emily left the hospital's car park, a nondescript hatchback started following them, dutifully, three cars behind. To the casual observer, it might have appeared that both cars were simply being driven very carefully. Neither exceeded the speed limit and all that could be said of the following car was that every time it pulled out to overtake, it returned to its original lane perhaps a little enthusiastically. Peter Stagg could not be described as a casual observer and was just beginning to find the whole thing faintly humorous from his position six cars further back when he realised that he too was being followed, or at least someone was not bothered about getting past him. A service station proffered itself and he left the motorway, pausing only to take the number of the car. One discreet telephone call later and he knew that the car that had been following him was an unmarked police vehicle. It was tailing Cotting, who, unknown to Jonathan and Emily, was tailing them. He toyed with the idea of calling Michael's car phone, but thought better of it. They didn't know and nothing was likely to happen to them, he hoped. More bizarrely still, none of the drivers or passengers in this cavalcade remarked that some 2,000 ft above them, all were being observed by armed officers of Special Branch in an unmarked helicopter. Nothing did happen to Jonathan and Emily. They simply arrived in good time at the airport, said their farewells and went their separate ways. A few minutes later, Jonathan was heading home once more followed at a suitably discreet distance by Cotting, the unmarked police car and, last of all, by Peter, who wondered at the sheer folly of it all. Tailing someone was not an enviable task at the best of times and with the attendant task of not being spotted by the 'tailee' it could be fraught with danger in heavy traffic or bad weather. Thus having determined that it was Cotting who was being followed and not he and having, in addition, extracted a promise that in exchange of information, he would be kept informed of police activities, Peter allowed himself a leisurely coffee break before heading back to the office to wade through the inevitable pile of mail and telephone messages and printed e-mails adorning his desk. There were a few cheques, an equal number of bills and a handful of enquiries that had the potential of becoming interesting cases. Among the telephone messages were one from Emily and one from Mike. She had decided at the last moment that she would not be leaving until the following afternoon and would be at the usual hotel if he would care to meet her for dinner. It did not sound like a summons, but it might be the last chance he had to speak with her face to face for a while so he called to confirm, left the tape of his chat with ADO Duncan for someone to type and headed back to his flat for a quick change. It was barely six miles to Emily's hotel but the last dregs of rush hour ensured that it was a very slow journey. He didn't care much for using his mobile phone in case there was a lapse in security, but he owed it to both his colleagues and the client to keep them informed, so he decided to take the risk. He knew that Tess, if she was there, would not be so stupid to answer without first identifying the caller by listening to the speaker on the answer phone and that is exactly what she did.

"Hi, boss. You sound as though you're mobile."

"That's right, so I'll keep it brief. Is Jonathan about?"

"He will be in a minute or two. He's just finished a stint in the pool and I think he'll be in need of something warm – is there a problem?"

"No – not as such, or at least nothing that we can't deal with given a little outside help. I just thought I should bring you both up to date on what's been going on, since I probably won't have another chance this evening."

"OK, fine. Jonathan is coming in now looking distinctly blue at the edges. Shall I put you on the speaker?"

"Please. You should both hear this. Hi, Jonathan."

"Hello, Peter." Jonathan replied, recognising his voice.

"Right, both of you. Things are getting a little dirty and you should both exercise a lot of care. And you particularly, Jonathan, since you are relatively new to this sort of thing. The bad news is that you were followed to and from the airport this afternoon and you can probably assume that it was neither the first time this has happened nor the last. It was Cotting. I'm afraid that we should therefore assume that he knows something that we don't. He drives a light blue Vauxhall Astra with a dented rear offside wing and with a Registration Number K383 PEG. I'll email you a copy of his duty roster so that you know when you should expect him. If you should spot him, do absolutely nothing and on no account give him any reason to suspect that you know that he is behind you. The good news is that he too is being followed, so there is no reason to believe that you will come to any harm. Are you about tomorrow or are you lecturing?"

"I'm lecturing in the morning and back here about one, or at worst, one thirty."

"Right, I'll be there at about three and my office will send you a transcript of my conversation with Mr Duncan, together with the roster. I think you will both find the transcript good reading. It will be safe for me to be around tomorrow since Cotting is doing a late shift. What are your plans, Tess?"

"I don't have any as such, other than mugging up on this new computer thing. Is there anything in particular you want done, or shall I just stay hidden?"

"A little bit of the former but otherwise mostly the latter, I think. I don't yet know why Cotting is tailing Jonathan, but it's a safe bet that he will also consider watching the Stables. I don't much like the idea of encouraging him to break in – Miss Pollard's sense of humour probably wouldn't stretch to that – but of course it doesn't stop us from watching him watching. I'll be delivering some more surveillance equipment tomorrow afternoon so that, as and when the time comes, we'll have some hard evidence to give to the police. Can you make time to set it up for me, Tess? I won't be staying very long."

"Was that the former, Peter?"

'Yes, unless I think of anything else in the meanwhile."

"Peter?"

"Yes, Jonathan?"

"Who exactly will be tailing Cotting? It's not that I'm a bit paranoid, but it would be reassuring if I knew what other car registration numbers I should be watching out for."

"Good point, Jonathan. It'll be the police – some people from their internal investigations department. I doubt that I will be able to get their names, but I'll see what can be done about what they will be driving. I'm seeing their boss tomorrow morning before I come out to you. Oh yes, that was the other thing, Tess – can you also fit a new battery in the homing bug on Michael's car?"

"No problem."

"Right then, any messages for Emily, Jonathan?"

"I thought she had flown out."

"So did I, but apparently she didn't and I'm dining with her tonight – in about twenty minutes time."

"Okay fine … no, I can't think of anything off hand."

The three said their goodbyes leaving Jonathan wondering again quite what he had fallen into. In the space of about two weeks he had: gotten himself unusually drunk, become a video star (albeit in a very small way), had his car stolen and burned out, moved home, swum more lengths than he cared to remember, been bounced and deserted by someone whom he hardly knew, his best friend had bloody nearly died, he had been arrested for murder for no reason at all and had been allowed to be followed by a bent policeman who seemed in some way to be connected with the person who had been murdered. As if all that wasn't enough to think about, Jonathan felt vaguely uneasy about something that had been overlooked and he just couldn't place what it was. He screwed up his face in concentration but nothing momentous came to mind. He was still wearing the bathrobe that he had put on as soon as he had completed his twenty-five lengths. If Cathy had been around he would probably have been coerced into doing more, but she wasn't so that, at least, was a relief. Normally he would have grabbed a mug of coffee before heading for his shower but Peter's phone call had intervened and he was now standing in a growing puddle on the kitchen floor, still wearing a screwed up face in addition to his swimming trunks and robe.

"A penny for them," Tess said, helping them both to coffee.

"Oh, sorry," Jonathan replied, relaxing his face to a smile and shrugging. "I was miles away and trying to think of too many things at once. Needless to say, I managed to think about none of them properly and I wish I hadn't tried."

"You should try to look on the bright side, Jonathan."

"I would if I could think of one, but what passes for my brain is just a bit overloaded at present. Tell me about the bright side before my willpower fades completely and I ask you for one of your cigarettes."

"The bright side is that on the assumption Mr Cotting is out there somewhere freezing his nuts off watching this place, we, or rather you, can draw the curtains and then we can stoke up the fire, have an intimate supper, drink ourselves silly and see how we feel…"

"On the face of it, that does sound quite attractive; I think I'll have a shower, while I am warming to the idea. But first, can I have one of your cigarettes?"

Chapter 24:

One Less to Worry About

David Cotting was having a bad day – in fact, a very bad day. He didn't dare use his position to try to find out how Frank's assailant was connected with the Evans man, but since she was, it obviously meant that he, Evans, had been lying all along. He could have been protecting her for purely selfish reasons, of course; every one of the witnesses had described what they had seen of her as being very attractive. However, the fact that nobody could give a full or, in some cases, even partial description of her face was at least unusual, if not downright suspicious. If he had any doubts on that score, they vanished completely at the news that, in all probability, the woman in question had booked accommodation at the village hotel and promptly disappeared, leaving a substantial deposit in cash, but nothing by which she could be traced. That in itself was unusual enough, but why had she bothered to rent a room at all if she knew Evans? Of course, he didn't actually care what she had done to Frank. The fool had had something like that coming to him for ages. However, having been obliged to investigate the attack, he had made himself vulnerable to scrutiny. Evans clearly knew more than he was saying and it was a great pity that Frank hadn't finished him off when he had the chance. The other man – Grey – was also a problem. He probably knew as much as Evans and worse still, he had managed somehow to avoid being arrested for Frank's murder. That, more than anything else, was really odd, unless of course he had a solid alibi. The investigating officers were unavailable and he wasn't about to risk being caught looking through the Crime Book. All he had managed to discover was that although Grey hadn't made any phone calls, his solicitor had appeared almost out of thin air and whisked him off to freedom. The only person who might be able to help was Bill Edwards, but he wasn't answering his phone. Cotting thought about leaving some form of coded message but decided, on balance, that there was too much risk. With all the works going on at the Hall, there was no telling who he might end up talking to. There was nothing for it – he would have to risk a visit. The trip to the village was uneventful enough and he saw no cars that he recognised. His knowledge of the back roads enabled him to avoid the high street and at about midday he found himself approaching the entrance to the Hall. Simply driving up to the door would not do, so he left his car hidden in woodland just a few hundreds of metres away. From there, he knew from previous nightly visits, that he could approach the staff wing without being seen. The roadway to the Hall bent round to the left in a tight semicircle, which was filled for the most part with young trees and ground cover. A reasonably well-trodden path had been made, forming a short-cut through the woods and this was the route that he took. As he got within a hundred metres or so of the building he started to hear the distant muffled sounds of contractors' equipment in use. After a few moments, he started to discern a few voices mixed with the mechanical sounds and he moved slowly closer. The trees were thinning out and he could begin to see the outline of the main roof with some of the ornate chimneys breaking up the line, and also the lighter colours of the contractors' huts between the woods and the Hall itself. He was able to inch a little closer without the risk of being seen and as he did so, he started to see movement. One of the voices seemed familiar – yes – it was Bill Edwards having some sort of argument with another short man, who seemed to be something to do with the ongoing work and was wearing one of those plastic safety hats that people leave on the rear window shelves of their cars for the sun to crack. Well at least he had found Bill without too much trouble; now all he had to do was attract his attention and get him away from the buildings. The argument was reaching a climax as the two men moved toward one of the site huts, but just as he was about to break cover so as to call Bill, Cotting caught sight of another man who was also eavesdropping. He had never seen this man before, but a sixth sense told him that something was wrong. The other man didn't look like a builder and was clearly intent on watching the argument. Bill and his adversary moved even closer to the site hut, shouting all the while and soon after the stranger moved off towards the Hall. Despite knowing where Bill was, it was beginning to seem unlikely that he would be able to gain his attention, so Cotting retraced his steps a little so that he could overlook the front of the Hall and the car park. If there were no visitors, he might be able to slip inside to see Bill while the workmen took their lunch break. No such luck. There was a fire brigade car and at least three other vehicles partly obscured by it, but he couldn't see their number plates without breaking cover. Cotting was beginning to think that all of this had been a dangerous waste of time and he sat down on a tree stump in the hope of having an inspired thought. None came, and after about thirty minutes, he started to weigh up the advantages of trying to see Bill now, as distinct from finding him later at home. Suddenly, the front doors of the Hall were opened and a group of people emerged. He could see the eavesdropper and the rich bitch Pollard – the two were obviously well acquainted. There was someone in fire service uniform, another woman whom he didn't recognise and another man, also unknown to him, who seemed to be chatting avidly with the man in uniform. The unknown woman left almost immediately, followed shortly after by Miss Pollard and the eavesdropper – who was he? The other two men showed no sign of getting into their cars and since there were still loads of workmen scurrying about, getting hold of Bill Edwards would just have to wait. If he were to run back through the woods he would be able to follow the Pollard woman and the eavesdropper and perhaps find out what they were up to. He knew that even if he ran, they would have a head start, but since the road serving the Hall was more or less straight once it got past the woods, he would be able to see which way they turned at the end. He guessed right and had joined the road in plenty of time to see his quarry take the right hand turn towards the city. The next seven hours were, on reflection, a complete waste of time and fuel. He patiently followed (had he but known it) Michael's car into the city, where its occupants got out and ate lunch while he sat in the car park opposite, listening to protesting noises from his stomach. His first inkling of the name of Miss Pollard's companion came when, following lunch, they drove immediately to the hospital. It was more or less confirmed when, following a tedious trip to Heathrow and back, he followed Jonathan almost as far as the Stables. Once he had satisfied himself that that was Jonathan's ultimate destination, he doubled back and almost collided with the car being driven by the police following him. He was too tired and too hungry to notice that the same car followed him home and that some while later another car containing two other policemen followed him almost as far as Bill Edwards's cottage.

"Evening, Bill," Cotting said, as he slid quietly into the gloom of Bill's parlour. "I'm sorry to have to trouble you in person, but I need your help. Is anyone else in?"

"No, we're quite alone. The missus is at a church meeting and Betty's gone up to one of the pubs with 'er mates. Do you want a drink or are you on duty?"

Bill already knew the answer and poured two large tumblers of single malt from an expensive-looking decanter which he then carefully returned to its hiding place. He didn't much like Cotting, any more than he had liked Frank, but he found him more reliable and knew that it would have to be something serious to bring him out in person. Anyway, with Frank gone he would probably be seeing more of Cotting and they would also have to divvy up Frank's share of the takings, so perhaps a personal visit was not so surprising after all. With thoughts such as these at the front of his greedy little mind, Bill could afford to be generous with the whisky – especially since both it and the decanter should, by rights, have been at the Hall. Cotting had to tread a little carefully to avoid implicating himself in Frank's death so he decided not to come to the point if it was at all possible, not unless it was absolutely impossible to obtain information otherwise.

"So how's it going, Bill? Is there very much more stuff to be shifted or are we nearly there?"

This was not at all the question that Bill had been expecting, not least because if that was all Cotting wanted to know, he could easily have phoned. There must be something else, otherwise he wouldn't have come in person.

"There are only about two – maybe three more rooms to go then we'll be just about done. One more load only."

"Right," Cotting went on, trying to ignore his mistake. "It's just that with Frank gone, I wondered if you needed any help getting rid of the car." That certainly wasn't the sort of question that Bill wanted to hear. He had just got used to the idea of having at least half of Frank's share of the takings when this bloke Cotting, who never seemed to take any risks until it was nearly all done, came muscling in. No, he didn't like this conversation at all – he'd have to start a different one.

"No! I'll manage just fine thank you. I'm sure you've got quite enough to do finding Frank's murderer. How are you getting on with that anyway?"

This was just great. Bill's insatiable greed had made him change the subject to the one that Cotting really wanted. He took a large gulp of whisky, frowned convincingly and ploughed on while at the same time gesturing for a refill.

"Well, not very well since you ask. C.I.D. pulled in Dr Evans's friend, what's his name?"

"Grey?"

"Yes that's right – Grey. Anyway my money's on that woman who did for Frank here in the village. The problem is finding her. No-one seems to have seen her since the event, so either she's in hiding or she has left the area completely."

Bill nodded in agreement as he refilled Cotting's tumbler. He knew of course that Frank had discovered the woman at the Stables just a few hours before he died, so Cotting could well be right. His problem was of course that if he told Cotting that, it would be like admitting that apart from the murderer himself - or herself, he was probably the last person to see Frank alive. If he was questioned, he might then have to explain why, in the middle of a rain storm, Frank would have shared this news with him rather than the police. He thought very carefully before he lied.

"Christ! I've just thought of something," he gasped, slapping his forehead as convincingly as possible. "I saw

Frank the day after he came out of hospital and he said that one of his mates had seen the woman down by the Stables."

"Really?" Cotting enquired. "I'm sure that that can be looked into by some of my colleagues – thank you very much, Bill."

He almost admired Bill for conjuring up such a plausible lie in such a short space of time. Obviously Frank had contacted Bill, or even gone to see him before, or shortly before their meeting on the bridge. Bill was obviously becoming too clever for safety – for his own safety, that was.

"Look, Bill," he went on, "we are going to have to meet at some time to sort out how to split Frank's share, so why don't we divvy up here after the last load? Just ring me at home when it's all ready."

"Oh, OK then. Right. Good. That's done then." Bill said, with some relief. "I'll just make sure there's no-one about. OK, I'll be in touch then."

Cotting left the gloom of Bill's parlour and retraced his steps to his car, smiling as he went. He drove off slowly with all the lights off for the first few miles, with a germ of a plan forming in his mind. Evans and Grey probably knew more than was good for them and, once it was all done, Edwards would have outlived his usefulness. He would have to be careful about the Stables since he knew from his previous visit that there was an alarm. There would be no such problem at the hospital, there was certainly no alarm there. It was just after nine when, after a brief meal and a few more drinks for courage, David Cotting set off to commit his first premeditated murder. Frank's death had been a spur of the moment thing – nobody was going to miss a no-hoper like Frank anyway. He was just another of life's congenital blind alleys and the world was probably better off without him. This, however, was quite different. Dr Evans, and for that matter, Dr Grey, had to die because they probably knew too much. He recognised the same strange thrill that he once experienced when, as a young detective, he had taken his first case to court and had secured a conviction. He became aware of a red light and stopped as if by instinct. It was not a traffic light but some form of advertising sign in a shop window. Summoning up what was left of his composure, he pulled into a side street to light a cigarette. Both of his hands were shaking badly and he wondered if he was really up for this. Three cigarettes later he was and, with renewed conviction, he started the car once more and headed for the hospital.

"Good Evening," he said to the receptionist, without even a trace of emotion. "I'm sorry if I'm a bit late for visiting, but I've had a long way to drive. Is it possible that I can see Mr Ewan?"

"Is there a first name, sir?"

"What? Oh yes, it's Lloyd – I was told that he was involved in an accident at work."

The receptionist touched a few keys and then frowned.

"I'm very sorry, sir, but we don't appear to have anyone of that name here. Do you know if his injuries were particularly serious? It's just that if they weren't, he may have been discharged, in which case his name might not be on my list."

"Well, from what I had heard, he was in a pretty bad way. Are you sure there hasn't been some mistake?"

"No! I'm sure that there is no mistake. Here – look for yourself, there's no 'Ewan' on this list."

She dutifully spun the screen toward him so that he could more easily see both Dr Evans's name and room number on the alphabetical list.

"Right," he said. "I've obviously made some sort of mistake. I'm sorry to have troubled you, miss."

"It's no trouble at all sir. I just hope that you manage to find your friend and that he is alright. Good night, sir."

"Yes. Thank you very much, miss, you've been most helpful."

Cotting went off in search of an alternative entrance to the wards, leaving the receptionist dealing with a phone call. He didn't have to look far and a few minutes later, he had hidden himself in the day room of Michael's side ward. It was in total darkness and in the reflection of the windows, he could see the last of the visitors straggling in and off to their homes. He reckoned that it would take the nurses about half an hour to troop around with the last of the day's medication prior to handing over to the night staff and he was only five minutes out in his estimation. At just after ten o'clock, he crept out of the day room into the now dimly lit corridor and, checking the names on the doors as he went, he worked his way quietly along past the side wards towards the nursing base. He could hear the subdued chatter of female voices somewhere just out of sight about twenty metres up the corridor, but he didn't have to advance further. The door on his left had a handwritten name wedged in a plastic receptacle fixed just below the small viewing window. The name read 'Dr. M. Evans'. Checking once more that he was unobserved, he left himself in and noiselessly shut the door after. The room was typical of small side wards and looked for all the world like a single hotel room with en-suite bathroom. The only way to spot the difference was that there was some form of waterproof covering on the floor in lieu of carpet, the bed was considerably higher than would be found in a hotel, and the services above the bed included oxygen and an emergency cord. Cotting hesitated briefly by the door to the bathroom to make sure that there was no sound or movement from the bed. There wasn't and he crept further into the room. His hands were shaking again but he couldn't risk a cigarette. Now was his only chance and, nerves or not, he had to take it. The room was even more dimly lit than the corridor outside. The curtains were drawn almost closed and a small, red light illuminated the service outlets above the bed head. The adjustable back support was fully down and only the nose and closed eyes of the occupant were visible above the bedclothes. Everything above the eyebrows and beneath the nose was neatly swathed in bandages. Cotting relaxed a little and checked quickly that there were no wires or monitors attached, before lifting a spare pillow from the chair next to the bed. He held it briefly in one hand while with the other he pulled the light bedclothes away and down to expose fully what little he could see of Michael's face. That done and with growing confidence, he gently but very firmly placed the pillow over the face and pressed down hard for a full five minutes. There was no struggle. A brief check of the nearest limp wrist confirmed no pulse. He replaced the pillow on the chair and, after replacing the bedclothes as he had first seen them and pressing an ear to the door to ensure that there were no footsteps or voices to be heard outside, he left the room just as noiselessly as he had entered. Five minutes later, he was in his car lighting a well-earned cigarette. "One down, two to go," he thought out loud as he started the engine and headed home for, so he reckoned, an equally well-deserved drink.

Chapter 25:

Mistaken Identity

Jonathan had slept very heavily, as was usually the case on the few occasions when he had had thoroughly too much to drink. He woke late and, suspecting that Tess would be in an even worst state than himself, he didn't even look at her side of the bed. He simply took the precaution of going to the kitchen to put on a pot of coffee before going for a swim. He fully expected the kitchen would resemble the same war zone that it had resembled the night before, but it didn't. Everything appeared to be clean and/or put away and, stranger still, the coffee maker was steaming gently away in its appointed place. However, much stranger than all of this, Tess was ploughing up and down the pool as if the world was about to come to an end. He helped himself to a small glass of cold orange juice before going out to the garden.

"May I join you or is this a private session?" he enquired, as she headed towards the end at which he stood shivering.

"By all means, do," she answered, turning. "It's your pool, after all and, as you know, it's warmer in than out."

"I didn't know you indulged in …" Jonathan couldn't think of a nice way of saying what he meant without giving offence.

"Exercising in the mornings?" she offered, laughing and then swallowing water.

"Well, yes, I suppose so," he agreed, enjoying her honesty. "It just seemed, well -"

"A little out of character?" she finished. "Why don't you get in and swim? It will be just as easy for me to finish your questions with both of us swimming and you won't have to walk up and down the side of the pool looking embarrassed and cold – unless, of course, you don't think you can keep up with me."

The challenge was irresistible as of course Tess knew it would be and Jonathan slipped off his robe and dived in. As it turned out, he was hard put to keep up with her speed and complete acceptance of the fact was avoided only be the arrival of the newspaper van. Tess climbed out of the pool to collect the papers, leaving Jonathan to finish his lengths at his own pace. They both showered and met about twenty minutes later in the kitchen. Tess had arrived a short while before Jonathan and her face was now haggard. The brandy decanter had joined the coffee pot and Tess's hand was shaking as she leant over to pick it up.

"Jonathan," she began, "I'm afraid that there is some very bad news. Look!" She passed him the newspaper, which was open on the fourth page. There was a small picture of Michael above a headline, which read:

COLLEGE LECTURER DIES IN HOSPITAL MYSTERY

"Surely there must be some terrible mistake?" Jonathan protested, as he topped up his own mug of coffee with brandy. "I mean, he was getting better, wasn't he?"

The room fell silent as Tess tried to light a cigarette without dropping it. Jonathan read the story in a mumble as tears began to fill his eyes. He nodded as Tess offered to light one for him. There was no mistaking who it was.

College lecturer Michael Evans, 33, was found dead in his hospital bed in Cambridge at eleven o'clock last night, shortly after nursing staff had changed shifts. Hospital staff representative Miss Hemsworthy expressed shock and surprise saying that Dr Evans was making what was thought to be a full recovery from head injuries and was due to have been discharged today or possibly on Saturday.

Jonathan wept openly and Tess leant over the table to hold his shaking hand. It was some twenty minutes or so before he could recover sufficiently to carry on reading.

Dr Evans was an orphan as a child and was brought up by an aunt, Miss Emily Pollard, 46. She was staying in a London hotel last night and apparently was due to leave for Italy this morning. Perhaps understandably, Miss Pollard was too upset to comment. A police spokesman said that they would know more once a post mortem has been conducted, but in the meanwhile, they are not treating the death as suspicious.

"Is there anything I can do, Jonathan?" Tess asked, with genuine concern. "If there's any way I can help, just say."

Jonathan remained silent and was shaking violently as if with some internal rage. He drank carelessly from his mug and sat with his eyes fixed on Mike's photograph. At length he stirred and looked up at Tess.

"This could have been prevented, if only I had thought."

"How do you mean?"

"I knew yesterday that there was something not being done, but I just couldn't think what it was. It's bloody obvious now of course – now that it's too late! While we were drinking ourselves silly and shagging each other senseless last night and being thoroughly smug about how we were going to get Cotting on tape while he was snooping about outside, we, or to put a finer point on it, your precious boss and the police, left Michael totally unprotected at the hospital. Damn!"

"I don't think that's altogether fair, Jonathan. Peter did say that the police were following Cotting, didn't he? – if it was Cotting that did it, of course."

"I know that," Jonathan snapped back, "but if they were, they did a fucking lousy job of it."

"Yes. I agree," Tess conceded. "I suppose we had better make some sort of plan. The chances are that Peter may not even know yet – I'd better see if he's sent us anything by email." Jonathan downed the rest of his mug of augmented coffee and shrugged before he refilled it and Tess's. He felt and probably looked a wreck.

"Hey, look, I'm sorry I shouted at you just now. I know it's not your fault. It's just that I'm angry at being helpless and I've just lost the best friend I've ever had."

"Don't apologise," she smiled, "I would probably have done the same, or worse, if I were in your position. Aren't you drinking a lot of brandy if you are going to drive?"

"I'm drinking a lot of brandy," he said, topping up his mug to the brim, "because I'm the poor sod who has to phone Jenny! At least I don't have to break it to Emily!"

"That's right. I'm not thinking straight, am I? If she knows, then Peter will most certainly know by now. I wonder that he hasn't rung. I'll just go and check."

"OK. I'll ring Jenny."

Jonathan reached for the phone and prepared himself for what he had to say. He then remembered that he had switched it off overnight. It was still quite early, so he tried Jenny at home first. The voice was hers, but it was a message machine. He put the handset down with some relief, because if she was at work, at least there would be a shoulder to cry on – someone to comfort her. He had found Jenny's office number and was just about to speak to the receptionist when Tess ran back in clutching a piece of paper. She appeared elated and launched herself at him in an attempt to prevent him saying any more. Her mouth flapped open and closed with words failing to make it out. With one hand she managed to free the phone from Jonathan's grip and with the other, she pulled him hard by the neck so that he fully faced her and then kissed him with a violence that took his breath away. He kept his eyes open, partly because he didn't know what might happen next, and partly in an effort to read what was on the email printout. Regaining his senses, he peeled Tess away from him and she sat down, trembling. Her mouth had stopped flapping long enough to say:

"Look. Look! He's OK!"

Jonathan eased the now screwed up single sheet from her shaking hand, unfolded it carefully and read it almost twice before falling into a dead faint on Tess's welcoming lap. He had got as far as the phone number that he or Tess was supposed to ring, and having eased him reluctantly to the floor, she dialled it. He woke again just a few minutes later to find himself in the recovery position and with Tess sitting quietly beside him. She was no longer shaking. In one hand there was the inevitable cigarette, while in the other was the phone.

"He's awake now – would you like to talk to him?"

The answer appeared to be 'yes' and she passed the phone to Jonathan as he clambered, embarrassed to another chair. Tess lit him a cigarette as, with obvious trepidation, he moved the handset closer to his face. He swallowed hard and took a long drag on the cigarette that Tess placed in his other hand. He was shaking again, but this time with anticipation rather than grief. He didn't really know what to say and was about to try something non-controversial like "Hello", when Mike said, "Hi Jon. I hear Tess hasn't wasted much time getting you on the floor. I hope you are not enjoying yourself too much in my absence. I wouldn't want the Stables to acquire that sort of reputation without my input!"

Jonathan's jaw dropped and he quickly passed the phone back to Tess, so that he could run and throw up somewhere in private. He returned a few moments later looking only slightly green at the edges and gestured to Tess to pass the phone back to him.

"Sorry about that, Mike. I'm not used to having my emotions jerked around like this and I know I'm going to regret asking this, but aren't you – well, how can I best put it – dead?"

"Yes, you're right Jon – about regretting it, that is. But I'm still alive, if not yet kicking. Look – Peter needs the pair of you in London this morning. Can you get out of your lecture?"

"Yes, I guess so. Why?"

"He'll explain when you come. I'll need some clothes. Can you manage that – oh and my passport?"

"Yes, but why?"

"Because I haven't got the front to fly to Italy in a hospital dressing gown and by boxer shorts. Okay?"

"Yes, okay. Look I haven't managed to get hold of Jenny yet."

"That's because she's here with me, Emily and Peter. Let me put you onto Peter. He thinks he owes you an apology."

"Morning, Jonathan. Are you okay yet?"

"Apart from yet another hangover – yes."

"Look, I really am sorry. I had hoped that you would read my email before you saw the papers. I didn't want to wake you in the middle of the night and the phone was off this morning – besides if you were silly enough to get into a drinking contest - and bed - with Tess, there probably wouldn't have been much point. Can you be ready to leave in thirty minutes? Tess reckons that neither of you is liable to be in a fit state to drive so an unmarked police car will collect you then. There will be two people in the car; they know nothing about Mike's unexpected health and must be told nothing. If they still haven't arrived within forty minutes, it'll be because they've spotted Cotting nearby too close to you and then we'll use Plan B."

"And what might that be?"

"I'll let you know when I've thought of one! Bye."

Tess made some more coffee which this time, by agreement, was not augmented with brandy and quickly cooked something just sufficiently greasy to weigh down what they had already drunk. Jonathan went round to Mike's room to pack a bag and returned in time for them both to eat without rushing before their car arrived. Jonathan switched everything off and set the alarm as he left himself out. They could hear the engine of the police car ticking over as they walked over to the gates, but before they reached them, Tess took a quick step forward so as to block Jonathan's path.

"Jonathan?" she asked, with some reluctance.

"Yes, Tess?"

"In case I don't get another chance before you see Cathy again, can I ask a very small favour of you?"

"Of course! Ask away. After today, I'm not likely to be surprised by anything."

"Thanks. It's to do with what happened earlier – you know – us last night. I would really prefer it if you didn't mention it to Cathy." She flushed, just a little, as she spoke and Jonathan pretended not to notice.

"Why, is it a breach of professional conduct?" he helped.

"Yes," she agreed, willingly, "just a bit."

"No problem – let me get the gate for you."

The question of not talking to their escorts didn't arise for the first few miles. They were uncommunicative and appeared to have been up half the night, as indeed they had. Only as the college came into view did the driver break the silence.

"You might as well know now that the car we narrowly missed hitting a few miles back was Cotting's. I hope your building is well protected."

"Well enough, I think," Tess replied. "Will anyone else be watching him while you're with us?"

"Oh yes – you can be assured of that," the other man replied.

Jonathan wasn't paying any attention to the conversation: his mind was elsewhere. As they approached the college he felt a moment of guilt about landing someone else with one of his lectures and as he looked at

the main gate, he recognised the unmistakable rear view of
his ex-wife going in.

"I wonder what she's doing, going in there?" he
muttered, to the little voice at the back of his head.

"Probably checking to see if there's anyone she
overlooked last time," came the reply.

Jonathan agreed with his alter ego, but not for the first
time, they were both wrong. Sara was there for business,
not pleasure and she was oblivious to anyone passing by
outside the college. She was far more intent upon seeing if
there was anyone in the car park who might recognise her.
She had left it until the very last moment to put the
ridiculous hat on, but perhaps better than anyone else she
knew that her figure could give her away. She had rightly
been proud of her body for many years and had devoted
many painful hours at her health club (at Jonathan's
expense) to keeping it just as she wanted it. Her view of the
more distant third of the car park was partially obscured by
some building work and after a moment's hesitation, she
walked quickly to the administration building checking to
make sure that Jonathan's car was not there – he was the
last person she wanted to bump into unless, of course, she
happened to be driving a bus. She had been less than
impressed by the most recent letter from her solicitors,
especially since their reaction to the terse missive from
Jonathan's new London lawyers appeared to be based on a
mixture of caution tinged with awe and outright fear. She
knew that she needed some new initiative, but didn't quite
know how to find and seize it. She had thought about yet
another abusive telephone call to Jonathan, but decided to

hold off, just in case he recorded it. No – she had to find something new and she had to do it herself – her solicitors were clearly too gutless. Still completely devoid of a plan, she opened the door to the administration building and headed for the staff photograph board in the hope of finding some inspiration there. Her eyes drifted over the serried ranks of mug shots and came eventually to an abrupt halt at Michael's crumpled face. They obviously hadn't got around to taking it down yet and despite how rude he had been to her the last time they spoke, she experienced the briefest moment of humanity. Jonathan's photo was also there, of course – his face a little younger than she remembered and there was a little more hair. More out of curiosity than any real plan, she started to look for other familiar names and in particular, that of Lisa Adams. She could, of course, have been a student, or maybe she had left, but it was a disappointment nonetheless. In desperation she risked a glance at the receptionist's desk and was comforted by the knowledge that she didn't recognise the occupant.

"Excuse me, miss?"

"Yes, how may I help you?" came the polite reply.

"Well, I don't really know if you can. I was looking for an acquaintance who I thought worked here, but I don't seem to be able to find her photograph on the board over there." She waved a hand airily in the direction that she had just left.

"If you could give me the name, I'll see if it's on our list. Is it staff or student?" the receptionist asked with a neatly manicured finger poised over the keyboard.

"Well I thought it was staff, but would it be any trouble for you to check the student list also?"

"I probably better had. It's only my first week here and I'm still trying to learn as many names as possible. Surname first, please," she said, trying to bring the appropriate database on screen.

"Adams – and the first name is Lisa."

There was a brief pause as the name came up on screen, was entered and quickly followed by the question 'spelling'.

"Try a zed," Sara almost snapped.

The same thing happened and the receptionist closed the file.

"Well I can't think of any other variations so I guess there has been some sort of misunderstanding," she said.

She was spared being informed in no uncertain terms that Sara didn't misunderstand anything by the entrance of one of the staff, who smiled at her and automatically handed over his car keys, which were exchanged for a small pile of mail from one of a bank of wooden letter holes. Sara scanned them at a glance, noticing that Jonathan's was still full of mail, thanked the receptionist with a forced smile and walked out. The reason for the passing of the keys was easy enough to see once she got outside to the car park. The construction vehicles and the building work itself were taking up so much room that the orderly rows of parking spaces had been abandoned in favour of what looked like an organised traffic jam three, and in some places, four cars deep. Her recently acquired disappointment at not finding Ms Adams evaporated in favour of a much better idea. She would wait until Jonathan was at college, turn up when Miss Pretty Fingers went to lunch and repossess her car. A brilliant plan!

Chapter 26: Yes, but No

The first part of the journey to London was fast and, thanks to the intervention of breakfast, surprisingly uneventful so far as Jonathan's gut was concerned. The two men up front remained wrapped in their own thoughts and Tess read through the case file, such as it was, to pass the time. Jonathan read Peter's email once more, to find out where they were destined and then, as the inevitable headache appeared, he sat back to endure the rest of his hangover. As they approached the outskirts of the city, traffic became heavier and the driver opened his window to put a blue light on the roof and switched on a deafening siren. After a few minutes, all the novelty and excitement wore off for Jonathan and was replaced by an entirely justified bout of nausea to accompany his headache. He was about to ask if they could manage without the sirens when they turned off automatically as a radio message came in.

"Golf Delta to Golf one # eight – are you receiving? Over."

The front passenger picked up the microphone and replied, "Golf one # eight receiving – go ahead – over."

"Golf # Delta to Golf one # eight. The target has now left the Stables and is now en route for his home. He has reconnoitred briefly, but made no attempt, repeat no attempt at entry."

"Golf one # eight to Golf # Delta – message received and understood. Do we now have full surveillance? Over."

"Golf # Delta to Golf one # eight. Affirmative, repeat, affirmative."

"Golf one # eight to Golf # Delta. Message received, thank you, over and out."

He replaced the microphone and switched off the siren before it could make Jonathan's headache any worse.

"Well, that was convenient," observed Tess, from behind a pile of papers. "I bet you were wondering when you would get the chance to bug his phone!"

"And his car," came the reply.

"I've already done that and I thought I saw yours there," she quipped.

"That's bloody odd – we've not had the chance yet. Are you sure?"

"Standard police equipment."

"That's illegal, isn't it?" the driver protested.

"So, arrest me!"

"Are you ex-job?" the driver asked.

"Yes."

"I thought so. The video doesn't do you justice though. I nearly didn't recognise you with your clothes on! That said, however, the boss ain't gonna like the fact that you found another bug on his suspect's car."

Tess suppressed a blush long enough to slide further down into her seat and grinned stupidly at Jonathan, who was failing badly to hide his amusement.

"There's always one!" she whispered.

"Two, actually," the driver's mate added, laughing. "It was me who set up the camera. It's nice to see you again."

Tess was steeling herself in readiness to give them both a severe tongue-lashing when her portable phone warbled. It was Peter.

"Are you far off?" he enquired.

"About ten minutes I would guess. Why?"

"No panic – it's just that Emily asked me to check so that she could organise some breakfast for those who want it. We are in suite two three eight."

"Right. See you in a bit then."

They were dropped off outside the hotel without any further embarrassing conversations, slightly less than ten minutes later and quickly made their way to Emily's suite. She, Peter, Jenny and Mike had been joined by another, somewhat older man and Peter took it upon himself to do the introductions.

"Tess and Jonathan, I'd like you both to meet Detective Chief Superintendent James Leonard from Scotland Yard.

Mr Leonard, I'd like you to meet Tess Williams from my office and this is Dr Jonathan Grey."

They all shook hands and agreed to dispense with formalities as Peter poured coffee and continued, "Emily, Jenny and Michael have, at best, two hours before they have to leave for the airport so we had better begin. I wonder Emily if you would mind chairing this so as to keep us all focussed on time? Tess, would you mind taping it all? I think I have enough battery to last that long."

The two women agreed and Jim Leonard was invited to speak first. He had quite a large file, but spoke mostly from memory.

"I work in the internal investigations department of the police here in London, but a few years back I was based out on division and for a while, was a superintendent at the same station as David Cotting. I know, or at least knew him well and it was partly as the result of his fall from grace that I was moved to my present post. We have continued to watch him for several years now, together with some of his known associates who remained here in London. Approximately three months ago, we got word that a particular 'fence' whom we had been watching had been receiving regular – as in once a week – deliveries of stolen paintings. We kept a lid on it for a while, as it was a relatively easy job to have them marked so as to keep track of them, and the port authorities were all given details."

"How did you manage all that?" Jonathan asked, innocently.

"They have a mole, Jonathan!" Tess replied.

"Do I know you from somewhere?" Jim asked Tess. "Well anyway, we got word about it from some colleagues in the Arts Squad and by coincidence, one of my men was due to be attached to them for a few days to see if he wanted to transfer. In the event, he wasn't bothered, but he did come back with a copy of a surveillance video. The quality wasn't good and it was mostly in infra-red but there he was – Cotting! We were about to arrest the whole gang when Peter phoned me last week about your business. I managed to persuade my boss to let it run a while longer, but since the death of that man in hospital, I'm afraid the pressure is back on and we'll have to act soon."

"Yes, who was he anyway?" Emily asked.

"I can deal with that," Mike chipped in. "His name was Jeff Mates and he had been transferred from another ward following surgery. He had been quite badly injured in a motorcycle accident about a week ago. Whey they operated to mend his head, they found a massive inoperable tumour, so they just patched him up and continued to look after him while they tried to find next of kin and left him to die with some dignity. They weren't getting anywhere and were still wondering what to do when, yesterday, there was an influx of new patients and not enough beds to go round in ICU. This was a few hours after you and Jonathan left, Emily. I was asked if I would mind being discharged a day early – which, of course, I didn't, and he was shipped into my bed to make more room in the main ward. I don't know how the administration cocked it up, but my name stayed on the door and on the computer listing until Mates's body was found."

"I'd better deal with the next bit, Mike," Jim cut in, "since you are probably not up to date. The night duty staff on the ward were supposed to change your name on the door and the computer listing was supposed to be updated the next day. We interviewed the night receptionist at her home as she has identified Cotting from his photograph. Obviously, my men followed Cotting to the hospital, but they didn't follow him in. Needless to say, the hospital authorities are acutely embarrassed by the whole thing and it is mostly for that reason that they have agreed to go along with our little charade. The coroner took a lot more persuading, especially about misinforming the media! You can carry on again if you like, Michael."

"Thanks. I telephoned Jenny and asked her to collect me and while I waited, I left a message at Peter's office. I was going to ask Jenny to run me back to the Stables for some clothes, but she had her own plan and we went instead to her flat, intending to go back to the Stables today."

"My turn now, I think," Peter said, as he passed round copies of some typed notes. "I found Mike's note and contacted Jim, which is why the people in the car tailing Cotting didn't bother to follow him into the hospital. They, at least, knew that Michael wasn't there! I'll get to these notes in a minute so don't bother to read them in any detail yet. They are an account of my meeting with the fireman yesterday. You should get someone to take a statement from him sometime Jim, he has a lot of information. So as to remain chronological, I should perhaps tell you what happened earlier. Emily decided to stay over last night because she thought that she had been followed to the airport – which, of course, she had."

Jonathan thought about announcing that he hadn't known that, but thought better of it, after some timely advice from the usual place.

"What neither of you knew was that he – Cotting – had started following you shortly after you left the Hall. I picked him up as Mr Duncan and I left shortly after you. I didn't bother to tail him then, as I knew he was following your car and I could find that remotely. Besides, I would have missed out on picking Mr Duncan's brain. After we parted, you two had just left the hospital and had Cotting in tow. I was heading back to London anyway and followed along until I realised that, as I now know, Jim's men were also there."

The little voice at the back of Jonathan's brain coughed politely before saying, 'I told you so'.

"Right, then," Peter continued. "Back to the present. According to Mr Duncan's records, in the last three months there have been seventeen incidents of cars being stolen and burned out on the outskirts of Cambridge. Both of those figures are well above the national average and are considerably above the previous local figures for the same period in the past five years. There are, I believe, a number of significant features associated with most of the 'real' fires, but the list that I have compiled is not necessarily in order of importance – apart maybe from the first – which is that so far, they have stopped since Frank died. The rest are as follows. They occurred at night. They were all at the same distance from the fire station, give or take a few hundred metres. In many cases there were false alarms, causing firemen to go in the opposite direction.

"In those cases where we have been able to examine the remains, we have found traces of 'red' diesel, which presumably was used to help the fire start – that's including yours, Jonathan."

"Is 'red diesel' the fuel used in tractors and off-road vehicles, Peter?" Michael asked.

"Yes, Michael and before you say it, there is a supply of it at the Hall – primarily for Frank's use, but of course it can also be found on most farms and building sites. The bad news, Emily, is that the distance I mentioned earlier is the same as that from the fire station to the Hall."

"I was afraid you were about to say that," she replied.

"There's another one for your list," Jonathan said, looking up from his pile of papers. "Each of Cotting's rest days occurred the day after each fire with a false alarm to another location."

The room fell suddenly quiet as the implication of the last item sank in. Peter, Jim and Tess looked at Jonathan with open admiration, but Mike and Emily took it in their stride, neither of them being particularly surprised. The silence was broken by Emily, who carefully drained her cup of coffee before speaking.

"We don't have much time," she said, thoughtfully, as she looked to see who else was in need of a refill. "I mean – assuming that it is my paintings that are ending up in London – the last rooms to be refurbished will be started at the end of next week at the latest. Do you have any idea how it is being done, Peter? You seem to have figured almost everything else out."

"I have an idea but, as yet, not much proof," he replied. "My guess is that Edwards would have ample opportunity to measure frames and even take photographs, but I don't know for sure that it would have been him. He could quite legitimately remove the paintings to storage pending refurbishment and then replace them with fakes once the work was completed. He, or perhaps Frank, could take them to Cotting's the night before a rest day and even use a stolen car to do it."

"That would certainly explain choosing hatchbacks," Tess said, sipping her coffee.

"I don't think that would have been the real reason," Jonathan said. "A hatchback is more convenient to carry a push bike for cycling home on afterwards. It would be a bit of a dead giveaway having a taxi pick you up next to a burning car twice a week."

"I think I preferred you when you had a hangover!" Tess said.

"I think we can safely assume it was Edwards," Jim broke, in quietly. "I should have told you earlier but I forgot – sorry. Before Cotting set off for the hospital to murder Michael, he went to visit Bill Edwards. My guess is that he was risking a meeting with him at the Hall earlier, but changed his mind and decided to follow Jonathan and Emily instead."

Several people started talking at once and Emily had to remind them of the time. When quiet returned, she asked if anyone cared to sum up. Peter offered – initially, at least.

"If I read this correctly, Cotting, Edwards and, before his death, Frank, have been systematically replacing Emily's paintings with fakes with the ultimate intention of burning the Hall down to destroy the evidence. The trial runs with cars and false alarms, I think, speak for themselves. Leaving aside for one moment the unfortunate encounter between Frank and Cathy, Cotting for some reason or other decided to dispose of Frank and try to blame it on Jonathan. The fact – if it is one – that he wanted to get shot of Frank is perhaps understandable, since it would mean a greater share of the spoils for himself and he could get rid of someone whom, I believe, was a blackmailer and whom, by any standard, would be a continuing liability. Cotting's interest in the Stables, Jonathan and Michael is more worrying, not least because I don't understand it. We have to accept that in at least one respect, he is one jump ahead of us and that therein lies danger. Michael is now dead so far as the media are concerned and the sooner he and Jenny are on the plane with Emily, the happier I will be. Jonathan here is another problem and, in a sense, I am relieved that Jim is about to take things out of my hands."

"That was a very good summary indeed, Peter. Thank you." Jim was standing now and looking alarmingly official. But as if he was undergoing some internal turmoil, he let his shoulders sag and he sat down again with a wry, resigned smile. "When I asked for this meeting, I did so with the intention of telling you that things had gone quite far enough and that I could no longer condone your interference in police business – no matter how professional or well-meant it was – and that is still the case. What's more, I now understand that there was already a bug on Cotting's car and I'm urgently trying to find out whose it is. The one thing I really hate is to be kept in the dark. Look, it's like this: I've only got two years to go before I retire and have my obligatory heart attack and I want Cotting's scalp before I go. Like Peter, I am immensely relieved that Michael is now out of the equation, but that leaves you Jonathan and I'm afraid we'll now have to replace you with a look-alike."

There was another silence as all eyes focussed on Jonathan. He was oblivious to it all – even the little voice at the back of his head didn't dare say anything he didn't want to hear. His only thought was about what Cotting had intended to do at the hospital and how much he loved Mike. Tears started to well in his eyes but he held them back with some effort. He felt Tess squeeze his hand and saw her look at him with complete understanding.

"I don't suppose there is any chance at all that I could have five minutes alone with Cotting, is there?" he asked no-one in particular. "No. I thought not," he said, deep in conversation with himself.

"Right, this is the plan," Jim said. "Tess and Cathy go to the Hall tonight?"

"That's correct," answered Peter.

"Good. I assume you will be at the Stables with Jonathan as often as you can?"

"All this week, if necessary," Peter replied, again.

"Fine. I will place an armed officer there at all times while we find an officer who looks like Jonathan. When do you have to go to College this week, Jonathan?"

"I don't have to go at all – it's vac time."

"Can you find an excuse to go in on Thursday?"

"I can find an excuse to go in any day – why?"

"Because we should have a replacement for you by then. It's the only day this week that Cotting is off duty and since he is on nights the rest of the time, it's my guess that he'll be watching the Stables every morning to see if you leave. Putting it bluntly, I want to encourage him to have a snoop around on his day off to get a bit of daylight footage. It's so much more juror-friendly than infra-red."

Jonathan nodded in understanding as Tess, who seemed to have moved a little closer, squeezed his hand again. He was still in conversation with himself.

"Well, unless anyone has got anything else to suggest, I think we're about done," Emily said, urging her papers together. "Michael, Jenny and I should be heading off for the airport in a few minutes and I also have to check out. If anyone wants to stay for lunch Peter can pay and put it on expenses. I'm afraid I really will have to leave you nominally in charge of the Hall this time, Jonathan, but I don't think you'll be bothered much. I've asked my architect to be there all week, with strict instructions not to contact you unless absolutely necessary. I've also sent a similar message to Edwards, explaining that you will be far too busy making funeral arrangements for Michael to be bothered with the Hall. I'll be back Tuesday week, whatever happens, and I expect that you'll have your work cut out between now and then, replying to sympathy cards."

"I should perhaps add something on that point," Mr Leonard intervened. "The local coroner was happy to assist to a degree, but no further. Consequently, I have arranged for Mike's coffin to be brought here to London to some special people that we have to use from time to time. I'll give you the details, Jonathan, in case we need more time and actually have to go through with a formal service. Also, on a personal note, I'd like to say how well you are taking this, Miss Pollard. I trust that you had the paintings insured?"

"Indeed I did," Emily replied, "but not for very much. They were copies – very good ones mind – the originals are in the villa in Italy. My late sister had the copies made when the originals were restored years ago – well before Edwards was taken on."

Peter smiled to himself but said nothing. No point in gloating.

"I didn't know that," Michael protested.

"Well, until today, Michael, very few people did – and obviously that doesn't include Bill Edwards. Anything else, Jim?"

335

"No – other than that, I really am done, unless you would like me to have you three driven to the airport, in which case I should make the arrangements."

"There is one more point," Jonathan broke in. "There will be no need to find a look-alike. I'll do it."

"I thought I had made myself clear on that point," Jim replied.

"You did," Jonathan continued, barely containing his mounting anger, "but I think you've actually missed the point completely. There is probably no doubt that Mr Mates would have died fairly soon, but that does not excuse the fact that there was no surveillance at the hospital. It doesn't matter that we, or some of us, knew that Michael was safely away. The fact is that there was a murder and because of someone's fuck-up, excuse my language, Emily, Mates was not allowed to die with dignity."

Jim made to interrupt, but Jonathan stopped him with the gesture of one hand. Peter and Emily looked at each other in silence and admiration.

"I very nearly lost my best friend last night and thanks to someone's incompetence – I'm not saying it was yours, Jim – someone else died in Mike's place. The press would jump at any chance of criticising the police and if I'm not allowed to follow this through, I'm going straight to them with all of this as soon as I leave here. Right, now I've made myself clear."

"You can't. You wouldn't," Jim objected.

"I can and I certainly will," Jonathan replied, with conviction.

Emily excused herself to check out, leaving the others to resolve the impasse. Her betting was that Jim would have to have to concede and such was her good judgement, he had done so by the time she returned. In fact, according to Peter, to whom she spoke later, Jim had little other choice and took it on the chin without rancour. Jonathan and Jim shook hands, as men do, and Jim added, "Any last questions?"

"I have one." It was Peter and it was directed at Jim. "Has anyone from your department been in touch with the Inland Revenue?"

Jim appeared genuinely surprised and Emily, genuinely interested. Jim replied, "Not to my knowledge and definitely not with my authority, why?"

"It's just that Emily has received a tax demand, which I assume relates to 'sale' of art and, via her accountants, I understand that the Revenue was tipped off by Scotland Yard."

Jim looked around the room to ensure that none of his colleagues was responsible and agreed to make enquiries, after which, the meeting was effectively over.

"I've been thinking about the car, Jon," Mike said. "You might just as well hang on to it for good, if you like. I probably won't be able to drive it for a few weeks anyway and I've been toying with the idea of buying an automatic for some time."

Jonathan protested, but to no avail and after joining the rest in saying goodbye to Emily, Jenny and Mike, he joined Tess and Peter for a light lunch in the hotel restaurant. Jim

Leonard had made his excuses, saying that on balance, he would be better off not knowing all their plans in case any more of them were less than legal. The three then drove back to Cambridge in Peter's car. Tess wedged herself quite uncomfortably on the 'plus two' seat behind Jonathan and Peter. They dropped her and her luggage off at the station cab rank so that she could make a semblance of independence for the final part of her journey to the Hall. That done, Peter and Jonathan went on to the Stables to await their armed guard. Jonathan, if no-one else, was relieved to think that some sort of end was in sight. As the evening drew closer, he buried himself in a good book and then helped himself to a well overdue early night. Before he went to sleep, he indulged an urge to phone Mike in Italy.

"Mike, I meant to mention this before you left, but do you sometimes find that you are talking to yourself when you are under stress?"

"I find myself doing it even when I'm not – under stress that is. I find I get a better class of audience that way. Why?"

"Oh. No matter, I'll sort it later."

"Are you really sure you want to do this?"

"Are you kidding? I was entirely serious about going to the press."

Chapter 27:

The Best Laid Plans

It didn't take long for Emily's prediction to come true. Soon after his swim and breakfast the following morning, Jonathan became inundated with phone calls of sympathy and/or condolence and he was hard put to it to make a list of all the callers' names and addresses. By lunchtime, it was beginning to look as though he might have to charter a special train to get all the would-be funeral goers up to London. By three o'clock he had had enough, and recorded a special message for the answering machine asking callers to leave their names, addresses (e-mail or otherwise) and telephone numbers so that he could get back to them in writing. He left the speaker on so that he could take any non-Mike calls and among those was the inevitable call from Sara. It was inevitable because it was a weekend, but in all other ways it was unique. He turned the machine off and lifted the handset.

"Hello," he said, still a little bit apprehensively.

"Hello, is that you, Jonathan?" The voice dripped with honey.

"Yes, Sara. How can I help you?"

"Well, I've been meaning to get in touch with you for some time, but I haven't quite plucked up the courage. Anyway, this awful news about poor Michael brought me to my senses, so here we are. I just wanted you to know that I really am sorry about what has happened and I just wanted to say that if you need any support – well, you know where to find me."

Jonathan didn't know what to say. This was a Sara that he just couldn't remember and certainly didn't recognise. The little voice at the back of his brain was no help. The best it could manage was, 'You married her, I didn't'. He sat, phone in hand, and mouth shut.

"Are you alright, Jonathan?" Sara asked, still dripping honey.

"What? – Err, yes. Sorry. It's been such a difficult time with all the arrangements to make – I'm sure you understand."

"Yes, I'm sure," she oozed "Look, I'm sorry to have phoned at such a difficult time. Do you think we could meet during the week some time? Just for a chat – I mean if you want to, that is. It might help take your mind off things."

"Yes, why not," Jonathan replied. Even the little voice at the back of his brain was shrugging its shoulders. "Do you know the café just opposite the college's main entrance?" he asked.

"Yes."

"Well, how about ten o'clock on Thursday then? That's the only day I'll be going in this week and I should have all the arrangements finalised by then."

"That'll be lovely. I'll look forward to it. 'Bye."

The line went dead but Jonathan sat in a trance and continued to look at the earpiece for some while, almost as if he was expecting a last-minute torrent of abuse to come screaming out of it. None came and he put the handset down, a very confused man. He wandered off to take another swim, thereby missing ten other phone calls, including one from Lisa.

Peter and the armed guard, Alan, had spent their day partly bemused at the spectacle of Jonathan trying his best to be a telephonist/secretary, and partly at the more serious task of watching out for Cotting. Much as Jim Leonard had anticipated, Cotting paid a visit first thing in the morning as soon as he had finished his shift. There was no need to tail him all the way from the police station, as one of the cameras that Tess had installed viewed straight up the approach road and his car was comprehensively bugged. He duly parked beyond the entrance at just after six-thirty, checked that there was a car inside the gates, waited three hours for Jonathan to go out, got tired of waiting and went home to bed. Monday was almost a carbon copy of Sunday except that there were fewer phone calls and an email arrived from Italy, saying that all was well there. Tuesday dawned so fair that even Peter, who was not known for his athleticism, was tempted to have a swim. Cotting arrived at six-thirty once more, this time armed with breakfast but as on the two previous days, he went away again disappointed.

Half an hour later, Jonathan, Peter and Alan sat quietly listening to Cotting making a telephone call to the college.

"Good morning."

"Good morning, sir. How may I help you?"

"I wonder if you could tell me if Dr Grey is in today?"

"I doubt it, sir, but I'll try his extension. No, there's no answer. It's vac time, you see, and most of the lecturers are not here."

"Oh yes, of course." Cotting cursed himself for not realising it. *"Thank you very much, miss."*

"Oh, sir, if it's any use to you, I believe he's due to be in on Thursday, if you would like to try again then."

"Right, thanks, you've been most helpful. Goodbye."

"Goodbye, sir."

Peter removed the memory chip that had been recording all the while and handed it to Alan, who placed it in an evidence bag which he then signed, dated and sealed.

"That was a stroke of luck, them knowing that you would be going in on Thursday," Alan observed.

"I doubt that it was luck," Peter smiled, looking at Jonathan.

"Well, whatever it was," Alan continued, "at least tomorrow we can all have a later start."

The moment of reverie extended to include lunchtime, but was curtailed abruptly by the first of the afternoon's phone calls. It was from Dorset and it was Lady Antonia

Lyle. Jonathan accepted her sympathies with practised ease and was about to terminate the conversation when to his complete surprise, she asked to speak to Peter.

"Good afternoon. Is that Mr Stagg?"

"Yes, Lady Lyle, how may I help you?"

"Emily gave me your office number with the strict instructions that I should use it only in an emergency. You weren't there so I deduced that you might be with Jonathan and, well, I think this may be an emergency."

"Please go on," Peter urged, as he beckoned Alan to within earshot and put Antonia's voice on the speaker.

"I have just learned from one of my staff that earlier today, a Mr Edwards from the Hall rang, enquiring about Miss Everet. Naturally, we hadn't told the staff about our little arrangement with Miss Pollard and, to cut a long story short, he was told that no one of that name had worked here. I do hope it won't cause a problem. I do hate to let Emily down – especially at this difficult time."

"Well, thank you very much for letting me know, Lady Lyle. Do you need to speak to Jonathan again?"

"No, thank you."

"Well, goodbye, then."

Peter replaced the handset, swore loudly and paced around the kitchen in search of inspiration.

"Fuck! I thought things were going too well."

"Well, at least we would have known about it if Edwards had shared the news with Cotting. We'll have to find some way of getting her out before he does, though," Jonathan added, without caring that it wasn't his decision to make.

If Peter minded, he wasn't showing it. In fact he had developed a healthy regard for Jonathan's views and opinions and right now, he could do with all the help he could get.

"We have three options," he said at length. "Either we leave a message on Tess's portable phone and hope she receives it soon, or we phone the Hall and hope to God we don't get put through to Edwards. Or, we send Alan up there with his warrant card, to arrest her on some pretext or other. Would you mind doing that, Alan?"

"Not at all, but what if she doesn't want to go along with it and tries to resist? I wouldn't want to start anything that might get back to Cotting."

"No problem. Just stay out of kicking range, show her your warrant card and tell her that you are arresting her in connection with a burglary at my office in London."

Alan made ready to leave and was just about to do so when the phone rang again. This time it was Bill Edwards. Jonathan didn't put it on the speaker but recorded it instead, in case it could be used in evidence.

"I'm sorry to be disturbing you at this difficult time, Mr Grey, but since I'm supposed to let you know about anything important, I made an exception on this occasion."

He sounded quite full of himself, but more than a little miffed that he had to tell anyone anything, what with the Pollard woman out of the country and her jumped-up nephew dead. Still, he'd only be in trouble if he didn't tell Jonathan what he had done, especially since it was too late to make any difference.

"Well, it's like this, Mr Grey. I've had to dismiss one of the serving staff for stealing some of Miss Pollard's silver."

Jonathan looked at Peter and Alan for ideas, but they both pulled faces and shrugged expansively. He played for time.

"Had this person been employed with you long enough to seek a tribunal?" he asked, as Peter passed a hastily written note.

"Oh no, sir, she's not been with us long at all – a matter of days only – she was just appointed by Master Michael."

"Then I'm sure you've done the right thing," Jonathan said, as he read the note verbatim. He also added, lying: "Miss Pollard was quite right in putting her trust in your judgement and I'm sure that she'll thank you personally when she returns to England."

"Why, thank you, sir." Bill said, puffing himself up.

"Not at all. Goodbye and thank you once again." Jonathan couldn't keep it going any longer, as Alan and Peter's expressions were becoming unbearable and he couldn't stop himself from laughing.

"Well, thank goodness he acted instinctively and didn't think things through." Peter said, after Jonathan finally regained his composure. "That was very nearly very nasty, not to mention having to abandon things before the finale."

"There's a car coming at speed," Alan interrupted, looking at the screen of the surveillance equipment. Peter moved over to take a look and smiled with relief as he recognised Cathy's car. He ran out to the gate and closed it again after she had driven in, almost without slowing down, and hidden her car beneath a tarpaulin in one of the garages. She stormed into the kitchen, accepting, en route, the generous glass of whisky that Jonathan held out in her path. She sat down at the table, red-faced, looking at the three men in turn as if daring each of them to be the first to speak.

Jonathan had seen her in action so he wasn't about to be the first. Alan realised how grateful he was that he hadn't had to arrest her and Peter just sat patiently waiting for her to explode. She finished her drink and shook the empty glass at Jonathan in certain expectation of a refill, which of course she got.

"Fuck! The bastard sacked me!" she shouted, at last. "The nasty little thieving bastard sacked me! Fuck! Can you believe it? He actually sacked me!"

"We believe you, Cathy," Peter said, firmly. "Now calm down and tell us exactly why he sacked you. No histrionics – just facts; it's important – believe me."

Cathy had seen Peter with that face before and knew that he was serious. She finished the glass and composed herself.

"He called me to his office at one-thirty this afternoon and confronted me with a bag full of Hall silver from my room. He asked me why it was there – I gave him no answer – and he sacked me on the spot. I tried bluffing it out by saying that it was planted, but then he threatened to call the police unless I went immediately, and knowing which police he might call, I opted to leave. We still have Tess there, after all."

"Yes, probably wise in the circumstances. Had he planted the silver in your room?" Peter asked.

"Only some of it. I already had a few pieces there and he didn't find all of those – look!" Cathy produced a handful of cutlery from her coat.

"I think I already know the answer, but what were you doing with the Hall silver in your room anyway?"

Cathy took one of the spoons with both hands and flexed it until it broke. She then gave the two parts to Peter.

"If you look carefully at the hallmark, you'll see it purports to be solid silver whereas if you look at the broken ends, you can see that it's not. My guess is that it's weighted alloy." Peter took the two pieces, nodded in agreement and then passed them to Jonathan and Alan. He then passed Cathy Jonathan's note of his conversation with Antonia Lyle. She whistled and poured herself yet another drink before sitting down again.

"As you can see, we've all just had a very close call. So far, Edwards has not called Cotting and we must just hope that he doesn't. Alan – I don't think it will do any harm if we buy ourselves a little insurance. I doubt now that Cotting will show his face here tomorrow so if you would, I think you should, after all, pay Edwards a visit tomorrow morning to make enquiries about someone who obtains jobs in service using false references and then absconds with valuables. As for you, Cathy, your cover was very nearly truly blown, so you can either stay hidden here or get back to the office once we know that Cotting is on duty. I leave the choice to you, but I should warn you that if you stay, there's a very good chance that Jonathan here will find you some tedious secretarial work! What do you say?"

"I'll stay, thank you," she replied, without hesitation. "I'd like to see this business through to completion and anyway, I'd like to make sure that Jonathan's bereavement doesn't interfere with his swimming."

Chapter 28:

Taking Advantage

Despite the fact that they weren't expecting a visit from Cotting the following day, they took no chances and got up well before six o'clock. The mobile team had long since been parked up, watching Cotting's house and reported his late arrival from work and then no sign of movement for the rest of the morning. Telephone messages of sympathy were starting to dwindle, only to be replaced by cards and letters and Cathy, without being pressed, offered to help out by setting up a database of names and addresses to help Jonathan, not least because at some stage they would all have to be informed of Mike's continued health! Tess made contact during the lunch break at the Hall and was brought up to date on Cathy's near disaster. Jonathan was clearly apprehensive about the next day and spent most of the morning trying to read. The only bit of light relief occurred when Alan went to the Hall late morning to see Bill Edwards. He was only gone about an hour and reported back in detail on his return.

"What was your impression, then?" Peter asked. "I would have come with you, but he may have seen me in another guise."

"I think the best description I can give you is that he was generally nervous, throughout. You might not get much impression of that from the recording – listen."

There was a noise of footwear on gravel, followed by the ascent of five steps and the remote ringing of a bell.

"Come right in," came a voice from a speaker.

More footsteps on stone followed by the same voice, but this time less electrically.

"Good morning, sir, how can I help you?"

A rustling sound of clothing as Alan removed his warrant card from an inside pocket.

"Nothing to worry about, miss, just a routine enquiry. Can I have a word with the owner, please?"

"I'm afraid the she's abroad at present, sir. You'd perhaps better speak to our Mr Edwards."

"Who is he?"

"He's the butler, sir, and he thinks he's in charge. I'll call him for you if you would care to take a seat."

"Thank you, miss."

More footsteps on stone accompanied by distant ring of bell, a pause and then the warble of a phone.

"Hello, Mr Edwards, there's a police officer in reception to see you. Shall I send him up? Right, thank you.

If you would care to go up those stairs, left at the top and then through the double doors, he'll be waiting for you outside his office."

"Thank you, miss."

More noise of footsteps until reaching carpet on the first floor, then a pause followed by, "Good morning. Is it Mr Edwards?"

"Yes, officer. What can I do for you?"

Alan stopped the recording at Peter's signal.

"What was his first reaction when he saw you?" Peter asked.

"I know what you are looking for and I think that he was a bit surprised, but I can't swear that he looked as though he was expecting someone else. He ushered me into his office, anyway."

"Okay," Peter said, "sorry about the interruption. Carry on."

"It's just a routine matter, sir but we're investigating a series of thefts of valuables from stately homes and I wondered if you had taken on any new staff lately. There seems to be a team of people who forge references to gain employment and then steal the goods."

A brief pause.

"No, officer, we've had the same staff here for years and I can vouch for all of them personally."

"And no-one's applied for a position lately?"

"No – nobody. Sorry I can't help you."

"That's quite alright, sir; you've been most helpful. If anyone should apply for a job, could I ask you if perhaps you could ring this number." A further rustle of clothing as Alan found a card. "There is a considerable reward being offered in the event that we find them. Thank you very much for your help, sir. I'll see myself out."

"And that was about it," Alan said, rewinding the tape. "As I said, he seemed to be nervous throughout, and certainly a bit pissed off when I mentioned the reward, and him not getting it. The card I gave him gives a general enquiry number at Scotland Yard, so it shouldn't do any harm even if he does tell Cotting. My guess is that he probably won't because he's feeling a bit stupid right now. I'm sorry about the improvisation, Peter, but once he had committed himself to lying about staff changes, I just couldn't resist it."

"That's okay, Alan. With being too near Jonathan, ad-libbing seems to be catching. Besides, if I'm honest, I might well have done the same myself. Seriously though, Edwards' reaction shows, if we ever doubted it, that we are on the right track. Not only does it confirm his involvement, but his haste to get rid of you was very telling."

Cathy copied the recording onto disc later in the afternoon and then the important call came in. Peter recorded it and then played it back to the others. It was from Jim Leonard. "Hello, everyone, we've just intercepted a call from Edwards to Cotting. Seemingly the refurbishment is going to schedule, and we are all set for tomorrow night! I will arrive tonight while Cotting is on duty, some more people will arrive late tomorrow morning when, hopefully, the coast will be clear and the rest of the team will go straight to the village in the afternoon. Are you still up for this, Jonathan?"

"Yes," he replied. "I can't forget what he tried to do to Mike. I'm up for it, alright."

"Good. We're set then. See you later."

Cathy finished collating all the recordings and then busied herself making final adjustments to the cameras using Alan as a stand-in for Cotting to make sure that, at no time, would he be out of sight. While all this was going on, Peter gave Jonathan what he hoped would be his only briefing for the following morning.

"It is always very important," he cautioned, "to act as if nothing different was going on. Just get up at your usual time – even if you think he's already arrived. He won't do anything until you have gone and the papers and post have arrived and then you can leave him to us – okay? Just have your usual swim, your usual breakfast, pretend that none of us is here and go to work. When you get to the road, don't act strangely even if you see his car, just head for the city, as usual. In the unlikely event that he changes his mind and decides to follow you, we will follow up behind and there will be the mobile unit to block his path at the end of the lane."

"You mean you'd call the whole thing off if he doesn't follow your plan?"

"No, Jonathan. For once, you're not thinking straight. We would abort only if there was any suggestion that you were in danger. Remember that he has already killed Mates and probably Frank too. We don't want to help him to a hat-trick, do we?"

"No, I suppose not. Sorry."

"No apology needed. For a relative novice, you are doing very well. I might even think about offering you a job when this is all over!"

Jonathan laughed nervously.

"Nothing personal Peter, but quite apart from coping with the full-time distraction of Cathy and Tess, I could probably deal with the 'cloak' bit, but certainly not the 'dagger!'"

"Fair enough. Now is there anything else you feel I haven't covered adequately?"

"No. I'm as ready as I'll ever be," Jonathan said, starting to head for his room and then pausing. "But if it doesn't all go to plan tomorrow, and he has to be taken in the lane, I'd still like five minutes with him. Three would do, at a pinch. Oh well, there was no harm in asking."

"For someone who professes not to like daggers, you seem to have a nasty violent streak just below the surface – even if it only relates to Cotting. No, sorry, Jon. We have to play it by the book. Besides, if the police did declare open season on him, Aunt Emily, Cathy or more likely, Jim Leonard would get there first. None of them has much time for 'due legal process' and Jim has been after Cotting for years. Take it from me, you are much better off with your books!"

"Okay, okay, you've convinced me. Anyway, I can't stay here chatting to you. I'm going to have another swim and then prepare the last supper."

"That's a point, Jonathan. It's about time that I did a kitchen duty, instead of shuffling all those pieces of paper around – although I must say that I'll miss your cooking."

Jim Leonard arrived later than planned and Alan stayed up to let him in. Jonathan slept quite well, despite constant bouts of nerves. He woke, swam, ate and drove off to the college as if it were any other day. He even managed not to give in to a panic attack when he saw the front of Cotting's car sticking out of the hedgerow about a hundred metres further up the lane. The papers had been delivered while he was eating breakfast and he passed the postman as he got to the end of the lane. The postman duly drove up to the Stables three minutes later, delivered yet another bundle of sympathy letters, reversed out and headed back the way he came. The cameras had started rolling the moment that Jonathan had left and one by one they traced and recorded Cotting's movements, as he carefully worked his way around the outside of the stables, first checking to see if there was anyone left at home and then trying, so it appeared to those within, to determine if there were any weak spots in the alarm system. After about fifteen minutes or so he concluded, quite correctly, that there weren't. He then returned to the gates at the front, cursed, scratched his head and went away a truly disappointed man.

"Well, that seems to have gone some way towards spoiling his day," Cathy observed, "and it's only just started."

Leonard started speaking into his radio in the next room, as Peter and Alan monitored the progress of their respective homing devices on separate screens in the study.

"He's on his way," Leonard said. "Give him plenty of leeway unless, repeat unless, he heads anywhere but home. Alan will keep you informed."

"Right, boss," the reply came back. "We see him – out."

Unknowingly, Cotting obliged all of them by heading for home. An hour later, he surprised everyone when he drove out once more. His house was in the first leg of a cul-de-sac off, so it was very simple for the mobile crew to park well away and still be able to keep a watchful eye on movements.

"He's on the move again," they reported.

"Yes, so I see," Jim replied. "We've got him on screen, so there's no need to get close. Just let us know where he stops and I will decide what you should do next – out."

Jim, Alan and Peter were joined by Cathy, and they all bent forward in concentration, trying to determine where Cotting was going, since it clearly wasn't toward the college.

"I'm buggered if I know what he's up to," said Jim, sighing. "I wish now I'd ordered up a helicopter, but with this low cloud predicted, there didn't seem to be a lot of point."

The moment passed and anyway, the vehicle first slowed and then seemed to have stayed put.

"Do you have him?"

"Yes, he's at a garage about two hundred metres further up."

"Fine. Can you get nearer without being seen?"

"Not unless we buy fuel."

"Okay, do it. But don't let him see you use the radio! Just report back as soon as you can – especially if he sets off on foot!"

The next ten minutes dragged and beads of perspiration appeared on Jim's forehead.

"Boss?"

"Yes?"

"Bad news, I'm afraid. His car's gone in for a service."

"I don't give a fuck about the state of his car!" Leonard shouted. "What's bad about that, for God's sake?"

"He had a courtesy car delivered to his house this morning and we've been following its driver."

Leonard went red, asked Cathy politely if she would mind covering her ears and screamed into the radio, using language guaranteed to make even the most hardened sailor blush. He remained more or less ballistic until the crew driver, who it seemed, was quite used to such outbursts, assured him that the garage proprietor had just given them the make and registration number of the courtesy car and they were now breaking every speed limit in the recently enlarged European Community, trying to get to the college before Cotting.

"How do you know that he didn't just stay at home?"

"We've just reviewed the video and it shows Cotting coming out of the junction in a courtesy car, even before his own was driven out."

"Right. Find him and report back – or start pressing your old uniforms! Is that clear?"

"Yes, boss – out."

"Damn it!" Leonard said, his face now returned to its usual colour. "We really should have sent one of our men out instead of Jonathan. I feel responsible for him, and if somehow we manage to rescue this farce, I might yet give him his five minutes."

"I could do it in one!" Cathy said, through gritted teeth, as she stomped out to the kitchen to make some fresh coffee.

"Right, gentlemen. I think we give it another ten minutes, at most, before we telephone Jonathan and have him collected from his office."

"There's no need," Peter said, coolly. "I have someone there."

"Well, you didn't tell me!"

"Sorry, Jim, but I had hoped that the situation wouldn't arise and with any luck it won't. You may be working for Queen and country and all that, but I have a far more demanding client; I had to take out some insurance."

In the event none was needed – the crew called back.

"Boss?"

"Speaking."

"We have him. He's parked just outside the college and we're about a hundred and fifty metres behind him. We are the other side of a railway crossing but can't move any closer without risking attention. If it becomes necessary, one of us will go on foot to the other side of the line so we'll have to go to three-way radio contact. Could you switch to the conference band?"

"Right. Well done."

After the initial trauma of leaving the Stables, Jonathan had completely recovered his cool and, once parked up, went off to his room to shuffle a few bits of paper before going out to see Sara. He had entertained numerous second thoughts about meeting her on this day of all days, but after a lengthy session with his alter ego, he and it agreed that he might just as well get all the crap over in one go. Thus with no outward care in the world, he set off through the car park, across the road and back a few yards toward the railway and into the café bar to meet Sara. Cotting saw him but did nothing and the mobile team didn't see him at all.

She was there and waiting, just as he remembered her, though with perhaps slightly shorter hair. She was wearing trainers, tight designer jeans, a shirt and a hip length camel coat, all of which looked new and had, in all probability, been paid for by him out of the maintenance. He swallowed hard and managed to produce a smile. He had been wondering what he might say to her ever since he had got to work, and dreading what she might say in reply. Eventually, he decided that by far the safest course would be to appeal to her vanity with something like:

"Hello Sara, you still look as beautiful as ever," or something equally banal – and perhaps add, "and if anything, you look even younger."

The opening gambit seemed to be having the right effect. She had been really quite friendly over the phone and he had done his level best not to imagine what that might portend. That said, it was still decent of her to have offered what appeared to be sincere condolences regarding Mike's death and he wondered mischievously what her reaction would be when she found out the truth. It was almost worth asking him to visit her before the rest of the world knew ... no, perhaps not. Anyway, she had seen him now and this was the big moment that he had been preparing himself for all morning.

"Hi," he said, kissing her on the cheek and sitting down.

"Hi," she returned. "Would you like some coffee?"

"Please."

There was an awkward silence as she poured him a cup. Perhaps this was a silly idea after all, but if there was a chance to call a truce, he would always regret not having taken it.

"Two spoons?" she enquired.

"Err – no, thanks. I've given up."

"Oh – right." She passed him his cup and continued. "Look, Jon, I've been thinking for some while that it was about time we stopped squabbling with each other and just got on with our separate lives, and sad though it is, I thought I might use this business with Michael to ask to meet with you and bury the hatchet, as it were. What do you think?"

Any other time, Jonathan would probably have seen through Sara, and told her precisely where he would like to bury the hatchet in her head, but having rather too much on his mind and more importantly, being a mere man, he fell for it.

"I've wanted that for a long time, but there has never been the right moment to suggest it," he replied, sincerely.

"No, I suppose not," she sighed. "Look – I'm really sorry to have to cut this short now that we've met but to be totally honest, I wasn't at all sure that you would agree to come and I didn't get around to cancelling a dental appointment. I don't want to presume, but if I dash off now, could I buy you lunch later?"

"Here – at one?"

"Why not, it's handy for you, isn't it? I must go."

"And no more asking for the car?" he asked, still not quite believing her. "Only I don't have it any more."

Sara almost stopped in her tracks, but managed to mask it by pretending that she had caught her coat on a chair.

"Really?" she said, composure regained. "What are you driving now – something newer?"

"Yes, I suppose it is. I'm driving Mike's Golf – he … he…. doesn't need it any more …"

"Yes, I'm sure that's what he would have wanted. Poor Michael. Look, I really must go now."

And she did. There was nothing to pay and after a few moments staring at the vacant space that Sara had left, Jonathan walked back to college and the sanctuary of his room. He was quite oblivious to Cotting, the mobile crew and the dust cart that narrowly missed mowing him down. He was dazed, struck dumb and bemused as never before had he been bemused.

Cotting was also bemused, but for a very different reason. The reconnaissance of the Stables had been a complete waste of time, especially since he was long overdue some sleep. He was just about to give in to that idea and return home when he had seen Jonathan cross over to the café bar and leave again a little while later. That perhaps was nothing strange, but his attention had been drawn to the woman who had left just before Jonathan. He had not had a very good view of her, as a bus had intervened, and when it had moved off, so had she. His devious brain started to review information and he tossed a mental coin to decide whether he should follow the bus or stay put a while longer. The coin landed and he stayed put. Jonathan was still bemused when at ten to one he set off again to see Sara. He had briefly considered the notion of ringing to let Peter and the others know, especially since Peter had cautioned him to behave normally. However, since he was beginning to doubt the concept of normality, he didn't believe that he was in any position to make a judgement and thus he decided not to decide. He just walked out of the college gates and across the main road to the café bar -- missing Cotting yet again -- ordered himself a drink and sat down to wait for Sara. He couldn't see the college gates from his table and hence he didn't see her get out of her taxi, put on her ridiculous hat, an equally ridiculous pair of sunglasses and walk quickly toward the main building. Cotting did of course see her and his devious brain was just about to convince him that two and three made four. Sara walked smartly up to the car park, noted the position of Jonathan's new car and then went into the building through the main door. She had planned to go straight up to the relief receptionist, cause some sort of diversion and take the keys from Jonathan's mail slot in the confusion. It was not to be, for as soon as she got inside the foyer, she recognised the person behind the desk and had to go straight back outside. There was nothing for it, she would have to use Plan B. This was more risky, since it meant going in through one of the other entrances and then through part of the building where she might well be recognised. Well if it happened, it happened. Anyway, her disguise would probably be convincing enough in artificial light. Five minutes later she was outside the toilets at the far end of reception. She had seen no one and, in her present position, she could not be seen by the receptionist. Checking once more that there was no one in sight, she turned her back to the fire alarm point just by the door to the toilets, and broke its glass with her elbow.

There was no panic, just a coarse ringing of bells. The relief receptionist picked up her area register and went to join the gathering throng outside the tennis courts. No-one saw Sara walk over to the reception desk to liberate Jonathan's keys and only Cotting saw her drive out of the gates about three minutes later. He tossed another mental coin in his devious mind and when it landed, he followed her.

Chapter 29: The Final Act

"Jonathan's on the move," Alan said, urgently. "I thought he'd be staying at college all day."

"So did we all," Peter replied, with equal concern. "You check with the mobile crew while I make a call. Cathy, you'd better wake Jim."

"Well?" Peter asked, as he returned to the study.

"More bad news, I'm afraid. They were both in the car when it happened and then everything else happened at once. They saw Jonathan's car being driven out of the gates and Cotting start to follow it, but no sooner had they started up themselves when the barrier came down as a train arrived. One of them went on foot over the foot bridge but by the time the barrier went up again, the road the other side was blocked with fire engines! We've lost him again."

"Well, I'm very confused," Peter said, "because *we* have not. I don't know what Jonathan is playing at but he is certainly not in his car. Geoff, my man at the college, saw him go off for lunch just before one and I am assured that he's still having it. I've told Geoff to make himself known to the mobile team so that they can work together. I don't have a clue what's going on and we'll have to leave it to them to sort out. The only thing I'm sure about is that for the second time today, your boss is not going to be a happy man."

"What am I not going to be happy about this time?" Jim said.

"Ah!" Alan replied, taking a deep breath.

Jonathan had been waiting for about fifteen minutes before he resigned himself to the idea that Sara wasn't going to show. It wasn't as if there had been nothing to distract him while he sat patiently at his table. There was frenetic activity outside as more and more fire engines jostled for position in front of the college. Then, just as they appeared to have got themselves sorted, the police in the redoubtable person of PC 'Jobmate' started organising the parking and made matters worse again. By one-thirty there was still no sign of smoke or Sara and in a typically magnanimous fit of generosity of spirit, preceded by another drink, Jonathan concluded that Sara couldn't quite bring herself to be nice to him more than once in the same day after all – and on reflection, *once* was something of a breakthrough. The fire engines departed slowly and the traffic got back to normal as he ordered and ate lunch on his own. At about two-thirty, he deftly folded his napkin, placed it on his table, left a tip and shambled back to his room, watched all the way by Geoff and the mobile team.

"He's safely back, boss."

"Good. Resume your stations for now."

"Do you want one of us to go after Cotting now that we have another vehicle?"

"No. We should just concentrate on Jonathan and only Jonathan. Once he is safely back here we can worry about Cotting. Anyway, we know that he is due to pick up his car at five, so we can locate him then or when he goes home. If plans change before that, we can probably find him by finding Mike's car. I'd hate to think what his insurers will say when he tells them he's lost another one. Where is he now, by the way, Peter?"

"I can't tell you," he replied, switching the range on his monitor. "I've had my set switched to Cotting's car. While Alan was asleep, it looked as though the garage took it out for a test drive and I've only now switched back to the Golf and it's not there."

"What's the receiving limit on your sender?"

"About a hundred and fifty miles and there's no way on earth it would have got that far in this time."

"How about under the earth? It could be in a tunnel."

"Yes, that's true. I'll just leave it searching and if we don't get a signal in a few minutes we'll just have to assume that, for some reason or other, it's stopped sending."

Sara, in her twisted little way, was feeling justifiably smug as she drove out of the city in her new car. Not only was it newer and faster than the one she had been expecting, but there was the added irony that she had got one over both on Jonathan, and Mike – albeit posthumously. Her original plan was to take it straight to

366

her friend with his collection of registration papers and number plates, but at the last minute, she decided that she could risk taking it for a spin first. She had calculated, in the event quite rightly, that since it had been parked so far from the main doors, Jonathan would not have seen it missing one his way back from lunch, hence time was very much on her side. To be quite safe, she drove entirely legally through the outskirts of the city and, foregoing the motorway, took it out to the south on the winding country lanes by the old gravel works. All went well until she noticed the lights in her rear view mirror. It didn't look anything like a police car and she slowed to pull into a passing place in the hope that all the driver wanted to do was overtake. She was wrong as, having overtaken, the driver of the other car stopped, got out quickly and flourished a warrant card at her. She summoned up her much practised honeyed tone as possible and quickly undid a couple of extra buttons on her shirt for good measure, but her luck ran out of the window as soon as she opened it.

"Would you mind stepping out of the vehicle a moment, madam?"

"Is there a problem, officer?" she oozed. "I'm sure I wasn't speeding, was I?"

"I couldn't say, madam. Just get out of the car, please."

"May I have another look at your warrant card, please, so I can be sure I've got the name right when I complain."

"Certainly, madam," he said, moving closer and placing it under her nose, "and now if you've seen enough, perhaps you would oblige me by stepping out of the car which, by the way, I have reason to believe is stolen."

There was nothing for her to do but comply, so she did.

"Thank you, madam – now could you tell me the registration number, please?"

'Well – err – no. I can't remember it. The car belongs to my husband you see," she lied, as she thought desperately.

"Right – and where might the two of you live, exactly?"

"In Grantchester, at the Stables, if you know them."

"I know them only too well, madam. Could you perhaps show me any documents relating to the vehicle?"

"No, I'm afraid I don't have them with me. Would you like me to bring them to the police station later? I could if you like."

"No I don't think that will be necessary, madam. Would you just open the boot for me, please?" he asked, almost pleasantly.

"Why?"

"So that I can see what you've got in there."

Sara neither knew nor cared what was in the boot, but since the man had shown no interest in her cleavage she might just as well humour him and try to be polite, in the hope that he would accept her offer to produce documents later.

"I was only joking about reporting you, of course." she smiled at him, as she moved round to the rear of the car.

"Yes, of course," he replied. "Just open it, please."

"There!" she said, smiling. "It's quite empty."

"Oh, that's good," he said, as he hit her hard in the stomach. "That'll make things much easier."

He bundled her roughly into the boot, shut and locked it and then got into the driver's seat to restart the engine for the short journey across the field to the nearest gravel pit. The bubbles had more or less finished erupting at the water's surface as he got back to the courtesy car and drove first to the garage to collect his newly serviced car and then home for a much-needed sleep.

"Well it took me quite a while to find her, Frank," he said, thinking out loud, "but that one was for you. Mr Grey will just have to wait a while."

It was Peter's turn to be asleep, when the little green dot representing Cotting's car started to wander across the screen once more. Jim Leonard was the first to see it and quickly radioed the mobile team to inform them and Geoff.

"It looks as though he's heading for home from the garage, rather than in your direction," he said. "If you can catch up with him before he gets there and can get an actual sighting of him without being seen, all well and good, but if you can't I'll risk phoning him with a wrong number just to make sure that it's really him this time. I know his voice, but I doubt that he'll recognise mine if I disguise it. Once I'm sure that he's there, I want Jonathan brought back here to safety. I'll leave that to Geoff if that's okay with him and ask him to make sure that he reports the car as stolen. I want everything done by the book and no more slip-ups. My guess is that Cotting is going to get his head down for a while, so once you've sat on his house for an hour, decide who takes the first break and I'll have you relieved at eight. Okay?"

"Yes, boss."

Geoff and an even more bemused Jonathan arrived at the Stables just after six o'clock, in the plasterer's van used previously by one of the many incarnations of Mr Phillips. Jonathan refused, point blank, to discuss Mike's car and tried in vain to convince anyone who would listen that it was some prank that Mike had devised just to embarrass him. Nobody really wanted to listen so first he went for a swim and then, feeling a bit of a spare part, he started to organise food for the masses. Cathy didn't appear to want to sleep and instead, she went to the kitchen to help Jonathan.

"You'd better prepare for two extra," she suggested. "If I'm right, the mobile team will turn up once they're relieved. They've been chasing that bastard Cotting around all day and I can't see them wanting to miss out on the kill!"

Her prediction came true and by nine-thirty, she and Jonathan were back in the kitchen dealing with the dishes.

"Was it my imagination, or did I sense some hostility between Peter and Jim, over supper?" he asked.

"You were right." she answered. "Peter is pissed off because Jim has insisted that when it starts, civilians are

370

off-limits. Peter knows it's a lost cause, but he's still trying to find a way to persuade Jim to change his mind."

"What about you? I mean, how do you feel about it?"

"I'm disappointed, naturally, but I expected it as soon as the police became involved. Besides," she added, smiling, "I have my own plan for this evening."

"And what might that be?"

"Plying you with drink and seducing you."

Jonathan gulped, but managed not to flinch under Cathy's intent gaze. He simply went through the ritual argument and counter-argument with his alter ego and replied. He also gave some thought to the concept of waiting for a bus all day and then three coming at once.

"Sounds like a good plan, in the circumstances."

"I hope that you'll take longer than five minutes."

"I hope it'll take you longer than one!"

They were fast asleep when, at one-thirty, the relief mobile team radioed through to say that Cotting was again on the move and heading towards the Hall.

"Yes, we have him," Jim said, as he looked in fascination at the moving dot on the screen. "The other teams are in place so we will go in on foot. Don't, repeat, don't follow him. I don't want him scared off by car lights and we have him on screen here with a radio link through to us on foot. Teams three, four and five report in sequence on the conference band now. Good, we're set and will join you in twenty minutes – out."

Peter had long since given up all hope of going with them and instead, consoled himself with the fact that while he monitored radio traffic, he could sit in the study in front of a roaring log fire and renew his acquaintance with Mike's best brandy as he telephoned Emily, Mike and Jenny to keep them up to date.

David Cotting awoke refreshed at one o'clock and showered in the dark, before dressing and quietly leaving his house. Most of the neighbours were used to his odd hours but there was no point attracting any undue attention to his departure. He drove carefully round the ring road, as would any law-abiding citizen and only as he approached Grantchester did he turn off his main lights. Once through the village, he turned the sidelights off and drove almost at a snail's pace to the Hall.

"Team three to leader – we have him now."

"Good – follow slowly and wait for my signal."

The bushes in the hedgerows began to thin out as Cotting neared the entrance to the grounds – good – Edwards had left the gates open, as planned, and he drove through. The coppice of trees to his left which, had provided him with a hiding place, days earlier, loomed grey in the moonlight, but apart from a few rabbits startled in mid-feed, nothing stirred and nothing would keep from his task. The Hall was just around the bend.

"Team four to leader – we have him now."

"Good – follow slowly and wait for my signal."

Edwards was waiting by the west side door and heard the slow approach of the vehicle. He peered into the gloom and, when he was quite sure it was Cotting, he flashed his torch once and then put it back in his pocket. Cotting pulled up close-by but left the engine running. Neither man spoke; they simply went in and out of the door several times and on each occasion carrying out sacks, which they quietly loaded into Cotting's car.

"Team five to leader – we have him now."

"Good – wait for my signal – team one, are you in position?"

"Yes, boss."

"Good – we'll all be with you soon."

After the sixth trip, Edwards got into the car and Cotting went back into the Hall. He made his way to the main stairwell in reception. Just behind the receptionist's desk was a panelled door serving the under-stair cupboard housing the gas and electricity meters. He removed a taped bundle of candles from his coat pocket, placed them carefully beneath an illegally soldered joint in one of the gas pipes, lit the candles and left. Moving at speed, he was back at his car before the solder had even started to melt and he and Edwards drove off into the night.

"Now! Repeat, now!"

Chapter 30: Unbridled Lust

One of the more curious and remarkably consistent features of the human condition is our unfailing ability to take things for granted. We blunder through life, emotions and hormones at the ready, but overlook or completely miss some of the minor details that, with hindsight, would have helped us cope with reality. Mother Nature is perhaps the most frequent victim in all this and it is greatly to her credit that she just gets on with things as if we didn't exist. Perhaps there is something to be learnt, there. Thankfully it is never quite too late to make an effort and we could perhaps spend a few useful moments dwelling on some minor details like: what became of the crushed tulips and Mr & Mrs Right Duck?

As for the tulips, those that were damaged during the brief prenuptial chase, (apparently ducks don't indulge in foreplay as we know it – per se, the males puff up their chests and strut about a bit and the females pretend disinterest until they start to lose a few tail feathers) they managed to recover after a fashion, so we need concern ourselves only with the final bunch upon which the duckling deed was done. These, sad to say, were crushed beyond repair. They spent a few days trying quite valiantly to right themselves, by osmosis, and after a further week of sulking, they decided to give up trying for the year and concentrated on the relatively safe alternative of bulb growth. As it turned out, this was a very wise decision since only two weeks later, the estate gardener won on the Lotto, got thoroughly bladdered and went berserk with the lawn mower. Mr & Mrs Right Duck missed all of this for they had long since returned to the river in order to find somewhere cat-proof to make a nest. A little later, nine ducklings were taught how to swim (easy), how to do so in line and, most importantly, how to do tricks for the tourists in exchange for bread. The stretch of the river which, by common consent, was set aside for this popular activity, stretched from the boathouses at the old hospital site up to the weir close to the city centre. Here, the banks of the river were too steep even to intrepid ducklings to climb and since they had not yet learned to fly, the mysteries upstream, including Grantchester village, Hall and Stables would remain temporarily out of their grasp. We, of course, suffer no such restrictions and, back at the Stables, all was peaceful. It was a midsummer's day, nine in the morning and a Sunday. The early morning sun had heaved its glowing bulk over the eastern horizon many hours before and was shining its benevolent light into most of the garden. It was quite used to this sort of work because it had been practising for weeks. There was only one shadow, to speak of, and even that was reducing by the minute; it was cast by the east wing of the building. Way up on the south-facing roof of the north wing, twenty solar panels were creaking gently as they tried to expand in response to the sun. Somewhere below them, a microchip accepted relevant data, thought briefly and decided what to do, a couple of relays clicked shut, the water circulating pump changed up a gear and the creaking stopped. Down on the patio, a couple of snails waited for the dog to go away and then made the snail equivalent of a quick dash from the relative safety of their home beneath the barbecue, over to the new vegetable garden for a quick snack of courgettes.

"Nice day again," One said.

"Yes – I can't stand all that rain like we had in the spring – too much of it plays havoc with my foot," the other replied.

"You too, eh?" One said.

"Yes. By the way, did I tell you where I went for dinner last night? – over to that hosta just beyond the herb garden," Two said.

"Any good?" One enquired.

"No – a bit of a disappointment really. It had the texture of cabbage, but far too bitter for me – I was up all night!" Two complained.

"Really?" One enquired.

"Yes – but I left a nice few holes," Two replied, with genuine satisfaction.

"Oh good – perhaps I'll take a quick look later," One pondered.

"The birds are late today," Two observed, pointing one eye stalk at the sky.

"It's Sunday, shell-head! Watch out – there's that dog again. No, it's alright; it hasn't seen us," One said.

"Have you booked a holiday yet?" Two asked.

"No, I can't see the point when the weather's like this," One said, pulling its foot back from a hot piece of paving.

"I agree. My cousin in planning to go on a container to France this year!" Two commented.

"Must be mad." One concluded.

To the left of them, the fig tree, obviously suffering from its daily bout of short-term memory loss, was flaunting its leaves and wantonly displaying its soft green fruit as if it was the first real day of summer. A little way to its south, in one of the deeper recesses of the garages lay the rotting remains of Jonathan's old car, still tethered to the far wall. In his great enthusiasm to drag the police trailer from beneath it months earlier, he had given no real thought as to how, later, it might be removed. Thus, there it lay as a crumpled, rusting tribute to automotive engineering, and a permanent reminder of his former life. To one side of it, barely an arm's length away, was a Mr Phillips's most excellent plaster-work. To the other side, just more than an arm's length away and in stark contrast, sat the TVR that Jonathan had purchased from Peter just the week before. To say that it 'sat' was perhaps doing it an injustice. In fact it positively quivered in its burgundy metallic red GRP magnificence – at least that was what Jonathan liked to think. Against all odds, it had been purchased courtesy of Sara, his late ex-wife. Ever since their divorce, and probably for some while before, she had been so preoccupied with bonking everything in trousers that moved, that she had forgotten to change her will or inform anyone officially that she was divorced. Consequently, as sole beneficiary, Jonathan got his old house back, complete with the remaining CDs and also the considerable residue of her savings – even after the credit card companies had taken their dues. He had the house fumigated – twice – and then put it on the market. Apparently the cats had buggered off for good the day after she didn't come home – so much for loyalty! It had taken the police two weeks to find Sara and that was only because the fishing season had just commenced and anglers had seen dead fish in the gravel pit as the result of oil and petrol leaking from Mike's car. The will wasn't Jonathan's only surprise however. In his typical absent-minded way, he had forgotten to change his insurance – his joint-life, first-death insurance – or tell his insurers that he was divorced. An oversight, yes, and possibly a little against the rules, but thus it was that in the same week during mid-May he received not only a surprisingly fat cheque from Sara's most recent solicitors, but also an obscene one from his insurers.

As the shadow from the east wing shortened further, flocks of birds arrived to take up temporary residence. After the usual squawking and jostling for position, each pair of proud parents set about the task of teaching their fluffy young some of the more important elements of avian existence, like:

➢ how to find worms and pull them out before anyone else did;

➢ which and where were the best rocks for evicting snails;

➢ how and where to sing loudly at four o'clock in the morning when most people wanted to be asleep, and

➢ which were the best places from which to crap on people's washing after a good meal of blackcurrants.

Fudge, the nine month old Labrador Retriever bitch, had been minding her own business and having a good sniff at the little froglets by the pond when her human, Jonathan, came out for his morning swim. She didn't really understand what he saw in this ritual, but he did it twice a day so he must have enjoyed it – it certainly looked more comfortable than walking on one's back legs all day. Even though she was still a pup and relatively new to life, the Stables and Jonathan, Fudge knew instinctively that, like most humans, he wanted to form some sort of relationship with her, and he seemed to enjoy having her pace up and down the side of the pool to keep him company until he got out. Some months ago, when she still lived at the kennels in the village, Fudge's mother had mentioned something about 'bonding', but she was too busy practising tail-catching to pay much attention at the time. Anyway, on the whole, things seemed to be going alright. Jonathan appeared to be good-natured with other humans and certainly enjoyed going out for a long run in the fields after supper. There was quite a lot of training to be done, though, and he was still nervous without the lead.

"How many is that now?" she thought. "Let's see; he's going back to the far end and so it's either thirty-seven or thirty-nine. Yes – he's getting tired now so it must be thirty-nine. Last lap, old son, and then you can have some food – that's good – now up those steps and put your fur on. That's quite clever when you think about it – taking your fur off to go in the water – it saves all that shaking afterwards. What? No! I don't want to shake your paw – it's all wet – yes I know, I know. 'Good girl, Fudge'. God what a boring conversationalist. Well go on then, go on, go and get the papers, they're over by the gate look. Fetch! What am I going to do with him? Oh thank goodness. Now, what's next? I know – go and play dead for the birds."

Jonathan smiled broadly as he watched Fudge lope over to her favourite spot on the lawn and then collapse in a heap. He was feeling good if a little tired, and thoroughly content with life. It had been about six weeks since he had had any conversation with his much-maligned alter ego, and that was about Sara. He had started to convince himself that she might still be alive if he had given her his car, and when he started to share that thought with some of his friends they told him to see his doctor, which he did. She sent him to see a psychiatrist, which didn't really help. Ultimately, towards the end of it, he sought further advice from his friends and they told him, collectively, not to think like a prat – so he stopped.

It was the day after Mike and Jenny's wedding. It had been just great, and Jonathan had the unusual satisfaction of knowing that, with the possible exception of the bride and groom, he was the only one without a justified hangover. The service had been at the college chapel and the splendid reception at the Hall; all of it recorded by Jenny's work mates. Overnight accommodation was available for those who needed somewhere to dry out – and most appeared well-qualified. The date had been decided quite deliberately to coincide with the end of the fifth training session and, thanks to a little arm twisting by Emily, Romulan agreed to forego the induction weekend due to start the sixth. Jenny's father was a little tearful at the service, of course, but Bev, her late mother, was there in spirit – her wedding ring on Jenny's hand. Jonathan met up with Lisa once more: it was inevitable, since she was matron of honour, and he best man. He had already learned from Jenny that Lisa's trial reconciliation with Greg was doomed from the start and lasted only two weeks, after which she had spent most of her time working abroad. Peter was on the guest list as Captain Phillips and turned up in full naval uniform.

"I haven't done this one for ages," he had confided in Emily, as they took the first dance.

"I've always admired men in uniform," she replied, gently squeezing his bottom.

Cathy had sent her apologies from somewhere in El Salvador and Tess, hers, from North America. Mike and Jenny had left just after ten, once he was finally convinced that no one was going to start a cricket match without him. He had made a full recovery from his injury followed by an unbeaten century against a team aptly named Henry's Hedonists. Jonathan was still leafing dreamily through the papers and mulling over the events of the previous day – in particular the finer points of his speech. The review of Mike's past history had taken a while of course. Suddenly, a tray of breakfast appeared in front of him. The other side of the tray was attached to Lisa.

"I thought it would be nice if we had this out here," she said, from behind a curtain of red hair.

"Wonderful." he said, getting up to move a chair out for her.

They sat quietly over their breakfast, listening to the birds and the occasional plop of a froglet as it executed a particularly difficult dive into the pond. Other than that and the odd contented snuffle from Fudge on the middle of the lawn, silence was complete. Jonathan had gone to the study to turn off the phone and fax earlier, on his way out to the pool. As time passed, the shadow retreated still further, the pile of croissants disappeared and the coffee ran dry – but who cared, if they didn't?

"They'll be taking off for Italy soon." Jonathan said, as he shaded his eyes from the sun to check if he really had seen a dragonfly. "Look!" he said, putting his arm round her, "just over there by the pond."

"Isn't it beautiful!" she gasped.

The silence continued while the dragonfly looked for somewhere to land, gave up, shrugged both sets of shoulders and went back to the river. More minutes passed before Jonathan gave up the pretence of being interested in the papers. He gazed smiling at the friendly face opposite.

"Are you ready for the rest of the story, then?"

"I am – unless you're ready for some more unbridled lust."

"Later – where did we get to, anyway?"

"The fire."

"Right – the fire. Once the word was given, the team nearest the main door went in to deal with it, but Tess had got there first. Despite telling Jim Leonard that he would keep her out of it, Peter briefed Tess as soon as the troops had left the Stables. Consequently, she was watching Cotting and Edwards as they removed the last batch of paintings from where Bill had hidden them and then followed Cotting round to the reception area. She just hid and then put the fire out after he went – as simple as that. By the time that the team got in, she was seated at the receptionist's desk and even asked if she could 'help them' – I thought that was rather a nice touch and so did Peter. Anyway, after that, things started to fall apart. The original plan was for the remaining teams to split up, two of them to deal quietly with Bill Edwards and the others, plus Jim and Alan -"

"Who was Jim?"

"The guy who was here protecting me and manning the radios. He subsequently quit the police to join Peter's firm. Anyway, this second group was to let Cotting get far enough away so that noise wouldn't matter before they took him. Once it was realised that Cotting and Edwards were still together, they regrouped hastily and followed them. In the confusion, they didn't catch up with them until they had got back to Edwards' house. In the time it took them to get organised and get people round to the rear, a fight had broken out and Bill was shot. No one is sure quite how it happened. Jim was more or less convinced that Cotting had planned to kill Edwards at some time or other, but not necessarily there and then. Bill's wife had heard them

383

arguing about something – possibly about the cutlery that Bill had been taking. Anyway, she intervened and when Bill produced his shotgun, Cotting got it off him and shot him with it. At that, Jim ordered all the cars to put lights on and ordered Cotting to surrender. Two of the teams had weapons and when Cotting tried shooting his way out using Bill's wife as a shield, Jim gave the order to shoot and they killed him."

"How awful," Lisa sighed, "but I guess it was unavoidable."

"Yes, and as Jim pointed out, Cotting was beginning to find killing was quite easy. So that was that – and it was all over apart from clearing up the London end of the operation. Except that that wasn't really the end of it at all, as that was when the cavalry arrived!"

"The cavalry?"

"Well, to be exact – the SAS."

"What?"

"Yes – did I mention the problem with Emily and the Inland Revenue?"

"Briefly, yes."

"Well, their enquiries were related to the thefts at the Hall. Jim Leonard never told us the full story, but piecing things together, it went like this: Cotting, Edwards and Frank were stealing paintings from the hall and replacing them with copies. Frank stole cars for transport and either he or Cotting took the stolen paintings to a fence in London. The original fence and most of the rest of the

384

original gang had disappeared to South America some years before and that part of the organisation had been taken over by more seriously organised criminals with connections to the Mafia and people with terrorist interests."

"Terrorists?"

"Yep – apparently they have fingers in any pie that is useful for laundering money and, in this case, they were fronting an art dealer."

"Sorry, you've lost me there."

"I was to start with also, but Peter, as usual, explained it very simply. Basically, if you've stolen something of value you can sell it for more if you pass it via a dealer with valid documents. In Emily's case, Edwards was forging sale documents for the dealers to use, and some of the documents came into the possession of the Inland Revenue. They contacted Emily's accountant and also tipped off the police. Normally the police would not bother much with such information, but the dealers were on a list of terrorist suspects. Peter first started smelling a rat when Tess told him she found an existing bug on Cotting's car when she planted hers. Anyway, the anti-terrorist squad let Jim Leonard do all the visible leg-work (without Jim knowing) while they sat back and waited. They were not too interested in the Cambridge end of the operation, but were there in force, nonetheless, on the final night – and it took everyone by surprise. No sooner had Jim's crew switched on their car lights than other fixed search-lights powered up, a helicopter appeared from nowhere plus two armoured vehicles stuffed full of SAS."

"Well, I'm glad now that I missed out on it all, but what happened to the people? Did Mr Leonard get a commendation?"

"No. In fact as I heard it, he was given a stiff reprimand for not bringing the case more quickly to a conclusion without such a bloodbath. Peter reckons that that sort of attitude was inevitable for official purposes, but that behind closed doors, everyone up to the Home Secretary wanted to thank him for sparing them the embarrassment of taking Cotting to trial. The dust settled and Jim felt that he had nothing left to achieve, so he retired early to take a pub outside Bath. Tess surprised everyone by resigning her job. Apparently, she had enjoyed what little she had done of the course so much she decided to complete it, and she now works for Romulan in America. Everyone thought it was a strange move, but according to Cathy, she had been looking for a new career, preferably one with less contact with the police."

"Is there anyone else?"

"Only one. Did you notice the new butler – Bill's replacement? He used to work as a breakfast waiter at the City Hotel and a very fine old gentleman he is too. Apparently he was fired for emptying a pot of hot coffee into some fat American's lap and following it by saying, 'have a nice day, sir'. When Emily got to hear of it she hired him on the spot – and then gave his former manager a verbal savaging – as only she could!'

"Thanks, Jonathan. Now – about that unbridled lust?"

"Right – it'll pass the time while they're on honeymoon. They are away for two weeks!"